Praise for
The Woman Between the Worlds

"It's a true original, a romp sinister around the back streets of a gonzo late-19th-century London very persuasively evoked, conducted with splendid verve, by turns macabre and very funny (and witty too)—and macabre again. Three rousing cheers for this uniquely warped and wondrous romance of eerie extraterrestrial dimensions."

—Ian Watson, author of *The Fire Worm*

"A stunning dark adventure with the flavor of H. P. Lovecraft, a hint of Edgar Rice Burroughs, and a richness of invention and language that could only come from this unique author's pen."

—Charles Ardai, editor of *Great Tales of Madness and the Macabre*

"An extraordinary debut novel, with a unique and chilling sensibility. Read it if you dare."

—Janet E. Morris, creator of *Heroes in Hell*

THE WOMAN BETWEEN the WORLDS

F. Gwynplaine MacIntyre

A DELL TRADE PAPERBACK

A DELL TRADE PAPERBACK

Published by
Dell Publishing
a division of
Bantam Doubleday Dell Publishing Group, Inc.
1540 Broadway
New York, New York 10036

The trademark Dell® is registered in the U.S. Patent and Trademark Office.

ISBN: 0-440-50327-2

Printed in the United States of America

Published simultaneously in Canada

February 1994

10 9 8 7 6 5 4 3 2 1

BVG

Acknowledgments

I am fortunate to have known so many people who have been helpful at crucial times in my life or career. In no particular order, I especially wish to thank the following people, alive and dead: James Blish, Isaac Asimov, George Scithers, Darrell Schweitzer, John G. Betancourt, Jeanne Cavelos, Lenore Nier, Lord Grade (ITC), Lord Russell (Penrhyndeudraeth), Lady Amabel Williams-Ellis of Plas Brondanw, George Markstein, David Tomblin, Ellen Datlow, Ellen Asher, Alexander H. Cohen, Herman Shumlin, Eva Holvak of the Alice, Anne Forbes Cooper, Elizabeth Burns Dendee, Vanessa Jones-Rutledge, Yvette Maurer, everybody at LaserSet Graphics, Janet Elizabeth Campbell-Waggott, Kate Renshall, Max Miller, Max Wall, Helene La Pointe, the research team at the University of Utah Medical School, William K. Everson, Dick Bujarski, Romano Tozzi, Patrick Rock of Saint Elmo's Fire, Allan & Beryl Williams, Billy Smart, Professor Tommy Shand of Chipperfield's, Herbert G. Goldman, Jenny Dawkins, Flanders & Swann, Elizabeth Jane Lash, Verity Lambert, Bron Waugh, Grant & Susan Tyler, Melinda Snodgrass, Jeri Taylor, Zayra Cabot, Brannon Braga, Fred Pohl, Terry Carr, Harvey Shild, Lula Adams, John Vanible, Angelique Pettyjohn & Charlie Watkins, Patia von Sternberg, the Earl of Clancarty, Jeff Goodman, Irving Feld, Giani Siri, Darbi Falen, Eric & Janet Kagan, the staffs of Somerset House and Saint Catherine's House, the villagers of Aberfan, the people of Thursday Island, and all the authors who kindly supplied favourable quotes for this book's publicity campaign. Thanks as well to David Kranis (World's Greatest Landlord) and Leonard Bernstein (World's Greatest Lawyer). Special thanks go to the people of the Noong'gubooyu and the Oenpelli, who showed me the path to the Dreamtime. And most of all, my gratitude to the schoolgirls who once befriended a frightened and crippled young day-girl: the gift you gave her has been passed on to me, and I shall pass it onward to another.

This book is dedicated
in loving memory to my wife:

DIANE M. MacINTYRE

who never heard the music,
but always knew the song . . .

and to my stepfather:

JEREMY S. WHITFIELD

who conquered all of his demons
except the one in the bottle.

Whatever I become, I owe to them.

The First Part

THE CALLER FROM ELSEWHERE

23rd November, 1898

There are houses in London that keep to themselves and say nothing when strangers walk by. There are buildings that squat dark and grim in the shadows, and wait for some unsuspecting human to pass, so that they can pounce upon his attention with a clatter of wrought-iron fence and a scrabbling of gingerbread eaves. There are taverns in London that laugh, now and then, at the joyous good times they once hosted within. There are factories that howl, and tenements that moan, and there is one ancient house in the Clerkenwell district, at the foot of the Pentonville Road, that occasionally screams.

My uncle's tattoo shop, in Nicholas Lane, seemed to grumble sometimes, from despair. My uncle began as a tobacconist, but in the back room he entertained clièntele desiring certain medical services of a highly intimate nature: young ladies seeking the discreet termination of a pregnancy, or gentlemen desirous of relief from an unfortunate dose of French pox.

In 1862 His Royal Highness Edward, Prince of Wales, returned from journeys abroad sporting a tattoo he had acquired in Palestine: an image of the Jerusalem Cross, emblazoned upon his right arm. Thus was created in London society a great vogue for becoming tattooed. Within a decade, several tattoo *salons* appeared within London, catering to fashionable gentlemen and ladies wishing coloured illustrations on their arms or more intimate regions. My uncle learnt the skills of the tattoo artist's trade, and reaped such profits from his needle that he soon abandoned his former illicit custom, and devoted himself solely to the art of the tattoo.

My parents having died when I was young, and my elder sister Sarah having been sent for by a maiden aunt in Orpington, I was raised by my uncle, and served a term as his apprentice. Many evenings I swept Uncle's parlour, or sterilised his tattoo needles, or refilled the tall glass jars of brightly coloured pigments that lined the walls of his shop. As I grew older, Uncle taught me the secrets of the needle. I learnt how to outline the chosen tattoo illustration on the skin with an iodine pencil, so that the client could approve each detail of the art before its permanent injection. I learnt how to fill in the outlines with carbonised lamp-black, injected well beneath the surface of the skin, to the juncture of the dermal and epidermal tissues. I learnt the recipes—frequently originating in the Orient—for the preparation of each pigment, and how to obtain the various chemical compounds and vegetable dyes required for each colour.

By the time of my twenty-first birthday I was doing most of the tattoo work myself, which left my uncle free to follow new pursuits.

There were callers, sometimes, in my uncle's small shop, whom I was never permitted to meet. He would send me upstairs to our cramped living quarters whenever any of them came, but I would often watch them through the stair rails, and listen. There were men who arrived with thick packets done up in brown paper, which my uncle would buy. There were other men, and women, to whom my uncle sold the contents of these packets. There were ladies of foreign appearance and peculiar attire who would call at strange hours, and oftentimes my uncle sent me out of the shop altogether whilst these ladies came to visit.

Most peculiar of all were the books. There was a man who came on Thursdays fortnightly, invariably after sunset, always clutching a dust-covered book or an ancient brown scroll. On one occasion I recall that he arrived bearing a set of clay tablets. My uncle would invariably suggest that I go out for a walk, whenever this strange gentleman arrived. I sometimes watched though, from the Birchin Lane crossroads, observing the shop for a glimpse of the visitor's departure. My uncle, whenever I returned to the shop, would always be in his study, the door locked from within, and his tremblous voice muttering strange words that came distorted through the door.

Early this morning my uncle sent me to Epsom on an errand that proved to be entirely false, to an address which turned out to be nonexistent, and by the time I returned to the shop in late evening my uncle was gone. There was a note addressed to me:

> *I must leave, and am unable to*
> *return. The shop is yours: keep it, sell*
> *it, or abandon it, just as you please.*

My uncle's possessions and clothes remained behind, and some small store of money; evidently he had left in great haste.

The door to Uncle's study had been torn off its hinges. The furniture within was intact, but there was a gap in the front of one bookshelf, where some score or double-dozen books had been removed. I was trying to recall the names of the missing volumes, when I heard the bell jangle at the front of the shop. As I approached it the door opened, barely half an inch, and a young woman's voice emanated from the shadows outside:

"Your shop was recommended to me by . . . *another,*" she said. "Can you provide me with the full-body tattoo?"

"I can do full-body tattoos," I replied, although the lady had not completely entered. "But they're a dicey business at the best. Are you certain that you want one?"

"I have just come from Smithfield's," the woman in the shadows went on, without coming within. Her accent was not English, nor anything I recognised. "I have seen the Zebra Man. Your work, I believe?"

"My uncle's." There is, on exhibit in Smithfield's, a living man, almost naked, whose body is covered from head to foot with broad black and white stripes, zebra-fashion. He was a former strong-man with Fossett's Circus, who had submitted himself to the tattoo needle to be assured of a steady income in exhibition halls. "My uncle created the Zebra Man when I was barely fifteen." I told the woman in the doorway. "I helped with the easy bits: the arms and shoulders and such. But have you any idea of the labour involved in a full-body tattoo? Surgical operations to tattoo the eyelids and throat and the genital organs. It's painful. Some of my clients who requested tattoo work upon their genitalia have reported a heightening of erotic sensation afterwards, but even so I cannot recommend . . ."

"I have come a great distance for the full-body tattoo," said the woman. "I shall have it. But not stripes, like the Zebra Man. Something *else* . . ."

I peered into the shadows surrounding this mysterious voice. "I must examine you thoroughly before I consent to do anything," I said, "so as to ascertain that you can withstand the ordeal of the full-body tattoo."

"I have withstood a great deal of pain, sir," she said. "I can endure a bit more. *Please.*" The woman's voice was thin, desperate. "You *must* tattoo me."

"And so I shall . . . *if* it is safe. Give us a look at you, then."

A pause. I saw the door open a bit wider, then shut, and I heard a footstep, yet no-one emerged from the shadows. "Where are you, then?" I asked impatiently.

"I am here."

I must have jumped when she spoke. The woman's voice was emanating from a spot in midair several inches to my left.

There was nobody there.

"Is this some sort of joke?" I said angrily. "If it is, you'll regret it." The thought occurred to me that perhaps some manner of electrical device had been employed to open my door, and that some female ventriloquist was projecting her voice from a distance. "Come out and show yourself."

"I am here," she insisted. "Give me your hand. Feel me, touch me."

I extended one hand, and found myself touching what felt like . . . could it be her *breast?* I traced its contours in midair: the taut curve, the heat of warm flesh, the resilience. Two of my fingers brushed a nipple, and I felt it grow erect at my touch.

This was no apparatus-trick: either I had gone mad, or there was an invisible *woman* standing before me. I decided that it was preferable to believe the latter. "Very well," I replied, "you are invisible. Or else I am dreaming, in which case your invisible colour is only a pigment of my imagination. How did this happen to . . ."

"My name is . . . hmmm . . . Vanessa Steele," said the invisible woman. "I'm a scientist. You needn't look so surprised; there are several female scientists these days. That woman Curie in France, for example, who announced the discovery of the peculiar substance *polonium* only last July."

"Was it *polonium* that did this to you?" I asked her.

"No. I was experimenting with keratogenic pigments, and stumbled upon a process for making organic tissues transparent. I tested the process on a guinea-pig, and then . . ."

"And then on yourself, obviously. Look here, this is astounding. Can you make your clothing invisible too?"

"No; I am obliged to keep quite naked. Fortunately we are having rather a warm November."

"All the same, invisibility drugs should be invented in the summer. How do you become visible again?"

There was a pause. "I cannot. That is why *you must help me* . . ."

I put out my hand again . . . there *was* someone there; I felt her throat swell and fall as she breathed. And now I perceived, in the flickering gaslight, a *wrinkle* of space in the dim room before me, as though a woman-sized portion of air were *thicker* than the air around it. "How can I help?" I inquired.

"I want you to tattoo me," she said. "Perform the full-body tattoo on every square inch of my flesh."

"Certainly," I said, still not altogether convinced that this was real. "What sort of tattoo do you wish? Does madame prefer stripes, or chequer-works, or polka-dots? Perhaps an excellent Scotch plaid . . ."

"Do not mock me, sir," said the she-voice. "I want to be tattooed a simple flesh-colour all over. The colour that I was before this happened." Invisible hands clutched me; I saw my shirtfront wrinkle, felt the desperate tug. "Make me *human* again!"

I disengaged the invisible woman from my shirt and took her hands. She was trembling. "I suppose it could be done. But certain portions cannot be tattooed: your hair, to begin with, would remain invisible."

"I shall dye my hair," she answered.

"And your eyes, of course, cannot be tattooed. You would appear to have empty eye sockets."

"I shall wear smoked-glass spectacles," she replied.

"But, confound it, how can I tattoo someone I can't even *see?*"

"I shall guide your hand," said Vanessa. "Don't you simply inject the pigment beneath the skin?"

"Ordinarily, yes. But ordinarily I can *see* what I am injecting it into. In your case, there is an element of risk . . ."

". . . which I must accept. This shop was recommended me, and I have come a great distance."

Again it struck me that her accent was certainly not English. "How far *have* you journeyed?" I asked her.

"Very far. How much will it expense me for the full-body tattoo?"

I thought this over carefully. A piece of full-body work was a serious undertaking. "One hundred guineas," I said at last. "In advance, as I cannot very well take back my pigments after I've worked them into you. Have we a bargain?"

"Done." I heard floorboards creak, and then the door was opened by invisible hands. "I shall have payment brought here."

"Yes. I had noticed that you weren't carrying any money when you came in," I told her. "We can begin tomorrow morning."

"No," said the voice of the unseen. "It is just before eight of the clock; I will return in an hour, and we can begin then." I heard her footsteps recede into the shadows, and then she was gone.

"Wait!" I ran out into the street, but could not hear her. And of course she was impossible to see.

From a faraway place I heard hoofbeats, and then the bells of St. Edmund's Church in Clement's Lane began striking the hour. I went back into my uncle's shop, and waited.

Some minutes later there came a rapping at the door, but when I opened it no-one was there. In the moonlight something glinted on the doorstep: a mysterious bundle. It was, as I discovered when I lifted it, extremely heavy.

With a knife I slit open the bundle, and poured its contents onto the bare wooden table. There were coins: dozens of them, round and shining Spanish doubloons and English spade guineas and Austrian guldens and Scottish bonnet pieces and bright new South African krugers and Renaissance florins and a battered lump that I took to be Roman, and coins with words and images upon them that I cannot yet decipher. And each and all of them were gold.

When I counted them I discovered there were precisely one hundred gold coins. The invisible woman had paid my fee in full.

23rd November, 1898, and the following day

I am one of those peculiar souls who never throws anything away. I took a fevered half-an-hour to unearth my old copies of *Pearson's Weekly* and skim through the back numbers for the summer of 1897 until I found what I was looking for: a serialised novel entitled *The Invisible Man, a Grotesque Romance,* by Mr H. G. Wells.

As it turned out, my recollection of the story proved correct: the Invisible Man of Wells's tale had lost all colour from his flesh, yet the corneas of his eyes remained slightly opaque. This was logical: if the eyes become invisible to light, then they cannot absorb it, and the Invisible Man is struck blind.

Yet the eyes of Vanessa Steele were as transparent as the rest of her, but she appeared to see perfectly well. So then how . . .

"Are you ready to begin?" She had returned.

I cleared some apparatus from the bench so she might sit. "I found the gold pieces," I told her. "Wherever did you get them?"

"Does it matter?" she asked.

"No."

"Then I shan't tell you. Let us begin."

"I have very little flesh-coloured pigment to hand," I said. "My clients, after all, are generally flesh-coloured to begin with. Perhaps if I combine crushed madder root with powdered carmine . . ."

"We will try that. Please begin."

I produced a bottle of ethyl chloride and some cotton-wool swabs. "This will prevent infection." I unstoppered the bottle, and as its fumes stung my nostrils I heard Vanessa moving rapidly away.

"That bottle's contents . . ." she hissed with peculiar revulsion. "The smell of *alcohol* . . ."

"Not alcohol, but ethyl chloride," I said. "They are closely related."

"I cannot abide alcohol, nor any of its cousins by marriage," quavered Vanessa. "Please. I am . . . *allergic.*"

"As you wish." I ground the pigments in a mortar. "I will clean each region of your body with water and surgical soap before tattooing it," I told her. "The soap film will reveal your invisible contours."

I coated a portion of her left arm with the soap and water. The filmy coating on her invisible flesh looked like an elbow-shaped soap bubble. "Will you need to find a vein?" Vanessa asked.

"No; the pigment is absorbed beneath the skin. I shall use, in your case, my electrical needles: their gentle rotation, as I insert them, will carefully push blood vessels and nerve tissues aside. Let us begin."

I rolled up my sleeves. My left arm is a patchwork of parti-coloured blotches and hues where I have tested my various pigments and practised the insertion of my needles. I found a small bare patch astride my left elbow, and pricked the flesh with a pigmented needle. Yes: the colour was a delicate rose tint; a suitable flesh-colour for this lady Vanessa.

I possess a copy of the electrical tattoo gun devised by my

colleague, the tattoo artist Professor Thomas Riley, and patented by him in 1891. This ingenious device consists of six small needles clamped into a brass tube, set to vibrating by means of a current from a small battery. I now switched on this tattoo gun, dipped its needles into the pigment, and touched them to Vanessa's arm. There was a tingling sensation as the needles met the skin; a slight pressure, and then the flesh yielded, and the needles entered within.

The first application worked perfectly: a small patch of Vanessa's left elbow now bore a definite rose-hued complexion.

"Can't you work any faster?" she asked.

"No." I nodded towards a tintype "Gem" photograph on the wall, of a man whom I had tattooed in the Japanese *horimono* technique. Every inch of his chest was decorated with dragons and mermaids. "Nice bit of work, that was. Fellow took me six weeks. In *your* case, of course, I'll save a great deal of time; your desire to be tattooed a single colour all over eliminates the need for complicated linework. But the surface area of your skin is the same size no matter if I use one colour or twenty."

I worked in silence for an hour. Vanessa's breathing was soft and rhythmic, somehow oddly reassuring.

"Look here," I said suddenly. "I've just realised: now that I've begun tattooing, you'll have to stay here until I've finished. It would hardly do for the neighbours to see a solitary arm perambulating through Bishopsgate, with no visible body attached."

"Very well," she agreed. "But I may have to leave suddenly, before your task is completed."

"Whatever for?"

"I have not been permissioned to say. Have you some female's clothing here?"

"Being neither a husband nor a pervert, I do not," I replied. "But I daresay that I can obtain some."

"I shall need a complete outfit," said Vanessa, "plus gloves and hat and a veil. I shall get you the money required. Whatever clothing-size is most easily obtained, that size will fit me."

This was a peculiar statement, but I let it pass. By now I had worked most of the way down her arm to the wrist. "I'll do the hand later," I said, proceeding towards her shoulder. "Hands and feet are among the more difficult areas to tattoo. The *most* difficult, of course, is the face."

Vanessa said nothing, though I felt that she nodded assent. As I continued my work on my client's invisible arm I found myself wondering, for the first time, what her face might look like.

30th November, 1898

My work was very nearly unceasing: I took just enough time to attend to eating and washing, with a few hours of sleep whenever I could get them. My invisible visitor begrudged me these respites, and was constantly prodding me to resume my task. By the end of the first week I had completed tattooing her arms from the shoulders to the wrists, and one lower limb from the ankle to midway up the thigh. The legs, which make up the largest portion of the human body's surface area, would in Vanessa's case require the most attention from my needles.

"I've been wondering," I said to her, as she placed herself on the workbench and I went to work on her thigh. "How is it, Vanessa, that you never seem to sleep, nor do you take food and drink?"

She twisted suddenly, and I nearly tore her skin with my needles. "I sleep when *you* do," she replied hesitantly.

She was lying; I had set up a folding camp-bed for Vanessa the night of her arrival, and its bedclothes were still neatly folded. "Why don't you ever eat anything, then?" I inquired.

"But I *do* eat. I help myself from your larder, but take very little. It seems to be some side effect of the invisibility process; I require very little food or drink to sustain myself indefinitely."

"It seems to me," I said, quite certain she was lying, "that if an invisible woman were to eat, she would no longer be invisible; everyone could see the food inside her, long after she had eaten. Might I impose upon you to eat something? I should like to observe the process."

"Oh, very well." She crossed to the sideboard, where I had laid the dinner things. Knife and fork in invisible hands floated just beyond visible arms as she sliced bread and cheese, lifted it to the space above her shoulders, and chewed. The food tore to shreds among invisible teeth, and then shuddered convulsively, tumbling downwards as she swallowed. The chewed mass suspended itself in midair within her invisible stomach; the food, I assumed, would fade away gradually, as Vanessa's gastric juices broke it down.

"I should like to see you drink something," I suggested, pushing a decanter forward. "Perhaps some Madeira . . ."

"Wine? No, I cannot touch alcohol."

"Tea, then."

She hesitated. I saw the tea-kettle pour as invisible hands lifted it, and then saucer and cup flew upwards as she drank. I watched very carefully as the hot liquid formed a clear outline of her mouth and invisible throat, then descended, passing the epiglottis and revealing the contours of the alimentary canal. "Enough?" she asked, as a puddle of tea joined the food in her midair invisible stomach. "Perhaps now we can continue."

I worked for another hour at tattooing her thigh. Then, when I thought I might not arouse suspicion, I excused myself and went into the study.

From a bookshelf I removed my uncle's copy of *Gray's Anatomy,* and found an illustration of the human digestive system: the throat, the alimentary canal. I mentally compared the picture before me with the contours of Vanessa's internal organs that I had glimpsed an hour ago.

The organs did not match.

There was an invisible creature in my parlour who claimed to be a woman, who was apparently *shaped* like a woman, but whose internal digestive system was something unutterably alien.

And I was helping her assume the disguise of a human. What was she planning to do when the full-body tattoo was completed?

1st December, 1898

"I should like to perform an experiment," I told my visitor the next evening.

She was sitting at my bench, unclothed as usual, but her nudity was only now becoming apparent as Vanessa became increasingly visible. I had tattooed her arms from the wrists to the shoulders, and begun an assault at the base of Vanessa's breasts. One of her legs had been treated from ankle to pelvis, and the other one nearly completed.

Those portions of Vanessa which I could now see were exceedingly feminine, and I confess that I found the sight of her quite arousing.

"What sort of experiment do you propose?" she asked me.

"A small quantity of vegetable dye," I told Vanessa, "injected into your bloodstream, will delineate your circulatory system most admirably. The blood vessels of the hands, feet, mammary regions, and of the face are so densely compacted that colouring them will reveal to me the precise contours of those portions of yourself, so that I can tattoo them the more accurately. The dye will fade as your body absorbs it."

She hesitated. "I am not certain it will be safe to . . ."

"Safe as houses! Much safer than getting tattooed when all I can see of you is a soap bubble." I had the dye ready-mixed in a syringe; before she could stop me I grasped her half-visible left wrist, found the pulse of her vein, and injected the bright crimson dye.

Vanessa shuddered. *"Take it out!"*

"It is harmless," I said. "Harmless, at least, to *human* blood."

Vanessa was weeping and moaning uncontrollably. I endeavoured to calm her, but she thrust me away with one invisible hand. "You do not know . . . *you cannot imagine what you have done!*"

I soon found out. The colouring spread through her body rapidly. The primary vein in Vanessa's left arm became clearly outlined in scarlet. The dye then progressed past her shoulder to form a crimsoning pattern of red vessels and organs inside her invisible chest. In a few moments her entire circulatory system became visible.

The creature had two hearts.

"Suppose you tell me now," I suggested gently, "what sort of being you *really* are, and where you come from."

The visitor straightened, and faced me. The blood vessels of her head became visible, but gave little indication of the nature of her face. "My real name," she said, "is not pronounceable in your language. I am not from any region of your world, but from an else-place . . ."

I had read Mr H. G. Wells's latest novel, published in April of this year: *The War of the Worlds*. "Are you from Mars?" I asked my visitor.

"Not so far away as that. My world is separated from this one by perhaps an inch of space, but that space lies in a direction which you cannot perceive. An unseen dimension . . ." She sat down, and crossed half-invisible legs. "There are many of my people in your world, and ever have been. Have you never felt the sensation of being *watched*, yet when you turned you could see no-one there? *We* were watching. Invisible."

I shuddered, perhaps from the cold. "Go on," I prompted her.

"Did you ever lose something, and be unable to find it again?" she continued. "Some common object: you know precisely where you left it, but when you look again it has vanished. We *take* things. We take them back through the *vacua* with us to our homeworld, and study them so as to learn about your race."

"Those gold coins you paid me," I asked her then, "the hundred guineas? Were *they* taken from my world into yours?"

"From your world, and from others. Over centuries, my people have collected many else-world artefacts. From their distant realms of origin, they vanish without trace . . ."

"Sometimes," I said slowly, *"people* vanish. The French scientist Louis Le Prince, for example, who stepped into a railway carriage eight years ago and never came out. Or the Viennese actress Ludmilla Hubel, upon whose sexual exploits Arthur Conan

Doyle based the adventures of his creation Irene Adler: I recall that Miss Hubel vanished in mysterious circumstances in 1891, while *en route* to Montevideo. And there was that Swedish aëronaut Andrée, who went aloft in his hydrogen balloon just last year, and never came down. The vanished ones must gather *somewhere.* There was a plague of disappearances in London in 1881, and I recall that my uncle once showed me an old newspaper cutting—dated 1872; I was too young to appreciate it at the time —concerning the peculiar fate of the crew and passengers of the *Mary Celeste . . .*"

"We took them," said the she-thing with infinite calmness. "Perhaps not the ones whom you mentioned, but we have taken many people from your world. We needed them to teach us the speakings of humans. Some of them fell by accident into a hole between the worlds. Others came willingly."

"I don't believe you," I said. "The ones who vanished . . ."

"Always, *always,*" she responded, "they find our world very beautiful once they arrive there. Always they choose to remain. Did you ever hear music from a faraway hill, and when you tried to find its source you could not? That is the music of my people's world, far and beautiful. And it leaks through the crevices from one world to the next."

"How is it," I asked, "that your eyes are invisible, and yet you are not blind?"

"I *am* blind, at least to the colours of your visible spectrum: red through violet. I know the names of your colours, and yet I cannot ever see them. But there is another range of colours, beyond the violet, that my eyes perceive quite clearly. I can see *you* because your skin reflects a portion of the ultra-violet-coloured light which it receives from the rays of your planet's Sun. And my own body, as well, is visible to anyone who can see the ultra-violet colours. For these are the colours of my world."

I said nothing.

She changed positions and then recrossed her legs; a bit of visible thigh traded places with its invisible counterpart. "Now then," she went on, "be good enough to continue the full-body tattoo."

"Why?" I asked her. "Why do you wish to become permanently visible to human eyes? Why not simply attain impromptu visibility, by coating your skin with flesh-coloured theatrical paint?"

"Is it not obvious?" she responded. "I wish to attain, as nearly as possible, the appearance of the people of your world. I want to be a *woman.*"

"Yes, confound it, but *why?*"

For a time she said nothing at all. Then at last the faint words came from her alien mouth: "The *vacua,* the Openings between my world and yours are fleeting, random. Our people have used them for centuries, but we know little of how the *vacua* materialise, or why. Sometimes a dozen such portals will appear within one day, a walk-distance apart. Sometimes only one or two will appear in the same century, on opposite ends of the Earth. We cannot predict their arrival in advance."

"Go on," I said, intrigued.

"I came to your world through a hole in the sky. Two weeks ago, by your time-longs, the *vacuole* opened to your world. How can I describe the beauty of Earth to one who has known it from birthing? How can I express the cool smell of the grass after rainfall, or the warm taste of sunlight at morning? We have no such pleasures on our world. There is in your city a place, between Billingsgate Market and the northern end of London Bridge, where the fishmongers' barrows converge with the stalls filled with oranges and cheese, to form what is probably the most fascinating scent in all the Universe's everness. It is unique."

"And . . . ?"

"I stayed here too long." Her invisible voice seemed to tremble as she spoke. "When I tried to return to my own world the *vacuole* was gone. I am trapped here."

"Can you never get back?"

"Perhaps. But I have fallen in love with your world, with the cities of men, and the forests and rivers and smells. And the humans themselves are most visit-worthy of all . . . they delight me."

"But surely your own people must . . ."

"Touch me!" she cried suddenly.

"I beg your . . ."

"Touch me! Feel me, sense me, *touch me!*" I saw her shoot out one half-visible arm, felt invisible fingers touch my face, sensed the warm fingertips gently probing my flesh.

"My people, we cannot do this," whispered her invisible mouth. "There is a sort of . . . a *polarity,* a charge within our bodies that makes physical contact between my people painful. Like magnets repelling one another. The time of birthing one's young is sheer agony. We can *grasp* one another, hold fast by sheer physical force and shut our eyes to the pain, but we cannot ever simply *touch* . . ." I felt Vanessa breathing in the stillness as she spoke. "That is why I now wish to remain here, in the world of the humans who are able to touch one another. I want to be able to *feel* . . ."

For a very great while I said nothing. Then after a time I heard the bells of St. Edmund's distantly chiming the hour, and then the bells of All Hallows joining in, and the great bell of St. Paul's, until it seemed as though all of London was clanging at my eardrums. I turned suddenly and left the shop, fleeing into the night. I spent many hours of that evening in a Whitechapel pub, staring into one whisky glass after another as I wondered what manner of creature I had left in my shop, that had the voice of a woman and sought to wear human flesh, but that dwelt in an alien form. And more and more as that grey evening crept over me I thought of Vanessa, and wondered why I felt such an overpowering desire to see her invisible face.

2nd December, 1898

I left the pub at closing time, and spent the night seeking shelter where I dared; feeling somewhat unwilling to return to my shop and the half-visible creature within it, I set out through the dark

London streets, towards my sister's house in the Marylebone district.

I felt the most peculiar mixture of sensations towards the creature Vanessa—or whatever her name was—and these feelings were in need of sorting out. I felt repelled by her alien nature, yet at the same time there was something else, an arousal of sensations towards Vanessa that I had never felt before, that were not altogether unwelcome. There was no-one on Earth who might help her, excepting myself, and I found myself wanting to protect her and wanting to chuck her out in the street both at once.

Shortly after daybreak, I reached my sister's house in New Cavendish Street. Her husband Henry saw me coming, and ushered me into the house. "Look who's here, Sarah: that prodigal brother of yours!" Sarah fetched coffee, steaming black in the pot, and a jug of fresh cream. "You're only just in time for breakfast," Henry told me. "A good big plate of slap-up prog is what you . . ."

"Thank you, no," I answered. "I've already drunk my breakfast."

My sister Sarah was more perceptive than her husband. "What's wrong, then?" she asked me.

"Supposing I were to tell you," I began, "that there is an alien creature in London. It speaks, it walks and feels and behaves much like a human, yet it possesses the most bizarre appearance that I have ever encountered."

"Perhaps it's an Irishman," said Henry, refilling his pipe.

"Joke if you like," I told him. "I have *seen* this creature. It was invisible, until I . . ."

"*Seen* an invisible creature?" asked Henry. "*That's* a rum go. And talking of rum, I'd say you've had a few over the . . ."

"Don't talk rubbish, Henry," said my sister. "Just because some creatures haven't been put in cages yet doesn't mean they don't exist. Think of the Himalayan Snow-Giant, for an instance, or these recent Australian reports of the Bunyip. And remember Springheel Jack, and St. Columba's ancient tale about the creature in the River Ness, in Scotland . . ."

"And leprechauns and unicorns, neither of which I believe

in." Henry tamped down his pipe. "See here, man; Lewis Carroll has been dead since January. If Looking-Glass creatures ever existed they've all gone extinct. This is the modern age, the nineteenth century!"

"I can see that you do not believe me," I said. "Right, then. I'm off. Good morning."

"Don't go yet." Sarah put one soft hand to my arm. "Wait a bit until I've changed my things. I should like to meet this invisible creature of yours. Henry, call for a hansom."

Half-an-hour onwards, Sarah and I were cabbing it back towards Uncle's shop. "Your house looks more beautiful each time I visit," I remarked to Sarah as we set off. "Even your back-garden privy is welcome, in contrast with my chamber-potted quarters in Nicholas Lane."

"Next year, Henry and I mean to replace the outbuilding with an indoor water-closet," Sarah ventured. "They say that by 1900 all the best homes will have one. Now tell me about this monster of yours."

"It isn't a monster, quite. It's a sort of a *woman* . . ."

"So now my young brother is frightened of women."

"No, Sarah! There's a . . . *creature* in Uncle's old shop. Had I not touched it, and heard it speak, I should have sworn it was not . . ."

" '*It*,' not '*she*'? You said this was a woman."

"*She,* then. A female being from another world."

I told my sister everything about Vanessa then, beginning with our uncle's curious disappearance. Sarah seemed little disturbed by this first part, for she had never been fond of Uncle, and had long suspected him of peculiar behaviour. My description of Vanessa aroused my sister's interest, however:

"But why do you call this mysterious female a *creature?*" Sarah asked. "Has she behaved like a beast of the forests?"

"No," I admitted. "But she has lied to me."

"Lying to a man is every woman's prerogative. Has she committed any crime, either against the laws of Her Majesty or those of God?"

"Not to my knowledge."

"Has she exhibited unlady-like behaviour?"

"None whatever," I said, "except for parading through the streets of London stark-naked. However, since many fashionable ladies have been wearing their skirts above the ankle of late, and may be exhibiting an inch of their lower limbs any day now, perhaps this Vanessa is merely ahead of the fashion."

Sarah smiled. "Then I believe that you have got all excited over nothing. Really, this acquaintance of yours sounds rather a delightful young lady."

I sat bolt upright, nearly smashing my skull on the roof of the cab. "But she is *invisible* . . ."

For the first time my darling Sarah seemed confused. "Is she a ghost, d'you mean? A phantasm?"

"No. But her flesh is of a colour that lies beyond violet in the spectrum, and is invisible to us. She is transparent to the wave-lengths of visible light, and so . . ."

"Nicholas Lane, then." The panel overhead slid open, and the driver peered through. "Here you are, squire."

We alighted and I paid him, and as the cabman drove off I took out my latch-key.

The door of my shop was already ajar.

"Sarah, *stay here!*" I pushed open the door, and went in.

The room was a-shambled. Phials of pigment and trays of equipment lay shattered and strewn in every corner of the shop.

Something groaned beneath the wreckage at the far end of the room.

"*Vanessa?*"

I could not see her, not even the portions of her flesh which my tattoo needle had made visible.

Another groan, and drawing nearer I saw an overturned cabinet stir as if pushed. Had Vanessa relapsed into total invisibility?

"*Vanessa?*" I struggled to lift the cabinet, saw the puckering and wrinkling of the air beneath it as something invisible stirred. I heard the floorboards creak, as the unseen thing tried to stand.

"*You will die now,*" it said, and *its voice was not Vanessa's.*

And then the invisible thing was upon me, with its hands at my throat.

I found myself fighting for my life against a creature that *could not be seen*. I struggled desperately, but the damned thing seemed to *flow* on top of me. I was unable to breathe, feeling the invisible fingers tightening round my neck . . .

I had my penknife in my waistcoat pocket. I took this now, and sliced at the air, hoping to strike some vital spot of my unseen attacker's anatomy.

I felt the blade strike something. There was a howl, and I managed to pull free. But an invisible fist struck my nose, and I let go the knife.

"No escape for you, human," slurred a voice from midair.

Something lunged. It knocked me backwards into the ruins of my shop, and as I crumpled under the impact I felt a weight on my chest and a hand at my throat. One of my uncle's surgical knives slithered out of the wreckage and dangled aloft, firmly grasped by invisible fingers. And then the blade whistled down towards my . . .

I heard a thud, and then a groan; when my head cleared, the invisible thing was slumped across my chest, and Sarah was standing over me. Her velvet-gloved hands held a chair, and I noticed a dent in its frame where she had smashed the chair against an invisible skull.

"I heard the noise, and came in," said my sister as I managed to stand up. "At first, when I saw you clawing at the air, I thought you were having a fit of epilepsy or syncope. But then, when I saw that knife jump up *all by itself* . . ."

We found Vanessa in the pantry—what was *left* of the pantry—moaning gently in the wreckage of the place. The portions of her form that I had made visible were all over scratches and bruisings. The invisible parts of her body seemed damaged as well, and I could not even guess the extent of her injuries.

"Those cuts want medical attention," said Sarah.

"A doctor?" I asked. "D'you think we can find one whom we can trust to keep Vanessa's existence a secret?"

"You do me a dishonour, dear brother," said Sarah. "I've not forgotten *all* my medical skill." My sister had been an army nurse during the Afghan campaign of 1879, and Henry had been a lieutenant. They had met during the Kabul Massacre, and it was love at first sight.

"You can patch up Afghani cavalrymen, right enough," I told Sarah, "but Vanessa *is not human.* Her internal organs are differently arranged, and have the further disadvantage of being invisible."

My sister smiled. "I'd be a poor nurse if I didn't fancy a challenge. Is there a chemist's hereabouts?"

The nearest chemist's shop was at the bottom of Fenchurch Street; I gave Sarah the directions, and some money. By now the invisible thing that had attacked me was regaining consciousness. I located some rope, and secured the wretch quite firmly to the chimney-piece. "You needn't struggle," I said, as the coils of rope began to writhe from the contortions of their invisible prisoner. "Escape is quite impossible."

"Fool!" croaked the voice, from the empty air close to my face. *"These ropes will not hold me. As soon as I regain my strength . . ."*

"I'd like to see you try that," I said to the invisible thing. "In fact, I'd like to see you *at all.* Now, then: who and what *are* you? Why did you come here, and why did you attack Vanessa?"

"She is a . . . criminal . . . on our world." The invisible intruder's breathing was laboured. *"I was sent here . . . orders . . . bring her back through . . . Opening from your worl' to . . . ours. She mus' be sentenced for . . . her crimes . . ."*

"What crimes?" The door opened as I spoke and Sarah entered, her arms laden with medical supplies. I nodded towards the pantry where Vanessa lay, and Sarah went to work. I saw the look of determined excitement on my sister's face, and I knew that Vanessa was better off in Sarah's care than among the best surgeons in Harley Street.

I gripped the throat of the invisible intruder. Its flesh was cold, and unpleasantly damp. "If Vanessa dies, I shall very certainly kill you," I said. "Right, then: what crime has she committed?"

The creature laughed; an invisible laugh, full of mockery. *"The Dreadful Eye will send more of us . . . an army of invisible*

men . . . pouring into London through holes in the sky. . . . They
will seek out the criminal-she, and capture her. . . ."

The room must have been cold, for I felt myself shiver. "Tell
me something of Vanessa," I bargained, "and I may let you return
to your own world without her."

The invisible laugh was more horrible now. *"And shall I tell*
the Dreadful Eye of my failure?" The thing made a ghastly noise in
some part of its throat. *"I would rather . . . die here. You can-*
not . . ."

And then nothing. I waited, and in another minute the rope
coils went slack and the stench of the dead thing came up from
the floor.

I have mentioned that the alien visitors—both Vanessa and
this intruder—were not totally invisible; there was always a slight
rippling of the air, a refraction of light, such as that of a transparent bit of ice within a glass of clear water. Now, however, the dead
monstrosity in my parlour became *wholly transparent,* and as it did
so its smell grew more sickening.

I left the dead thing where it was and I bandaged my hands
as best I could, with some court-plaster from my uncle's wrecked
cabinet.

Sarah, when I found her, appeared to be probing Vanessa's
back; I could just see the visible bits of the alien woman. "Spine's
not broken, at least," my sister reported. "Let's get her to bed."

We carried the unconscious Vanessa upstairs as gently as
possible, and into my bedroom. I left Sarah to her patient, whilst I
attended to the alien corpse in my parlour.

I dragged the invisible thing down to the cellar, and went
for a shovel. The wooden floor of the cellar was rotted through in
spots; I dug a hole in the damp earth below, and when it was
grave-sized I pushed the corpse in with the blade of my shovel. I
could not bear to touch the dead thing with my hands.

I started to fill in the grave. The earth beneath the cellar
floor was damper than I had suspected, and a quantity of clay
began to form. There was a single awful moment—when I tossed
a shovelful of clay across the dead creature's body—when I could
see the shape and contours of the invisible form clearly outlined in

the pit. A thin layer of clay had formed across the features of the thing, and I saw—clearly outlined for one terrible instant—the dead creature's hideous face. And if I may live to be a hundred years old, every nightmare in all of my life will reach into that cellar, and force my memory to see again that ghastly face within the pit.

10th December, 1898

For a week and more Vanessa lay still as though dying, and her body was cold. Sarah and I by turns spent long hours sitting up through the night with her, and one particular night stands out with especial clarity in my mind. I had sent Sarah home to her husband until morning, and I kept my night's vigil alone. The portions of Vanessa that were visible lay cold and unmoving. And then, slightly after three o'clock in the morning, she started to twitch and to shudder and moan, and then a cold ray of light from my lamp fell across her, and she suddenly bolted erect in the bed and flung out both her arms as she screamed:

"They have come! I hear the beating of their wings! A thousand servants of the Eye!"

And then words, terrible words, in some alien tongue. And she collapsed and lay moaning for the remainder of the night.

On the morning of the eighth day of the vigil, I was breakfasting in the pantry when Sarah came from upstairs, and laid a hand on my arm.

"She is asking for you, I think."

I ran up the stairs two at a time, and entered the bedroom.

Vanessa was standing, unsteadily, her visible lower limbs waving precariously on invisible feet. I ran forward, and caught her as she fell. Her body had recovered its warmth, and I found it surprisingly pleasant to hold her, and feel her hands upon my face.

I made the most brilliantly clever remark that came into my mind: "Are you all right?"

"Yes," she whispered, quite weakly. Then: "You must get

out of this place. Quickly! They are coming for me, and if you are here they will kill you."

I held her, and stroked her invisible hair. "*Who* are coming, Vanessa?"

"The disciples of the Dreadful Eye."

"And what, pray, is . . ."

"The Dreadful Eye? He has enslaved all my homeworld. I have never seen him; I do not know what he looks like. He possesses knowledges and abilities that I cannot even begin to understand."

"Go on, Vanessa."

"I have heard that he can walk through walls and read minds. I am told that he can bridge the dimensions to your universe at will. You recall that I told you of the *vacua*, the Openings between my own world and yours? They appear randomly, at odd-fashioned places and of differing durations. But the Dreadful Eye can create such passageways at his will, and walk between my universe and yours."

"I cannot conceive of such power," I said, "except in the hands of either God or the Devil. I thought you had told me that your planet was beautiful."

"It *was,* once. A time ago *he* came. What he is, I do not know. One day, quite at once, a dozen people of my world began proclaiming the advent of the Dreadful Eye. They hailed him as our ruler, to be obeyed without question. Every day after that, a few more of my race—male and female—became disciples of the Eye, and devoted themselves to forcing his laws upon the rest of us. Rebels and dissidents disappeared of a sudden, or were slain."

"And are you a rebel, Vanessa?"

"Yes. They came for me, but I escaped. I took with me a sack of gold coins from our Museum of Artefacts, intending to escape to Earth. I located a *vacuole* between the worlds, and emerged here in London."

I helped Vanessa to the bed; she was clearly in pain. "I have two desires," she said slowly, halting for breath. "For myself is the easier desire: I want you to complete my full-body tattoo. As soon as I am visible to human eyes, perhaps I can then live among humans, as a woman, with only little difficulty. My birthworld was beautiful once, and will be so again when the Dreadful Eye has passed, but I have fallen in love with your planet of Earth-ones. Yet I cannot remain here in peace until I accomplish my desire for my people."

"And that desire is . . . ?" I asked her.

"I must assemble weapons, or allies, or power, with which I can return to my homeworld and destroy the Dreadful Eye, so that my people can be free."

There was a knock at the door just then, and Sarah entered carrying a bundle. "I brought these this morning from home," she said, displaying a lady's frock, some undergarments, shoes and gloves, and a hat with one of the new-fashioned motoring-veils. "You had better put these on, dear," she said to Vanessa, "and we'll see how they fit. Will you be wanting any help?"

"Yes, please." Vanessa reached into the bundle of garments and drew out a corset. "Whatever is *this?*"

"A mediæval torture device," said Sarah, helping Vanessa dress. She stopped when she saw I was watching. "Really! What sort of gentleman are you, to stand gape-a-goggling while a lady gets dressed?"

"The practical sort of gentleman," I said. "Since Vanessa is invisible when she is naked, and visible when she is dressed, it stands to reason that her body is more revealing to me when she is dressed than when she is naked. Therefore, I feel that in the interests of Science I must observe the phenomenon of a woman who exposes her body by putting her clothes on."

"I didn't understand that," said Sarah. "But I expect that you're rather enjoying this."

To Vanessa, as she stepped into a pair of camisole-knickers, I asked: "Why is this Dreadful Eye bloke so determined to send his invisible thugs after you?"

"Because he knows I intend to lead a revolt, and destroy him. He cannot allow me to remain on Earth; my freedom would inspire others to oppose him. He wants me brought back, alive or dead, and he means to make an example of me. His disciples, I am told, are highly skilled in the art of torture."

Vanessa was dressing herself as she spoke. Sarah's clothes fit Vanessa precisely, as if they were tailored for her. This struck me as rather too neat a coincidence, and I resolved to question Vanessa about it—but not just yet. Instead I asked: "Why doesn't the Dreadful Eye come after you *now?*"

"He will not come himself, I think. There is a great deal of dissent and unrest in my homeworld just now—I am partly the cause of it—and the Dreadful Eye will not risk leaving, and thereby weakening his grip on the minds of my people. If he were to come after me personally then my people would see that he considers me a threat to his power. He prefers to treat me as a minor annoyance, and he sends his mind-slaves to capture me."

I watched Vanessa slip into the stockings, drawing one and then the other up her thighs. The gas bracket was lit, and the effect of the light streaming *through* the silk stockings, unimpeded by Vanessa's invisible feet within them, was remarkable indeed. I asked her: "Was that one of the Dreadful Eye's disciples who attacked you week last, and nearly killed me?"

"Yes. The Dreadful Eye created a pathway between our two worlds, no doubt, and then sent one of his disciples to capture me. I was found in your shop, and we fought. I knocked him unconscious, and then I collapsed."

"Well, he's dead now, no fear," said my sister proudly. "I parted his hair with a Chippendale."

"Just the same," said Vanessa, "now that the Dreadful Eye knows that his assassin has failed, he will undoubtedly send others."

Sarah produced a button-hook, and showed Vanessa how to button her shoes. The shoes fit Vanessa as though they were made for her, and again I resolved to ask about this later. "I think," said Sarah, "that perhaps this is a matter for the police, or the Home Office."

"The Home Office?" I shook my head. "No; invasions of London by extraterrestrial fiends are seldom within the jurisdiction of the Home Office. Try the Foreign Office."

"But surely the police . . . ?"

"The peelers would never believe us. If we came to them

howling tales of invisible men they'd promptly book us for a lecture tour at the Colney Hatch Lunatic Asylum."

"We could show them Vanessa," said my sister. "A half-visible woman? They'd have to believe us if . . ."

"Show them Vanessa? Not bloody likely! They'd cut her up for a specimen, or clap her into the Regent's Park Zoo for a freak, or something worse. We can't . . ."

Vanessa suddenly clutched my arm. *Something,* at the far end of the room, very quietly coughed.

"Human," said a voice. It was slurred and alien, and the source of the voice was invisible. *"Human, you will be good enough to stand aside from the female. She is ours."*

My sister Sarah turned pale, and I reached for her hand. I could see, in the far corner, a distortion of the air, but I was unable to tell how many invisible men had arrived. "Can you see them, Vanessa?" I asked.

"Yes. There are three of them this time."

I took a poker from the fireplace. "Then I will have to kill all three of them."

Something invisible laughed, and a chair arose from the floor and came towards my head. That was a mistake, for so long as the invisible intruder held onto the chair, I could guess his approximate location. I shied away from the chair as it came at me, then I dodged and swung the poker with all of my strength. There was a loud and very satisfying *thunk,* and a groan, and then I saw the floorboards flex as an invisible body pitched forward across them.

And then the other two attacked me. I managed to give them as good as I got, but then one of them pinioned my arms from behind, and the other caught hold of my throat.

Vanessa, the only one of us who could *see* the attackers, was still too weakened to fight. But Sarah, bless her, seized the coal-scuttle from next to the fireplace and dipped it into the ashes of yesterday's fire. Then she flung the ashes at my attackers.

I coughed, in a thick cloud of ash, and struggled so fiercely that I broke the invisible creatures' grip. And I perceived, in the shower of coal-dust, that I could *see* my attackers now: two invisible men covered with ashes and soot, partly visible in moving silhouette. Sarah struck one on the head, *hard,* with the coal-scuttle, and the half-visible thing groaned and fell. The last of the three, howling: *"No! You shall not defy us! Death to the enemies of the Dreadful Eye!"* suddenly turned and flung himself through the casement window, to land amid a shattering of glass and splintered wood upon the cobblestones below. The last I saw of him was a weird figure, a dust cloud of ashes in the shape of a man, running off into the shadows toward Cannon Street.

"He's for it now," Sarah decided. "So long as he's got that soot on him, he can be seen. And if he tries to wash it off, he'll look like a great walking bubble of water until he dries."

"He'll escape," said Vanessa. "The Dreadful Eye's disciples are too clever to get caught. He's sure to hide somehow."

The two invisible men on the floor, all over soot, were still unconscious, although one of them showed signs of coming round. I coshed him with the poker and then sent Sarah to fetch some rope from the cellar whilst I stood guard. To Vanessa I asked: "The one who escaped: will he report back to the Dreadful Eye, d'you think?"

"Perhaps not," said Vanessa, adjusting the petticoat my sister had lent her. "To go back would be a confession of failure, and the Dreadful Eye does not permit his disciples to fail. The penalty is torture until death."

Sarah returned with the rope, and I tied our prisoners, flinging some more ashes on them to sustain their visibility.

"That rope won't hold them," said Vanessa. "As soon as they come to consciousness, they'll . . ."

One of them *did* revive at just that moment, and the other one came round a moment later. "Now, gents," I prompted them, "some answers, if you please: does your master know that Vanessa is here?"

"Be hanged," one of them rasped.

"Pour some alcohol on them," said Vanessa, arranging herself in Sarah's borrowed frock. *"That* will scare them, right enough."

"I've some isopropyl alcohol in my medical bag downstairs,"

Sarah told me. "You watch these bodger-boys while I stravage it up."

As soon as Sarah had left, one of our prisoners prodded the other, and spoke in some alien tongue: *"Hac iklakic."*

"Look out!" Vanessa shouted.

The two intruders *changed*. I saw the invisible men—at least, I saw their outlines in ashes and soot—suddenly shift to new shapes. Their limbs attenuated, transforming into writhing tentacles. They squirmed free of the ropes in an instant, and bounded straight towards Vanessa.

I seized the first thing to hand, a brass andiron, and flung it full into the face of one ash-dusted creature. I watched in horror as the face—still half-covered with ashes—suddenly melted, changed shape, and *engulfed* the andiron. Then the hideous thing, with a laugh out of Hell, spat my weapon right back at me. The andiron struck me square across the shoulder, and then the creatures were upon me.

There were some toilet articles beside the bed; I snatched the razor. It had a blade eight inches long, freshly stropped, and could slice a throat as easily as shave one. I slashed towards the animated ash-heaps, at the nearer one's throat, and was rewarded by an alien scream and a sudden loathsome smell.

My sister came in, clutching a phial of clear liquid. "What's all the . . . *my God!*"

"Throw it, quickly!" said Vanessa. "But mind that you get none of it on *me!*"

Sarah flung the jar's contents at my attackers. They both yelped, and one of them fell backwards and crashed through the grate of the fireplace.

The creature, coated in ashes and alcohol, immediately burst into flames. Howling in agony, the gibbering thing began running round and round in a sort of blind fury, setting fire to the furniture and drapes as it brushed against them.

"Get out of here, you two!" I shouted, pushing Sarah and Vanessa towards the stairs. Vanessa, still weak and unsteady, had managed to put on a pair of Sarah's gloves and to drape the motoring-veil over her face. She was thus entirely covered with clothing; an odd appearance, but one that concealed her invisibility. "Ring for the fire-brigade," I told Sarah, "and then both of you wait for me at the crossroads, King William Street." I watched them go, then I turned to face the swift inferno drawing towards me.

One of the invisible creatures was dead. The foul odour of its burning flesh was unbearable. The other creature, having lost an arm in the blaze, was writhing horribly in the centre of the carpet. By now the whole room was in flames.

In the cellar my uncle had installed a Chubb safe, to which I possessed a duplicate key. I went down to the safe now, and extracted its contents: some family papers, the gold coins that Vanessa had given me, and a revolver that my uncle had obtained illegally in the Seven Dials district ten years ago, during the notorious Whitechapel slayings that had terrified all London. There were a carton of bullets as well, and I had cleaned and oiled the revolver when I left the gold coins here. I pocketed the weapon. Just then, from the bedroom upstairs, I heard the agonised screams of the remaining invisible thing. It was being roasted alive.

I ran upstairs, and hurried from the house. In the distance I heard the bells of an approaching fire-engine, and the hoofbeats of the horses drawing it. Ahead of me, Sarah and Vanessa were waiting. I made to rejoin them, but on a sudden impulse I turned and looked back towards my house, the tattoo shop in Nicholas Lane.

The roof was entirely swallowed up in flames now, and the fire had spread downwards to nearly ground level. As I watched, there came a great roaring bellow and a shower of sparks, as the roof collapsed inwards and was eaten by the blaze. The walls were next, and I hoped that the alien corpse beneath the cellar floor would never be found, and that the two dead things upstairs would be so cremated as to thwart official inquiry.

And then the building fell in upon itself, as the hydrant-waggons came galloping up from the Metropolitan Fire Brigade's station in Leadenhall Street. A man in bright red flannels, with an even redder face beneath the brim of his fireman's helmet, ran towards me. He was clutching a brass fire-trumpet in the crook of his arm.

"Is that your house, man?" he asked.

"It *was.*"

"Rotten luck! Is anyone still inside?"

"No," I answered. To myself, I added: "No-one *alive.*"

I walked away, and left him there. He was shouting to his crew on the steamer-engine to unfasten the cagings and move back the horses. I ignored him. My uncle had vanished, our house was destroyed, with never so much as a fire-insurance policy to cover the loss. I went to join my sister and our strange guest, at the crossroads down the way.

Later, the same day

I still have most of the hundred gold coins that Vanessa had paid me. A few of them I had in past weeks converted into more conventional currency, and either spent the proceeds or deposited them with my bankers. Some of the older and more esoteric coins had proven so obscure that several coin dealers to whom I had shown them were reluctant to purchase them, despite the coins' gold content. A few of the pieces, in fact, bore images and lettering that I was certain could never have originated on Earth.

But those of British, European, or Yankee mintage are negotiable. I thus have some small quantity of funds, and the prospect of more when necessary. My position, though unenviable, is not yet hopeless.

When I reached King William Street I began to speak, but Vanessa cut me off with a single gloved gesture. "We must find new lodgings straight away," she insisted, "so that you can continue my full-body tattoo."

"But all my pigments, all my tattoo needles were destroyed . . ."

"We will get others. Did you think, having decided to give up my invisibility, that I would be content to stop halfway? I cannot become a true woman of Earth until you complete the full-body tattoo."

"I'll complete bugger-all," I replied, "until you give me one hell of a good many answers." I flagged down a passing hackney coach, and we all three stepped in. "Bank of England, Threadneedle Street, please, driver."

"Today's Saturday, sir," he replied. "Bank's shut."

"So it is. Number Seventeen, Piccadilly then, if you please." I slid shut the partition, and we were able to converse without the driver overhearing.

"About this Dreadful Eye now," I asked, as the hackney drew away from the kerb. "How were his invisible thugs able to trace you to my shop?"

"They can *sense* me," said Vanessa through her veil. "Do you recall what I told you, that the people of my world have a sort of polarity within our bodies? One pole of this charge is internal; the other external, on the surface of the flesh. There is a slight internal resonance that we feel at all times, and it grows stronger as we approach each other. The disciples of the Dreadful Eye were very likely prowling the London streets, aware of their own inner resonance, sensing it grow stronger as they neared me."

"Next question," I asked. "How did they get into my house? The door was locked."

"Locked to *humans,* it was. We are shape-changers, my people. By contracting and attenuating our forms, we can slip through a letter-slot."

"This is extraordinary!" said Sarah. "Are you like an *amœba,* then? A Proteus?"

"Not so elastic. We have two arms, two legs, an abdomen and head; that much remains the same, although the length and thickness of each can change. Did you notice how thin and drawn out those two assassins became, when they escaped from your ropes? *That* is the extent of our shape-changing ability."

"I rather wondered," my sister said then, "why my clothing is precisely your size."

"I altered my figure to fit the clothing."

"And most commendably you do," I pointed out.

We arrived a few moments later in Piccadilly. At Number Seventeen is the firm of Messrs Spink & Son, dealers in coins, gemstones, and curios. They were shut until the Monday, but I knew that Mr Spink, Jnr, would be keeping accounts in the back room of the shop, for I had done business here before. My sister and Vanessa waited in the hackney whilst I alighted and rang the doorbell.

Mr Spink, having purchased several gold coins from me this past fortnight, knew that I always gave good value for money, and offered ten guineas for the gold coin I showed him, which he informed me was a Roman *aureus* of the emperor Lucius Verus. This transacted, I rejoined the others, giving the coachman my sister's address in New Cavendish Street.

"Where are we bound?" Sarah asked as I climbed into the hackney.

"To *your* house, to drop you off. I fear that I have involved you in this dangerous interplanetary affair quite long enough."

Sarah laughed. "In my army nurse days, *I* was dodging Jezails while *you* were still in short trousers. I've seen ten thousand howling Afghani tribesmen come screaming down from the mountains with daggers in their teeth and Martini rifles blazing instant death. Rather exciting, I thought it was. Bring on the danger, then: I'm ready!"

"But surely your husband . . ."

"Henry is in Rutlandshire just now, on business, although what business anyone has in Rutlandshire is beyond me. We'll stop in at home long enough for me to pick up some things and leave a note for him, then we press on."

It was raining slightly when we arrived at my sister's house. I paid the coachman, and we three went inside. Vanessa abruptly announced that she wished to go walking for a bit, to see something of London. "I'll go with you," I offered.

"Thank you, no. I desire to go . . . *alone*."

"Do you think it's safe?" Sarah asked.

"I do. Look at how lovely the streets are, in this rain. I never dared to be touched by the rain before, on your world, because rain against my flesh would make me visible to your people. But now, in these clothes, I am a woman of Earth. A proper lady of London!"

And Vanessa went out. I made to follow her, but Sarah's hand upon my arm restrained me. "Let her go. This Dreadful Eye fellow's assassins won't attack her in public while it's raining; they'd be visible."

"That's not what worries me," I told my sister.

"What, then?"

"Sarah, Vanessa hides something from me. I have known her for more than a fortnight; during that time she has never, to my knowledge, taken any food—except for some bread and cheese one night, at my insistence. Nor had she slept, before we found her unconscious in the pantry. Yet she claims that she eats and sleeps as we do. She is *lying* to me, Sarah, and I must think very carefully before proceeding with the full-body tattoo."

I was tired then. Sarah loaned me Henry's bed; I slept fitfully, amid nightmares in which I was pursued by invisible beings through dark London streets. When I awoke, all the bedclothes were covered with sweat.

At ten that evening Vanessa returned. She was still dressed in the clothes that Sarah had lent her, but I marked that the veil was disarrayed. "Are you all right?" I inquired.

"*Splendid!*" Vanessa answered through the veil. "To be able, for the first time in my life, to go among humans, and be accepted as one of them! And the people here are *free,* unlike the people of my own world."

"In the morning, Vanessa," I said, "you and I have some things to discuss. But just now Sarah and I were sitting down to some cold bird and a glass. Won't you join us?"

"Food? No, thank you. I have already . . . *partaken.* I wish to lie down for a bit."

The woman-thing came closer then, and as she approached me I made to straighten her veil with one hand. "Permit me . . ." But she passed me so quickly that my hand only brushed the skin of her invisible face. I touched the corner of her alien mouth, and felt something damp. I waited until Vanessa went upstairs, then I examined my hand. There were, on the forefinger and thumb, faint dark traces of *blood*.

I heard the floorboards creak above me, in the spare bedroom that my sister had offered Vanessa. The creature, having fed, was now retiring for the night. But I did not believe that she was sleeping.

11th December, 1898

I told Sarah this morning of the previous night's incident, and of my deep suspicion that our guest was in the habit of drinking blood.

Sarah grimaced. "You never told me that your lady friend had such distinctive . . . *table manners*. I vote we wake her up and discuss this."

We rapped on Vanessa's door and, receiving no answer, went in.

The creature was asleep. She had removed all her clothes, and lay naked, curled in upon herself. The bed was unused; she slept in a corner near the wall. The visible fragments of her body, all jumbled together in shadows, looked faintly grotesque just now.

There was a quantity of some organic mass inside her belly, clearly visible through the half-visible portions of Vanessa's stomach.

As I approached her, Vanessa awoke. "Are you here to resume the full-body tattoo?"

"Not yet, but . . ."

"Then go away, and please do not awaken me until you are ready to proceed."

I found her veil where she had left it, and pointed to the clotted bloodstains. "What do you call *this?*"

She took it with one invisible hand, and examined the stain before answering: "Left-overs."

"It appears to be human blood," I remarked.

"Either human, or some other flavour," said Vanessa.

"Might I trouble you for an explanation?"

"I do not feel obligated to offer one."

"Then I shan't feel obligated to continue the full-body tattoo," I replied, "and will chuck you out into New Cavendish Street, in your nakedness."

I could feel Vanessa's eyes fixed upon me, even though they were unseen. "You have been kind to me, sir. But do not interfere with my privacy, or I will regretfully but certainly turn unpleasant."

I had anticipated this. "Sarah, please fetch the alcohol."

"*Alcohol!*" The change in Vanessa's demeanour was astonishing. "You would not dare . . . you would not endanger my life . . ."

"When my own and my sister's lives are in peril?" I asked, as Sarah left the room. "I think I am entitled to your trust."

Vanessa saw that I was in earnest, and paused. "Very well. Yes: the blood is . . . *was* that of a human's. A man's."

"Did you kill him?" I wanted to know. Sarah returned just then with a bottle of very passable Bordeaux; Vanessa, seeing this, grew somewhat more docile.

"Yes, I killed him," she said. "In Liverpool Street. He was a ruffian; I tore out his throat."

Sarah gasped, and I took the Bordeaux lest she drop it. "Pray continue, Vanessa."

"There is little to tell," she went on. "I killed the man. And then I ate him, of course."

"That somehow seems logical," I admitted.

My sister hastily poured herself a glass of Bordeaux. "Whatever did you do with the blighter's *clothes?*" I asked our visitor.

"What do *you* do with the wrappings on *your* dinner?" Vanessa replied. "I flung his clothes down a sewer. Also one or two portions of his remains which I found quite indigestible. One must be careful of whom one eats nowadays."

"I quite agree."

My sister had swallowed the wine at one draught, and now gazed at me reproachfully. "We cannot keep this . . . this *vampire* in my house, in my husband's house! I forbid it."

The half-visible creature sat erect against the wall. "Do not condemn me so readily, human. What were you eating last night, when I came in?"

"Cold chicken," said Sarah.

"Did you kill it yourself?"

"Of course not; a poulterer did."

"I see. So I am to be reviled because I kill my own food, whereas you have a tradesman do your killing for you."

"What rot!" I protested. "Killing chickens isn't murder. *You* have killed a human being. A member of my own species."

"And *you,*" said Vanessa, "killed two members of *my* species, when they entered your shop."

"That was different. I didn't kill them to go grocery-shopping. I killed in self-defence."

"Ah! Just so!" There was triumph in the invisible woman's voice. "And I *also* defended myself. The man in Liverpool Street mistook me for a lady of the streetlamp profession, and tried to purchase my services. I refused, and he attempted to ravish me. Do you blame me for defending myself?"

"Against rape? Of course not," said Sarah. "But . . ."

"*Ah!* He was stronger than I, and had more freedom of movement, on account of his trousers. I say, these clothes you Englishwomen wear—these long skirts, and these ridiculous corsets—imprison me like a cage. One would think that your corset-makers wanted women to be as helpless as possible."

"We were discussing cannibalism, not corsets," I pointed out.

"Yes. My assailant had a physical advantage, but I fought back. Then he decided I was no longer rape-worthy, and he tried to strangle me. So I killed him."

I said nothing.

"And having killed him, of course," Vanessa went on, "it would have been wasteful not to eat him. Wastefulness is a sin."

I poured myself a very large glass of Bordeaux. "Excuse us a moment, won't you?" I left the room, and Sarah came with me.

We debated, my sister and I, every possible moral and ethical aspect of our visitor's act. Sarah was not entirely unsympathetic towards Vanessa's behaviour; the fact that Vanessa had not attacked the man until he had endeavoured to molest her made Vanessa's dietary habits somehow less hideous in my sister's eyes. At length, having made our decision, we rejoined our carnivorous houseguest.

"Vanessa," I asked her, "is this event likely to repeat itself in future?"

"I have eaten," she answered. "Now I am sated for the next two Earth-weeks, or thereabouts."

"And in two weeks' time, what then? Will it be necessary to kill another human so that you may eat breakfast?"

"Not likely; any large meat-form of your planet should do. A pig, I think, would make an excellent substitute for a man."

Sarah and I exchanged glances. "Very well," I told Vanessa. "I must insist that, so long as you are with us, you confine your menu to the lower animals. If you desire meat, we will obtain it for you. If there is another incident like this, I shall have to give you in charge to the authorities. No doubt it is perfectly legal to dine on human flesh in the various backwoods provinces, such as Canada, and cannibalism may well be considered a gourmet experience in France—the Frenchmen eat frogs' legs and snails, and would therefore probably enjoy eating something even *more* disgusting, such as other Frenchmen. But this is *England*, Vanessa, and Englishmen simply do not go about eating one another. It just isn't *polite.*"

The Second Part

ALEISTER CROWLEY,
Esq.

11th December, 1898

After Sunday church services, I hired for the day a light dog-cart, and a horse to draw it. I travelled with Vanessa and Sarah to a chemist's warehouse in the Clerkenwell Road, where I purchased the basic implements of the tattoo-artist's trade. The establishment was shut for the Sabbath, but the proprietor lived on the premises, and having dealt with me before he was most eager for my custom. By similar stratagems, I next obtained a supply of pigment earths and oxide bases from the establishment of Messrs Winsor & Newton, in Rathbone Place.

I dare not keep Vanessa in my sister's house any longer, lest the invisible men mount an attack upon the place. We three have agreed, then, that Vanessa and I seek haven elsewhere; once settled, we will send word to Sarah to join us, whilst I resume work on Vanessa's full-body tattoo.

I feel an increasing certainty that Vanessa can be trusted. She had seemed to regard me at first as a tradesman hired for her convenience; now her manner towards me is increasingly that of an ally. And there is no doubt at all in my mind that, whatever this strange Vanessa may be, the forces which oppose her—the disciples of the Dreadful Eye—present a far greater threat to the people of London than Vanessa ever will.

I drove the dog-cart to Sarah's house in New Cavendish Street, whereat my sister took my hand and guided me away from the door of the house, towards Great Portland Street, that we might converse for a few moments at some slight distance from Vanessa.

"Are you quite certain that you'll be all right?" my sister asked me.

"Invisible men may slit my throat at any moment, but other than that everything is just tickety-boo," I replied. "Uncle's shop is gone, of course, and so is Uncle. But I've money, a bit, and I intend to survive."

My sister glanced at the veiled figure sitting alone in the dog-cart. "I worry about leaving you alone with . . . whatever she is."

"Vanessa? I daresay I can handle her."

"That is not what I meant. What if this Dreadful Eye or his disciples attack her again while you are with her?" Sarah asked.

"All the more reason," I answered, "why she needs my help. She has paid me to create upon her body a full-body tattoo; I am honour-bound as a businessman and a gentleman to complete it. Besides, I see now that Vanessa is genuinely in trouble, and I am the only one who will aid her, excepting yourself. It must be terrible for her, to be so completely alone on this planet."

"And nothing else?" my sister asked. Her eyes, china-blue in their clearness, looked intently into my face. "You have no other reason to wander off with this she-thing?"

I thought a bit before replying: "Until Vanessa came I spent my life in a dark little shop, among dust-covered jars. This woman has changed that forever: for the first time in my entire wretched dust-covered life, I do not know what is going to happen next. She has shaped my tomorrows. There is risk if I stay with her, I know, but there is also something else. It is a thing I cannot name, because I have never known it before. But, Sarah, I want that something else."

I kissed my Sarah good-bye, rejoined Vanessa, and rode off slowly towards Great Portland Street beyond. Vanessa, in the dog-cart beside me, was strangely silent. At the edge of Oxford Circus a slight wind sprang up, and I saw the corner of Vanessa's motoring-veil briefly rise. Her face, underneath, was still invisible, of course. But as we rode on in silence, towards Waterloo Bridge, I found myself wondering more fervently than ever what it might be like to *see* Vanessa's face.

11th December, 1898

I obtained lodgings for myself and Vanessa that evening, in the Lambeth district, at Number Sixteen, Walcot Square. The entire neighbourhood seems filled with rather much of London's old and sick and poor. Our lodging-house stands some five minutes' walk from the Asylum for the Blind. And even closer to hand, practically lurking on our doorstep, is that shuttered apparition, the Bethlehem Hospital for the Insane—the notorious *Bedlam*.

I paid our landlady three shillings in exchange for a fortnight's lodging and her promise not to disturb us. She was a curious old witch, asking far more questions about the contents of the dog-cart than I was willing to answer, and when she caught sight of Vanessa—all bundled and gloved, with the motoring-veil —the old woman's curiosity was aroused even further. Eventually, though, I managed to get Vanessa and myself and my crates of chemicals and supplies up the stairs and into our rooms. I shut the door on the landlady's prattle and turned the key in the lock.

"Excellent," said Vanessa, peeling the clothes from her half-visible body as soon as we were alone. "And now we will resume the full-body tattoo."

"Not just yet," I told her. "I must return the cart and horse to the livery stable where I hired them, in Clerkenwell."

"Can the horse not wait until morning?"

"What, in Lambeth? Not likely! The local Yahooligans will make a proper horse-meat stew out of him. Yes, and some dustman's family will set up housekeeping in the dog-cart."

I left then, ignoring Vanessa's protests, and drove off in the dog-cart. I reached Clerkenwell without mishap and, having divested myself of the livery rig and paid for its hire, I proceeded towards the nearest station of the electric tube-railway, in Farringdon Street. But at the Hatton Garden crossroads, something which I could not see quite suddenly and firmly *touched* me.

"This is the man," said a voice.

There was no-one standing before me. I turned.

"Should we kill him, do you think?" asked a second voice, more slurred than the first.

I saw nobody. My accosters were invisible.

A third voice: *"Perhaps he can lead us to the she-fugitive."*

Invisible men. I *assumed* that there were only three of them. There was a slight wrinkling of the air before my face, a vague refraction. I could not tell how many of these creatures were watching me, ready to attack.

The streets all round me were deserted, this being Sunday evening and the Hatton Garden diamond market closed. There might conceivably be any number of invisible men in those streets.

"How is it that you know me?" I asked, in a tone that I hoped would seem calm.

"Do you not remember me?" rasped the first invisible voice.

"I do not, sir; all invisible men look alike to me."

"We fought in your house, you and I. My companions here arrived in London some hours ago."

"I assume that you are hunting Vanessa."

"Aye. The fugitive-she. You have sheltered her, human. Take us to her immediately."

"And if I refuse?"

"Then we shall kill you, and hope that the experience will prove a lesson to all Earthers who would defy us."

"It would certainly be a lesson to *me.*" I was trying to think of some means of escaping these fiends, but how can one escape a menace that one cannot even *see?* I slowly reached into the pocket of my greatcoat, where I was carrying my uncle's old revolver. "How did you find me?" I asked, endeavouring to seem as calm as possible.

"We did not expect to find you so soon," said the voice of the first invisible. *"We were searching London, hoping to sense the internal emanations of she whom we seek. When you passed us just now, human, I recognised you at once."*

Another spoke: *"Earther, give us the fugitive."*

"Sorry. Shan't. Come and kill me, then," I replied, "if you're quick enough."

Something moved. I drew my revolver, and fired at the rippling air in front of me. There was a groan, and a thud; the sound of an invisible *something* sprawled across the cobblestones.

And then the other two attacked me.

I *felt* the cold dampness of their flesh clawing and grasping against me. I *felt* the peculiar sensation of the alien limbs which held me slowly changing from arms into tentacles. I *felt,* as I approached the borderlines of death, the numbing pressure of invisible talons.

I pulled free, and fired my revolver again. There was a sound like a gasp, and I saw the bullet suddenly stop in midair. I must have wounded one of the fiends, and the bullet was lodged in his invisible flesh.

Something cold struck my face. I fell . . . and my revolver, knocked from my hand, clattered off amidst the shadows.

I rose to one knee, but before I could stand something *bit* me, through the fabric of my waistcoat and shirt. I screamed. A mass of cloth, with blood on it, tore away from my chest, clamped in the invisible thing's jaws. I felt weak . . .

"I say, there! *You!*" piped a voice. "You invisible men! Stop, I say!"

My attackers, evidently as startled as I was, let go of me. With one hand to my injury, hoping to stanch the blood flow, I turned towards the source of this voice.

A man was running towards us. He was large, wore *pince-nez* spectacles, and looked to be in his sixties. Well-dressed, with a pointed white beard, and a Malacca walking-stick that he swung wildly as he came.

"Take *that!*" He swung again, and the stick landed smartly on the patch of air in front of me. I heard a crack, and a hissing noise, like the sound of a wounded serpent.

"And *that,* sir!" He swung once more, and something invisible yelped.

"Stand and fight, you transparent cowards! Ha! Good riddance!" Something rushed past me, and then I saw the bullet that had lodged within one of my unseen assailants go galloping off towards Leather Lane, bounding along in midair with a peculiar limping gait.

"Are you all right, man?" my deliverer asked. Behind his beard he was quite red in the face.

"I shall live, I suppose." The bite in my chest was not deep, but was nearly two inches wide. I showed it him, while I recovered my fallen revolver. "This wants medical attention."

"I've a motorcar round the corner," he offered. "Come on, then; the nearest surgery, I think, would be the Bluecoat School at Christ's Hospital."

The motorcar proved to be an Acme & Immisch electric. I tried, as carefully as I could, not to bleed on the seat covers as we got in.

"I am in your debt, sir," I remarked to the stranger as we motored into the Farringdon Road.

"Forget it, fellow; any other chap would do as much. I saw you being attacked by those invisible men, so I . . ."

"*Saw* them, you said?"

The stranger grinned through his moustache. "Oh, I *frequently* see invisible men; they're so much more interesting to look at than the visible sort." He laughed so heartily that he nearly let go the steering-tiller. "I say, they looked funny enough just now! Two of them galumphing away, and dragging the third one behind them." He laughed again, and I was positive that I knew him from somewhere.

"Your face seems familiar to me, sir," I ventured.

"It should. I was knighted last year, at the Queen's Jubilee. I am Sir William Crookes."

"Indeed! I have read of your work, sir, in chemistry and physics."

He harrumphed. "Yes. Of late, however, my efforts have been in the fields of spiritualism and mental telepathy. I am president, sir, of the Society for Psychical Research. I was on my way to a *séance,* in fact, in Chelsea, at the home of my good friend Bram Stoker, when I met you. I say, does it hurt much?"

"Like Billy-O," I admitted, clutching the gash in my chest.

"Steady on; we're nearly there." Sir William suddenly looked up from the road, and watched me. "How comes it, sir, that you are attacked in Hatton Garden by invisible men?"

"And how comes it," I countered him, "that *you* are capable of *seeing* invisible men?"

Sir William Crookes smiled, with the air of a conspirator divulging a secret. "I was born, sir, with abilities that science cannot yet explain. I *perceive,* sir, objects and creatures in the streets of London that can only have been spawned on some world other than this. The Russian mathematician Loubachevsky has theorised that the universe contains an infinite number of dimensions of space. The invisible men, I believe, inhabit one of those alien else-planes."

"Yes, but you can *see* them, and other men cannot!"

"Ah, my friend! Have you heard of the American mysticist Daniel Dunglas Home?" Crookes inquired. "Amazing chap. I worked with him in 1871, and for three years thereafter. The fellow was in the habit of floating in and out through second-storey windows, scrubbing his face with red-hot coals to no ill effect, causing objects to move without touching them, and elongating his body until he touched ceiling and floor both at once. Rather a talented fellow."

"Yes, and great fun at parties, I should think. Those were conjurors' tricks, I daresay. Maskelyne could have done them, or David Devant," I remarked.

"Do not mention your Egyptian Hall stage-magicians to me, sir," said Crookes. "Daniel Home performed his psychic feats in strong light and in a place of my choosing, unencumbered by mirrors or wires, in the presence of myself and other witnesses. Those feats were *real.* There are men born into this world, sir, who have hold of an alien realm. Home was one. I, to a lesser extent, am another: I can *see* the invisible men. It is a birth-talent, not an acquired one. And there are women, sir, spiritualists such as Florence Cook and Mrs Besant, or the late Madame Blavatsky, who have knowledge of the back streets of reality. Hulloa, this is our stop."

We had just passed Newgate Prison, across the way, and now

we stopped at the gates of Christ's Hospital. "Can you make it from here, lad?" my benefactor asked as I alighted.

"Yes, thanks. I hope you won't be late for your *séance.*"

Crookes grinned again, and twisted his white moustache into points. "They can't start until I get there; I'm bringing the ectoplasm." He gave me his card. "I live in Notting Hill, sir; look me up one day. But mind you don't bring your invisible vampires with you to frighten the chambermaids; I've enough trouble keeping good servants as it is."

And then, with a wave of his hand and a hum of his motor electric, the greatest scientist in all England drove into the night.

13th December, 1898

The events of the next thirty hours are of no great concern to this narrative. I told the Christ's Hospital attendants that my injury was a dog's bite, and although they treated it expertly I was still in great pain. I paid two guineas for this medical care, and proceeded with difficulty towards my lodgings. By now it was morning. At the post office in the Kennington Road I wrote a penny postal card, and sent word to Sarah of my new address. When I returned to Walcot Square—bandages, bloodied shirt, and all—Vanessa was there, concerned at my long absence. I told her of my run-in with the invisible men, and then went straight away to bed.

I awoke in late afternoon, and resumed my work. After blending some flesh-coloured pigments, and inspecting the few tattooing implements I had managed to buy on Sunday, I bade Vanessa undress.

I had previously rendered one of Vanessa's lower limbs visible from the ankle to the base of the pelvis, and left her other leg nearly completed. I finished this now, then resumed my labours at the base of her breasts. It is a necessary factor of the tattoo-artist's craft that he not spend too many consecutive hours on one portion of the subject's anatomy, lest the skin in that region become too sensitised, and thus inflamed. Hence I coloured Vanessa one bit at a time.

After some hours at my task my eyes grew tired, and I could not immediately continue. "I'm going out for a pub-crawl," I told Vanessa, "and a bit of a nosh. Can I bring you back anything?"

"Thank you, no; I am not hungered. The humans of this district look most unappetising."

I spent much of that evening in a pub in the Kennington Road, consuming bitter and considering my options. I did *not* want Vanessa and myself to remain in Lambeth—nor in any part of London—so long as her enemies were still after us. Sooner or later the invisible assassins would catch up with us, and innocent lives would be endangered if the attack were to come in a well-populated district.

I was wondering whether I ought perhaps to disengage myself altogether from this Adventure of the Invisible Men. I was in danger so long as I stayed with Vanessa; the Dreadful Eye and his carrion-slaves seemed hell-bent on recapturing her. Surely, in sanity's name, would I not be better off almost anyplace else than in the middle of this interplanetary battle?

I kept thinking about the tattoo shop in Nicholas Lane. It had brought, to my uncle and myself, fewer customers each year. The vogue for tattoos among the Mayfair set had long since faded, and up until the night when Vanessa first entered the shop my career—and my life—had been very much a failure.

I had scrabbled, like some human blackbeetle, for twenty years. In all that time I had been unwilling to risk what little security I possessed, too reluctant to strike out on one single adventure that might bring some small but genuine *accomplishment* to my undistinguished days.

Vanessa, strange Vanessa, had changed my life forever. A month ago my life had been one of decay masquerading as stability. Now I was homeless, down to my last fifty guineas, and being pursued by a horde of invisible horrors from some land beyond the borders of reality. But, by God, I was *alive,* yes, and whereas a month ago I would have hidden from the shadows of bill collectors, tonight—full up with my own excitement and several pints of Whitbread's Bitter Ale—tonight I felt ready and able to fight ten thousand slavering battalions of bloodthirsty invisible men.

I resolved, then, to continue this adventure . . . for the moment. If things grew too dangerous later . . . well, perhaps I might then turn tail and run after all, and leave Vanessa to her own devices whilst I scurried back to my dusty shelves and jars.

And then again, I might stay till the battle was ended.

13th December, 1898

At eleven this morning, having been several hours at my tattooing, I laid down my needle and informed Vanessa that I was going out.

"Again?" she protested. "When you have so much left to do?"

"I cannot continue the full-body tattoo much longer," I informed her, "without help. The arms, the legs, the breasts: these are easy enough to tattoo, and you see quite plainly the quality of my work. But, Vanessa, my needle must soon begin entering regions of your flesh where tattoo work is both difficult and dangerous. The method of tattooing a person's throat, for example, or near the sockets of the eyes . . ."

Vanessa stood. "The Zebra Man, in Smithfield's . . ."

". . . was tattooed, yes, quite all over his body. But my uncle and I never tattooed *all* of him; we never tattooed his genitalia, for an instance, yet you expect me to perform such a service for *you*. And tattooing the Zebra Man's face and throat, as well as certain portions of the groin and lower spine, required surgical operations of the greatest delicacy. The epidermal layer must be lifted from the cutanea, injected with the pigment, then retracted and—frequently—sutured. It is difficult, time-consuming, and painful. It also involves, on the part of the patient, some element of physical risk."

"Bother the risk."

"Easy enough to say. But how, Vanessa, can I perform surgery on invisible flesh?"

"You have tattooed me satisfactorily thus far."

"Yes. By coating the skin with a soap-film, so that it becomes visible as a sort of great bubble. By sense of touch and from years of practice, I can sense with quite tolerable accuracy how deeply to insert the needle. Having injected your circulatory system with dye, I know where your blood vessels are, and how to manipulate the needle to avoid them. But so far there has been some slight margin for error. In the matter of tattooing near the eyes, upon the throat or genitalia, where the blood vessels and nerves lie so closely together, I must have pinpoint accuracy." I stood up then, and put on my coat. "I cannot complete the full-body tattoo by myself, but I believe I know of someone who can aid us."

The nearest station for the underground was at Elephant and Castle. I boarded the East London Line, transferring at the Embankment for the District Railway to Notting Hill Gate. I emerged from the depths there and, slightly blinking from the sunlight, I went to seek Sir William Crookes.

I had never been to Notting Hill before, and was astonished by its splendour. The mansions, the tree-lined avenues, the electric streetlights: so very different from the dark and smoke-filled tenements and alleys, the incessant stench of coal-gas squalor and despair that I had left behind, one hour ago in Lambeth.

I had endeavoured, before my arrival, to render myself as presentable as possible: a shave, a good wash, and a handkerchief tucked into the hole in my waistcoat where the invisible fangs had bitten me, to conceal as best I could the bandaging and bloodstains. The clothes I wore now were all I possessed; I'd had no time to purchase others since my escape from the fire in Nicholas Lane.

The calling card that Sir William Crookes had given me stated his address as Number Seven, Kensington Park Gardens. The entrance, when I reached it, was magnificent: bluebottle windows, and four fluted columns at the top of the stairs.

The entrance bore one of these newly invented electrical doorbells, and I recalled having once read that the home of Sir William Crookes was one of the first private residences in London to have been electrically wired. I pressed the bell stud, and a moment later there came footsteps.

The door opened as much as two inches, and a manservant —I took him for the butler—appeared. "Yes, sir?"

I showed him the calling card. "Sir William Crookes told me that I might call on him . . . that is, if he is not indisposed."

The butler had a nose like the beak of a heron: he looked down the entire great length of it at me. "You cannot see him, *sir.*" His stress upon that last syllable appeared faintly contemptuous. "As it happens, Sir William is in Bristol, attending a congress of the British Association for the Advancement of Science. He is that body's president. Good afternoon."

I knew that something was wrong here. "Sir William told *me,*" I said slowly, "that he was president of the Society for Psychical Research."

"So he is, yes. Also a Fellow of the Royal Society. Very busy he is, sir. As am I. Good afternoon."

"Wait!" The butler had begun to close the door, but I deftly inserted my foot in the opening. "If I may make so bold as to ask: why did Sir William depart London so suddenly?"

"Suddenly, sir?" Until now the butler had behaved as though I were merely some ruffian. Now he seemed to regard me as a proper lunatic. "You are mistaken. Sir William has been in Bristol since September, and has not returned."

"But I saw him two nights past, in Hatton Garden. He was driving his Acme & Immisch."

"I think not. Sir William owns no such machine. Good day, sir."

At that moment a strange man bounded up the steps behind me and shouldered his way to the door. He was clad in green, purple, and orange, and his funnel-shaped hat was painted all over with gilt symbols: stars, and crescent moons, and other cabalistic shapes. "I have come to see Sir William Crookes, my man!" he cried, slithering past me. "My perpetual-motion machine has stopped again, and I . . ."

The butler, clearly, was used to this sort of thing. "Sir William is in Bristol. Good day." He gave me a look which indicated that this newcomer and I were, in the butler's regard, interchangeable eggs from the same cuckoo's nest. Evidently Sir William

Crookes, with his highly publicised dabblings in the spirit world, must be a target for all the crackpots and treacle-brains in London, and his butler obviously thought me quite as demented as this spangled jackanapes beside me. *"Good day,"* he said to both of us.

And then the door *was* closed, quite firmly, and the parti-coloured jabbernowl beside me was clutching at my coat. "How do you do, sir? I am the reincarnation of Nostradamus, and . . ."

"What a coincidence," I remarked. "So am I."

"What?" he stammered. "You *too?* But . . ."

"Yes, we are both Nostradamus. Leave me alone, as I have no desire to be seen talking to myself."

I disengaged my coat from the lunatic's grip and hurried away. Behind me, the man was still shouting: "Come back, sir! I am soliciting funds for a balloon expedition to the South Pole, to witness last night's solar eclipse!"

"If the eclipse was last night," I called over my shoulder, as I made my escape, "how can you witness it *now?*"

"Better late than never. Pledge a thousand guineas, sir, in the name of Science! Come back!"

The last I saw of him, as I turned the corner into Ladbroke Grove, he was explaining to a very large policeman that the end of the world would arrive at any moment. "It will for *you,* mate," said the policeman, and lifted his truncheon.

Later, that same day

"Sir William is a brilliant man, Vanessa; perhaps the most brilliant in England. He fully grasps the notion of a bridge between the worlds. He would make a valuable ally for us in the battle to come. Unfortunately, I haven't the faintest notion of how to get hold of him. Either Sir William Crookes has learnt the art of existing in London and Bristol both at once, or else his butler is lying."

I continued my work on Vanessa's full-body tattoo until well into that evening. I found it increasingly disturbing that—as my labours rendered Vanessa's anatomy more and more visible beneath my tattoo implements—it was becoming rapidly more obvious that Vanessa's feminine physique was exceedingly shapely indeed. One might go so far as to consider it *voluptuous.*

But I know now that Vanessa is a shape-changer. How can I determine if her present form—which undeniably arouses me—is in fact her *true shape?* I still remembered the ghastly appearance of the dead thing that I had buried in the cellar in Nicholas Lane. What if *Vanessa* is actually shaped like that as well?

At some time after ten in the evening, our landlady rapped on the door and informed me that I had a visitor. I went downstairs and found my sister Sarah carrying a basket.

"Come, this *is* prompt!" I said, kissing her. "I only wrote you yester-morning."

"Is she here?" Sarah asked.

"Vanessa? Yes. I'll take you to her."

I could tell, by the look of distaste on Sarah's face when we entered the lodging-rooms, that she was bothered by the darkness and filth of the place. I put another penny into the gas meter, and turned up the lamps.

My sister, bless her, had brought some small quantity of food, and the makings for tea. Without my asking her, she at once went to the gas-ring and put up a kettle. "What happened *there?*" she asked, touching the bandage poking out at my shirtfront.

I told her, then, of my battle in Hatton Garden, of my rescue by Sir William Crookes, and of the curious behaviour of the butler.

When tea was ready, Sarah and I ate. I offered Vanessa some food, but she was getting dressed. She put on her hat and adjusted the motoring-veil. "I'm going out for some air," she announced, and left.

"Is it safe to let her just go like that?" Sarah asked me. "The last time she went out she ate somebody. I wonder she hasn't made sandwiches out of *you* yet."

"Perhaps I don't taste very good," I suggested. "I'm beginning to see why Vanessa eats human flesh; it saves her the need of washing dishes. Perhaps we ought . . ."

Someone screamed, down below in the street.

"That was Vanessa!" I shouted to Sarah. *"Come on!"*

I bolted down the stairs three at a time, with one hand on the bannisters and the other hand gripping my revolver. Sarah was not far behind me.

I rushed into Walcot Square and ran towards the sound of the screams. Several streets farther on, in the darkness, I suddenly tripped over something. I landed face-down in the street, and had to feel about among the dimly lit cobblestones to find out what I had stumbled over.

It was the body of an invisible man.

"Oh, dear God." It was Sarah who spoke. *"Look! Look up at the sky!"*

On my knees in that gutter in Lambeth I looked up, and saw.

A ball of violet-coloured light was approaching us above the rooftops of the Kennington Road. I saw it turn, change directions in midair, until at length it hovered some thirty feet above us.

"What is it, in God's name?" asked Sarah.

The ball of light grew larger, and began to change shape. It went flat, like a huge flying disk, and then the disk became a hexagon. And then the hexagon turned in upon itself, and became —upon my honour—a hole in the sky.

I saw a tunnel in midair, beginning in the sky above the Kennington Road, and its other end—far away in the dimness and distance—leading into a place that I could barely perceive and did not want to see.

A high wind began to spring up, pulling at my coat. The very air of London was being sucked into that vortex in the sky, and the wind clawed and howled and it clutched at me as it rushed headlong into the hole.

"He is coming," said a voice at my elbow. It was Vanessa. The veil had been torn from her hat, and in the gaslight I saw the empty space above the collar of her frock, where her invisible head was. "He is coming for me. The Dreadful Eye is approaching."

In the dimness of the passageway from our world to the alien place, I saw a figure coming towards us. It squatted at the far end of the sky-hole at first, but then it came. Leaping, capering, bounding towards us, it beckoned obscenely with a pair of upper limbs that clawed the air as it approached. The thing was still too far away, too indistinct, for me to see its outlines clearly. But the leaping horror was approaching quite rapidly, in the howling of the wind.

I did not want to see the thing's face.

"Where are the police?" Sarah asked. "Why doesn't someone send for them? Are we the only people in London who can *see* this?"

"That tunnel is only just above the rooftops," I told her. "It cannot be seen, except from almost directly below. And there is so much crime in this quarter of Lambeth that few residents dare come out at night. I fear no-one will help us."

"But they must have heard Vanessa scream. They will come out to see . . ."

"They heard her scream, yes. That is *why* no-one will help us. They are hiding indoors, with the shutters latched."

The bounding, capering thing clambered out of the hole in the sky, and squatted in the shadows of the nearest rooftop, like some misshapen gargoyle come to life. *"Give up the she-one,"* it hissed. *"She is mine."*

"Are you the Dreadful Eye, then?" I shouted against the wind, whilst I reloaded my revolver.

"I am he. That is, I am a portion of the whole. What you witness before you is not the totality." The thing came nearer, scuttling crabwise amongst the rooftops.

"Then show yourself," I said, making what I hoped was a convincing show of bravery, for the sake of Vanessa and Sarah. For myself, what I wanted was to *run.* "Come and give us a look of you."

"My true shape, human?" hissed the leaper in shadows. *"If you saw my true shape, you would covet insanity. What colour are your nightmares, manling? What shape is your death? Shall I trace you the outlines of fear?"* The thing laughed, and flung itself headlong off the rooftop towards my face.

"Run, Sarah!" I shouted. "Vanessa, get away!" I put one arm

across my head, to shield my eyes, and fired my revolver at the oncoming thing. Either I missed, or no bullet could slaughter the horror, for the Dreadful Eye kept coming.

It landed twenty feet away from me, atop the cobblestones of Kennington Lane. I started to run, and although I knew I must not turn and look back, still . . . I looked.

The thing in the gutter began to change shape as I watched. In the gaslight and fog of Kennington Lane I could not see it clearly, but it began to assume the form of a naked human *leg*. It drew erect now, with its toes pointing towards me. At the top of that single pale leg, sprouting out of its stump where the hip should have been, there grew a human head. The head opened its eyes, and it saw me. The face, in that terrible darkness, seemed familiar.

"Oh, my God . . ."

The single disembodied leg came towards me, bounding over the cobblestones, and its mouth was split open in a gibbering laugh. And as it came within a yard of me I saw that *the thing had my face.*

I fired my revolver again, point-blank. I saw the bullet strike the face, and the face collapsed inwards on itself. The dead thing laughed, and its laugh became a howl of grinning triumph. I saw the head-legged thing change its shape again, altering itself into a writhing mass of tentacles and eyes. There was a mouth, in the centre of the mass, which dripped saliva as it spoke:

"What shape shall I copy next, human? Any object you see may be me in disguise. If a lamp-post sprouts eyes and calls to you in the dark, that is I. If a faceless mannequin climbs out of a dress-shop window and follows you, beckoning, that is I. I may be the person beside you in a crowded room. I am anyone and all. If the lady whom you kiss suddenly sprouts tentacles from her face, that is I. If you see your own face in the mirror, and your reflection in the glass suddenly speaks to you and changes to another, I am there."

"Keep away," I said, holding the revolver, although bullets were apparently useless against this thing.

"I want the fugitive, manling. The she-one you are sheltering from me."

"You shan't have her."

"*Such bravery as yours is commendable, manling. I reward you, by permitting you to live. For the moment. Tomorrow they will come for you, a battalion of invisible men. You will give the she-fugitive to my disciples, manling. If you refuse, they will kill you.*"

And then the tentacled thing sank into the ground and vanished, laughing. The screaming wind faded from a howl to a whisper, then was gone. I looked up: the gap between the universes, the sky-corridor above the Kennington rooftops, had vanished.

All the way back to Walcot Square, I kept looking over my shoulder. When I returned to the lodging-house, Sarah was there, gathering up the tea-things. She seemed unusually quiet. Vanessa knelt in the corner; she appeared to be injured, and was binding up her wounds with some strips of cloth torn from the drapes.

"We cannot remain here," said my sister after I had come in. "Now that the invisible men know where we are, they may attack again."

"They do not know precisely where we are," I ventured. "Only that we are living in this approximate area. I saw nothing follow me here."

"Nothing *visible,* you mean."

I saw what Sarah meant.

"You are right, Sarah," I said. "*You* must leave. Your life is in danger so long as you remain with Vanessa."

"So is yours."

"I accept that."

"And do you think that I cannot take the same risk," Sarah asked, "just because I am a woman?"

"No; because you are married. If the Dreadful Eye were to kill you, do you think that I would be able to face your husband, and tell him what happened? Go home to Henry, Sarah; for his sake and mine, and for your own sake as well."

There was a cut on Sarah's forehead; she touched it now, and winced. "There is something you should know," she said to me quietly, so that Vanessa would not hear. "I have had, all this time, some doubt as to whether this Vanessa could be trusted. But now I believe that I was wrong to have doubted her."

"Why, what happened?" I asked.

"On the way back here just now, at the bottom of Union Street, I was attacked by an invisible man."

"Sarah!"

"Vanessa saved me," reported my sister. "She could have got away while I was struggling. Instead she injured herself in coming to my aid."

I kissed Sarah and accompanied her to the door. "You had better go. Vanessa and I will get away as soon as we can. I shall contact you as soon as we are safely hidden elsewhere. I must get Vanessa out of London immediately." I kissed my sister again. "Be careful, won't you?"

"Be careful yourself, you mean. If you get your throat slit by invisible Martians, don't come running to *me.*"

We held each other once more, perhaps for the last time, and then Sarah was gone. I closed the door of the lodging-room behind her.

Vanessa, in the corner, was not moving. She had bandaged herself, and fashioned another veil from a corner of the drapes. Now she seemed to have collapsed from sheer exhaustion. I sat on the cold floor beside her, and touched her invisible face.

I knew her for a refugee, a fugitive from a tyrant's domain, alone and fleeing for her life. I felt a strange bond with her; for though I was born in London and have lived here the whole of my days, there are times when I feel so out of place and cut off from the rest of humanity that I might as well be an invisible man from an alien race, adrift in London. I felt that . . . in some rare, peculiar way . . . I knew this strange alien female as intimately as I understood myself.

She was moving now: still unconscious, but beginning to stir. I knelt beside her, in that wretched little room in Walcot Square, and held Vanessa's hands in both my own. There was a fire in the grate; it was beginning to die, and as the last embers faded to sparks, and grew cold, the rays of morning appeared dimly through the window, and I felt my growing weariness begin to overtake me. I had to get up. I had to get Vanessa away, before the invisible men might find us. But I was so tired; I needed to rest for a moment. Vanessa's hands felt warm in mine, and with my eyes closed it seemed as though I could see her invisible face.

14th December, 1898

"What time is it?" Vanessa asked.

"Hmmm?" Out of reflex, I reached for my pocket to take out my watch. Then I realised that I was lying on the floor, and that Vanessa was sprawled half on top of me, my chest and stomach pillowing her head, and daylight was streaming through the tattered drapes. What time *was* it? I sat up, and opened my watch. *Good Lord!* Half past seven!

"We must get *out* of here, Vanessa. *Now!* Get dressed; cover your invisible parts as best you can. We haven't . . ."

At that instant there was a sound at the door. I had barely time to help Vanessa veil her face when suddenly the door—which I was certain had been locked—flew wide open, and a stranger came in.

He was a broad-shouldered man, clean-shaven and lantern-jawed, and scarcely twenty years of age. He wore an open-collared shirt, and a large flowing four-in-hand cravat, tied into the clumsiest of all possible bow-knots. His mouth was a glistening obscenity in the centre of his face. The thickened lower lip dangled pendulously, his grotesque tongue surmounting it like some moist-coated leech. His teeth, I observed, had been carefully filed into points. I had never previously beheld any man who looked quite so satanic.

"Sir William Crookes suggested that I visit you," remarked the stranger, extracting some small bits of wire from the keyhole as he spoke. "May I come in?"

"It seems as though you already have," I replied, whilst he closed the door and pocketed his picklocks. "How did you find us, sir?"

He stroked his forehead with a theatrical flourish. "All

knowledge is accessible to one who comprehends the universal secrets. Besides, I followed you here."

"Indeed? From where, pray?"

"I was in Notting Hill yesterday, reclaiming the motorcar that I had loaned to Sir William. An Acme & Immisch electric, it was."

"So the butler *was* lying." I nodded. "Sir William *was* home."

"Indeed," said our strange visitor. "Sir William returned from Bristol in October. But there are certain . . . *activities* . . . in Sir William's private life which necessitate occasional . . . *evasions* . . . as to his whereabouts. At any rate, Sir William suggested that I learn your address, so I followed you here from his house. I would have called upon you last night, sir," the stranger went on, "but after ascertaining your address I had to leave immediately, owing to a pressing engagement with three naked virgins and a pentagram in Chelsea."

"The social event of the season, no doubt," I remarked.

"Yes. However, this is not a social call," said the visitor. "Are you aware, sir, that this house is entirely surrounded by invisible men?"

I heard Vanessa gasp, and I very likely turned pale, but the man with the file-sharpened teeth was quite calm. "No fear: they don't seem to know which house you're in yet. If we try to leave now they'll find us, but if we wait here for a time they may pass on. The people outside in Walcot Square cannot see them, and the invisible men are taking care not to be touched by any passersby. So no-one knows that they are here. But *I* can see them, for I am able to perceive the invisible world."

I was aware that Sir William Crookes possessed the ability to *see* the invisible men; it was not wholly impossible that this stranger perceived them as well. "What is your name, sir?" I inquired of him.

"My name is unimportant," said the visitor. "I have taken many names: Baphomet, Therion, Adeptus Minor, Frater Perdurabo. The world will one day know me as the Great Beast. My earthly family's name was Crowley, but I attach no importance to such mundane cognomena. I am a student, sir, of the arcane and other-worldly. Sir William tells me that you have dealings with these invisible men, and it is clear that they have come to Earth from elsewhere. I have need of your help, sir, in obtaining knowledge of their invisible realm."

"He cannot help you," said Vanessa to Crowley, or whatever his name was. "He cannot show you the way to the invisible world. *But I can.*"

She took off her hat and the veil, and revealed her invisible face.

I give Crowley credit for this much; he never blinked. "An outworlder!" he said, as though meeting invisible ladies was quite the most natural thing. "I am honoured to meet you, Miss—?"

"I am calling myself Vanessa Steele just now. What do you wish to know of my planet?"

"The invisible dimension?" asked Crowley. "I seek knowledge, higher learning than can be obtained in this smokestack-world of London. I have travelled extensively in the Alps, and visited St. Petersburg, and I am currently planning an expedition to the Himalayas. The more realms I visit, the more wisdom I acquire. Knowledge is power; therefore I desire absolute knowledge over all."

"Which means," I observed, "that you also desire absolute *power* over all."

"Of course," said Crowley. "Doesn't everybody?"

"For myself," answered Vanessa, "I seek only the power to accomplish my cause. *I must free my people.* If I show you the path to my homeworld, sir, will you aid me in my battle against the Dreadful Eye?"

"A battle, or a thousand battles!" said Crowley gallantly. "When do we set forth?"

"There stands the fugitive." The door quite suddenly burst open, and I heard the tramping of invisible feet. *"You will come with us now,"* an invisible voice rasped.

"What do you want of us?" Crowley inquired. He seemed calm, yet I sensed that he was fully aware of the danger. "What business have you, breaking in like this?"

*"With you, Earther? Stand away and we will leave you alone.
The same applies to that tattoo-scribbler beside you, although he has
been much trouble to our cause. Our business here is with the she-one.
Stand aside."*

"You shall not have Vanessa," I said, "unless you deal with
me first."

"Steady on, laddie," warned Crowley. *"I* can see these invisible bastards; you can not. There are at least seven of them in this
room, and Great Pan knows how many more are coming up the
stairs. D'you think that we three can take the lot of 'em?"

I took out my revolver. "We shall ruddy well *have* to."

Several voices laughed—an *alien* laughter—and then suddenly all fell silent. Something was wrong, and I knew suddenly
what it was.

The noises, the street sounds of London, were gone. The
human voices from the shops, the hoofbeats, the barrow-trundle
sound of wooden wheels, the rattle of broughams in the Kennington Road; all had stopped. The only sound still left in all the
world was the soft, hawking gasp of Vanessa's breath, gently warm
against my shoulder. I felt for her hand, and held it. She was
trembling.

Vanessa whimpered something: *"No!"*

A sound. It came from someplace far away. It was a hum, a
deep and sonorous throb, that seemed to come from the farthest
extremities of the universe. A hum that could not be ignored, for
its sound and its tone seemed to clutch at every level of my being.
I felt the floor begin to throb beneath my feet, and the walls and
the roof and the gas-pipes throbbed as well. And the hum, that
seemed to originate from someplace past the stars, beyond the
borderlines of sanity and time, the hum that had travelled across
all eternity with the specific destination of this filthy lodging-
house in Lambeth, came in through all the walls and pipes and
rafters.

The colour came. A tiny pinprick of light, that wavered
slowly to the rhythm of the hum. And then, as the humming grew
louder, the light began to grow. A circular aura of violet-coloured
light, it spread and dangled humming in the space above the

hearth. And then the sound increased, and loudened, until the hum was a roar that grew dynamo-loud, and the violet-coloured circle of light had transformed itself into a hexagon.

The winds came. A breeze at first, to set the curtains dancing. Then the breeze was a gust, then a gale, and the wind came roaring madly all around us. The drapes, the tablecloth began fluttering. All the air in the room was being *drawn,* with incredible suction, into that glowing hexagon. The thing became a hole in midair, an alien vortex swallowing everything it touched.

The curtains, with a sudden tearing sound, pulled away from the window and fell, spinning rapidly like wreckage in a whirlpool, full into the centre of the vortex. I saw the curtains touch the glowing violet light . . . and then they *vanished.*

The wind was louder now, and so was the gathering hum. Crowley had both hands clapped over his ears; I should have liked to do the same, but I was holding Vanessa with one hand and my revolver in the other. I found it difficult to breathe, as the air was sucked out of the room and into that vortex of light.

The window-panes began to rattle. The vibrations of the glass became more insistent as the humming sound increased, until at last, with a splintering crash, all the window-panes shattered, and the slivers of glass hurtled into the growing hexagon of light. The implosion of the windows caused a great rush of air to flow into the room, but as fast as it came the purple vortex consumed it, in a torrent of wind. I felt a smothering sensation.

The hexagon of light was now roughly four feet across. Until this moment the six-sided thing had been more or less equilateral, but now its topmost and lowermost edges began to move towards the ceiling and floor very rapidly, causing the four remaining edges of the hexagon to lengthen. The pulsating aura was now some eight feet high, and half that distance wide. Its hexagonal form had now taken on the shape and outlines of a *coffin.*

The humming stopped, and the vortex ceased growing. It remained motionless now, as though waiting.

The wind continued howling; for so long as the vortex existed, it would continue to draw all the air of London through the shattered windows of that room, to be consumed within itself.

Vanessa was trembling quite violently. "I will *not* go back to that place," she managed to say. I held her, with her invisible head cradled between my shoulder and neck. I could feel her half-visible breasts pushing against the still-painful wound in my chest; the pain increased, yet was somehow tinted with pleasure by Vanessa's touch against it.

I discovered, at precisely that instant, that I loved her.

"You will come with us now," rasped the voice of an invisible brute, near my arm. *"Our master, the great and Dreadful Eye, has fashioned this corridor between the worlds. The she-fugitive will now step within it."*

I cocked my revolver. "And if I will not permit you to take her?"

"Then we shall kill you, or force you to accompany us into the passageway between realms. When you discover what awaits within, you will wish then that you HAD been killed."

Crowley appeared to be somewhat less frightened than I was, or else he was more capable of concealing his terror. He stepped towards the throbbing hexagon of light, and slowly stretched out a forefinger so as to *almost*—not quite—touch the glowing cavity.

"High-intensity particle waves, right enough," he remarked. "I daresay that if I were to bump into this thing edge-on, so that one side of me passed through it and the other side did not, I would be neatly cut in half."

I decided to act. The constant torrent of onrushing air pouring into the room made breathing difficult, but it also did something else: I could *see,* more distinctly than before, a refraction as though certain portions of the air were thicker than other parts; the peculiar wrinkling that indicated the presence of invisible men. I perceived the bare alien outline of one, standing directly in front of me, and another one to my left.

I attacked. I fired my pistol at the being to my left, and at the same instant I lowered my shoulders and *butted* the creature in front of me. I felt the body collapse as I struck it, heard a howl in some alien tongue.

I must have knocked the creature up against the vortex. For

an instant *I saw the thing's body,* as the howling invisible man fell headlong against the hexagon of light. He struck the edge of the vortex as he stumbled against it, so that the upper portion of his body plunged through, as his waist touched the edge. And then I saw him, in outline, as *his body was sliced cleanly in half.* His uppermost portion vanished, presumably into the alien realm; the other half fell to the floor, and emitted a sickening odour.

Something grabbed me; *two* somethings, and they were wrestling me towards the vortex. Orders were barked in some alien speech.

I caught a glimpse of Crowley in the struggle. He, at least, could *see* the invisible attackers. He kicked, punched, and thrusted, his hair contorting wildly in the wind. He seemed to be using some arcane form of self-defence; the Oriental *ju-jitsu,* perhaps, or the French *savate.*

I fired my revolver and hoped that the bullets struck invisible flesh. I was running out of bullets, with no time to reload.

Vanessa changed shape very suddenly; I saw the visible portions of her body elongate right out of her garments. She appeared to be battling at least three of the invisible assassins. I fired again, and heard an alien moan.

"The window!" Crowley shouted. *"Get out, man! The window!"*

Something clutched me round the ankles, and I fell. I took out my pocket-knife and slashed at whatever thing held me. I *felt* the blade slice into invisible flesh, and scrape against something unseen that was probably bone.

I fired my last bullet at the gibbering thing. I pulled free and leapt to the window sill, amidst the broken glass, and balanced for a moment on the ledge. I turned to look back into the room, and that was when I saw it.

The violet-coloured aperture of light, the gateway to the Dreadful Eye's dimension, slowly turned until it faced directly towards me. And now I saw a many-legged *something,* scrabbling about within the violet passageway, far in distance but rapidly closer . . .

"Vanessa! Crowley!" I yelled. *"Bloody hell, let's leg it out of here! It's . . ."*

Something snatched at my collar; I lost my balance and fell. There was a tearing sound, and then I saw the cobblestones of Walcot Square come rushing up to strike me in the face.

I fell against a drainpipe, careered off it at an angle, and landed, most ingloriously, in a rain barrel. I climbed out of the rain-butt dripping wet, with sharp pains in one shoulder and knee, and a robin's-egg lump on my head. But at least I had avoided landing face-first on the cobblestones, which would have made a deep impression on my outlook.

I heard a crash from above, and saw Vanessa's visible portions—with the invisible parts of her presumably attached—plunging headlong out of the window. I limped to the kerb, and managed to catch her as she fell. Her shape-changer's body went slack in my arms.

"Look out below! Gardy-loo!"

Crowley stood on the window-sill. There was blood on his shirt. "Jump, man!" I shouted. "I can catch you, I think."

"Jump?" he answered, in withering scorn. "My dear sir, you are addressing a magus who has divined the sacred mysteries of the East. I shall *levitate,* slowly and gracefully, with the utmost of . . ."

"Jump, you bloody idiot!"

Something seized him, apparently; I saw Crowley twist in midair, and then he fell towards the street. Vanessa shape-changed to her full height, and caught him as he plummeted. I heard her gasp at the moment of impact; it was clear that her pain was intense.

We ran. Crowley and I took Vanessa by either arm, and the three of us clattered down the street towards Ship Lane.

"My motorcar!" shouted Crowley, pointing to a machine parked at the kerb near to hand. It was the Acme & Immisch that Sir William Crookes had used. "Climb in, then! We're off!"

I helped Vanessa in, and we roared away in a thick cloud of dust.

"I say, that *was* fast!" I remarked.

"Precisely why I purchased an electric," said Crowley, guiding the steering-tiller as he spoke. We were roaring down Lambeth Walk now and gathering speed. "These electrically-driven motorcars can be switched on instantly. Had I bought one of those petrol-driven machines, you would still be battling invisible men whilst I was struggling with the hand crank. I have no doubt that, if common sense prevails, the inefficient petrol-driven motorcar will go belly-up before 1900."

Vanessa was peering towards the road behind us. "We seem to have lost them," she reported.

"Keep your head down, fair outworlder lady," said Crowley. "These motorcars attract the stares of all the horse-drawn antiquated oafs of London. It wouldn't do for 'em to see an electric go rattling past with a half-visible woman inside." He unshipped the throttle, and twisted the steering-tiller. "Cry halloo if you see any monsters; I know of a circuitous escape route."

By now we had crossed Lambeth Bridge, and reached the Horseferry Road. Crowley drove, as rapidly as possible, through several of the alleys and side streets of Westminster, through turnings of decreasing access and increasing obscurity—from Old Pye Street to Strutton Ground, to Greycoat Place, to Artillery Row—proceeding steadily northwards through Soho and Bloomsbury.

"We *have* lost them," breathed Vanessa. "I can no longer sense any nearness to my pursuers. We are safe, then."

"For *now,*" I added, amid the rattling of the engine.

A few crossroads later, Crowley motored into Chancery Lane, past the stone arch of Old Serjeant's Inn on our right, and parked in front of a large grey stone building just south of the High Holborn. "Here we are," announced Crowley, switching off his machine.

"Where is *here?*" Vanessa asked.

"Numbers Sixty-seven through Sixty-nine, Chancery Lane," said our mysterious companion. "Come in, and refresh yourselves. This is my home."

14th December, 1898

The house at 67–69 Chancery Lane did not appear—from the outside, at least—particularly strange. Then I saw, among the row of seven windows on the building's second storey, a most peculiar thing: all the windows were bracketed by floral ornaments, cut into the masonry, but *one* window—the second casement from the left—was flanked by a pair of stone faces: a bearded male image on the left, and a feminine likeness upon the right. They seemed to watch us, silent-countenanced and grim. No other window of the house, I noticed, displayed any faces.

"That window borders on my rooms," said Crowley, opening the front door. "I regret that several other tenants lodge within these walls. Fortunately, we have only two flights of stairs to negotiate."

There was nobody on the ground floor at the moment, but Crowley and I put our coats over the half-visible Vanessa as she left the motorcar, lest some passer-by appear.

We went upstairs to the first floor without incident, and thence to the second. At the door to Crowley's second-storey flat an astonishing sight awaited us. Crowley's doorpull was a pewter ornament, fashioned in the shape of a hideous face: a demon, with horns and pointed ears. It thumbed its nose obscenely with both hands, and its pewter tongue dangled out from its porcelain lips to form a leer of the most grotesque depravity. The cord of the doorpull projected from the demon's lips. Beneath this grinning demon was a card frame, bearing a neatly lettered card:

COUNT VLADIMIR SVAREFF, M.M.

"That stands for *'Master Mage,'* my rightful title," said our host, producing his latch-key. "'*Svareff*' is one of my current aliases. My detestable parents cursed me from birth with the unfortunate name Edward Alexander Crowley. I changed my Christian name to Aleister last year, when I abandoned Christianity."

"By what name are we to know you, then?" I asked him.

"My friends call me the Antichrist. Easy to remember, is it not?"

"The Antichrist. Yes. Simple and distinctive."

Crowley opened the door and ushered us into a darkened room. I hesitated, but Vanessa rushed past me and into the flat. She seemed most eager to explore its contents.

Crowley lit the gas bracket, and turned up the lights. "You behold my abode," he informed us. "Splendiferous, what?"

The man's home was a wreckage. The furniture within the place—tables, chairs, a writing-desk, a couch—were all of exquisite design, yet in the most hideous condition imaginable. Every corner was battered, the panels and table limbs were scratched, the polished surfaces scarred by cigarette burns and stained by unknown chemicals.

On every flat surface, as well as the floor, were littered and strewn and hung and scattered every conceivable object of utter uselessness. A beaker of some noxious concoction lay fermenting on a tabletop. A quantity of white powder was scattered across half the sideboard. A glass jar filled with some cloudy liquid stood close by my hand, and a grotesque *homunculus*—resembling certain apparitions beheld in the drawings of the late Aubrey Beardsley—floated silently within. Upon closer inspection, I discovered that the jar's occupant was a bloated and malformed human *fœtus*. I withdrew, and kept as far away from the jar as possible.

In a corner perched a human skeleton, coated with some peculiar variety of slime. "I see that you have a room-mate," I remarked to Aleister Crowley.

"That? It is my latest experiment."

"Might I ask where you obtained it?"

"Oh, I dug it up someplace. Its original owner had no further use for it."

There were, in every cranny of the rooms, a great quantity of books. At least a dozen of them lay dog-eared and dusty in the most unexpected portions of the flat. Evidently this Crowley was either a highly educated man, or else a charlatan parading as a sage.

"Sit down, my friends!" Crowley swept several notebooks, a mummified lizard, three hypodermic syringes, and a Haitian voodoo devil doll off the couch to the floor. I chose to remain standing, and said as much, but Vanessa perched uneasily amongst the cushions. "Let us begin now," said Crowley, "to review our predicament."

"I am pursued," said Vanessa, "and my people are enslaved. I must have weapons if I am to stand against the Dreadful Eye's disciples. Revolvers, if you can obtain them."

"Martini rifles would be better," I observed. "So that we can keep as much distance as possible between the invisible men and ourselves. Oh, and alcohol is deadly poison to these creatures: several barrels of raw spirit may prove helpful to us."

"Alcohol is always useful," acknowledged Crowley, and reached for a nearby decanter.

"I must acquire," said Vanessa, "every possible instrument of warfare, take them to a place of seclusion elsewhere on your planet, where no innocent human lives may be endangered, and then wait for my enemies to come. Eventually the Dreadful Eye will create more *vacua* between the worlds, through which to strike at me. When that happens, I shall enter one of his pathways between these two worlds, bearing my weapons. I shall confront him, and kill him, or die in the attempt."

"And what about *me,* Vanessa?" I asked of her.

"When my enemy comes, I cannot expect you to follow me. There is too grave a risk . . ."

"Confound the risk. D'you think I'd pass up a chance to meet this Dreadful Eye? He's gone to a good deal of trouble trying to kill us. It would be impolite if I did not return the compliment."

Vanessa took my hand, and placed it to her invisible face so that I could touch her gentle smile. "Your help is welcome," she said. "But you can best help me by completing the full-body tattoo, so that after I have freed my homeworld's people I may become what I most desire to be: a woman of Earth."

"I'm not getting all of this," said Crowley, as he poured himself a second glass of brandy. "If you're going to war against this Dreadful Eye wallah, won't it be a strategic advantage if you remain *invisible,* instead of becoming more flesh-coloured than you already are?"

"What has colour for one set of eyes is often colourless for another," said Vanessa. "I was surprised to discover that your human eyes can see through window glass; to my own eyes, which perceive only ultra-violet light, a sheet of glass is solid *black.* My form, which is invisible to humans, can still be seen by the people of my own world, for my flesh is of a colour that reflects the ultra-violet spectrum's light. Your human flesh *absorbs* some ultra-violet rays, and you are thus faintly visible to me . . . but as a shadow, an outline."

"Is that how *I* appear to you, Vanessa?" I asked her. "When you look at me, do your alien eyes perceive only a shadow?"

She kissed me, on the corner of the mouth. "Some shadows, dear human, are more inviting than others. Give me the full-body tattoo, make me woman-coloured as the Earth-shes appear, and I will then be nearly invisible to the eyes of my people. Their *minds,* I fear, are already possessed by the Dreadful Eye. But give me the full-body tattoo, and I will become so transparent to my people's eyes that I can easily slip past them, and enter the fortress of the Dreadful Eye."

"Very well; I shall do what I can," I told Vanessa. "But certain areas of your anatomy—the eyelids, the lining of the mouth, the more intimate regions—can only be tattooed by procedures involving quite delicate surgery. How can I ensurgeon the unseen?"

Aleister Crowley threw his head back and laughed. "Is *that* your difficulty? Have you forgotten, laddie, that I perceive the invisible? Like William Crookes, I *see* the ultra-violet waves; no doubt he and I are among the vanguard of a forthcoming superior race. My good man, I can *see* every portion of this outworlder Vanessa as easily as you can see King's Cross Station. Come: with your expertise and my eyes, and the hands of us both, the fair lady will soon receive what she covets. Tattooing fascinates me, sir;

there is something about the act of imprisoning an image within willing flesh that arouses all my instincts."

"You do not understand the risk involved to Vanessa," I told him. "The possibility of abscess, or septicæmia . . ."

"I am willing," she answered. "I have faith in your skill."

"There is the further difficulty," I added, "that I was obliged to leave my tattooing implements in the lodging-house in Walcot Square. At this rate, the expense to replace them . . ."

"*Expense!*" chortled Aleister Crowley. "My good man, there is nothing which income cannot accomplish. My father died when I was twelve years old—the only kindness he has ever done me—and upon attaining my majority I came into an inheritance of some forty thousand pounds. With great wealth comes responsibility, sir; the day I inherited my fortune I swore a holy vow to devote my entire existence to the sacred cause of squandering every last farthing of it. I propose to offer you, then, three hundred guineas for the completion of yon outworld maiden's full-body tattoo."

Three hundred guineas! This was more money than I had ever seen in my life; far more money than the average Londoner can hope to earn in three years' labour. "Your offer is tempting, sir," I admitted. "But I repeat that the physical risk . . ."

"I am ready," said Vanessa, very softly.

"If my needle were to slip," I told her, "you might never . . ."

"I am ready," she answered. "Don't you see that I *must* do this, in order to have what I want? It will make me less visible to the Dreadful Eye's unholy disciples, so that I can defeat them. And then, once my birthworld has been freed, I can return here to Earth, to the world of the humans-who-touch. With the full-body tattoo, I *can* be human, very nearly. I believe that, to be a woman of this planet—a woman of England, for your land is so beautiful —must be very delightful. I want this, and I mean to have it."

I said nothing. Crowley, for once, was silent as well. I had my doubts about Crowley the Beast, but I had no doubts now about my feelings towards Vanessa. I was certain that nothing was more important to me now than to have this else-world female remain in England, with me, and find her happiness. And I knew that, if I were to complete Vanessa's full-body tattoo, then I would be able—once and for all—to behold her invisible face.

"If this is what you desire, then," I said to Vanessa, "and if you accept the physical risk, then I shall give you . . ."

Aleister Crowley leaned forward, mouthing the words silently as Vanessa and I spoke them to each other:

". . . the full-body tattoo."

THE CURIOUS INCIDENT AT PADDINGTON

16th December, 1898

All is, for the moment, well. Crowley has provided sufficient funds for me to outfit myself with some much-needed clothes and some tattooing implements. A young lady of Crowley's acquaintance, whom he introduced to us as Sister Hecate, has assisted Vanessa in obtaining a supply of ladies' garments, including the gloves and veiled hats that she must wear when setting forth in public.

Vanessa has regained much of her strength, and already she has come for several walks with me through the streets of this London that we both love so much. Does Vanessa know, I wonder, how the thought of her arouses me, how pleasured I feel in her presence? I have never been entirely at ease with any woman—my dear sister Sarah excepted—and I find myself somehow afraid that if I reveal my feelings to Vanessa she will laugh at me. Why is it that I am brave enough to face the Dreadful Eye and all of his grinning assassins, yet I am too afraid to let one woman know that I love her?

Crowley's behaviour presents other problems. The man is a drunkard, and while I do not hold that against him—my uncle was likewise a slave to alcohol, and thus I know that Crowley has no control over his weakness—nonetheless Crowley's grip upon reality is not so strong as it might be. It amuses him to fill his flat with waxwork heads, graven images, and effigies portraying the most grotesque and depraved sort of poses. He has purchased, at auction, some arcane weaponry: an iron morning-star mace, and two halberd battle-axes, which it amuses him to wave about amidst cries of "Death to the Sassenach foemen!" and other war slogans. There are, at strange and inconvenient hours, a constant parade through Crowley's living quarters of every peculiar representative of humanity to be found amid London's environs. Last night Crowley played host to a one-legged prostitute, three dwarfs of uncertain gender, an individual whom Crowley assured me was "a hermaphrodite, warranted genuine," and a bevy of Negro sailors off a ship just arrived from Jamaica. These last hardy souls Crowley introduced to me as "stout Blackamoors, with whom I mean to enact the unholy rituals of the high priests of Sodom and satisfy my taste for seamen," or some such clamjamphery. But I have learnt the explanation for Crowley's peculiar tastes: he is an alumnus of Cambridge University.

Crowley babbles impossible plans of how we will march into the fortress of the Dreadful Eye with a thousand soldiers at our disposal, and of how the Great Beast—that is, Crowley himself— will reign over the invisible world once the Dreadful Eye is vanquished. There is every reason for me to believe that Aleister Crowley is insane.

I am proceeding with Vanessa's full-body tattoo, but each hour draws me closer to the point from which I can no longer continue without resorting to surgery.

I have, however, hit upon the notion of coating Vanessa's invisible teeth with white dental enamel, the primary ingredient from which dentures are made. The procedure was time-consuming for us both, and disagreeable for Vanessa, but she is now endowed with a smile of pearlescent whiteness such as any young lady might envy. It is startling, however—since the rest of Vanessa's head is still invisible—to see those smiling teeth suspended in midair above her torso, with no visible throat intervening.

Early this morning Vanessa, hatted and veiled, went out by herself. I offered to accompany her, but she desired to go alone, expressing the wish for more practice at passing as a human female unaided. She left, promising to return within the hour.

Aleister Crowley's quarters in Chancery Lane are furnished in the most bizarre of fashions. His southernmost room contains an altar that he refers to as Jachin: it is painted entirely white, and furnished with six looking-glasses arranged in curious patterns. The room immediately north of this contains an altar dubbed Boaz: this is painted all in black, and decorated with obscene statuary. I assume that both altars are consecrated to the worship of Bacchus, for both are filled with empty bottles from the local wine-merchant's establishment.

The white altar Jachin, which stands by Crowley's windows, provides an excellent work surface; I was mortaring tattoo pigments on top of it when, through the doorway, I saw Crowley carrying the articulated human skeleton, which he proceeded to prop up within the black altar Boaz.

"I cannot thank you enough," I told him, looking up from my work, "for permitting Vanessa and myself to stay here for a few days."

"I've been meaning to ask you," said Aleister Crowley, coming closer. I smelled whisky on his breath. "If I may be so bold, sir," he asked, "since your relationship to Vanessa is ostensibly that of tradesman to client, how comes it that you two were sharing living quarters in Walcot Square?"

I explained to him then how I had lost my shop in Nicholas Lane, and with it my home, and how Vanessa was likewise now homeless and adrift in London. Crowley listened in comparative silence before he spoke: "You care for this outworlder, don't you?"

"Is it that obvious?"

"What's obvious is that you know not what you're getting into, laddie. This Vanessa isn't *human*. Were you planning to *marry* her?"

"And what of it if I *am?*"

Crowley shuddered, and took a drink from his pocket flask. "Such an unholy alliance could produce no children. No *human* children."

"A coupling between man and woman may be rewarding," I answered him coldly, "without benefit of children."

"There's more than that. Can a male human being and a female what-d'ye-call-her collaborate in the, ummm, *physical* sense? Can she be a woman for you in *that* way, m'lad?"

"It is fortunate for you, sir," I told him, "that I know a drunkard when I smell one. Otherwise, I should knock your teeth in. A gentleman does not discuss a lady's . . . *abilities* . . . without her permission."

"Yes, damn it, but *can* she?"

"She can," said a voice from within the black altar.

The skeleton within the altar stood up, and clattered towards us. The mandible of its skull clacked grotesquely as it groped with bone fingers. *"Shall I tell you, then,"* it whispered, *"of Vanessa the slut? Of Vanessa the whore?"*

The voice which emerged from the clattering skull was the voice of the Dreadful Eye.

"It has taken me a time to find you," whispered the thing. *"I have been too busied elsewhere with my disciples to devote much effort to locating you. But now you are found, and the she-one Vanessa cannot be far afield."*

Crowley reached into his writing-desk and produced a Lancaster's Enfield revolver. He fired at the skeleton's face. The skull shattered into bits, and the skeleton toppled.

"Most talkative skeleton I ever met," remarked Crowley, wiping off his pistol. "I wonder if . . . *look out!*"

The headless skeleton stood up and capered towards us, its fingers groping towards Crowley's throat. He fired again and shattered one of the skeleton's ribs.

In a corner of the room, scattered among bolts of cloth and wax images, were Crowley's mediæval weapons: I seized a large battle-axe, and brought its blade crashing down upon the skeleton's neck. At once the rib cage and spine bent and snapped, and now the half skeleton remaining—the bones of the pelvis and legs —bounded madly across the room, then toppled at length in the corner.

"Is he gone?" Crowley asked.

"I am never gone," said a waxwork head in the corner, opening its eyes. I screamed and flung the axe at it. The head dodged nimbly aside and then commenced bounding towards me with a hideous grin. *"I should have conquered this world when first I had*

the opportunity," spoke the head, leaping closer. *"I shall begin to do so now."*

"Go *away!"* shouted Aleister Crowley.

"To rule this world I need a body," whispered the terrible head. *"This head will not sustain me for long. I require a living body, with its occupant scooped out and flung aside so that I can dwell within. Will one of you gentlemen volunteer?"*

I struck the head with a poker from the fireplace. The head cracked, and I struck it again and again until it shattered and lay still. Then Crowley's devil doll sat up and began crawling towards us.

"I need a body," whispered the oncoming thing. *"Either one of your two will do nicely. Or perhaps the slut Vanessa will give me her body? She has offered it to so many others."*

The devil doll leapt at Crowley, and sank its teeth into his hand. I seized the fireplace tongs, and caught the shrivelled *homunculus* by the scruff of its neck. There was a fire in the grate; I rammed the tongs into the blaze, and saw the devil doll burst into flames. "Burn in Hell, then!" I shouted.

"I *am here,"* said a voice, and I turned.

In the centre of the room there stood a shadow. It was fashioned like a groping, twisted man. The shadow stood without any support, without a wall to cast itself against, quite alone within the centre of the room.

"The one I seek, the she-one, is not here," whispered the Dreadful Eye's approaching silhouette. *"So I shall leave for a time. But when you least expect me, I will be there. You are marked, manlings. I shall destroy you and pillage your flesh."*

Crowley's pistol fired once, and the shadow was gone. From some unknown place, I heard the laughter of an invisible mouth.

"Now what?" I asked after a time, when it seemed that no further attacks were imminent.

"Now we prepare," answered Crowley, wiping blood off his hand, "for a battle with Earth as the prize. You must go and find Vanessa. Do *not* bring her back here."

"She has nowhere else to . . ."

"Do not bring her back. The Dreadful Eye has marked this place. Find Vanessa, and take her to Paddington."

"What, the railway station? Or d'you mean the electric?"

"Railway, laddie. Ask for the Great Western terminus and wait for me there. *Keep Vanessa with you.* I shall arrive presently, unless the Dreadful Eye gets me first. Good God! He may be listening *now.*"

I put on my greatcoat, and had gone as far as the door, when Crowley called after me: "Wait."

"What is it, man?"

"I owe Vanessa an apology," he said, "for the remarks I made against her. I owe *you* an apology as well." He extended his hand. I hesitated for a moment, then clasped it. "I was wrong," he admitted. "Even an Antichrist can make mistakes."

"As Antichrists go," I replied, "you are the most civilised Antichrist that I have ever met."

And then I collected my wits, and my hat, and ran out.

There are two entrances to the house at 67–69 Chancery Lane; by standing outside the more southerly one I had a clear view of the other. After some five minutes' vigil, I saw Vanessa's veiled figure approaching up Cursitor Street.

"Taxi!" I bawled at a passing brougham and bundled the startled Vanessa into it. "Paddington Station, driver," I said through the trap, and closed it. Only then, as the cab horse clopped off towards the High Holborn, would I tell the protesting Vanessa what had happened.

"The Dreadful Eye wants you dead, Vanessa," I said, when I had finished my account. "And so long as I am with you, he seems quite willing to murder me too."

"Do you regret being with me, then?" she asked.

I lifted her veil, hoping to see a woman's face where I could only behold invisibility. How could I tell this else-woman about the thousand empty days in the dusty tattoo shop, or the nights when my uncle was drunk in some pub, and I had only unpaid bills and the rats in the walls to keep me company? Vanessa had altered my life, touched it forever, and despite the present danger I did not for an instant regret having thrown in my lot with her.

"No, Vanessa," I answered. "I will never regret being with you." There was more that I wanted to say . . . but how could I expect this alien woman to comprehend the feelings I held, when I did not fully understand them myself? "Hulloa, here is the station," I said.

I paid the cabman at Paddington Station, and we alighted at the terminus of the Great Western Railway. "What now?" Vanessa asked me through her motoring-veil.

"Now we wait, I suppose, and see what sort of plans Aleister Crowley has hatched in that fiendish little mind of his."

At the left-luggage counter, several well-dressed ladies were sporting with a little grey mongrel dog, who wore a green tin collection box round his collar. I recognised this fellow as Tim, the famous Paddington Dog, who for the last six years has collected coins for the widows and orphans of deceased railwaymen. I put a shilling in the slot of his coin box and patted his head. Vanessa approached him and extended her hand, but the dog sniffed her gloved fingers and suddenly stiffened, backing away whilst emitting a low growl.

We continued our wait. Half-an-hour later we were approached by a lady of astonishing physical beauty. She was dressed all in black, in a tight-fitting frock that emphasised the delightful curves of her physique, and her raven-black hair was worn hanging straight down, in defiance of proper ladies' fashion. She was carrying two large Gladstone bags; they looked heavy, yet she bore them with evident ease.

She set her burthen at Vanessa's feet. "Frater Perdurabo has instructed me," this dark lady announced to us both, "to seek a pair of travellers bearing your descriptions."

"Perdurabo? Is that Crowley, d'you mean?" I asked her.

"Yes. I am his acolyte: Sister Cybele." She gestured significantly towards the Gladstones, and departed before I might stop her.

The bags proved to contain my tattooing supplies, as well as my own and Vanessa's garments. Atop my tattooing gun lay an envelope; I opened this, and discovered within one hundred quid in ten-pound notes, wrapped in a letter scrawled in Aleister Crowley's spidery hand:

> *This bit of chink should cover your travel expenses. I had hoped to meet you at Paddington myself, but certain difficulties have arisen.*
>
> *You are both in the gravest possible danger. Purchase tickets for the next train to Bristol. I have made telephonic arrangements with useful allies in that region.*
>
> *You will be met at the Temple Meads station in Bristol by a coachman in black. Say to him:* 'The Widow's Son has travelled from the East'. *If the coachman gives answer thus:* 'Contine te in perennibus studiis', *then you will know that he may be trusted.*
>
> *Do not believe that in fleeing London you have escaped the Dreadful Eye. He may be sitting beside you in the railway carriage. His unseen disciples may be squatting in the baggage-rack above your head: invisible, waiting.*

I showed Vanessa the letter. "It all seems rather much," I remarked, while Vanessa lifted a corner of her veil to read the words. "Not even Crowley, surely, is lunatic enough to expect us to go haring off to Bristol on a madman's rendezvous."

"It would seem," replied Vanessa, "that we haven't much choice."

I went to the ticket-agent's window. "A pair of Bristols, my good man. No, on second thought: make that a private compartment." I regretted the expense, but a first-class compartment would spare us the necessity of sharing a second-class railway carriage with other passengers. So long as we are pursued by the Dreadful Eye, Vanessa and I must avoid *crowds*. Our enemy might be anywhere, and wearing anybody's face. . . .

The Bristol Flyer was waiting on Platform Number 4. A good many travellers were already waiting, and Vanessa's appearance aroused no little curiosity among them. "I wonder what *she's* hiding, then, underneath that there veil," I heard someone mutter nastily.

"She's the daughter-in-law of the Elephant Man," I snarled. "And I'm Jack the Ripper. Mind if I cut through?"

The crowd was all round us, and I searched among their faces. Any one of them might be the Dreadful Eye in disguise; any person we passed, however commonplace, might be our enemy dressed in stolen flesh, observing us.

I helped Vanessa into the train, then hauled myself and the Gladstones aboard. The engine started, and I stood by a window as our carriage began to move, so that I might have one more glimpse—perhaps my last glimpse—of my own beloved London.

Someone screamed.

A man was running, pushing his way through the crowd in the station, rushing madly towards our departing train. I saw a fragment of a hand, a flash of upturned face; it was Aleister Crowley. His eyes, as he ran, held pure *fear*.

And then I saw, at the far edge of that Paddington crowd, the gatherings of panic. There was a *hole* in that crowding of people; an empty space in which no-one seemed willing to stand. The men, women, and children at the edges of that gap screamed and struggled and pushed to get *away* from it. Now I saw that the hole, the uninhabited gap within the mob, was *pursuing* Aleister Crowley. It chased him through the crowd towards Platform 4 and our train, brushing up against bystanders as it came. Something large and *invisible* was hounding Crowley, and it pushed its way headlong through the crowd of the frightened, in its haste to overtake its prey.

Tim the Paddington Dog stood his ground in that panic-crazed mob, barking and growling at the approach of the unseeable thing. I heard a *thud,* and a howl, as something fetched an invisible kick at Tim's ribs; I saw the dog sail through the air in a shower of coins from his shattered collection box. The dog landed, dazed but apparently unhurt, ten feet away, while Crowley's unseen pursuer rushed onwards.

I saw this through the railway carriage's window, and as our train gathered speed I was transported farther and farther away from the Paddington spectacle, until at length I could perceive only the barest details. I saw the railway guards at the boarding gates shouldered roughly aside by the frantic Crowley, and then the iron gates themselves were pushed aside and bent double by the onrushing invisible *thing* that hurtled forwards in pursuit of its prey. I saw Crowley at the edge of the platform as he turned to face the oncoming shadow. I saw his body twist and stagger roughly backwards from the impact of some great and invisible mass. I saw him struggle, writhing in its grip, and as Platform 4 receded into the distance I saw Crowley suddenly slip backwards and tumble off the platform's edge, plunging onto the rails. I saw him try to get up . . .

And then our train hurtled into a tunnel, and Paddington was left behind in darkness.

I located our private compartment; Vanessa was there, and I told her what had happened. "They must know we've left London," I said. "If the invisible men have killed Crowley . . ."

"No, I think not," said Vanessa through her veil. "Mister Crowley is merely an obstacle between the hunter and his prey. *I* am the one whom the Dreadful Eye seeks."

I still was not entirely convinced that the invisible men had not done for Crowley; but with no way to find out, I could only hope that Vanessa was right. The railway guard came through; he punched our tickets, and I bolted the compartment door behind him.

There were gaslights within the compartment; I extinguished the gas-jets, drew the blinds down to blot out the early afternoon sun, and I sat beside Vanessa in the darkness.

"Why did you do that?" she asked, although she offered no protest.

"So that we may be equal," I told her. "In the darkness, we are both invisible."

In the shadows, I felt her warm fingers slip into mine. She had unbuttoned her gloves; my hand touched her invisible fingers.

"Thank you," Vanessa said softly, "for helping me, in my fight to free my people."

"We've quite a battle yet, before it's ended."

"But you will help me, I know. How long is the journey to Bristol?"

"About a hundred and thirty miles by rail, I should think." I struck a match in the dark, and consulted my pocket edition of *Bradshaw's Railway Guide.* "With several stops on the way, plus engine changes, I expect it will take us three hours."

"I am weary," said Vanessa. "I think, perhaps, that I would sleep for a time . . ." I began to draw away, but her hand kept me close. "I can still see, in my mind," she said softly, "the outlines of the Dreadful Eye. It seems that I have acquired *one* human trait, at least: I begin to have nightmares. I am wearied, yet for me to sleep alone in the darkness is frightening. Will you stay here with me, while I sleep?"

I think that, in the darkness of that railway compartment, I reddened. "I shall visit the buffet carriage," I told Vanessa, "so that you may sleep undisturbed. I am a *gentleman* . . ."

"And a gentleman ought not to refuse a lady's request. Stay with me, do! I am frighted . . ."

I have stated, truthfully, that I have always felt uneasy in the company of women. The physical intimacy between the sexes is something I have long desired, yet never experienced beyond the most superficial fumbling encounters with women who mocked my inexperience. And Vanessa, this alien female, aroused me in ways that I had never sensed from any Earth-born woman. And yet, and yet . . . all my powers of judgment warned me to avoid this arousal which my instincts all welcomed. A gentleman ought to respect the privacy of a lady, even when she displays no regard for it herself. And yet . . .

Vanessa drew me closer to herself. In the darkness I felt her motoring-veil brush against my face. She unfastened the veil, and it suddenly dawned on me that, in the darkness of this railway compartment, an invisible woman looked exactly the same as any female of the visible sort. A curious notion . . .

I held Vanessa close, while she unbuttoned my celluloid collar. And as it would not be proper for a gentleman to disclose the intimate behaviours of a lady, let it merely suffice for me to say that Vanessa and I shared the darkness . . .

The Fourth Part

SEE ME, FEEL ME, TOUCH ME

Mr. Blackmore has lent me his camera. Mr. Millard & Vanessa have kindly consented to pose.
23rd December, 1898

16th December, 1898

We arrived at the Temple Meads station, Bristol, in the gathering evening. A row of hansom cabs and broughams stood beside the station, soliciting fares. Vanessa pointed to a long black coach that waited at a distance from the others. "Perhaps he is the one."

The coachman's four-horse team were breathing heavily, as though they had come some great distance. The coachman himself sat in shadows, between the high knife-boards of the carriage. If he saw me watching him, he gave no indication.

I thought of Crowley's note. "I beg your pardon, sir," I told the shadowed driver, "but *the Widow's Son has travelled from the East,* and I thought you may have seen him pass this way."

The coachman's answering whisper: *"Contine te in perennibus studiis."* I still could not see his face in the darkness. "Did you come alone?" he asked me.

"No," said Vanessa, through her motoring-veil. "I am here."

The coachman hesitated. "I was given to understand, from Frater Perdurabo's telephone call, that he would be journeying with you."

Apparently "Frater Perdurabo" was Aleister Crowley. Recalling the sight of Crowley pursued through Paddington Station by invisible fiends, I told the coachman: "The man you mention has been . . . *detained."*

The coachman hesitated again. At length a hand reached down from the shadows at the top of the coach, and unlatched the passenger door. "Please to step in."

I helped Vanessa enter, and we took the Gladstone bags. I opened the coachman's roof-trap, to ask of him our destination, but he suddenly whipped up the horses; next moment, we were galloping through the streets towards the Gloucestershire coast.

"I say, up there! Answer, you Barkis! Where are you taking us?" I shouted up through the trap. But if the coachman heard me speak above the sound of the clatterous hooves, he gave no sign.

I watched, through the blinds, and tried to see by the coach lamps the route we were taking. The mysterious coachman took us through Bristol and on towards the coast. Then, reaching the cliffs and the sea, he turned south and west towards the Somerset border, still following the coastline.

We were carried, at a gallop, through parishes and villages unknown. Here and there within the darkness I saw, illuminated by the coach lamps as we passed, signposts and road markers bearing place-names of which I held no previous knowledge: Abbot's Leigh, Portishead, Clevedon, Kewstoke . . . and all the while, outside the right-hand window of the coach, we heard the rumble of the sea.

After a journey of some hour's time, with the smell of salt air growing constantly stronger, the dark coach rode into a town larger than any we had seen since leaving Bristol, and the horses slowed to a canter. I saw a street sign set into a wall at the nearest crossing: SAINT JOSEPH'S ROAD. There were mansions on our right; as best I could, I read the name of each residence, incised upon the gate-posts as we passed: *Penallt, Aylmer House* . . . the third was *Sherwood Lodge,* and our carriage turned in at the gate.

The horses stopped. I helped Vanessa to the ground, then retrieved our two Gladstones. "What happens next?" I shouted to the coachman.

He gave no answer, but reached down and closed the carriage door behind us. *"You've* been a treasure-house of information, I must say," I told him, as he whipped up his steeds and drove off.

There were several figures standing in the doorway of the house. "Come in and rest 'en," boomed a deep voice from within.

The inside of the house was larger than the outside. At least, so it seemed to me when I first entered. Great glass globes of electrical light hung from the ceiling, and naked Swan bulbs depended from a row of brackets in the nearest wall. The rooms of the place were inhabited by every conceivable species of clutter: there were Turkey carpets and Chinese festoons, and weird primitive sculptures of the sort found in Yucatán and Peru. An Egyptian mummy-case stood its upright vigil in the corner and glared at us through glass-bead eyes. The place seemed rather more like the lumber-room of the British Museum than any sort of human residence.

"Guid morra t' ye, *m'sieu, et vous, m'am'selle,*" said a voice at my side. Vanessa and I turned round, and were confronted by an apparition which I assumed to be our host.

He was a man, but not in any conventional sense of the term. He was large, with ice-clear eyes and broad jug-handle ears, and a moustache like brown furry caterpillars. He was clad, for some unfathomable reason, in a Scot's kilt and *sporran* and a Frenchman's beret. His feet were quite bare altogether. The pupils of his brown eyes were dilated, as though from the effects of some narcotic.

There stood behind him three figures—two female, one male—dressed in tight-fitting black, their faces concealed by black velvet domino masks.

The large man came forward and bowed, took Vanessa's gloved hand, and elaborately kissed it. "*Frère* Perdurabo of our Order—ye ken en's name as Alasdair Crowley, I think—rang I oop this arternoon, and says as ye'd be arter comin'. *Eh, bonsoir.*"

The man's lingo made no sense to me. It was a hash-up of French and a haggis of Scots, forced together so tightly that no room was left between them for the grammar nor the sense. He spoke in some execrable dialect that fancied itself to be now French, now Scottish, now both together . . . yet underneath his drawn-out consonants and slurring verbs, I detected the thick accent of a Bedfordshireman. I introduced Vanessa and myself, and then remarked: "Aleister Crowley did not tell us, sir, by what name we might know you."

"*Mais non?* He didna'? *Ceud mille pardonnez-moi! Je suis, m'sieu,* MacGregor Mathers, *le compte du* Glenstrae."

The Count of Glenstrae? Now I knew him for a liar or a madman. There was, to my knowledge, no such Scottish estate as Glenstrae. And there are no counts to be found in the Scottish peerage, although the odd earl and the occasional duke may be seen skulking about in the thistle brakes. The Count of Glenstrae? One might as well call himself the Emperor of San Francisco, or the Duchess of Puddledock!

"You must forgive my husban'," said the taller of the masked women. Her English was excellent, but thickly encrusted with accents of French. "Permit the introductions: I am Moïna Mathers—Soror Vestigia of the Order, yes?—and these they are Frater Emrys and Soror Circe. *Monsieur* Crowley, 'e telephoned us to expect you. He spoke of the *mademoiselle's* invisibility, and . . ."

"Then I need not wear this beastly veil," said Vanessa, and removed it. The sight of her, a well-dressed lady from the collar downwards, with pearl-white teeth yet no visible head to contain them, was still bizarre to me even now. The second masked woman, the one called Sister Circe, made a gasping sound at the sight of Vanessa.

Moïna Mathers spoke to the black-masked man—Brother Emrys, she had called him—in what I took to be Latin, and that worthy bowed and exited. "Do you mind very much," Vanessa asked our hosts, "if I remove these garments? I find them stifling, and as there is no need for me to pass as human amongst you . . ." The lady Moïna Mathers nodded graciously, and Vanessa at once attenuated her body to nearly twice its normal height and half its thickness, so that her clothing tumbled off her to the floor. "I believe that whoever decreed your planet's fashion in clothes was no lover of women," said Vanessa. "That *corset!* I had thought, before I submitted myself to corset stays, that your Parliament had passed laws against torture."

"The men who comprise Parliament," I informed her, "are not known for wearing ladies' corsets, although I have heard certain rumours . . ." Just then Brother Emrys returned, steering a tea-cart laden with victuals. Seeing Vanessa's unclad arms and lower limbs and naked torso, patched all over with invisible spots where my needle had not yet done its work, he blushed scarlet round the edges of his velvet mask, and hastily busied himself with the tea-things.

"Does *la m'am'selle* fancy *la cuisine du* planet Earth?" Mac-Gregor Mathers asked Vanessa. "Ye will find, *sur la carte, tout le* vittles 'en might possibly desire. If there be aught else ye wants . . ."

"Yes, I *do* want something else, please," said Vanessa. "Would it be too much to ask, sir, that you speak in plain English?"

Mathers turned pale, and his wife burst into laughter. Brother Emrys suppressed a grin, and Sister Circe was suddenly extremely busy with an arrowroot biscuit. MacGregor Mathers muttered something in Latin—it sounded like *"cave canem"*—and stalked out of the bric-à-bracked room, tripping over a Phoenician ceremonial urn as he left. "Have I insulted him, I hope?" Vanessa asked.

"Never mind," said Moïna Mathers. "I shall show you to your rooms. *Alors, Monsieur* Crowley 'ad said we might expect a gentleman and a lady, but he did not say whether you wished the separate bedrooms, or together."

I looked to Vanessa, yet it was impossible to read her invisible face. "The question of beds," I declared, "is for Vanessa to decide."

"One bedroom, I think, should be sufficient," she replied. "The people of my world can only touch one another with great difficulty, and pain. How curious this world of yours—where touching brings pleasure—seems to me. But if I am to become an Earth-she . . . an Englishwoman . . . then I must accustom myself to the ways of your world." She raised one half-visible arm; I felt her unseen fingers touch my face. *"One* bedroom, then," Vanessa whispered, "is enough."

17th December, 1898

To set down an account of a lady's sleeping habits, even those of a lady from an alien world, would be unworthy of a gentleman. Yet I feel that—in the interests of science—I must set down one particular detail of yester-evening.

Last night I couched with Vanessa, by her choice. I have never before *loved* any woman—my sister Sarah and our departed mother excepted, of course—nor have I partaken of sexual congress with any woman except for the most fumbling attempts. Yet, last night, I experienced an *attraction,* a drawing of my own flesh towards Vanessa's, as though she were a lodestone and myself a needle. The closer I drew towards Vanessa, the more strongly I felt this attraction.

Vanessa has told me of how her planet's people are *repelled,* one from the other, like magnets of identical charge. Is it possible that humans possess some charge opposite to this, that draws this alien female and myself towards each other? Or is it some purer attraction, a bonding of the flesh and heart and soul, which draws us together? Confound my inexperience! Have I discovered some force hitherto unknown to Earthly science, or is this how *compassion* feels? Past inexperience with women denies me an answer. There are disadvantages, it seems, to virginity.

On other matters: We are in the town of Weston-super-Mare. It was Aleister Crowley's plan that Vanessa and I remain here, whilst I complete Vanessa's full-body tattoo.

There is, apparently, an international secret society—a paganist cult of some sort—called the Hermetic Order of the Golden Dawn. Crowley has been a member of its London sect since mid-November of this year. MacGregor Mathers is one of the Order's founders, and high priest of its chapter in Paris. Moïna Mathers reports that she and her husband were visiting the sect here in Weston-super-Mare on some casual errand—to borrow a cup of warlock's toenails, I assume—and were present when Crowley telephoned. They agreed to shelter Vanessa and myself whilst Crowley enlists the London members of the Golden Dawn against the coming invasion of invisible men.

But what has happened to Aleister Crowley? I still recall the incident in Paddington. I have rung the London exchange and requested a connexion to Crowley's telephone, but his wire does not answer. Is Aleister Crowley alive or dead?

And how long can we hide here in Weston? The Dreadful Eye found Vanessa in Lambeth, and managed to locate our brief haven in Chancery Lane. I must assume that there will be some new encounter. Until then, every footstep on the path, every creak of stair and trembling of gaslight may mark the approach of the Dreadful Eye.

18th December, 1898

The Matherses and our hosts—who call themselves Brother Emrys and Sister Circe whilst in the service of the Golden Dawn, but who in all other pursuits are Mr and Mrs Francis Blackmore—have proven two quite charming couples, and in their separate ways quite spiritual. This morning the Blackmores and I went to Sunday church services and returned to find MacGregor and Moïna Mathers dancing naked round certain goat-headed pagan effigies in the parlour.

I have resumed Vanessa's full-body tattoo. Each day she spreads herself, for as many hours as my eyestrain allows, upon a sheet across the table in our room. I have readied her invisible skin for my needle by coating each portion of her flesh, just before I inject it, with a soap film combined with red vegetable dye. The effect is rather like sculpting a large pinkish woman-shaped soap bubble. By now I have completed Vanessa's limbs, excepting the hands and the feet, and pigmented all of her torso excluding the base of the spine. Remaining also are the genitalia, throat, and face. These are the regions wherein a slip of the needle can bring paralysis, or death.

"How am I to pigment your face, Vanessa?" I asked her late this morning, whilst enfleshing her left armpit. "The eyelids, the ears, the lips can be tattooed by only the most complex surgical procedures. And since you are invisible . . ."

"I have been thinking on that," said Vanessa, "and I believe that I have an idea. You must do as I bid you."

She rolled over face-downwards, and at her direction I sponged her lower spine with the soap-dye solution. "Can you see where my invisible bones would be, just beneath the flesh?" she asked.

"Yes; the coccygeal ridges are well formed. But plunging my needle into *there* would cripple a normal woman. The vast network of nerve ends . . ."

"Ah, but I am not a normal woman. *Look!*"

Something rippled in her flesh. I saw the skin lengthen, separate itself from her spinal column, and extend itself beyond her buttocks to form a caudal appendage . . . no, a confounded living *tail!* . . . of some six or seven inches.

"Took some practice, that did," Vanessa panted, face down, "and I don't know how long I can hold it."

"Does it hurt, Vanessa?"

She stifled a gasp. "Shape-changing's painful work. It's dif'cult for me to . . . change shape of skin *without* changing . . . nerve ends 'long with it. Hurry, please."

We are proceeding, then, for as long as Vanessa can endure a session. Normal shape-changing, she has told me, causes her alien form only minor discomfort, but to distort her frame so as to lengthen her *skin,* while retaining her nerve tissues' and veins' normal positions, thereby creating a gap between vessels and flesh, causes no little agony. She cannot now submit to my needle for more than five minutes at a time, with half-an-hour's rest betweentimes.

But bit by bit, filling in each fragment one by one, I begin to see my alien Vanessa.

21st December, 1898

"I say, Vanessa: what would you like for Christmas?"

We were sitting, she and I, in the back garden of the Blackmores' house, Sherwood Lodge. The high stone wall round the property kept us hidden from inquisitive neighbours. I wore an ulster, in the bare Decembered chill, but Vanessa, seated on the grass beside me, was by her own choice quite naked. She showed no chill, and this leads me to suspect that her birthworld is a far colder place than these Somerset hills.

"Christmas will be here on the Sunday, Vanessa," I went on. "What would you like me to give you?"

"For Christmas? But I am not a Christian."

"No matter," I told her. "The spirit of giving, the joy of the season; these are Christian traits, yes, but not exclusively so. A poor holiday Christmas would be, if only Christians could taste it! So: what would you fancy for Christmas?"

"I want," Vanessa said, "to confront my enemy the Dreadful Eye . . . to *kill* him, or die in the attempting. If I live, and if my people are freed, then I want to return here, to Earth, and live out my days among its fascinating humans. Can you give me *that* for Christmas?"

"I shall certainly try." I felt for her hand among the grasses, and found it. "And after returning to Earth," I asked her, "would you then remain with *me?*"

She touched my hand, very gently. "Yes, perhaps. I think that such would be pleasant."

Outwardly, I said nothing. But my inner self was turning cartwheels and handsprings, and bounding over the hedgerows.

"You will do the face last, will you not?" Vanessa asked.

"Pardon?"

"My face. You are watching my body turn visible bit by bit. Do you intend to save for last the pleasure of seeing my face?"

"The *pleasure?*" I kissed her. "Vanessa, there is little pleasure for me in tattooing *any* face. So many delicate vessels so near to the eyes, to the mouth: one slip means disaster. My mind would be on the edge of its chair every moment. But still . . . yes, confound it, Vanessa; I want very much to see your invisible face."

She brought my hands to the unseen place above her shoulders; I felt my fingertips touch soft invisible flesh. "Can you *feel,* then, the shape of my face?" Vanessa whispered.

"I feel the separate components, yes. And yet I cannot link them up to form an image in my mind."

"You man, you stumbling human." She kissed me now, on the mouth, on the throat, as she loosened my celluloid collar. "Why is it so mattering for you to *see* me?" she asked. "Blind men live without seeing. Lovers touch in the darkness, unsighted. You can hear me, feel me, taste me, fill me, sense me. Why is it so vital, Earth-one, that you *see* me?"

"Not vital, perhaps," I admitted. "But desired. Your face is a mystery to me. I catch glimmerings of it: outlines, brief flashes, just enough to tantalise . . ."

"And if I showed you that mystery, would you still show me desire?" Vanessa asked. "But come; it is time we resumed the tattoo . . ."

22nd December, 1898

This morning a council of war was held, presided over by Mac-Gregor Mathers; attended by myself, Vanessa, Moïna Mathers, and the members of Osiris, Weston-super-Mare's chapter of the Order of the Golden Dawn.

Founded ten years ago, they tell me, by local Freemasons seeking "the ancient true magicks," the Osiris sect has since then lost several members. All who now remain are Mr and Mrs Francis Blackmore; Major James Partridge Capell, retired army officer and local solicitor; Mr William Millard, landlord of the Three Queens tavern in Oxford Street; and Mr Henry Butt, coal merchant and member of a distinguished local family (he is descended, in fact, from a long line of prominent Butts). These five, with Vanessa, myself, and the Matherses, may be the first line of defence in the coming battle against the forces of the Dreadful Eye.

Our hosts the Blackmores have children, whom none of us wish to endanger should the Dreadful Eye mount an attack on this house in pursuit of Vanessa. Mr Millard has therefore offered to billet Vanessa and myself, temporarily, in his rooms in Burlington Street.

Major Capell and Mr Henry Butt, it would seem, are dubious allies at best. Capell, of the legal firm of Capell & Melsome in this city, expresses the thought that perhaps a lawsuit can be brought against the Dreadful Eye. But Butt butts in to suggest that our best chance against an onslaught of invisible men is to contact the War Office. Mr Millard, on the other hand, possesses neither military aptitude nor legal expertise. He is merely a publican, a dispenser of whisky and ale—and therefore a far more useful member of society than all the soldiers and lawyers put together. Mr William Millard has expressed the opinion that Weston-super-Mare has already been invaded by invisible men, owing to the fact that several of his tavern's steady customers hold frequent conversations with unseen companions, especially after five or six pints. I venture to suggest that his steady customers may be more unsteady than he realises, and at this point several members of the Golden Dawn jump up commencing savage incantations to pagan gods, who may or may not be listening, and they call upon dark entities with whom I share no acquaintance. I regard this behaviour as rather useless: I hold no faith in "magick."

And yet, less than five weeks ago I did not believe in invisible women . . . and now I find myself aroused and empassioned by one. Is it possible that some sorcery also exists, some magickal rite, which can be called upon to aid us? In the battle yet to come, we shall need every tool at our disposal . . . whether or not those tools have been properly introduced to Science.

23rd December, 1898

I have nearly done tattooing Vanessa's hands and feet, and have begun work on the more intimate regions. Her pain is considerable as I work upon increasingly sensitive portions of her flesh. I have offered to dose Vanessa with laudanum, but she refused this; the laudanum's alcohol content would be fatal, she says, to any member of her species.

Tomorrow we will pack our few belongings, in preparation for the exodus to William Millard's home. Complicating our manœuvre is the weather: this morning it began to snow.

Vanessa has witnessed no such phenomenon as snow upon her homeworld. "I can see them!" she cried, as the first drifts of winter came down. "I can see shining crystals descend from the sky, and in a thousand different colours! I must feel, I must *touch* them!" And although she was naked on my table, in the midst of a tattooing, the alien woman watched the snows pass our room's slightly opened window. Then the alien woman jumped up and hurried towards the door, to reach the garden beyond.

"Vanessa!" I ran after her, clutching a blanket to fling over her nakedness. But she would not wait, and thus the three of us— Vanessa, myself, and the blanket—were soon in the garden of Sherwood Lodge, beside the high stone wall.

"It is *light!*" sang Vanessa, outstretching herself to the snow-flakes as they fell, softly touching her flesh. "It is *light,* rainbow colours, sunlight frozen like crystal and shattered into countless tiny pieces! Oh, my world has no such miracle as this!" she shouted, flinging herself upon the grass and offering her limbs, her face, her upturned flesh to the icy tricklings of softly falling snow. "Oh, the sky itself has frozen," she breathed, rolling over and laughing as the snow fell. "The sun has frozen, shattered open, and split into fragments. It is *light!*"

And I found myself, hatless, coatless, collar open, standing gape-a-goggle in my shirtsleeves, and I wondered at this alien woman, to whom such a mundane thing as the first December snow became such shining spectacle. For she rolled in it, danced in it, leapt about like some outworlder porpoise in an ocean of frost. She snatched up great shimmering handfuls of snow, smelled them, tasted them, rubbed them over and into every portion of her flesh, shrieking, shouting with excitement. "It is light! It is shatterings of *light!*"

"Are you not cold, Vanessa?" I asked.

"It is a trifle," she said, all enfolded with snow. As she spoke, her frosted breath outlined the form of her invisible face. "My own planet, too, is often colder than this, so I am used to the chill. But this crystal rain—*snow,* you call it?—I have never felt this thing. Oh, it is *beautiful!*"

And she shouted, and laughed, and joining in with her voice the great bells of All Saints' Church, across the St. Joseph's Road, all sprang into their brass-clangoured song. And I found myself joining Vanessa; rolling, whooping, rubbing snow against this woman while she pressed white crystals and half-visible flesh against myself. And we tumbled in the snowdrifts, while the bells sang out our love.

Christmas Eve, 1898

This morning Vanessa and I gathered up our few belongings, and moved into William Millard's upstairs room at Number Sixteen, Burlington Street. Here, I hope to at long last complete Vanessa's full-body tattoo.

I have purchased, from the chemist's shop of a Mr W. H. Webb of this locality, a quantity of raw alcohol and some glass pint flasks. It is my intention to carry these upon my person at all times, for—recalling the aversion of the Dreadful Eye's disciples to alcohol—I must have a weapon in the event they attack.

One advantage brought by the snowfall is that Vanessa is now able to go out in her usual disguise—heavily bundled, gloved, hatted, and veiled—without arousing suspicion. In winter, all Englishwomen are so bundled.

Mr Millard's home is small compared to the Blackmores' great mansion, but it will serve us as haven. In the afternoon we accompanied our host to his tavern, the Three Queens, where Vanessa aroused no small attention amongst the customers in the public bar, so we retired to the comparative privacy of the saloon. "What sort of realm is this?" Vanessa asked me. "My homeworld has nothing like it. Is this a gathering place for ceremonial rites?"

"Not exactly," I said. "It is a *pub.* Here mortals worship the great god Bottoms-Up, and they practise the ancient ritual of I'll-Have-Another, upon the brass-railed altar of Alcohol."

Vanessa shuddered. "Alcohol is poisonous to my people."

"Mine too," I admitted. "Which is why some of us consume so much of it."

Millard was busy with his customers. For today is Christmas Eve, and—tomorrow's Christmas falling on the Sunday—there will be no taverns open for holiday merriment. Vanessa and I took our leave, then, and stepped into the throng of humanity outside.

There were wives with net bags filled with oranges, men fetching pheasant and goose from the poulterers' shops. The tram horses wore sleigh-bells, and the whole great vast crowd of Decembering people were lightly dusted with a sprinkle of new-fallen snow.

"There never *was* such a Christmas as this," I remarked to Vanessa, as I took her gloved hand and we walked down Union Street. A passing Quaker, rushing homeward from the nearby meeting-house of the Society of Friends, tipped his hat to my veiled lady as he passed us.

"Merry Christmas, good woman!" cried that worthy. "Merry Christmas to thee, sir! God rest ye merry!"

"And to you, sir!" I called. Then: "Do you see, Vanessa? You are treated precisely like any Earth-born woman; a lady of society. Is this not what you wanted?"

She said nothing, but the shoulders of her travelling suit were heaving strangely. I placed a hand beneath her veil, and I touched the invisible face.

Can an alien woman shed tears? Can an outworlder weep? I felt moisture; my Vanessa was sobbing. "I am so happy," she gasped, between sobs, "among you creatures the humans. And with *you,* most especially. But how can I remain here, when my people are enslaved? I have no right to this. You *must* find Aleister Crowley; find out if these sorceror-friends of whom he speaks are now ready to aid us. If not, I *must* return to my homeworld without them and fight the Dreadful Eye. Alone!"

"Not alone, Vanessa," I whispered. "I am with you."

"You would leave the safety of England for my carrion-planet?" she asked.

"Without hesitation, Vanessa."

"Why?"

"Because," I answered her, "I spent last Christmas in my gas-lit tattoo shop in Nicholas Lane, surrounded by rusting hypodermics and cobwebbed glass jars filled with crush-powdered colours. These were my Christmas decorations. The Christmas before that, likewise. And the Christmas before *that*, and on through a backwards procession of catchpenny Christmases. To my sister Sarah and myself, the memory most intimately connected with Christmas is the death of our mother. She succumbed to influenza one year, in the holiday season, between Stephenmas and Twelfth Night. It was agony, I tell you, to know that there were homes abroad in London where Christmas flap-dragons burned merrily, roasted geese were crackling brown, and all the plum puddings in Bloomsbury were stuffed fat with sixpences, while my mother lay dying for want of a shilling's worth of medicine. This was Christmas for me, this has *always* been Christmas for me, every year of my barrow-load life. Until now. My Vanessa, *this* Christmas is the first and only one in which I have ever known joy . . . because *you* have entered my life. And if all that you ask in return is that I accompany you to your birth planet, and hazard my life—a life that was empty and wasted before you came into it—then I am yours to command. I love you, Vanessa. And there never was, before, such a Christmas as this."

Then we went up the High Street towards home . . . *home* being, just now, friend Millard's upstairs room. With the door latched, shutters drawn, and the gaslight extinguished, for a time Vanessa and I explored each the other's self in darkness. And I marvelled at this mystery Vanessa, whom I love as I have loved no Earthish woman.

In early evening I resumed my labours on Vanessa's full-body tattoo. I have, by this time, tattooed Vanessa's entire hands and feet, with the exception of her nails. "There is only one method," I told her, "of tattooing *underneath the nails,* and it is painful. The entire fingernail, or toenail, must be drawn out with forceps, the cuticle sterilised, and the pigment injected. There is a risk that the new nail as it regenerates may become ingrown, and turn septic."

"I have been watching the women of England," said Vanessa. "I mark that some are in the habit of lacquering their nails."

"Some, yes. Prostitutes, mostly," I informed her. "It is a code in the Whitechapel district: shilling tarts paint their nails cherry-red, whilst fingernails of the mauve or magenta variety are sported by ladies offering more . . . *peculiar* services."

"And how is it that *you* know of this?" Vanessa asked me.

"Eh? Well, that is, ummm . . . the *point* is, Vanessa, that the ladies' vogue for lacquered fingernails expired in Regency times. In our modern Victorian age, nails coloured scarlet are those of a harlot."

"Then I shall lacquer mine in pale pink," said Vanessa, "and render them visible by painting them so delicately that few humans will suspect that they are painted at all. It will be a relief not to wear gloves every moment, to hide my invisible fingertips."

We resumed the tattoo. By this time I had pigmented Vanessa's entire abdomen, and I was surprised to discover that she did not possess a navel. "I have no need of one," she said, when I asked, "and I cannot think why anyone bothers to *have* a navel. Whatever would I *do* with one?"

"Precious little," I admitted. "They are, however, the fashion."

By the time that the hall clock chimed midnight I found that I had pigmented Vanessa's entire body excepting the nails, the genital and perianal regions, the *aureolæ,* her head, and a bit of her throat. I have saved these areas for last because they are the most awkward to tattoo. And I am tired just now, and cannot proceed just yet.

"Good night then, my love," said Vanessa, and kissed me. And then, with difficulty, for the words were alien to her unearthly tongue, she added: "Merry Christmas."

And for the first time in my life, I found myself looking forward to the holiday.

Christmas Day, 1898

I was awakened this morning by the unusual yet pleasant sensation of Vanessa gently licking my face, as though she were a cat. "Is this a custom on your own planet?" I asked my beloved alien.

"It is *my* custom," she told me, and her invisible tongue continued to delight me.

From belowstairs, I heard the baritone voice of William Millard singing "I Saw Three Ships a-Sailing," and a moment later he rapped on our door. "Hi! Hulloa in there! Merry Christmas! You're wanted on the telephone!"

"Who is it?" I asked through the door, whilst I trousered myself.

"Wouldn't give his right name. But he says he's the Antichrist."

"The Antichrist?" I kissed Vanessa, and reached for my shirt. "That must be Aleister Crowley!"

"Are you certain?" she asked.

"Positive! How many Antichrists do we know?" I opened the door and, following Millard, I bolted downstairs to his telephone. I seized the earpiece, and stood close to the wall box so that I could use its speaking apparatus. "Is that you, Crowley?"

"None other," came the electrical voice through the wires. "Frank Blackmore said I'd find you here. How's our interplanetary wench?"

"Vanessa's well," I answered. "Good God, man, I've been trying to raise you for days! We were beginning to think you'd been Paddingtoned to death by invisible men."

"Oh, *that.*" Crowley's electrified laughter in the earpiece was positively satanic. "Took me a proper bit of explaining, it did, to keep *that* little incident scotched up. People swearing they'd been trampled by invisibles! I finally persuaded the *gendarmes* it was a case of mass hysteria. Told the police I was one of Madame Blavatsky's pet clairvoyants from the Theosophical Society, come to Paddington Station to practise levitating steam-engines. They locked me up for inducing a panic; I only just yesterday managed to contact Billy Crookes. *He* set things to rights, soon enough!"

"What happened to the invisible men who attacked you?" I asked.

"They escaped through the Praed Street railway tunnel," said Aleister Crowley. "It seems they'd come to Paddington to catch Vanessa, or kill her, and when they saw she'd escaped they decided to kill *me*, as a sort of consolation prize. Would have done it, too, if you hadn't told me the blaggards cannot stand alcohol. Fortunately, I always keep a flask of alcoholic spirits with me for —ahem!—medicinal purposes; I unstoppered it. The filthy brutes got one whiff of absinthe and promptly legged it for daylight."

"Any sign of the Dreadful Eye, then?" I asked.

"No. It's Vanessa they want: I doubt that they'll attack me again now that she's scarpered off. I haven't seen hide, hair, nor collar buttons of a single invisible man since you and Vanessa left Paddington. That's what worries me."

"How so?"

"I assume," declared Aleister Crowley, "that the invisible men knew you and Vanessa were on that train. They've left London, I think; they must be searching every town on the Great Western Railway route, hunting Vanessa. They'll likely work their way to Devizes, then Bath, and next Bristol. After that, I shouldn't wonder if they turn up in Weston-super-Mare."

I gripped the telephone's hand crank to steady myself. "What if they find us?"

"Shoot any invisible man you lay eyes on," said Crowley.

"Easily said is difficult done. I cannot see them. And I have a revolver, but no more bullets."

"No bullets?" Crowley asked. "Pity. Useful things, bullets. No home should be without them. Tell you what: Billy Crookes was planning to spend the Christmas hols with his wife Nellie, but I'll send him down to Weston. Owes me a favour. Meantime, the Hermetic Order of the Golden Dawn are assembling their forces in London. *Think* of it, laddie: a battle royal between interdimensional cut-throats and the greatest sorcerors in England! The sky over London will rain blood and ectoplasm for a fortnight!"

"But what about . . ."

"Vanessa? Tell her to keep an eye out in case the invisible bolly-goblins come calling. Meanwhile, since I am the one and only genuine Antichrist—accept no substitutes—I bid you a merry Antichristmas."

"Crowley, wait! We must . . ."

Click.

He'd rung off. Nothing for it but to go back upstairs and tell Vanessa the news.

She was lying on the bed, outstretching languorously, yet I saw her visible portions grow tense when I told her that the invisible ones might be near. Then I went and hunted up Millard. "I cannot permit myself to conceal from you," I told him, "the risk you take by sheltering us. I have reason to fear that the Dreadful Eye and his invisible legions are approaching Weston, in search of Vanessa. They are perfectly willing to kill anyone who opposes them. I am grateful, sir, for your hospitality, but honour compels me to inform you that so long as you shelter Vanessa and myself you share our danger."

The publican grinned. "If any danger comes, I'll cut myself a slice of it. As for lodging you, squire; well, I'm merely returning a favour."

"A favour? Sir, you owe us nothing."

"Not for you, man. I've been asked to shelter you and your she-stranger there, as a favour to . . . *the Widow's Son.*"

As he spoke, Millard fingered the Freemason's charm dangling from his watch fob. Crookes and Mathers were Freemasons too, I recalled. Evidently there was a greater alliance at work here than I realised.

In late morning, having breakfasted, I made arrangements to attend the Christmas services at St. John's Church, nearby. Vanessa expressed the desire to accompany me, and we set forth, Vanessa suitably veiled. I made certain to carry, in the pocket of my greatcoat, a flask of raw alcohol for protection.

Vanessa was quite excited at the prospect of visiting a terrestrial church. "I have never witnessed the sacred rituals of Earth-folk," she said as we entered Meadow Street. "Does your church have human sacrifices?"

"You have obviously mistaken me for a Methodist," I replied. "Mind you, there *were* human sacrifices at the dawn of Christianity—the pagan Romans served Christians to the lions at regular intervals—but nowadays that seldom happens. This is regarded as an improvement by the Christians, but a great inconvenience to the lions."

St. John's was crowded; Vanessa and I endeavoured to remain inconspicuous, but the parishioners *would* keep staring at her grey motoring-veil. And then, at the beginning of Communion, as the church's great organ struck up the hymn *"Panis Angelicus,"* the throb and swell of its music soaring rafter-high throughout the walls, Vanessa grew so excited that she cried out: "Oh! What is this vibration that fills me? I must touch it!" And she rose from her pew and began changing shape beneath her clothes; I felt her body attenuate within my grasp. A red-faced verger appeared—from the smell of his breath, he had been taking inventory of the sacramental wine—and next moment Vanessa and I were summarily ejected.

"Do we have to leave *now?*" Vanessa asked, as a curate passed us bearing the bread and chalice. "See, they are just beginning to hand round the refreshments . . ." Someone opened a door, and Vanessa and I found ourselves ushered hurriedly out of the church and into the snowdrifts, left to freeze amongst the heathens.

"And a merry Christmas to *you,*" I remarked, as the heavy door swung shut behind us. "Henceforth, perhaps I shall take my business elsewhere."

We returned to Burlington Street, where I presented Vanessa with her Christmas present: a Chinese box of scented face powder that I had purchased two days earlier. "Wear this, my Vanessa, and I will be able to see your invisible face. Merry Christmas."

She kissed me. "And I have something for *you,* although your holiday is strange to me." She pressed into my hands a small object.

It was warm to the touch. There was a *gleam,* between my fingers, as of some incandescent gem, but I perceived only the briefest outlines of some faceted shape. I felt the *weight* of the object, as I held it—a few pennyweights—yet I was unable to see it clearly.

"It is a stone, my love," Vanessa said.

"An invisible stone, from your alien world?"

"No," she told me. "The stone is from your Earth. I see such pebbles occasionally, scattered on the pathways of your world, yet Earthish people appear unable to see them. Have you never stumbled against some small object, yet looked back and found nothing there? These are the stones which no human can see; silent crystals. I have taken one, polished it, and now it is forever yours."

I held her. "My Vanessa, when I think of how miserable I was two months ago . . . and now I find such happiness with you. There never *was*, before, such a Christmas as this."

For an hour, and more, we shared the darkness of that room, our passionings illuminated only by the soft unwinking spark of the gemstone my Vanessa had given me. Afterwards, I renewed my labours upon Vanessa's full-body tattoo.

By late evening, after much progress, I decided that a diversion was called for. I arose, stretched, dressed warmly, and—Vanessa being wearied from shape-changing, and uneager to accompany me—I donned my greatcoat, left the house, and set forth down the hill towards the shore. A pleasant glass at the Royal Hotel, and then I enjoyed a brisk walk through the neighbouring field towards the far esplanade and the sea. Overhead, the moon —quite nearly full—cast its silverness upon the snow all round me. I paused a moment at the shingle of the beach and watched the waves come lapping nearly to my boot tops while the . . .

Skrunch. Skrunch.

There was, behind me, a quiet sound approaching. *Skrunch.* I turned. The beach was empty, save for myself and my long trail of boot prints in the snow. Then I saw, *skrunch*-approaching in the distance, *a set of footprints*, made with no visible feet, appearing one by one, and coming towards me. The marks were crescent shaped, and I saw as the imprints approached me that the appendages which made them must be shaped like *hooves*. In a straight line, *skrunch-skrunch,* the hoofprints came directly towards me, and I was alone with the unseen.

"Who's there?" I called. "The Dreadful Eye? Or merely one of his faceless disciples?"

"I have found you," came a harsh voice. The invisible thing's breath *condensed* in the cold, forming a small cloud of vapour, just as humans' breath does in the winter. I could see, faintly limned by the vapour, the outlines of alien lungs, the insides of a throat, and some hints of an exhaling nose and mouth. The mouth was not human. *"You eluded me in Hatton Garden, manling,"* rasped the now-familiar voice, *"but now you are found. The she-one Vanessa is sure to be nearby. My master will be pleased."*

"And where, pray tell me," I asked, casually taking my watch from my waistcoat pocket, and just as casually examining the time, "where is your master, the Dreadful Eye?"

"He comes," said the vaporous outline. *"I have summoned him."*

"If I am not here when he arrives . . ." I said, closing the watch-case, and casually placing it in the pocket of my greatcoat, ". . . make certain that you give him *this!"*

My hand came out of the greatcoat, clutching the alcohol flask, and I raised it towards the vaporous face.

The alien thing was too fast for me. Something heavy slammed into my chest; I fell backwards into the snow, and dropped the flask. I felt the shape-changing flesh *ooze* across me, its invisible mass flowing over my chest, moving up towards my shoulders and throat. The thing's breath, on my face now, was cold and foul-odorous.

I fought, but the creature outstrengthed me. Its invisible form pressed down harder, burying me in the snow. I felt the moonlight slip away; the darkness gathered, and the snow rose up to envelop me. But if it was so cold, then why couldn't I *feel* anything? The invisible hands clutched my throat, and the vapours of breath that outlined the half-visible face whispered promises of death. *"Easy. Lie easy, manling. Do not resist. A moment more, and all your struggling is ended . . ."*

I tasted blood in my mouth. The indentations in the snow beside me offered some hints of the *shape* of this invisible thing. I felt my winter-numbed fingers close round something cold and hard in the snow, shaped like . . . *yes.* The flask I had dropped. I grasped it now, and—too weakened to uncork it—I brought the vessel smashing down upon the invisible shape, just in back of its outlines of face. I heard glass shattering.

There was a scream; the half-visible face changed its shape, twisted into forms writhing in agony as the alcohol, soaking its way into alien flesh, suddenly burst into flame. The thing writhed, contracted into itself, and by now very nearly its whole body was encrusted with flames. I saw it rise, fully visible now in the light of its own hellish combustion. I saw the thing turn away from me and run, shrieking, gibbering, down the hill towards the sea. And its footprints, as it hurtled through the snow, became now hoof marks, now claw-shaped impressions, now prints of splayed toad-like appendages as the outworlder thing took a dozen different shapes in its flight. I saw it plunge into the sea, heard the bubbling hiss as burning flesh kissed freezing water.

My greatcoat had caught fire in the struggle; I treaded it out in a snowdrift. One of my fingers had been slashed by a fragment of the shattered flask, but the cut did not seem very deep. I bandaged it with my handkerchief and went to see what remained of my assailant.

The dying thing was visible: its flesh, charred and blackened by combustion, had undergone some physical change that rendered the creature opaque. It floated face downwards in a smouldering heap, moaning and hooting to itself, its limbs contorted into some half-completed shape-change. After a time the brute ceased to move. There was a terrible smell, and then I knew the thing was dead.

A gull was shrieking someplace in the distance as the dead thing face-down in the sea was carried off by the tide. Behind me, as I turned, I saw the still-descending snow filling in the creature's footprints, and my own. When I looked back again to the sea, the alien corpse had floated far into the distance.

"There never *was,* before," I whispered, "such a Christmas as this."

Boxing Day, *1898*

It was past midnight when I returned to Burlington Street and informed Vanessa and Mr Millard of the incident.

"Was the creature that attacked you alone?" Millard asked.

"I saw no evidence of others, but we must assume that they are close. Weston-super-Mare can no longer hide us; Vanessa and I must seek Aleister Crowley's mysterious allies in London."

"And begin the battle for my homeworld," said Vanessa, though she gave no indication of how we might journey there from Earth.

A council of war had convened this morning in Sherwood Lodge, with all members of the Osiris coven attending. Moïna Mathers has departed for France *via* London, to recruit the Parisian disciples of the Golden Dawn to our aid. MacGregor Mathers remains, and he took charge of affairs. It was voted that Vanessa and I, accompanied by Mathers, will set forth for London to join Aleister Crowley tomorrow. Vanessa desires to begin the journey *now,* but she has been outvoted: as this is Boxing Day, all the thousands of merry-makers who have spent their Christmases with Aunt Agatha or Uncle Diggory will be travelling homewards today; the trains and railway stations will be crowded. Far better to wait, then, until tomorrow; take the first train up to London, and reach Paddington before noon. Mathers has rung up Crowley, and told him our plans.

Meantime, we are all still in danger. Tonight Vanessa and I will encamp in a place where, I fancy, the invisible men are not likely to seek us. Francis Blackmore is the proprietor of a butcher's shop at Number Fifteen, West Street; Vanessa and I shall spend the night hours within, behind shuttered windows and door bolts. MacGregor Mathers has volunteered to accompany us, offering protection of a sort he refers to as "sacred Druidickal magicks." So much for the hocus-pocus brigade.

Major Capell has supplied me with an excellent repeating pistol of German manufacture, a Borchardt "Prometheus," and donated a quantity of bullets as well.

All is readying. Tomorrow we're for London. Next we must find some means to shift the battleground to Vanessa's native planet.

The Fifth Part

THE MAN
MADE OF SAWDUST
AND SAUSAGES

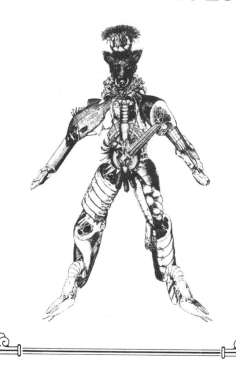

Late evening, Boxing Day, 1898

Vanessa is asleep, having surfeited her ravening hunger with a meal. I have managed to dissuade her from the highly antisocial habit of dining on Englishmen; she has therefore made do by devouring a side of raw pork, which she considers a reasonable substitute for human flesh. Indeed, as I sit in the butcher's shop now, with several hundredweight of raw pork piled up in front of me, and MacGregor Mathers squatting beside it, I note a definite resemblance between them.

The walls of this shop are entirely festooned with butchered flesh. Pork and gammon and mutton and salt-beef and veal hang from hooks all round us, and the floor is half-buried in a layer of blood-soaked sawdust. Quantities of ice blocks and salt are at hand, to delay the inevitable putrefaction of the meat. The smell of this place, the thick odour, is too strong to be ignored.

Upon our arrival, Mathers began to leap and prance through every room, performing some unholy ceremony "to protect against ensorcelment," as he explained. This apparently required that he rub garlic on all the door handles, throw hellebore seeds in the air, consult the entrails of the nearest butchered sheep, and invoke the spirits of thirty-seven Babylonian gods, none of whom condescended to reply. Why Mathers neglected to take off his clothes, stand on his head, and whistle three choruses of "Elsie from Chelsea" as an additional precaution is something I cannot imagine. Nor do I wish to.

"Beastly place, this *salon au boucher*," Mathers grunted,

pounding the butcher block disapprovingly whilst he pocketed a sausage. "The entrance to this shop has the audacity to face *south*. A proper entrance ought to face *east*. Far greater harmony *avec les forces du* Nature."

"Far greater chance of tripping over the watchmakers' shop next door," I corrected him, "since they're directly east of us. Why don't you *avey-voo* some sleep? Vanessa and I will guard *le* door."

I do not know which is worse; the sound of Mathers speaking, or the sound of Mathers snoring. He speaks in that Godghastly jabberment of French and Scottish, but he snores like a Bedfordshireman. Some men are more honest asleep than awake.

Some hours later Vanessa rose from sleep, and—since we had brought our baggage with us pending our trip Londonwards —suggested that I continue work on her full-body tattoo. I began to explain that a butcher's shop was not the most felicitous setting for my work, when MacGregor Mathers suddenly stopped snoring, and sat bolt erect.

"*Listen!*" he hissed, standing up on the shop counter. "Do ye nae *feel* it?"

"Feel *what?*" I asked.

"The etheric vibrations. The psychic aura. It *approaches!*"

"What the hell are . . ."

"*Evening, all.*" A butchered sheep corpse in a corner of the shop suddenly stood up, and walked towards us on its tottering hind legs. "*How thoughtful of you,*" the thing whispered, "*to surround yourselves with so many corpses whose lives have departed, leaving their bodies emptied for me to inhabit. You know me, I think. I am the Dreadful Eye.*"

Vanessa screamed. MacGregor Mathers, to his everlasting credit, did not panic. He turned pale, but stood his ground and asked: "How did you get in, past my circle of protective incantations?"

"*Your quack-fakery magicks are powerless against me,*" said the dead thing, juddering towards us. "*My methods touch science, not magic,*" the dead voice rasped. "*Your mumble-jumbleries are false parlour tricks. But I am real, and your death is real, and it comes. I shall play the death-bearer.*"

The thing reached us. I had a flask of alcohol ready: I threw it at the oncoming corpse. Nothing happened . . . and I realised that the dreadful sentience inhabiting this dead animal flesh did not share its disciples' vulnerability to alcohol. My weapon was useless.

I struck a Vesta-match, and flung it at the creeping thing. The animal-corpse, already wet from the alcohol, immediately burst into flames. It still came towards us. The entity within the roasting flesh showed no sign of discomfort. *"I have come for the she-one Vanessa,"* it whispered.

Mathers cursed, snatched up a meat cleaver and rushed at the animated corpse. He swung the cleaver and chopped the dead thing in two with a stroke. "Right, you can't be in *both* halves at once," shouted Mathers.

"I am elsewhere and allwhen," came the harsh voice. A string of sausages, coiling snakelike in the shadows, suddenly jumped towards Vanessa and wrapped themselves about her throat, writhing like some hideous serpent as they tightened their stranglehold grip. I rushed to help her, seized two handfuls of the squirming meat and tried to break its death grasp. The sausages *writhed* in my hands, twisting like alien worms. One sausage suddenly sprouted *eyes* and a *mouth* and admonished me: *"Do not interfere, manling."* I screamed, dropped the thing, and kicked it away.

The sausages fell from Vanessa, and then the very sawdust of the floor rose up and gathered itself in midair, became a whirlwind of wood particles shaping themselves into something very like the image of a man . . .

"Whatever once lived and has died, I inhabit," said the sawdust thing. Sawdust mouth, wooden voice of long-dead trees. *"I shall kill you, and then your dead mind and rotting flesh become mine to possess."* The sawdust thing attacked Vanessa.

I tackled it, but the wooden flesh came apart in my hands, disintegrated into sawdust, and the pieces reattached themselves to the primary mass. Vanessa struggled desperately against the sawdust thing. Her upturned face was outlined in a coating of saw-dust, and as I watched I saw the wooden horror, changing shape like some giant *amœba*, flowing its sawdust self into Vanessa's mouth and her nose, promising death by suffocation. She was drowning in sawdust.

"*Mathers, you ass! HELP ME!*" I gripped the sawdust man, tried to pull it away from Vanessa. Mathers helped, but fighting this thing was like wrestling a mound of oatmeal. We tore out the sawdust in handfuls, but each fragment torn away from the mass reattached itself a moment later. And then I heard, from far away, a grim, loudening hum . . .

A point of violet-coloured light appeared above us, swelled and enlarged until it formed a glowing sphere, and then flattened into a hexagon. The vortex grew larger, became coffin-shaped. "Jesus Christ, what *is* that thing?" MacGregor Mathers whimpered, and sank to his knees.

"They've come for us," I said, still trying to free Vanessa from the sawdust man. "God help us; that hole in the air leads to the place of invisible men."

The sawdust man let go of a now-unconscious Vanessa, and I watched as the dead wooden thing turned and faced us. "*And now I vacate this form,*" the Dreadful Eye whispered. "*My disciples arrive . . .*"

The figure of sawdust pitched forward, and fell. It was man-shaped as it collapsed, but then its mass became formless, un-shaped, as it scattered across the floor of the shop. A mound of sawdust . . .

I rushed to help my Vanessa, but something pushed me aside. Invisible hands clutched my collar, gripped my arms. I heard Mathers cry out, saw him struggle with something unseen. The invisible men had arrived.

"*We will take her to the Master's realm,*" said a voice with no visible face.

I saw Vanessa's body rise, dangling limply in the grasp of invisible hands. I took out my Prometheus pistol and fired, heard an alien screech and a thud as something fell; I had struck an invisible man. But already Vanessa had been pulled halfway into the violet-coloured orifice of light between the worlds.

I flung myself towards it, determined that they would not take Vanessa without bringing me along to protect her. Invisible arms pulled me away from the hole in the world. "You filthy bastards!" I howled in the roar of the gathering wind. "Cowards! If you want Vanessa you must have me as well . . ." Something struck me, sent me sprawling, and when I got up all I could see of Vanessa was one leg, in torn stocking and half-buttoned shoe, being drawn into the hexagon of light. Already the orifice was turning smaller, drawing into itself . . .

"Vanessa!" I shouted. And then she was gone. The corridor between dimensions—now a disk, next a dot, then a pinpoint of light in midair—suddenly winked out of beingness. It was gone, and my Vanessa was within it.

The wind died down as abruptly as it had come. The humming silenced. The only sound within the shambled butcher-shop came from a heap in the corner: MacGregor Mathers was sobbing hysterically. "I am a fraud," he wept. "I speak of magicks, but in the face of true sorcery my enchantments run dry. *Zut, je suis un canard . . .*"

Vanessa had been abducted by hell-fiends, yet this Frenchified idiot Mathers was only concerned that his quack-salvered "magicks" had been shown up for an empty-lardered hoax. Vanessa's imperilment was bloody bugger-all to him. "Och, *je ne sais,* I dinnae ken . . ."

The meat cleaver lay where it had fallen; I suppressed an urge to use it on Mathers. The door to the shop opened, and a paraffin lantern appeared, followed by Francis Blackmore. *"Good Lord!"* he said, surveying the wreckage. *"What happened?"*

"We are too late, it seems," said a familiar voice. A white beard and pointed moustache in a cloud of cigar smoke came past Blackmore and entered the shop. "How are you, lad?" I was asked, and I found myself shaking hands with Sir William Crookes.

"Thank heaven you've come," I said. "They've got Vanessa." I felt my left hand tighten round something as I spoke; I looked, and saw that I was holding the cleaver. "Sir William, I *must* save Vanessa. But they've taken her to some alien world I cannot . . ."

"I know the place," said William Crookes, very softly. "And I believe I can show you the pathway to reach it."

"Then let us *go,* sir!"

"We will go, yes," said England's greatest scientist. "We will go to the East Road railway station and take the next up train to Paddington. The Dreadful Eye may have ten thousand pathways from Earth to the alien realm, but I know of only *one,* and its door stands in London. Let us hurry."

THE RAILWAY HORROR

27th December, 1898

Sir William Crookes, MacGregor Mathers, and I took the first train for London. We reached Saltford without incident, then Keynsham, but in Bristol were obliged to stop for an engine change. Impatient with worry as to Vanessa's fate, I found the delay maddening. Sir William, too, was clearly worried. "I should have chartered an express," he told me sourly, consulting my dog-eared copy of *Bradshaw's*. "We'd be halfway to Paddington by now, instead of hobnobbing with hedgerows in Gloucestershire. Yes, a chartered express!"

"That would be . . . you will pardon my saying it, monsieur," Mathers said, "extremely expensive. Several hundreds of pounds . . ."

"A pittance, man! A few guineas of rhino! Lord knows I'm wealthy enough to cover it. No; *time* is what we must conserve."

As we left the through-station at Twiverton, Sir William arose and had a word with the railway guard. The guard nodded and left to consult the engine-driver.

A few minutes before eight o'clock in the morning, we arrived at the Manvers Street Station in Bath. I saw, through the window of our compartment, the engine-driver leaning from his cab to speak with the stationmaster. That gentleman nodded and came into our first-class compartment to speak with Sir William. The scientist produced his cheque-book, and wrote out a bank draught.

One quarter-hour later our solitary first-class carriage, plus the engine and coal tender, had become an express rail to Paddington. "They'll put an extra train on for the passengers we've left in Bath," Crookes informed me. "And of course my name will be left out of this . . . courtesy of *the Widow's Son.*"

And then I recalled having seen a peculiar talisman upon the stationmaster's watch-chain: an eye producing golden rays, enclosed within a compass: the emblem of the Freemasons. Our cause may have more allies than I had dared hope.

After passing through Devizes our train reached open countryside, rocketing through the Wiltshire fields at the astonishing velocity of nearly fifty miles per hour. Sir William Crookes stepped onto the observation deck and lighted a cigar. We came, just then, to the station at Woodborough and sped through without stopping.

"We are, at this moment," said the scientist, "entering the most astonishing region of England, at an appropriate moment in time. There will be a total eclipse of the moon this morning, visible from here—although it may be viewed to better advantage from more westerly longitudes." Crookes consulted his turnip watch. "The penumbral stage of the eclipse will begin soon. As for our present location: ten miles to the south of us, gentlemen, there waits Salisbury Plain, site of an ancient encampment of the Roman warlord Vespasian, and home of that eternal mystery, Stonehenge. Within six miles of us, to the north, are the ancient stone monuments at Avebury, the enigmatic pagan mound known as Silbury Hill, and the peculiar crypts of West Kennet Long Barrow. There are more far-ancient and mysterious vestiges of pre-Christian Britain crowded into this one darkened corner of Wiltshire than may be found in any region of comparable size in all of Europe." Crookes paused to relight his cigar, as our train rounded an embankment. "We are now approaching Windmill Hill, the most ancient place in England; the sacred burial site of England's earliest known inhabitants."

"Druids?" asked MacGregor Mathers.

"*Before* the Druids, man! Before the Romans! Prehistoric men; the first men to set foot in Britain dwelt *here.* If anything lived in Windmill Hill before that time, it could not have been human."

"What's that on the tracks behind us?" Mathers asked suddenly.

We were travelling eastwards now, and—looking back in the direction from which we had come—I saw a great shadowy thing on the western horizon. It was moving rapidly towards us, along the railway tracks, and approaching so rapidly that it would eventually overtake us.

"It must be a train," said Crookes, peering through his *pince-nez* spectacles at the shape in the distance. "I can just make out two yellow lights in the front; those are surely the headlamps."

"Those are not headlamps," said Mathers. "Unless headlamps can blink."

The shadowy thing was closer now, but still so far away as to be only dimly perceived. The morning sky was unusually cloudy; I could see the moon overhead, but the sun had buried itself behind the clouds. The yellow lights on the horizon came closer.

"I will stay and observe this phenomenon," Crookes informed me. "You go forward, man, and tell the engine-driver to put on more speed. Tell the brakeman to help the fireman stoke the burner. *Quickly* then!"

I went to the coal tender, and explained our difficulty. "Train behind us," I said, although the shadow that approached was almost certainly no train. "We want more speed."

The fireman, a huge red-haired Geordie, looked dubious. "We're gang fast enou' 's it is, lad. The engine . . ."

"Bother the engine. More speed; my friends and I will answer for it. Didn't the stationmaster in Bath tell you to co-operate with us?"

The fireman nodded, and the brakeman slung himself across the gap between the coal tender and the footplates of the engine. He pounded on the door of the engine-driver's cab: "Oo-er! Full throttle in there, Bill! Gent wants t' reach London by quarter-past yesterday!"

"Did the engine-driver answer?" I asked, when the brake-man returned.

"Yes. Heard him grunt, I did; that means O.K. It ain't wurf the sayin' more 'n that, above the chundering o' the Castle-Farish."

"Above the *which?*"

"Over the roar o' that there steam-engine, squire."

I returned to the observation deck. There was a jagged tear in the clouds overhead, and I saw a hole in the lowermost edge of the moon. "The eclipse has begun," said Sir William Crookes. "Do you know how the ancient Britons regarded a lunar eclipse? They believed that an invisible monster was devouring the moon."

The thing behind us on the tracks was nearer now. It was enveloped in a thick cloud of darkness, and carrying the darkness along with itself as it approached. I could see, peering out from the depths of the oncoming shadow, two bright circles of light with dark centres. They looked, more than ever, like a great gaunt pair of yellow eyes.

And the clacketing noise of the rails underneath our train's wheels seemed to summon me: *coming behind you now, coming behind you now* . . .

Somebody screamed, at the front of the train, and I heard a strange chittering cry.

Coming behind you now . . .

MacGregor Mathers ran towards the sound; I came hard behind him. Overhead, there was a large crescent-shaped bite taken out of the moon.

"Good Lord!"

The engine-driver was dead. His body, what remained of it, was slumped within a corner of the cab. The fireman and the brakeman, with an axe and a sledgehammer, were backing into the coal tender, attempting to escape from . . .

I could see it, despite the gathering darkness. In the centre of the engine-driver's cab squatted a black inhuman face that gibbered and howled. Its eyes were like huge yellow saucers, and its jaws were elongated into some sort of a snout. There was blood on its fangs. The creature, the hideous thing, had a bone-thin appendage at each of the four corners of its abdomen, and each limb terminated in some sort of a hand tipped with claws . . .

No-one was driving the train. The throttle was held down by the weight of the engine-driver's corpse, and the wheels rattled faster than ever across the rails: *Coming behind you now, closer now, closer now . . .*

"What in God's name *is* it?" asked the brakeman.

I drew my pistol, and then the hell-thing attacked. It flung itself at the brakeman; I fired, but the thing seized its prey, and its jaws tore out the brakeman's throat. I fired again, and the fireman swung the axe. Mathers seized the brakeman's sledgehammer, and hurled himself at the chittering thing. It lashed out with its talons, and I saw Mathers fall between the train's carriage couplings, towards the wheels . . .

Coming to kill you now, kill you now, kill you now . . .

"*Mathers!*" I shouted.

MacGregor Mathers was a large man, and powerfully built; his brawn may have saved him. He had flung wide both arms and outstretched his legs as he fell; he caught hold of the undercarriage of the engine, and pulled himself up. The fireman's axe struck again; I saw some dark fluid oozing from a gash in the railway horror's face. Then it caught the fireman in three of its claw-fingered limbs.

I fired again. I saw the horrid thing lurch, and then it tumbled from the train. *The wheels will crush it,* I thought, but then I heard a hoot and an inhuman cry. The horror emerged from beneath the engine, and bounded off through the increasing darkness of the Wiltshire countryside. Above us, the moon was now a pale sliver of light.

"The brakeman is dead," said Mathers. "And the fireman's been done for. Nobody's driving this train!"

Nobody's driving us, clattered the wheels . . .

I slung myself over the gap between the couplings and entered the steam-engine's cab. "There's a tiller here, and some sort of a brake," I told Mathers. "Perhaps I can stop the . . ."

"Don't stop! FASTER, man!" I heard the voice of Sir William Crookes. I turned.

Crookes was standing by Mathers, in the coal tender. Behind us, on the rails, the giant pair of yellow eyes were so near that I could now perceive a red network of veins running through them. The darkness surrounding the oncoming face had by now enveloped our train as well. There was no light at all, except for the fire in the engine's boiler grate, and from the twin yellow glows of those two monstrous eyes. Overhead, there was the barest toenail-paring of moon.

"We're not lost yet!" shouted Mathers, and hurried back to the passenger carriage. I saw his plan, and rushed to join him. Together, we pulled our meagre baggage from the passenger compartment, and flung it into the tender. "I hope," said Mathers to Sir William, "that you can reimburse the Great Western Railway for the loss of a passenger carriage. *Cast off!"*

He unfastened the coupling, and we leapt aboard the tender as the passenger carriage was left quite behind, in the path of the oncoming thing.

Coming too close, went the clacketing wheels.

And now, as our runaway engine thundered through the railway station at Pewsey, the moon was entirely gone, swallowed up by the total eclipse. The fire in the engine grate was dying, and the only light in all the world came from those two monstrous eyes. Now they sprouted a face, with a huge gaping mouth coming towards us. Something howled. I saw the abandoned railway carriage rumbling madly down the track behind us, saw it strike the giant face of our pursuer. I saw the railway carriage splinter apart. I saw the great hideous mouth gaping larger, and then nearly all of the shattered railway carriage was swallowed within. I saw that immense monstrous face pause for perhaps the tenth part of an instant, and then it continued rushing headlong towards us down the tracks.

It's too close, it's too close, it's too close, roared the wheels.

I gave my full attention, of necessity, to the Castle-Farish steam-engine. The gauge proclaimed that we were rocketing along at the nearly unprecedented speed of eighty miles per hour, yet that hideous face was still gaining distance upon us. "We *must* have more speed!" I cried, seizing a shovel and stoking coal into the boiler grate as rapidly as I could. Then I tied down the safety-valve, and opened the throttle.

"Let me help!" shouted Mathers, taking great quantities of coal in both his fists and flinging the stuff into the hopper.

"It's still coming!" I heard Crookes report, but I didn't look up; I dared not cease stoking the boiler for even an instant . . .

"You're the scientist," I heard Mathers tell Crookes. "Can't you throw an equation at it, or beat it to death with an hypothesis?"

"That thing is older than any science that I know," said Sir William. "The hills, I tell you, and the *countryside* in this region of Wiltshire are crawling with such ancient nameless horrors."

Coming too near, it's too near, almost here, roared the wheels of the runaway train . . .

I chanced a look at the thing. It was still some small distance astern, but approaching so rapidly as to be nearly upon us. I could make out the shadowy outlines of a form beyond the face.

I heard a scraping noise, as though something were scrabbling at the framework of the engine. Suddenly a pair of clawed hands appeared, grasping at the edge of the machine, and then a face pulled itself up. I beheld the same creature that had killed the engine-driver: the identical brute, or its twin. I drew my revolver and fired. The thing plummeted onto the tracks, gibbering and screeching, but then two more creatures just like it clambered over the side.

"This is it," I said half aloud. "We will die here, on an engine moving along at nearly ninety miles an hour." And, expecting to die, I found that I was thinking not of myself, but of Vanessa.

I fired again at the claw-fingered creatures. One screeched and hurtled down between the rails. The engine lurched; I was flung backwards, and fell across the engine-driver's corpse.

The corpse sat up, and its dead arms embraced me. *"I have come,"* said the Dreadful Eye's voice through the corpse's black lips, and in the firelight from the grate I could see where several bites had been taken out of the engine-driver's flesh. *"I have come to take dominion of your soul."*

I could not kill him: the corpse which this creature infested was already dead. I might destroy the engine-driver's remains, but then the Dreadful Eye might step out of the dead flesh, and show his own form . . .

"Oh God, the face! Look at the terrible face!"

It was Crookes who had shouted. The great yellow-eyed face was now directly behind us. Our train was travelling at more than ninety miles an hour, but the face was moving faster. Its jaws snapped at the figure of Sir William Crookes, and the scientist squealed like a rat and scrambled into the coal tender. The hell-jaws closed about the carriage coupling, and tore away a piece of cast iron the length of my arm.

"Behold the face of my most intimate disciple," whispered the Dreadful Eye's voice within the engine-driver's dead mouth. The corpse's arm rose and pointed, grotesquely, towards the face which pursued us. *"Beyond those jaws lie the borders of madness. None who pass through them escape. If I so bid, they will devour you."*

The Dreadful Eye plucked at me with the engine-driver's hands, and I felt the dead-cold fingers snatching at my throat.

"Let him go, damn you!" shouted Mathers, and seized the dead thing. Together we gripped the engine-driver's corpse, and flung it over the side of the hurtling train. Next moment the ghastly corpse containing the Dreadful Eye fell towards the tracks and plunged directly into the mouth of that oncoming face.

The face screamed.

The steam-engine chose that particular moment to rumble over a set of imperfectly closed switching points between the rails; there was a lurch, and I was thrown face-down across the foot-plates. By the time I managed to stand up, the face pursuing us had vanished. Overhead, the disk of the moon had a dragon's bite taken out of its rim . . . but the bite was smaller now. There were holes between the clouds through which I could see a few fragments of daylight as the sun crept out of hiding.

"It's over," said Crookes. "We'd better spill some pressure from that boiler, before the steam-engine explodes."

"But the engine-driver . . ." I began, as we raced along a curve.

"Dead, of course," answered Crookes. "I shall see that his family, and the brakeman's and fireman's, are provided for. The damage to this train I can pay for—I am a shareholder in the Great Western—but I cannot undo the loss of human life."

Mathers and I managed to slow the engine, and as we continued into Berkshire towards Surrey the boiler gradually quieted its rumblings. "Is the Dreadful Eye dead, then?" Mathers asked Sir William Crookes.

"I think not, sir. But he summoned a thing of incredible evil, and it swallowed him. We have flung him into a hell-pit that he constructed for *us,* but I believe . . . no, I am *certain* . . . that he will return."

"He is *mine,*" I said, gripping the engine's tiller. "Unless the Dreadful Eye releases Vanessa alive and unharmed, he is *mine.* I shall fight all the hell-spawn he throws up at us, if necessary. But *he is mine.*"

Crookes examined his turnip watch and lighted another cigar. "The next battle, I promise you, will be the last. Aleister Crowley has gathered our forces for the battle in London."

"In *London?*" Mathers protested. "But the danger to London's inhabitants . . ."

"The danger is to all of Earth," said Crookes. "If we lose this next battle, we have lost all to come."

I thought of Vanessa, in the hands of the Dreadful Eye's torturers, and I shuddered as our train continued eastward. Above our heads, the lunar eclipse had ended, but the edges of the moon glowed blood-red . . .

THE EDGE OF THE WORLD LIES IN HAMMERSMITH

27th December, 1898

The runaway steam-engine carried us well into Berkshire before Sir William Crookes and I determined a means of shutting off the boiler. The screeching wheels protested to a halt within hailing distance of the station at Shrivenham; we were able to summon the aid of several railway navvies, and another engine was brought to haul the remains of our vehicle into Shrivenham.

There was a small inn nearby; MacGregor Mathers went in search of a hire-telephone to ring up Aleister Crowley. Sir William Crookes, meantime, went into seclusion in the Shrivenham stationmaster's office. Through the door, I could hear the stationmaster shouting, and Sir William replying in murmurous tones, but I could not discern the individual words. Agonising at each further delay that kept me here while Vanessa was in danger, I took the opportunity to perform what seemed the most logical action under the circumstances: I went quietly looney.

I have been cursed, since childhood, with a mind that fashions monsters in the shadows and devils in the dark. Detained in Shrivenham, my fears for Vanessa took full hold upon my brain, and the nightmares came beckoning. I saw, in my mind, Vanessa tortured and ravaged by the Dreadful Eye's prison warders, employing torment-procedures so ghastly that I cannot bring myself to render them on any page more permanent than the foolscap of my mind. And the worst of it was . . .

"A penny for your thoughts," said MacGregor Mathers, his

Scotchman's kilt switching madly about in the wind of that wooden railway platform.

"My thoughts, just at present," I told him, "are not for myself. What news of Aleister Crowley?"

"*Frère* Perdurabo reports that all is in readiness. Are you prepared to leave Earth and set foot upon alien shores?"

"If they lead to Vanessa," I answered, "I shall walk through the gate-posts of Hell. If they bring, into the bargain, a chance to kill the Dreadful Eye, then I am that much the readier."

"We are *all* ready, then," said William Crookes, coming out by the stationmaster's door. He held the remains of his hat in one hand, whilst his other hand was thrusting some small object into his pocket. I did not see the thing clearly, but it looked like a cheque-book.

Five minutes later we were proceeding, by special train, towards London . . . and half-an-hour further on, we reached Paddington Station. "I will be delayed here," said Sir William, withdrawing his cheque-book again, "squaring matters with the directors of the railway. I learnt in Shrivenham that the three men whom the Dreadful Eye's minions killed all had families; I must see to it that their widows are provided for."

"Will they be told," I asked, "the manner of their husbands' deaths?"

"The stationmaster at Shrivenham has been persuaded—in the name of the Widow's Son—to concoct some story of a railway accident," said Crookes. "I shall make attempts to minimise publicity. You lads must carry on without me; find Aleister Crowley."

"What, in Chancery Lane?" I inquired.

"No," said Mathers. "Elsewhere. Come: we must see Willie Yeats."

Mathers and I left Paddington in haste. We hailed a hansom cab, and moments later we were clocketing down Praed Street.

At early afternoon we arrived in the Somers Town district of London; under Mathers's direction the cabman took us to the north end of Tavistock Square. "Is this our destination, then?" I asked Mathers.

"Nae, it isna," brogued the counterfeit Scotsman. "We must

walk the last wee tich of it, as our host's abode disnae have a carriage-way." He pushed open the hansom cab's door and stepped out. "Er, pay the driver, will you?" he asked me. "I seem to be fresh out of . . . ahem! . . . pocket change, for the noo. These kilts, ye ken, dinnae have any pockets. *Merci beaucoup.*"

The fare was two shillings sixpence; I gave the cabman a half-crown, and a moment later Mathers and I were alone outside the blank-faced wall of Number Eighteen, Woburn Buildings. There was no door; only a narrow alleyway leading to the dark interior of the Woburn complex. We entered this.

At the alley's far end stood the window of a cobbler's shop. On the shelves within, rows of boots and shoes stared out at us through the glass, with their unwinking brass-button eyes. Outside the shop, gazing covetously upon a delicate pair of ladies' high-heeled calf-leather pumps within, waited Aleister Crowley.

He looked up as we approached. *"Ave,* Frater Deo Duce," said Crowley, extending a hand towards Mathers, and consummating some sort of bent-fingered handshake.

"Well met, *mon Frère* Perdurabo," came Mathers's response.

"And *you,* sir," Crowley went on, shaking hands with me in the conventional manner. "I was saddened to learn, *via* Deo Duce's 'phone call, of Miss Vanessa's abduction. No fear; we shall avenge her."

"Avengements be hanged," I said. "I'd lot rather *rescue* her. What's our business in this cobbler's shop?"

"None," answered Crowley. "Our business is *above* it. D'you know the Irishman, William Butler Yeats?"

"What, the poet?" I asked. "I have read his poem *Fergus and the Druid,* and I have attended one of his plays at the Avenue Theatre. We have not met."

"But you shall." Crowley stepped forward, and I saw—beside the cobbler's window—a grey and undistinguished wooden door. "This is the home of Willie Yeats," said Aleister Crowley.

There was a stairway just beyond the door. Crowley led us up the creak-protesting stairs, his voice providing a running commentary as we ascended. On the first floor, he said, just above the cobbler's shop, resided the cobbler and his family. In the third floor attic dwelt a pedlar who dabbled in water-colour landscapes. Between these two, on the second floor, lay our destination. "Mr Yeats holds literary receptions in his rooms each week, upon the Monday," Crowley told me as we climbed, whilst Mathers came huffapuffing up the stairs just behind us. "All the finest minds in England have ascended this staircase. I need not mention that I am among them."

"Heaven forbid any contrary thought," I replied.

"Every Monday, I say," explained Crowley, "William Yeats's front parlour is positively swarming with celebrated Englishmen. The earls and duchesses are laid end-to-end across the wainscoting, and the dukes are popping out of the woodwork. However, as today is merely an undistinguished Tuesday, when the English nobility prefer to stay home and annoy one another, Yeats is making do with a couple of Irishmen. One of his two visitors is a cripple, and the other is a physician."

"A convenient arrangement," I noted. "Cripples and physicians depend upon one another for survival."

"Indeed," said Crowley, "I am told that the physician helps the cripple get up Yeats's beastly stairs, and at the top of the steps he hands him a prescription. 'Follow this carefully,' says the doctor, and the cripple flings the prescription down the stairwell. 'No, *you* follow it,' answers the cripple. 'Head first, preferably.'"

We had reached the second floor; I could hear three voices roaring somewhere close to hand. One voice was high and shrill, one deep and gruff, and the third pitched sidelong between them. Crowley rapped on the door. "Let us in, you potato worshippers!"

"Come in, and meet your betters," piped the high voice.

We entered, and there were three red-headed men. One was tall and quite thin, in a dirty black cloak. He was clean-shaven, and wore *pince-nez* spectacles. His long reddish-dark hair straggled in a comma down his forehead, nearly concealing his left eye. The second man was tall and broad; he must have weighed at least seventeen stone. He sported a walrus moustache and clutched a cricketer's cap. The third man was bearded and lean, and looked slightly dyspeptic. He sat perched on a settle by the fireplace, his left leg thrust out before him and his foot crusted over in bandages. Two crutches stood sentry duty beside him.

The room itself was remarkable, its walls given over to art. I saw some engravings by Blake, depicting nudes of a pseudo-religious nature, and several Aubrey Beardsley works that were decidedly obscene. There were at least two Rosettis by the mantle. A deck of Tarot cards lay splayed across the tabletop, beneath two high green candlesticks. The windows were draped in blue chintz, and one wall held a bookshelf populated by those two peculiar Williams: Morris and Blake. And on a chair, in the very centre of all this exotica, was a plate of boiled cabbage and pork chops.

"Bonjour, mes amis," said MacGregor Mathers, his beastly French resurrecting itself from wherever he'd buried it. "Ye ken Frater Crowley, o' course." Turning to me, and indicating the trio of red-headed Irishmen, Mathers added: "I have the honour of introducing you to Mr William Butler Yeats, to Dr Arthur Conan Doyle, and to Mr George Bernard Shaw."

I had heard of these men, surely, but had never suspected that they knew each other, much less that I might ever meet them. It developed, in our course of introductions, that Conan Doyle and Bernard Shaw are practically next-door neighbours. "My house is just *under* Shaw," Doyle told me, laughing at some jest he did not offer to explain. He and Shaw, they told me, both live in the village of Hindhead, southwest of London, and—because they are both good friends of William Yeats—they find it convenient to visit him in tandem. As Bernard Shaw lacks the use of one leg, and regards Dr Doyle and all other physicians as parasite nuisances, I can only conclude that Conan Doyle must be a very patient man, to have assisted such a violent-tempered cripple up those narrow winding stairs.

William Yeats, his *pince-nez* twinkling, drew me aside and requested a full rendering of our struggles against the Dreadful Eye. Yeats listened, his bone-thin fingers twitching nervously, whilst I recounted the details of Vanessa's abduction. "Sir William Crookes assures me," I finished, "that he knows of a route to the Dreadful Eye's realm. I am prepared to take it, sir, in order to rescue Vanessa . . . whatever the risk to myself."

"If Crookes says that a pathway exists between worlds, then it most certainly does," piped the poet Yeats in reedy-throated tones. His accent was Irish, though heavily Englished. "Has Crookes told you where such a dimensional corridor may be found?"

"It is somewhere in London," I answered.

"Then that narrows our search considerably." Yeats beckoned to Mathers. "Brother S'Rioghail, has the Temple been prepared?"

"All is ready," said Aleister Crowley, but Yeats ignored him.

"*Tout est* in readiness, Frater Daemon," said MacGregor Mathers.

"Indeed?" Yeats examined his pocket watch. "Then we have no enemy but Time." He turned towards Conan Doyle: "Arthur, might I prevail on you to stravage up a cab? We shall be journeying to Hammersmith."

"Right enough." Conan Doyle put on his cricketer's cap and a greatcoat and went to the door. "Mind you keep your foot up," he bellowed to Shaw. I marked that, although Crowley had spoken of him as an Irishman, Conan Doyle's accent was decidedly Scots-English. "Foot up, mind!" Doyle repeated, and then he was gone.

"Foot up your great-grandmother," answered Shaw, filching one of Yeats's pork chops and raising it towards his mouth. He was about to take a bite, when—discovering that I was watching him—the bearded playwright hastily dropped the purloined meat and reached for a leaf of boiled cabbage instead. "I find a vegetarian diet to be so healthful, sir, that meat is never required," Shaw informed me through a mouthful of cabbage, while his eyes masticated the pork chop. "Abstinence, sir—from meat, and from other unnatural pleasures—is of the utmost importance for a disciplined existence. For example, take sex."

"Gladly. Where shall I take it?" I asked.

"I speak rhetorically," said George Bernard Shaw. His left eyelid, I noticed, was slightly paralysed; it did not blink as readily as did its right-hand counterpart. "The consumption of meat, sir," said Shaw, "and the indulgence in sexual intercourse both defile the body's health and dissipate one's bodily energies. I speak from experience, sir. Would you believe that I have performed the sexual act *only once?* It occurred in my twenties, more than fifteen years ago, and I have never felt the urge to perform it again. When one does things properly on the very first attempt, there is seldom any need to repeat them."

I was concerned by the delay: must Vanessa's rescue wait while Conan Doyle prowled all the London streets in search of hire-carriages? Yeats and Mathers, meanwhile, were conducting a heated discussion in the corner. I heard the term "Diabolism" flung about in piping tones by Yeats, whilst Mathers gesticulated and jabbered his impenetrable French. I saw that Crowley was endeavouring to invade their dialogue, but Yeats was pointedly ignoring him. It is clear to me that Aleister Crowley and William Butler Yeats detest each other, although I do not know *why*.

"Tell me, sir . . ." began Shaw, plucking at my arm. I had looked away from him for only a moment, yet somehow in that interval a large quantity of pork-chop grease had materialised in Shaw's red beard. "Tell me, sir: how come you to know Samuel Mathers?"

"D'you mean MacGregor?" I asked. "Mathers is leader of . . ."

"Not tied up in all that Egyptology twaddle, are you?" Shaw asked. "Witchcraft and jiggery-pokery?"

"Well . . ."

"Listen to me," said George Bernard Shaw. "Willie Yeats fancies himself a magician, and Mathers encourages him. Crowley's a sorceror, but his magic is nine-tenths illusion, and the tenth part cocaine. He and Mathers are frauds, both as shameless as that mountebank Louis de Rougemont who swindled his way into the headlines a few weeks ago. *Witchcraft!* One would think, in this modern and electrified nineteenth century, that such superstitious sardoodledum would be discredited. Yet it is not, sir. My beloved friend Mrs Emery believes herself the reincarnation of a conjure-mongering Egyptian priestess. My own wife, Charlotte—to whom I have been married for less than seven months, but whom I am rapidly learning to detest—my own wife, sir, believes in leprechauns. I don't know why I tolerate that woman; she serves me hell-fire for breakfast, she reads my diary without my permission, and—most unforgiveable of all—while countless millions of people are stifled with poverty, my wife has the infernal audacity to be heiress to seventeen million pounds sterling. I cannot imagine what possessed me to marry her. Forget sorcery, sir. Forget witchcraft. I have no use for such exotica. I was foolish enough to insert a few references to paganism and sun-cults into my latest play, *Cæsar and Cleopatra,* completed only three weeks ago, and the result is disaster. The play will very certainly never be performed. Disbelieve yourself of witchcraft, sir; the only possible salvation for mankind lies in socialism. In socialism, and in the arrival of the communist state."

"Given a choice, sir," I said to Bernard Shaw, "between an England overrun by witches or an England governed by communists, I should likely cast my vote for the witches, whereas the communists would seek to take away my voting rights altogether. Witches are the lesser of the two evils, undoubtedly. Witches' brew, I believe, is far less poisonous than the communists' diet of blood-pudding and gunpowder tea. I recall a certain excellent quatrain by that fellow Ebenezer Elliott:

> *'What is a communist? One who has yearnings*
> *For equal division of unequal earnings.*
> *Lazy, dishonest, or both; he is willing*
> *To fork out his tuppence, and pocket my shilling.'"*

Aleister Crowley guffawed. I was now long since anxious to depart, and leave this lunatic cripple Bernard Shaw to his pork chops. What was keeping Conan Doyle and the carriage? How long must I remain here, while Vanessa is in danger?

"I would advise you, sir," Shaw continued, brandishing one of his crutches at me, "not to criticise communism before you have tried it."

"You are wrong," I replied. "Communism must be criticised *before* it arrives, since we will all be forbidden to criticise it *afterwards.* That charlatan Marx . . ."

"Karl Marx was a genius," said George Bernard Shaw. "I had the honour of knowing his daughter Eleanor, until her tragic suicide last March. I wish to stress, sir, that my relationship with her was above the crude sexual plane. You see, I am a member of the Urnings: that curious third sex, the twilight gender neither female nor male, yet encompassing both. I am just as much woman as man. In fact . . ."

That final statement passed all limits. I ran for the door and went clattering downstairs and into the streets, where I might find safe deliverance from all one-legged hermaphrodite vegetarian communist Irishmen named George Bernard Shaw.

At Tavistock Square I encountered Arthur Conan Doyle; he was only just now finding a brougham for hire. The driver hooted his horn; I saw Yeats's window fly up, and his wild mop of dark reddish hair appeared. "Cab, sir," called the driver. "Gent says as you'll be wanting Hammersmith."

"Right. We shall be down directly," said Yeats, and the red mop went in again.

As we waited, I thanked Conan Doyle for his assistance. "Between yourself, Yeats, and Shaw," I remarked to him, "I seem to have stumbled upon a veritable 'Red-Headed League.' "

"No Sherlock Holmes jokes, if you please," said Conan Doyle. His eyes, I observed, were grey; most unusual in a red-headed man. "It's bad enough," Doyle went on, "that William Yeats's brother Jack is drawing that beastly character 'Chubblock Homes' for the *Comic Cuts* and *Funny Wonder* papers. I dislike the parody as much as the original."

"What, you dislike your own creation, Sherlock Holmes?" I asked the famous Conan Doyle.

"I detest him," Doyle answered. "I threw Holmes off a cliff six years ago, and he continues to haunt me. He is dead, yet he comes back in my sleep. I perceive you have been arguing with Shaw."

"How the devil did you know *that?*"

"Simple observation. You have just left Shaw's presence. It is impossible for Shaw to exist for more than twelve seconds without speaking. It is impossible for Shaw to speak without arguing. *Ergo,* you have been arguing with Shaw. Come, what d'you think of him?"

"Are you the physician, sir," I asked the medico Doyle, "who treated George Bernard Shaw's foot?"

"No, but that doctor is a colleague of mine," answered Doyle.

"Then tell him, if you please, that when he treated Shaw he bandaged the wrong end. Shaw's head is far more swollen than his feet."

Conan Doyle laughed. "Pay no mind to either of Shaw's extremities; neither his head nor his foot is precisely so diseased as it may seem. I have every expectation that the abscess in Shaw's foot will heal within six months. As for his mind: well, Shaw's remarks are designed for shock effect. Shaw pretends to be an abstainer from sexual congress and meat because he fancies the guise of an ascetic; I happen to know that the old liar makes fraudulent entries in his diary so that his wife thinks he's meeting theatre managers when he's off somewhere beering and wenching."

"And carousing with communists," I suggested.

"Not *all* of Shaw's politics are so foolish as his communistic moods," said Conan Doyle. "By any chance, sir, will you be in Surrey next month? On the twenty-eighth of January, I shall be chairman at a meeting of the Pacifist League, in Hindhead Hall; Mr Shaw to be principal speaker. I invite you to attend."

I thought of Vanessa, imprisoned on an alien world, very possibly dying even at this moment. Oh, God! I would risk my own life if I could save her. "By the day of your meeting," I said to Doyle, "I may quite possibly be dead."

"Then attend in spirit form," said Arthur Conan Doyle, with perfect calmness. "For I am certain that the spirits audit our physical world. The Society for Psychical Research has appointed me their special investigator, and I have met several ghosts. No doubt you recall the publicity attending the celebrated artist Charles Altamont Doyle, who illustrated my *Study in Scarlet* and ended his life a morphia addict in a madman's padded cell? He was my father. His ghost visits me at night, sir, and . . ."

"I really *must* see what's keeping the others," I said hastily, drawing away.

"Ah, yes. Mathers and Yeats. Are you a member of their unholy cabalistic society, the Golden Dawn?" asked Conan Doyle.

"Their league is known to me," I answered.

"Indeed?" said Arthur Conan Doyle. "A few months ago I was offered membership in the Hermetic Order of the Golden Dawn, but I saw fit to abstain. They meddle, sir, in supernatural events of the most hideous nature. Have you read my novel *The Parasite?* Or my magazine piece, 'De Profundis'? I assure you, sir, that the alien horrors described in those tales are far less frightening than the spectres conjured up by the unholy Golden Dawn. In fact . . ."

Just then there came a great clattering from the alley. William Yeats and MacGregor Mathers rushed out, the former's cloak and the latter's kilt flapping madly in the shrill December wind. Behind them ran Aleister Crowley. "See that Shaw gets home safely, Arthur," said Yeats to Conan Doyle, as Mathers vaulted into the waiting brougham.

"We mayn't go directly home," said Doyle. "On the way back to Hindhead, Shaw wants to stop off in Woking and throw stones at H. G. Wells's windows."

"Could we *please* get on with it?" I said to anyone who might listen, as I entered the brougham. "If you knew what may be happening to Vanessa . . ."

"At once. Driver!" Yeats slid aside the coachman's partition. "Hammersmith, if you please. We want Number Thirty-six, Blythe Road. You know the way?"

"I can find it," said the cabman, and took up the reins. A moment later we were, blessedly, onward at last. Conan Doyle remained behind, to attend to the invalid Shaw.

"I apologise for the delay," Yeats told me, shutting the driver's partition. "I was awaiting a 'phone call of the gravest importance, which has only just come."

"Vanessa's life is important as well," I reminded him grimly.

"I agree." Yeats took off his *pince-nez* and polished the lenses on his Windsor tie. "When Billy Crookes contacted me by tele-phone yester-e'en, I was staying with friends near Dublin. I had hoped to pass a pleasuring fortnight with a dear woman-friend of my acquaintance—a former member of the Golden Dawn—but upon learning of your lady Vanessa's dilemma, I rushed straight away back to London to help, on little notice. I shall postpone my woman-friend's pleasures until after your departure."

"My departure?"

"Of course," cut in Mathers. "Your flight to the invisible world. Its entrance lies in Hammersmith, at the sacred temple of the Golden Dawn."

"Look here," I said as our brougham reached Hyde Park Corner. "I can't just go slogging off through interdimensional barriers as though I were planning a holiday jaunt to the seaside. This is an expedition, and a dangerous one. I have a weapon, of course," I went on, feeling the Prometheus revolver in my waist-coat pocket as I spoke, "but I will be needing supplies."

"Billy Crookes's 'phone call assured me that supplies have been obtained," said Yeats. "Provisions, water bottles, hiking rig. D'you know the terrain of the invisible world?"

I confessed that I did not. All that Vanessa had ever told me about her homeworld was that it was cold, and incessantly dark . . .

"I say, what about breathing apparatus?" Mathers asked. "The air of the alien world may be too rarefied for human lungs."

"A diving helmet and some oxygen cylinders might prove useful," I admitted. "But I daren't lose the time to fetch them, while Vanessa is in danger. If I can breathe London's air, I can breathe anything. Vanessa displayed no difficulty in breathing Earth's atmosphere, so I must gamble that her homeworld's air is similar to Earth's."

"A serious gamble," said Yeats. "If you are wrong, you will die."

"And if I do *not* go as quickly as possible, *Vanessa* may die," I said desperately. "I know the risks. I accept them."

"As do *I*," put in Aleister Crowley.

"*You?*" I stared at him. "I don't recall inviting *you* along."

"An obvious oversight," said Crowley cheerfully. "Did you think you could explore the elsewhere-dimensions without a suitable travelling companion? I nominate myself for the honour. Who else is more suited to face the Unknown? I am destined by Fate to see the unseeable, to sense the insensible . . ."

". . . and to screw the inscrutable," I added. I was beginning to see why Yeats dislikes Crowley. "Look here, Antichrist, old boy," I told him, "I know nothing at all of the Dreadful Eye's domain save that it is exceedingly dangerous."

"All the more reason," said Crowley, "for a two-man expedition: twice the resources, and half of the risk."

It pained me to admit this, but Aleister Crowley was right. We had already shared danger once, he and I—in the attack of the invisible men in Walcot Square—and I knew that Crowley was a man of genuine courage, for all his braggart-dances.

"Very well," I agreed. "We are confederates. Only see you do not get in my way."

The brougham drove on. Yeats and Mathers were conducting a heated debate in some tongue that I took to be Gaelic. Aleister Crowley, for want of aught better to do, began singing some raw gutter-ballad about the sexual exploits of the Man in the Moon. I took out this very memorandum-book in which I have set down the account of my adventures, and proceeded to bring them up to date. Beyond this I kept to my silence and thought of Vanessa.

She had told me that her world lies in a dimension of space that is somehow parallel to our own, separated from Earth at a distance of something less than an inch . . . yet that brief inch extends in a direction through which the human body cannot readily pass. A fourth dimension of space? Can such things be? I find it maddening to know that my Vanessa is now a prisoner only one inch beyond London's borders . . . and in a place which I cannot see, nor ever hope to reach, unless Yeats's plan works. But how can any mere three-dimensional man find a pathway to fourth-dimensional provinces?

Our brougham by now had reached the Hammersmith Road; I could see the Olympia Hall just ahead, to our right. In another minute we should reach our destination. I watched the buildings as we drove past them, for these precious kerb-stones and chimney-pots may be my final memory of London before I forsake her and die on an alien world.

It is still not too late for me to turn back; to flee the Dreadful Eye and scurry back to the barrow-grub existence that I knew before Vanessa came into my shopkeeper's life. But I will not, and I know I *cannot*. For I am now in the Hammersmith Road, with all the wonders of London around me, and I find there is no joy to reach me here, now that I am in London without my Vanessa.

27th December, 1898
Early dusking and nightfall

We arrived in the Blythe Road in Hammersmith. William Yeats paid the cabman, and I found myself standing before an undistinguished building; a brass plate by the door informed me that herein were the offices of *Chas. E. Wilkinson, Architect.*

Our objective proved to be abovestairs, one flight up. By the sign of the compass-and-eye hanging over the door, I knew this to be a meeting-hall of the Freemasons. We entered, Mathers leading the way, and as we came in I saw an astonishment.

The place was filled with strange people, of various sexes. Some among them were garbed in weird fashions, apparently meant to suggest an ancient Egyptian *motif.* Several others wore evening clothes of the most expensive style: the gentlemen's collar studs were all diamond or pearl, the ladies' gowns were watered silk or Belgian lace. In several instances a single costume might include both modern vogue and Oriental regalia: I saw one fellow dressed in an opera-coat with matching Assyrian headcloth, arm in arm with a lady whose turquoise pendant was engraved with the image of Thoth.

The walls of the seven-sided room were painted in singular fashion. Mystic gods and strange beast-headed deities paraded the walls, hands outstretched and faces in profile. Geometric designs cast their patterned festoons towards the high-vaulted ceiling.

There was an obvious attempt to emulate the Egyptian line of painting, but the overall effect was merely grotesque. There were too many bright colours, too great a reliance upon blue and orange, and the depictions of the ancient gods placed rather too much emphasis upon their sexual regions. Hardly Egyptian at all, but more like . . .

"Do you fancy my frescoes?" said a voice. I turned, to meet the dark eyes of Moïna Mathers. She was tricked out in a costume that apparently meant to represent a Babylonian priestess, but its drape was calculated to emphasise the slim contours of her female physique.

"Is this all your own work, then?" I asked her, indicating the daub-coloured pantheon.

The Frenchwoman nodded. "I am the noted *artiste:* I 'ave just completed, two months ago, the illustrations for a book of the spirit-poetess Fiona MacLeod. You will read her, yes? *Excusez,* there is my 'usband. Zan, *ma cher amour!*" She rushed towards MacGregor Mathers, embraced him, and they passionately kissed.

Many others hurried forward, greeting Mathers in English, Latin, or French. He was clearly of great importance to this peculiar band of masqueraders. "Yes," said William Yeats, when I asked him about this. "Brother S'Rioghail—Samuel MacGregor Mathers—is one of the trinity who founded our sacred Order. Three men birthed the Golden Dawn, ten years ago, and only Mathers survives."

"What became of the other two?" I asked.

"One of them died," answered Yeats, "and the other encountered a far ghastlier fate: he took a job with the government."

At one end of the room stood what appeared to be an altar, atop a flight of wooden steps. To cries of *"Speech!"* Mathers ascended the steps, and introduced me to the cheering throng: "Yon laddie is nae yet a member of our roodsome covenant—though I hereby offer him entry to the Golden Dawn as a novice initiate— yet he is withal a visitor of singular importance. We will unlock tonight the aperture betwixt dimensions: a passageway leading from our Temple to a far alien realm. Our friend here has volunteered to enter yon orifice . . . and Aleister Crowley, *le Frère* Perdurabo, has chosen to accompany him."

The assemblage hurrahed, and several called for me to speak. As this attention did not ease Vanessa's danger, I found myself growing increasingly frantic. "Might we dispense with the speeches?" I asked Mathers. "And will you show me this passageway you mentioned? If it leads to Vanessa's homeworld . . ."

"All in time, *m'sieu*," burbled Mathers. "I must prepare for the ritual. Ten minutes, lad."

Then he vanished through a doorway, and the crowd of masquers were upon me.

At another time I might have welcomed their attentions, for as they introduced themselves I realised that many members of the Golden Dawn were public figures of major celebrity. In the space of some five minutes' time I found myself introduced to the following:

· Mr Bram Stoker, the manager of the Lyceum Theatre, and I complimented him on the success of his two latest novels: *Miss Betty* and *Dracula*. Less than three weeks ago, so he tells me, Mr Stoker returned to London with the Lyceum's company; their touring production of the drama *Madame Sans-Gêne* was forced to cancel in Glasgow, owing to the sudden illness of their leading player, Sir Henry Irving.

· Miss Mabel Beardsley, the popular actress, who informs me that she is a neighbour and friend of William Yeats. I asked if it was she who provided Yeats with the peculiar sketches by Aubrey Beardsley that I saw hanging in Yeats's rooms. "No," she replied. "My brother Aubrey, just before he died, asked that I destroy all his erotic sketches, preserving only his religious artworks. I wish that Willie Yeats would honour my brother's death plea, and destroy all of his Beardsley erotica."

· Miss Florence Farr, the well-known and enchantingly beautiful actress, central figure in several recent scandals of a sexual nature. I had seen her before, from a distance, when she "starred" in the cast of Bernard Shaw's play *Arms and the Man,* at the Avenue Theatre, four years ago; I had never suspected we might one day actually *meet.* Miss Farr has succeeded in surprising me, delighting me, and embarrassing me all at once, when—before we had been properly introduced—she came up to me, exclaimed: "Come, *you're* a Jack I haven't done yet," embraced me suddenly, and pressed her lips to my startled face, as though searching for entrance. I felt her tongue's firm thrust against my own as it entered my mouth, and I was astonished at this woman's forwardness. Surprisingly, no-one paid any notice: apparently this is normal behaviour on the part of Miss Farr. As we drew apart I tried to speak to her; she quickly smiled, touched one opera-gloved finger to my lips, and melted into the throng. Despite my genuine love for Vanessa, and my determination to save her, I find myself desiring to know this lady Florence better.

· Mrs Edith Bland, who, under the pen-name "E. Nesbit," is the well-known poetess and song gatherer. I conversed with her, surprised that such a treacly and whimsical authoress might dabble in sorcerous activities. But upon listening to her I was distressed to learn that Mrs Bland is a political intimate of George Bernard Shaw. She thrust upon me a leaflet written by herself, praising Shaw's communist endeavours and blaming the world's current difficulties on the Jews. I tore the leaflet to shreds and flung it away. And to think that *this* is the work of a woman who pens fancies for children!

· Mr Arthur Machen, the Welsh reporter for the *Pall Mall Gazette.* He is, he claims, not yet a full initiate of the Golden Dawn, and is attending this meeting in the status of a novice. When I inquired as to his business here, Machen tapped his briar pipe against a small red leather notebook he was carrying, smiled, and said: "I'm doing research." He offered no further enlightenment.

There were present a good many others besides, all members of this confraternity of the Golden Dawn, and I noticed one curious fact: no two celebrants will address a third in identical fashion. MacGregor Mathers, for example, is addressed as "Zan" by Moïna, but dubbed "S'Rioghail" by Yeats, and hailed as "Deo Duce" by Aleister Crowley. Moïna Mathers, on the other hand, is spoken to most lovingly as "Bergie" by Florence Farr, called "Vestigia" by Yeats, and Crowley refers to her scornfully as "the Great Whore Mina." A society of aliases, then, is the Golden Dawn.

Presently the evening tightened its grip upon the hour of eight o'clock, and odd fellows and singular ladies were still entering the great hall. A woman clad in diaphanous garments arrived, whirling madly about. Behind her came a man clothed entirely in black, with a cowl over his shoulders and head, and a mask in the form of a death's-head concealing his face. He was drenched in some over-ripe perfume, by the smell of him. Immediately behind this fellow came a stout red-whiskered man, who was sweating profusely and dressed in the too-small garments of a fashionable girl. He wore a green silk frock, a lady's scoop bonnet, stockings, and green velvet slippers. I could not help staring at this bloated specimen, and he—discovering that I observed him—waddled towards me, waving his fan like any coquettish maiden.

"Do ye know me, sir?" he asked, simpering like a virginal girl.

"I hope not," I said. "Pardon me for staring: I mistook you for a ten-year-old girl of my acquaintance, who wears a similar outfit. She does not, however, wear her chin-whiskers *quite* so long as yours."

"Ye mock me, sir," said the newcomer, in an accent that was Scottish baritone masquerading as Irish soprano. "This body afore ye is that o' Mr William Sharp, but its flesh is presently occupied by the spirit o' Fiona MacLeod, the ethereal poetess."

"So you're a man *and* a woman, eh?" I asked. "Please don't both of you answer at once. I met another pair of sexes in one body today; they called themselves George Bernard Shaw. The four of you should get together sometime; it might make for an interesting game of bridge-whist."

Just then the door opened, and I was greatly relieved to see Sir William Crookes enter. "Pardon me, both of you," I quickly said to the man-maiden. "Perhaps you might dance with yourself, if you can figure out who leads . . . *Sir William!*" With immense relief, I left the two-sexed poet, and hurried towards Sir William Crookes. He was wearing evening clothes, quite the picture of elegance. "I'm delighted to see you here," I told him. "A clear-headed scientist makes a refreshing change from the lunatic ghost-mongers of the Golden Dawn."

"Indeed?" Sir William was plainly amused. "I should tell you, my boy, that I *too* am a member of the Hermetic Order of the Golden Dawn . . . although I took pains to remove my name from the membership rolls shortly after I joined, owing to the scientific community's prejudices against sorcery. I find the Order's magicks quite valid from a scientific viewpoint. There *are* such things as phantasms . . ."

William Yeats, overhearing us, came over. "I quite agree, Crookes. Have you told our friend of your experiments in psychical research?"

"He has mentioned them," I admitted.

"Ah!" Yeats nodded, and toyed with his cloak. "But did you know that I *too* have performed *séances?* It is by means of a *séance* that we shall tonight unlock the orifice 'twixt Earth and the alien realm."

"Impossible," I said. "One cannot breach the fourth dimension by performing mumbo-jumbo. Not even scientists . . ."

"I do not deal in mummy tricks," said William Butler Yeats. "I believe in this doctrine: the borders of our minds are ever shifting, and many minds can join together and create a higher mind, a stronger energy. I believe that this central mind can be unlocked, by means of the proper sensory stimuli. It only remains to find the stimuli required. So: incense, to arouse the olfactory senses. Music, to form the auditory stimulus. The bright colours and curious decor of this place stimulate the optic nerves. Then there are the methods of tactile arousal. These stimuli permit me to *see* the other realm, beyond the gulf between all worlds," Yeats went on. "In my *séances,* I have beheld emissaries from that else-place: sinister spirits in the company of evil men. Aleister Crowley, for instance, is followed about by a hideous goblin in the form of a small green elephant. *I have seen this.*" Yeats's eyeglasses glittered as he spoke.

"You're not the only one who sees goblins," said Aleister Crowley, entering our conversation uninvited. "Have I told you of my Alpine expedition last year, when I encountered those ghastly gnomes amid the Switzerland cliffs? The little brutes fled in terror, of course, when they witnessed the strength of my magick, but . . ."

There was a rapping, just then, as of some gavel or staff, and a sergeant-at-arms dressed in flowing red robes called for order. The masquers present fell instantly silent . . . and I knew that the purpose for which I had come here was starting at last, and that soon I would be rescuing Vanessa.

27th December, 1898

Someone extinguished the gas-jets, and the Temple was plunged into darkness. I waited for something to happen; nothing came, except darkness and silence.

A sudden wild thought filled my brain: *What in God's name am I doing here?* From what I had seen, the Golden Dawn's initiates were more concerned with weird costumes and bizarre sexual practices than with any sort of scientific skill. How could these harlequins possibly help me to reach Vanessa? Then I tried to dismiss such dark notions as panic: the Golden Dawn is my one hope remaining. Sir William Crookes is a world-famed scientist; surely *he* would not ally himself with this unholy band if their covenous rituals were not genuine. William Yeats and Arthur Machen are not scientists, but neither are they fools; surely, if the Golden Dawn were a legion of frauds, Yeats and Machen would not waste their time upon it. And Arthur Conan Doyle had seemed genuinely terrified of the Golden Dawn: Doyle is a physician, very nearly a scientist; surely *he* would not fear the Golden Dawn, if they were nothing more than a coven of mountebanks.

No! They have promised to aid me in saving Vanessa, and their power *must* be genuine. It *must!* For *I have no other hope . . .*

Someone lighted a taper and touched it to a salver. A moment later, the harsh pungent odour of burning incense stung my nostrils. Somewhere in that Hammersmith room I heard the ringing of a gong.

There was no light at all save for the single glowing taper. A woman appeared in its halo of flame; I could not distinguish her face in the dimness. Then she spoke, and by her voice I knew her to be the actress, Florence Farr.

"Konx Om Pax," she whispered, and the voices all round me replied: *"Pax Om Konx."*

"I am the Priestess and High Chieftain of our Isis-Urania Temple," murmured Florence Farr. "Tonight I yield that office to one more adept than myself, a *savant* long gifted in the supernatural arts. *Ave* the sacred founder of our Order. All hail our mind-father, Deo Duce Comite Fero."

A torch was lit, and by the light of its guttering flame I beheld MacGregor Mathers as he mounted the steps of the altar. He was garbed in what I took to be the raiment of a high Egyptian priest.

"There is one among us tonight," intoned Mathers, "who is not of our Order. Will the outsider now come forward?"

Several hands plucked at me in the dark, and at a gesture from Mathers I joined him by the altar. He indicated that I should stand beside the incense salver; I did so, though its smoke and its sickly-sweet odour were highly unpleasant.

"This man has come to us for aid," Mathers told the assemblage. "There is a being whom he loves: an else-woman, a she-one wearing woman's shape, from an other-world realm. She has returned to that place, against her will, and this man has pledged himself to her rescue. I have promised to send him forth upon his mission to that else-world, which lies in a dimension next-door to our own."

"Konx Om Pax," intoned the voices of the Temple.

"Let us beseech the Elder Gods to succour us," said Mathers. "Is Frater Perdurabo present?"

Aleister Crowley stepped forward. There was a light in his eyes which I had not seen there before: an eagerness that seemed to be bordering on lust. "I am ready to *embark*," he whispered huskily.

"Brother Perdurabo has volunteered to accompany this outsider on his quest, to serve as guide through the netherworld realm," Mathers murmured to the gathering. "As Virgil accompanied Dante through Hell, so Perdurabo shall usher this traveller."

"*Pax Om Konx,*" breathed all the faces pressing round us.

If there was some sacred significance to this ritual, I was unable to grasp it. I had difficulty concentrating on Mathers's words because of the incense burning quite near me. Its smoke stung my nostrils and eyes, and its smell was overpowering. I felt a gnawing certainty that I *knew* this strange odour, that I had encountered the twin of this aroma somewhere before. But its identity eluded me.

Mathers, his ceremonial garb enswirling all his movements, came towards me. He dipped his right forefinger into the ashen residue of the half-burnt incense and touched my brow. With the ash-daubed finger, he traced some mark upon my forehead.

"This is the sign," whispered Mathers. "It is your passport to the other-world terrains, the talisman by which all minds may know you." Then he beckoned to Crowley, and repeated the daubing. The symbol which Mathers traced on Crowley's forehead was apparently meant to represent a globe: it consisted of a circle intersegmented by a criss-crossing of lines resembling longitudes and parallels. Flanking this image were two crescent moons, their horns pointing towards the central planet. I assumed that the mark upon my own forehead was similar.

"*Pax Om Konx,*" said Florence Farr, and the assemblage repeated her phrase.

"Now," Mathers whispered to Crowley and myself, "the time has come for you to breathe the vapours. Inhale ye the winds of another far world and feel your minds become transported through the ether. You must link with the centre, the all-mind . . ."

Breathe the vapours? It was more difficult *not* to breathe

them; so pervasive had the incense smell become. Mathers lifted the salver, and Aleister Crowley, palms extended, received it. Crowley drew the smouldering dish towards himself and inhaled its dense smoke; I actually *saw* the thick billowing vapour creep into his nostrils. Crowley's chest grew barrel-round as his lungs expanded to accept the smoke into himself. A beatific expression came over his face, a raptured smile . . .

"It is your turn," said Crowley, passing the incense to me. "Breathe deeply, and loose the chains that bind thine inner self."

I did not like the form these rites had taken, and I saw no way that this might save Vanessa. Yet I could think of no other plan any likelier to aid her. William Crookes had sworn that Mathers was a genuine magician; I disbelieved in magic, but I had a high respect for science, and Crookes's credentials as a scientist are proven. So be it, then: for Vanessa, I had to do this.

I raised the tray of smoking incense. The smoke felt surprisingly *moist* against my face. Its odour—very distantly familiar— was unpleasant, and bitter, but for Vanessa's sake . . . I closed my eyes and inhaled.

The stench caught hold, and it clawed at my lungs. I dropped the dish and I stumbled, gasping, coughing. I must have knocked something over: there was a crash, and I fell. I heard Mathers shout, and then everything was darkness.

"You *ass!*" whispered Aleister Crowley.

I ignored him. I *knew* what that odour was now, that peculiar smell of the incense. I had encountered it years ago, in more youthful a time. My father had enslaved himself to it a long time ago, after my mother died, in the last year of his own life. I *knew* this smell, that had begun my father's death.

"*Opium!*" I stood up. "You *frauds!*" Someone touched me in the darkness; I pushed them away. "Liars! Is *this* your magic, that you said might save Vanessa? *Opium!*"

"Take care, novice," said a man's voice. "Mock you not our rituals . . ."

"Rituals and rubbish! Give me some *light,* then!" I demanded. "Are your trick-fancies so fragile they only work in the dark? *Give me some light!*"

Someone lighted a gas-jet, and then another, and the lights came back on. Several members of the Golden Dawn began to leave, and several others seemed eager to follow. Aleister Crowley lay sprawled in the corner, in the grasp of an opium jag.

"Liars!" I fetched a kick to the heap of opium-laced incense that had spilt across the altar. Mathers came towards me, and I flung the salver at his head. *"Liars!"* I howled. "Is that why these people obey you, Mathers? Did you think I don't know that Hindoo *fakirs* use opium to delude their disciples? Confess it! You meant to make me hallucinate, you hoped I'd mistake your drug-visions for magic. Did you think I would forsake Vanessa, and join your Hell-cult, Mathers? *Confess it!"*

For one instant Mathers wore a look of injured innocence; in that moment I nearly believed I had accused him unjustly. Then his features shifted to a look of craftiness, and I knew I had my man.

"You do not comprehend the magicks . . ." he began, and with a howl I was upon him.

"Magicks!" I knocked him down and grabbed his throat. "Bother your magicks! I'll give you magicks that you'll wish you never saw! *Fake!* My Vanessa is abducted, and you dangle cheap lies and empty promises of saving her!" I struck him, and was pleased by the sound of his whimpers. I was aware of shouts and murmurings behind me: I ignored them in my fury towards Mathers. *"This* is your magick!" I thrust a fistful of opium dust and incense ash into his face. *"This* is your power! Vanessa may be dying, while you peddle your lies! *Take* them, then!"

Someone grabbed me; several someones. I was plucked off of Mathers, hoisted upright, and Arthur Machen pinioned my arms. "Hold him, sir!" hissed a woman's voice. "He dares to strike our leader!"

"You've all been proper rooked!" I shouted, furious at the thought that this mob defended Mathers. "His magic's only opium and lies!"

"Who wants a sailor, then?" spoke up Aleister Crowley from the floor. Evidently his brain was knee-deep in opium.

"What about it, MacGregor?" asked the gruff voice of Sir

William Crookes. "You've shown *me* miracles, but only through a thick cloud of incense. I should hate to find out that you've swindled me. Is your magic all opium-coated?"

I had regarded Mathers, until now, as more a bumbling fraud than an outright mountebank. But now he made a peculiar sign with his fingers and lapsed into mumble-utterings of Latin. No-one present understood his bosh, and thus they all mistook his jabberments for great words of high wisdom. Even Crookes, I saw, seemed taken in.

Only Florence Farr appeared to retain some grip on sanity. She came forward now, touched a hand to my forehead, and placed her other hand upon Arthur Machen's arm. "Let him go," she instructed. "He will do no harm." Machen released me, and she took both my hands in her own. "It appears, sir," she said, "that you are owed an explanation."

"Rather more than that," I muttered.

"An explanation, and no more," said the stage-priestess. "Brother Deo Duce's enchantments *do* work, if one is a believer and accepts the high magicks. If you do not *believe,* sir, then *no-one*—no matter how skilled in the dark arts—can take you to the realm where your Vanessa is hostage."

"*I* can take him there," said someone very quietly.

We all looked up, except for the semiconscious Crowley. The remaining members of the Golden Dawn were standing near the altar. Now one figure among them stepped forward. I had seen him before: he was dressed all in black, with a cowl covering his head, and a death's-head mask concealing all his face. I had noticed, before, the thick smell of perfume that enveloped his body. Now he came closer, and I detected beneath that perfume the foul scent of . . . *something else.*

"I can take you to the alien dimension," said the dark one, advancing. I did not recognise his voice—the wild, slurring tones of a Wiltshireman—but I felt that I knew him. He came to the edge of the altar, extending his hands. They were sheathed in black gloves.

"Who are you, sir?" whispered Florence Farr. There was a

general shift in the crowd, as the masquers drew away from this pungent intruder. "Who *are* you?" asked the actress to the mask.

The stranger reached up and gently took Florence Farr's hands into both his black gloves. Her body stiffened with growing revulsion, but she did not resist the stranger as he drew her hands towards his face, and placed her fingers upon his mask. *"Remove it,"* he whispered, and I saw her fingers curl about the edges of the mask. Then he guided her grasp, very gently, and her hands came away from his face and brought the death's-head away in her fingers. He was unmasked.

Several people screamed, and they stampeded towards the door. Florence Farr dropped the mask; I saw it fall and roll across the altar. She gave a fragile little gasp, and fainted.

The stranger in the cowl still held his back to me. But now he turned, and then I saw the stranger's face.

It was the dead face of the railway engine-driver, whose corpse I had flung from the train several hours ago. Now the corpse had come back for a visit, and its dead eyes looked at me, and the dead mouth laughed. There was dust in its voice . . .

"So you thought to seek my domain, then?" asked the dead thing. "Did you think to free your dolly-poppet, Vanessa?" The corpse began dancing; it capered with glee, and as it laughed its tone shifted from the voice of the dead engine-driver to the voice of another, who had never been alive. *"I am here,"* said the Dreadful Eye's voice within the corpse. *"Dressed in a dead man's remains, I come calling. All that is dead lies within my dark province."*

"You're not dead enough to suit *me*," I said, hoping I sounded more brave than I felt. "Where is Vanessa?" There was a wind rising now in the room: the engine-driver's remains stood at the centre of the gale. I had to shout in order to be heard above the wind. "What have you done with Vanessa?" I asked the dead one. "I demand to see her!"

"You demand it, manling? Does the slave command the master? Very well." The dead thing whispered, in a voice of such power that I could hear each whispered syllable through the full rage of the wind. *"So be it, then. I shall open the gate to the dark world. Pass*

through it, if you possess much courage and little sanity . . . pass through it, yes, and lose courage and sanity both."

The Opening came. I saw the violet-coloured aperture of light appear, and it then began to widen, in the space above the altar. By now very nearly all the members of the Golden Dawn had fled the seven-sided room. A few remained; shrieking in terror or fainting utterly away. In a corner, William Yeats—his *pince-nez* astray, his great mane of auburn hair and Windsor tie flying loose in the wind—huddled underneath his cloak, moaning words of despair: "This is none of it happening." Yeats whimpered, "I have never left Dublin. I must go back there at once. This is nightmare, illusion . . ." The only spectator not paralysed with fear was Aleister Crowley. He was perched upon a corner of the altar, gazing awe-struck at the oscillating vortex, his mind still enshrouded with the dust of the opium poppy. "Look at all the lovely colours," said Crowley.

The *vacuole* grew larger and took the forms I had seen it assume in the past: first a sphere, next a hexagonal prism, then coffin-shaped. The wind, the incredible suction that was caused as the very air of London was drawn into this hole between the worlds, grew so fierce that I had trouble standing upright in its howling. The wind clutched at my greatcoat, it tore at my clothes, it wailed and beckoned and keened, and its shrillness pervaded the room.

"Let my foul dominion claim you," said the dead thing in the engine-driver's form. *"If you flee now, if you turn and run away, then the portal grows wider."* The dead thing gestured with one corpse-fingered hand, and as the creature spoke the howling vortex widened. *"It will grow larger, and engulf all of London, all England, all Earth. It will swallow the planet. Surrender, then; let the vortex devour you, and I shall close it behind as you enter. The Earth will be permitted to remain, and its ant-race of humans will survive a time longer, so that I may enslave them."*

Then the thing laughed again, a dead laugh, and it discarded the engine-driver's form. I saw the empty corpse topple forward and sprawl at the base of the altar. The Dreadful Eye was gone . . . but still watching me, surely, from some vantage point else-place. I was alone now, with the glowing void that beckoned me to enter its beyondings.

No . . . not *quite* alone: I heard a shout and saw Aleister Crowley, the opium jag still enflaming his face. "I see a place beyond all worlds," uttered Aleister Crowley. He stepped towards the Opening, both arms outstretched, as though he meant to embrace it. "Enter," he said now, "and witness dark secrets beyond man's imagining."

"Crowley!" I shouted into the wind. *"Keep away, man!* Save yourself before . . ."

Did he hear me? If my words pierced the wind, he ignored them. I saw Crowley smile, hurry forward, and offer himself to the vortex. How much of his manic behaviour was caused by the opium, and how much of it was born within his own madness? "Realms beyond Earth," Crowley shouted to the waiting dark beyond, "reveal yourselves to Baphomet!" Then he *leaped.* I saw his face, as he touched the howling orifice that bridged the far dimensions. I heard him scream then—in terror? in pain?—as the Opening seized him. For a moment he hovered, suspended in time, held fast between London and elsewhere. Then the glowing maelstrom swallowed him, *and Aleister Crowley vanished.*

"Bloody wonderful," I thought, half-aloud. "Now I've *two* people to rescue: Crowley, and Vanessa." I looked down at the engine-driver's remains . . . the dead eyes confronted me, the lifeless mouth appeared to be grinning in triumph.

The worst part of stepping into this vortex would be the . . . *unknowing* . . . of what might lie waiting beyond it. I examined my revolver: it appeared to be in order. I drew my greatcoat about me and buttoned it, and prepared to depart.

I looked round at the Temple of the Golden Dawn, with its sorcerous murals and charlatan furnishings. It seemed rather unfair, somehow, that this seven-sided room—so thoroughly pseudo-Egyptian, so purposely un-English—might be the last glimpse I would ever see of my beloved London.

The Opening howled: it had waited quite enough, and would no longer be denied. It gaped, hungering, demanding to be fed. "Right, that's it, then," I said. "Nothing for it but to *go.*"

I thrust my hands into my pockets, felt the pistol in my grasp. I took a deep breath, a double lung's worth of good English air, savoured it . . . and then, without exhaling, I closed my eyes. *I love you, Vanessa,* I thought, and then I ran towards the centre of the winds. I felt the air grow unbearably cold, and I *leaped.* Then the darkness engulfed me.

There was a sudden sharp pain, and I screamed. With my eyes shut, I experienced the sensation of being *pulled inside out.* The pain worsened, and at length it became so severe that I suddenly realised—I was thoroughly certain of it—that *now I am dead* . . .

The Eighth Part

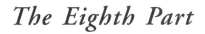

THE VOICES
IN THE PIT

The Other Place

I was falling, eyes closed, in a place of the most absolute *silence*. I managed, with a genuine effort, to open my eyes as I fell, and what I saw now was wholly unexpected.

I saw *nothing*; I was falling through impenetrable blackness. It was exactly as though I had been struck blind and deaf; there was no trace of light nor sound within this place. I flung one arm out in front of my face as I fell, and when I looked for my hand I saw *nothing*: the darkness of this place was absolute.

Perhaps I no longer exist . . .

As I fell I became aware, dimly, of a gradual increase of light. I appeared to be falling head downwards; there was some small sensation of gravity: an *upwards*, a *down*. I was falling to-wards a vast expanse of *greyness,* some featureless grey place stretching flatwards out beneath me.

I fell, and at the bottom of my fall I struck the grey mass, and fell *through* it. It was water . . . at any rate, it *felt* like water, though I had no desire to taste it by way of experiment. I sank, with my eyes and my mouth tightly shut and my arms and legs thrashing desperately, trying to ascend. At length, I felt my body break the surface, and I came up, lungs bursting for air.

"Vanessa!" I shouted. There came no reply.

That was careless; I had shouted before thinking clearly. I was an alien upon this world, surrounded by enemies. An outcry would likely attract much unwanted attention.

On the other hand, if no-one came for me I would certainly drown in this place.

"I say, is anybody there?" I shouted into the darkness.

Silence.

There was, on the horizon before me, a faint glow. Land, perhaps? I swam towards this, and found comfort in hearing the noise of my own limbs thrashing through the water, for that was the only sound in all this world.

I settled into a slow, even rhythm for the swim. I was suddenly reminded of my first attempts at swimming, during a rare childhood visit to Brighton . . . and the memory of my childhood, of my parents still alive, made me feel quite suddenly and dreadfully alone.

The glow in the distance was by now almost certainly land, but I was unable as yet to distinguish its contours.

The air of this place was musty, and somewhat thin—yet breathable, and I therefore held some hope of remaining alive on this alien world.

It is entirely possible that I swam for more than a mile before, at last, I neared the shore. By the time I gained the shallows, and was able to stand up in waist-deep shoals, I was so exhausted that I could barely walk. I staggered out of the water and flung myself, gasping, upon the shingle of the beach.

It *was* a seashore, right enough, but the most alien breed of shore I had ever encountered. The place was silent, except for my own wracking coughs, and the only light in this place was a faint luminescence emitted by the sea and by the rocks. The sky overhead was utterly black, and the air all around me was clouded in mist. The alien sea was as flat as plate glass and completely unrippled, and then I realised why this was so.

"There is no moon here," I said, speaking aloud so that some sound might warm me in this silence. "There is no moon for this world, and so there are no tides. There seems to be no wind here either, and so there are no waves, except for the faint ripples caused as this planet revolves in its orbit."

I stood up when I had strength enough. The shore was a long stretch of rocks: stones and boulders of curious shapes; most of them looked quite horribly sharp. There was no sand at all; only a small band of shore at the water's edge in which the stones were somewhat smaller and more rounded than their jagged neighbours farther up the beach.

I started to walk, with the sea at my right, and the rocks to my left. Beyond the boulders rose a stretch of darkened cliffs; I was unable to see the top of their plateau through the mists all around me. But as the walls of the cliffs were too sheer for me to climb, I was obliged to walk parallel to the edge of the sea, and I tried not to think about what might be watching me from the top of those shadowy cliffs.

I walked for what must have been at least three hours. I was unable to give an accurate accounting of the time; my pocket watch had stopped, owing to the water having got into its works. I was still wet from my swim, yet I felt no sensation of salt clinging to my skin, as occurs when one bathes in the oceans of Earth. I placed my tongue-tip, gingerly, to the dampness on the back of my hand; the water, though musty in flavour, tasted *fresh,* not salt.

"A fresh-water ocean," I said quite aloud, to give myself some form of company. "The oceans of Earth are salt water because of the tidal erosion. But there are no tides here."

I kept walking. I could only hope that my journey was bringing me *closer* to Vanessa, and closer to freeing her.

There were no visible landmarks in this place, not even a sun nor constellations in the featureless sky. I had started counting my footsteps, but lost count somewhere after ten thousand. The silence of this place was maddening.

The empty coldness of this world might be explained by the absence of any visible sun: perhaps this planet orbits a star that confines its radiation to the ultra-violet spectrum. Such energy would be undetectable to an Earth-born observer, perceived as neither visible sunlight nor as infra-red heat. What little warmth this planet offered me was strongest near the ground—suggesting some subterranean heat source, possibly volcanic.

After a very long time I stopped walking and, shaken with thirst, I waded into the alien sea and took a hesitant sip of the stuff. I cannot call the water truly *fresh;* it had a dirty flavour to it, and a smell between brackish and bilge. But it was not salt water. I drank as much as I could stand of the stuff in one shuddering draught, then kept on walking.

After walking for what must have been at least seven hours, with brief rests whenever I found a flat place to sit down amid the rocks, I rounded a bend in the shoreline, and it was there that I discovered the Cross.

The Cross loomed some ten or eleven feet high, rising out of a large cairn of stones that had been erected here for some shadowy purpose. Had Aleister Crowley placed this here, I wondered, as a signal to me? It seemed unlikely. But then who else had passed here? And how had the thing been constructed? It *appeared* to be made from two lengths of timber lashed together at right angles . . . but where might anyone obtain wood, or a rope, in this place? And *why* was this Cross fashioned here? I did not know, and the stones would not answer.

I could no longer go on without sleep, and soon I would require food. Was there anything to eat in this place? Vanessa had told me nothing of the foodstuffs of her world, but all the same her people must eat *something*. Where were the crops, and the cattle-pens?

I sat down and emptied my pockets, examining the contents. Of food, I had nothing. My battered pocket watch had stopped, yet I kept it in case the chain or the crystal might prove useful. My box of sulphur matches were likewise ruined, and these I threw away.

I had my pocket-knife, though the water had got into it, some pencil stubs, and—for whatever it was worth—my latch-key from the tattoo shop in Nicholas Lane. My note case was a mass of damaged papers and a few sodden bank-notes; they might answer for tinder if I could somehow start a fire. I had, as well, the memorandum-book in which I continue to jot down as many of my experiences as time permits; its leather cover had protected it, somewhat, from the water.

I also had my Prometheus revolver. The cartridges in its cylinder were all swollen up from the water they had taken, and I threw them away. Six bullets wasted! But my box of ammunition was watertight, and its contents appeared to be undamaged.

I took the revolver apart and dried each piece as best I could. The entire weapon wanted oiling and cleaning, but that was impossible here. I decided to rest for a moment, before reassembling it . . .

I must have fallen asleep quite nearly as soon as I lay down, and my sleep must have harboured some nightmare. For I awoke to the sound of screaming, and I was startled to discover that the screamer was myself.

Second Day

How long had I slept? There was no way to measure time in this place. I felt less tired, but my limbs were cramped, and I could feel the gatherings of hunger.

I collected my belongings and reassembled the revolver. Was it dry enough to *fire?* I loaded six rounds into the cylinder, aimed the weapon out towards the alien sea, and squeezed the trigger.

The shot that rang out, high and clear across the alien wastes, was the most comforting sound I had yet heard in all this place. With this firearm and my wits, and some portion of nerve, I might yet find a means of rescuing my Vanessa.

I pressed on. After some two or three hours of following the shore I encountered the corpse.

It was a man—*had* been a man, once—and I thought at first that it was Aleister Crowley. The man had been dead for quite some time; his body was cold. From the expression on his face, he appeared to have died while confronting some unsurpassed terror. His clothes, and a quantity of his flesh, had been sliced off his body like ribbons. There were no bloodstains, but numerous small punctures in the flesh attested that *the blood had been siphoned from his veins.*

The dead man appeared to be young, but his hair had turned utterly white. I could not determine the style of his clothing, since so much of it had been razored to shreds. I found some papers, badly tattered and stained, in what remained of his pockets, and piecing together these document shreds I learnt that the dead man had been an American, and that his name was Alan Kane. I could determine nothing of the manner of his death, nor of how he had been brought to this place.

I remembered having wondered, several hours ago, if the invisible natives of this world kept cattle-pens, or slaughterhouses. Now, as I saw the remains of this dead man before me, *I did not want to know* if those cattle-pens existed, nor what species of food was herded into them. There have been incidents on Earth, of men and women disappearing, and their vanishings have never been explained . . .

There was something decidedly *wrong* with this dead man's remains, and at length I realised: there were no signs of putrefaction. He might have died here an hour ago, or a week, or a hundred years past.

I said a prayer over his remnants, and cast the dead man into the sea. I hope that, somewhere, his soul has found peace.

I walked on. The sea cliffs to my left were now progressively lower, and I came at last to a place where the plateau was barely thirty feet above me, and the face of the cliffs now a gradual slope. Perhaps here I might make an ascent.

I heard a sound behind me, a sort of jabbering hooting cry, and I turned. A thing, a great flapping white mass with shapeless limbs and the rudiments of a face, was standing a quarter of a mile out to sea and running towards me across the surface of the water. The thing sounded the most horrid ululations as it came. I remembered the corpse I had found, drained completely of blood, and I climbed up the cliff face as quickly as I could. By the time I dared look back, the flapping white thing had vanished.

I reached the top of the cliffs and was obliged to lie still for some minutes to recover my breath. Then I stood and got my first look at the crest of the plateau.

It was an immense and barren plain, like a stone tabletop built by giants. At random intervals across the flatness of this place there stood boulders—huge, round agglomerations of stone that were very nearly spherical. They were all between twelve and twenty feet high. I touched one of them . . . the thing must have weighed thirty tons, yet it was so utterly spherical, and so evidently uniform in its internal composition, that it *rolled* at the touch of my hand.

"Here," I said to myself, "is where the Devil plays at marbles."

Then I heard, in the distance, a sound of many voices . . . a *chant* of some sort, far and distant, but gradually louder. It seemed to be coming from behind me, towards the centre of the plateau.

I went towards it, ducking behind each available boulder as I advanced, so as to remain hidden from view. I did not want the chanters in the distance to see *me* before I might discover *them.*

The darkness of this alien world, and the mist, prevented me from seeing for more than perhaps a hundred yards in any direction. The voices in the shadows in front of me were louder now, and their chant was accompanied by the ringing of a very loud gong.

I could hear, now, the nature of the chant. There were voices: hundreds of them, all singing the same thing at once, as though one mind were in control of all their tongues. And the words they intoned, to the pulse of that gong, were so alien and harsh against my ears that I knew at once they could not have been spoken by any tongues born on Earth:

> *"Tekeli-li, tekeli-li!*
> *Tch'kaa, t'cnela ngöi!*
> *Tekeli-li, teka'ngai,*
> *Haklic, vnikhla elöi . . ."*

As I came closer, the chanting grew steadily louder, and mounted in pitch. And the voices themselves grew more frenzied: *"Tekeli-li! Tekeli-li!"* as I advanced. The distant ringing of the gong, as I approached, was now accompanied by the constant beating of a drum.

The place grew darker and darker the closer I came to the

voices. It was very nearly as if I were going blind, the way this . . .

Something touched me in the face. I thrust out a hand and felt the hard edge of a *wall;* I had bumped into it. I muttered an oath. The wall felt like stone, crudely mortared; there was so very little light here that I had blundered full into the thing without seeing it. An invisible wall, for invisible men.

Ahead of me, the drum and the gong were beating faster, and the voices still rose: *"Tch'kaa, t'cnela ngöi! . . ."*

I walked towards the right, the fingertips of my left hand brushing the wall's rough stone edge at all times, so that I might proceed along this wall to some gate, or opening. I kept my right hand in my pocket, ready to produce my revolver.

Vanessa had spoken to me of a faculty which her people possess, a sort of inner ability to sense the presence of other members of their race. Humans, I suppose, must have this ability too: how often has a man, believing himself to be alone, become aware of a sensation that he was being *watched?* I experienced, now, with a sort of sixth sense that had never announced itself before, an *awareness* that I was drawing nearer to the place of the invisible men. Quite apart from the increasing loudness of their chant— *"Tekeli-li! Tekeli-li!"*—and the presence of the dark wall beside my hand, there was some less definable trace of the invisible men that made me *feel* their presence in some portion of my senses that had never previously asserted itself. There was a sensation of something *demented,* inserting itself within my mind.

The gong and the drum and the chant were joined now by another sound: the long, drawn-out note of some sort of wind instrument. And the chanting grew louder. *"Haklic, vnikhla elöi . . ."*

I came to a corner of the wall, and went round it, and I was instantly staggered by a sudden fierce onslaught of light.

Below me was a valley. I had to cover my eyes with both hands, and peek between the finger-slits, so as to see without being struck blind by the dazzling glare streaming up from the valley below.

At the far end of the valley was a pit. A great fissure ran the

length of the valley: a sort of natural *cañon,* and this fissure terminated in the pit. A steady procession of chanting figures were
moving slowly along through the valley, and walking single file
into the pit. And the shapes in the pit were invisible men.

Now this was the strangest part. I could *see* the invisible
men: I saw them clearly and in detail for the first time since I had
encountered their race. I think that there was present in that alien
world some source of radiation wholly unknown on Earth—a
wave-length shorter than violet-coloured light yet longer than ultra-violet rays, and which is only just perceptible to human optic
nerves. It must be a very narrow wave-length, at the edgemost
border of human perception; if this colour existed on Earth, we
should be able to perceive it. But in the rays of this peculiar alien
colour, the invisible men became visible to me . . . and their
loathsome appearances filled me with horror and fear.

"Tekeli-li . . . tekeli-li . . ."

The things were shaped like parodies of men. Twisted, de-
formed; a thousand hunchbacks on parade. Their arms and their
legs and their barrel-shaped chests revealed a muscular develop-
ment astonishing in its prodigy. Their fingers and toes were long
and thin, and appeared to be prehensile. Their genitalia were as
distorted and oversized as the priapic appendage of some pagan
sex-god. They had no necks worth mentioning, and their chins
dangled down against the swellings of their ribs. Their noses were
broadened and flattened, and in several cases the face was so sharp
and elongated as to take on the appearance of a *snout.* The lips of
these creatures were thickened, slavering, and their teeth jutted
out of their grin-slitted mouths like so many fangs. The eyes, I
think, were most hideous of all: they bulged alarmingly as though
ready to burst from their sockets, and the irises and pupils had
narrowed to a pinpoint in the centre of each eye. The fiends
looked capable of feasting on human flesh.

They were creeping along single file across the bottom of the
cañon, with their long claw-boned hands clasped across their
bloated chests. As they advanced, their hideous mouths formed
the noises of the chant: *"Tekeli-li! Tch'kaa . . ."* There were,
perched atop three or four monoliths, several other members of

this invisible race. They squatted naked and joined in the chant, and their fingers guided the instruments I had heard: a gong, and a flute made of bone, and a drum with its drumhead made of something stretched taut, that appeared to be human skin. The musicians of Hell . . .

There were at least a thousand of the brutes. And I was fearfully certain that their gathering place was also where Vanessa was held prisoner . . . if she was still alive at all. I would have to somehow pass these fiends, then, in order to find Vanessa. Yes, but *how?* I could think of several ways of approaching the pit, but every one of them was certain suicide: I had not bullets enough for all this vast parade of ghouls. I thought of the dead man I had found on the beach; there were terrible ways men could die on this world. Perhaps I . . .

Something clawed at my shoulder. I started to shout, but a limb clamped itself across my mouth, and another one gripped my arms. I struggled, until a voice in my ear very quietly spoke: "Get out of that, lad. Help's arrived."

I looked. It was Aleister Crowley!

He let me go, but pressed a finger to his lips to indicate I should be quiet. "Saw you haring about among the rocks," he told me softly, "and couldn't resist the chance to test my tracking ability, by sneaking up from behind. Hulloa, I see you've found the demons' lair. Come on, let's get away from this pit until we've figured a plan of attack. There are a thousand of them, against only our two pistols and my intellect . . . we are very nearly outnumbered."

We retreated to a place behind three boulders and exchanged, in the quietest possible tones, recountings of our experiences from the time of our separate arrivals into this alien gathering place.

Crowley, who had plunged into the Dreadful Eye's vortex some few minutes earlier than I did, had materialised *above* the plateau, some ten or a dozen feet above solid ground, and had landed dazed but not seriously hurt. "I am unable to understand," I confessed to him, "why two men might plunge through the same hole within the space of five minutes and yet emerge at two different destinations."

Crowley shrugged. "Perhaps this Dreadful Eye shuffles his sky-holes roundabout so that no-one can find them. Perhaps they move by themselves. Interdimensional short-cuts within the space-time continuum are notoriously volatile."

"So I am told," I replied.

"I say, have you been on this planet long?" Crowley asked me.

"Two days, I think. Three at the outside," I said. "I've lost track; my watch is damaged."

Crowley unpocketed his own timepiece and tapped the watch-case significantly. "Genuine Cartier. Keeps time perfectly. The man I stole it from had excellent taste. I have kept track of each twelve-hour cycle of the watch hands since my arrival. I have been on this world for nearly a week."

"Impossible!" I protested. "You left Hammersmith only a few minutes before me!"

"What of it, man? Time on this planet holds no alliance with hours and minutes back on Earth. D'you think that all clocks in the universe keep time with the chimes of Big Ben? When we get back to London . . . *if* we get back . . . we may find that only five minutes have elapsed since our departure."

"Five *minutes!*" I echoed.

"Indeed. Or five days, or five thousand millennia. Fancy spending two weeks' holiday on this shadow-planet and returning to Earth to discover that five *million* years have gone by in our absence. All of humanity will be long dead, with the possible exception of my great-aunt Priscilla, and the insects will have claimed their rightful place as masters of the Earth."

Crowley seemed perfectly serious. I noticed now, in the dim light, that his face—which had been clean-shaven when we left Hammersmith—bore some six or seven days' growth of beard. Could it be that this madman was telling the truth?

"If you have been stranded here for a week," I asked him, "then however did you live? There seems to be a great absence of pubs in this neighbourhood. What did you drink?"

"Water, of course, from the fresh-water sea," Crowley answered.

"Good God, man: what did you *eat?*"

Crowley paused before answering. "I found food," he said, very quietly. "There *is* food on this planet, though it was never meant to be ingested by humans. I ate, because *I had to stay alive,* but I shall never tell you nor any man *what* manner of food passed my lips, nor how I obtained it." Crowley shuddered. "You must not press me on this matter, nor mention it again. Swear to this!"

"I swear it."

"Good." Aleister Crowley nodded, then made an obvious attempt to change the subject. "Well! We had best be rescuing your lady-love, hadn't we? Got a weapon handy?"

"Yes." I showed him my revolver. "I've the Prometheus, and some bullets remaining." I counted them. "Twenty-two left."

Crowley produced his own revolver: a four-shot Lancaster's Enfield. "Not much better," he said. "I've only two dozen rounds, and four more in the cylinder. Fifty bullets between us, then."

I cast a glance at the procession in the pit, several yards away. The voices of the ghouls had grown steadily louder. "There must be more than a thousand of those brutes," I said. "A pity we can only kill fifty."

"Only kill forty-eight, you mean," Crowley remarked. "We shall be wanting one bullet apiece saved . . . for *the end.*"

I said nothing. It was suddenly colder in this place.

"I believe we may safely assume," said Crowley, "that your Vanessa is captive at the bottom of that pit. It clearly contains *something* frightfully important to these invisible blackguards. Perhaps the Dreadful Eye himself is in that pit."

"If he is," I said, very quietly, "I shall kill him."

"An excellent proposal. What say we pay him a call?"

"All very well to *say,*" I told Crowley. "How do you propose that we get *in?*" I pointed towards the chanting figures in the shadows. "They'll kill us as soon as we show ourselves."

"I daresay they will." Crowley nodded. "I propose, then, that we *do not* show ourselves. All this time we've been battling invisible men. Right; I suggest that we give them a taste of their own medicine. Let us take off our skins, you and I, and become invisible."

I made the most brilliant reply that I could think of at the moment: *"What?"*

"Invisibility is easy to attain," remarked Aleister Crowley. "I myself have achieved it numerous times and have noted the results in my journal of psychical experiments."

"Impossible, sir."

"Not at all. The secret of invisibility lies not in some artful manipulation of the light waves, but in rendering oneself so inconspicuous as to be able to travel unnoticed."

"Since Englishmen, not counting ourselves, are in noticeably short supply hereabouts," I observed, "I rather think that you and I are highly conspicuous indeed."

"Not a bit of it," said Crowley. "Consider: the invisible men can see only ultra-violet light; Vanessa has told us that much. If they can see us at all in this tenebreous dimness, we must appear as an *absence* of colour, since the human body *absorbs* ultra-violet rays, just as black things absorb visible light. I should think that, to the invisible men, you and I must look like two great walking shadows. A pair of perambulating penumbrae."

"Confound your explanations," I told him. "None of this jawing will help find Vanessa."

Crowley looked distinctly annoyed. "Oh, very well. Scoff at my genius, then. Let's descend to the pit, and rescue your lady. If you fear discovery, become invisible."

"How?"

"Tell yourself that you cannot be seen. Construct a mental image of your own invisibility, and project this image into neighbouring minds. I have studied Zen contemplation from certain Buddhist masters whom I have met in my travels: their teachings may help us to attain the proper mental state."

"Not *me*, they won't," I said.

"Oh, bloody hell. Open your mind to my soul-force and permit me to guide you." Crowley extended the thumb and two fingers of his right hand towards my forehead, but I instinctively drew away.

"Nothing personal, old Antichrist," I said, "but you are rather an ungodly sort of chap. You are either the Devil's agent or a madman, and I am not particularly anxious for either one of the above to take up lodgings in my cerebellum."

"Oh, you *are* tiresome!" Crowley drew himself fully erect. "Do you show such distrust to *every* man who calls himself the Antichrist?"

"Most of them, yes. It is a prejudice I have."

"See here," said Aleister Crowley. "You want to find Vanessa, do you not? And return to London? To Earth?"

"Most assuredly," I said.

In the darkness behind me, the chantings grew louder: *"Tekeli-li, tekeli-li . . ."*

"Very well. I submit, sir," said Crowley, "that there is no way out of this place, except to enter that pit. And we'll be dead men before we reach it, unless we follow my plan. If you've some alternative course of action, let us hear it. Otherwise, do as I say."

I could hear the solemn chanting of the voices in the pit— *"Tekeli-li, teka'ngai . . ."*—and all that mattered to me now was finding my Vanessa. If she had come to any harm . . .

"Tekeli-li, tekeli-li . . ."

"All right," I said to Crowley. "There's nothing for it: for Vanessa's sake, I shall open my mind to your madness."

Crowley extended his hand, and placed its fingers on my forehead. "Concentrate," he whispered, and his fingers touched my mind.

"We are now," whispered Crowley hypnotically, "totally at one with our environs; indistinguishable from them . . . and therefore totally invisible. Let us proceed."

Crowley's powers, I decided, were limited to those of a mesmerist: I did not *feel* any different, except for some increase of confidence. But perhaps this confidence, and my wits, might prove sufficient.

We made our descent to the pit. The ringing of the gong was much louder now. In the darkness I was unable to see Crowley at all. Had he abandoned me? I heard a voice at my elbow: "I'm here, laddie," and I saw him briefly flicker into existence,

then fade away into the darkness. I caught a glimpse of his sharp-
ened triangular teeth in a Cheshire Cat grin for an instant, and
then they vanished. Confound the rogue; *was* he invisible, or
merely talented at hiding in the dark?

"*Tekeli-li . . .*"

We reached the edge of the pit. The procession of chanting
invisibles were all entering at its opposite side; if they were aware
of our presence, they gave no sign. I recalled Vanessa having explained to me that humans were only dimly visible to her own
people's eyes. But perhaps they could *smell* us . . .

I crouched behind a narrow lip of rock at the mouth of the
pit, and here Crowley suddenly turned visible again. Or had I
merely shaken off the hypnotic delusion of *unseeing* him?

The entrance to the pit was so narrow that the invisible men
were obliged to enter it one at a time, single file. I could think of
no way to pass them without touching one or more, and thereby
informing them all of our presence.

"*Haklic vnikhla elöi . . .*"

"*Now* what?" I whispered, beneath the voices of the chant.

"Courage," whispered Crowley. "Watch *this.*"

He pointed a finger towards one of the invisible men. The
creature was just now some thirty feet from the edge of the pit: at
the procession's current speed this particular brute would reach
the edge within three minutes. Crowley continued to train his left
forefinger at the head of this creature, as it approached. At the
same time, with the fingers of his right hand, he began to stroke
his own forehead . . . slowly, rhythmically . . . and to pull the
most extraordinary faces. His eyes bulged out horribly, and his
lips worked up and down as though his life depended on them.

"*Tekeli-li, tekeli-li,*" whispered Crowley, in perfect unison
with the creature whom he had chosen.

At first, I saw nothing. Then, about fifteen feet from the
mouth of the pit, Crowley's victim began to twitch its facial mus-
cles. Another five feet, and the creature began to shudder uncontrollably. Two feet more, and it broke off the chant and started
gasping for breath.

"*Get ready,*" whispered Aleister Crowley.

At the edge of the pit, Crowley's chosen prey suddenly pitched backwards, and fell against the disciple next behind it in the queue. They both toppled over like dominos, taking another three disciples down with them. The chanting of *"tekeli-li . . ."* broke off suddenly, and now there were shouts and confusions.

"Now!" Crowley vaulted over the outcropping, and plunged into the mouth of the pit. I held back for a moment—but then I thought of Vanessa and regretted my fear. I took a deep breath and plunged into the pit after Crowley.

There was darkness. Ahead of me stretched a long narrow tunnel, carved out of the rock. Every eight feet or so along the tunnel's walls were hollowed-out niches, and a small lump of blackened stone had been placed within each of these hollows. I have read that certain minerals on Earth emit a quantity of ultra-violet radiation; perhaps the creatures on this world could *see* by the light of these alien stones.

But my own eyes could barely see a thing. Ahead of me in the passage Crowley struck a match, and I caught up to him.

"Where to?" I whispered.

He pointed. Ahead of us, the tunnel abruptly forked into two separate shafts. The procession of disciples, resuming their chant, passed onwards down the left-hand tunnel; I could hear their voices receding into distance. And there was light ahead in the right-hand tunnel—*bright* light, fit for human-born eyes. Crowley now drew his revolver and went into this shaft. I followed.

We came into a chamber carved out of the solid rock. I thought at first it was some sort of natural cavern formed by volcanic upheavals or glacial tides of some sort. Then I saw, in the surface of the wall, countless pick marks and scarrings of the rock, formed by tools.

"Who could have done this?" I wondered aloud. "Were they miners, do you think?"

"Not miners," said Crowley. "Slave labour. Look, *there are the slaves.*"

And I saw, in the rubble before us, the rotting corpses and the whitened skeletons of the dead. They were slaves, right enough—*had* been slaves, for the shackles and chains were still fettered to their bones. And then I realised a greater horror still.

"Crowley," I said very slowly. "Those are *human* remains." Men and women, from Earth, had been brought here, enslaved, and they died here.

Crowley gave no answer.

What becomes of the people who vanish, and never are found? Can it be that some people are *snatched,* taken by force from the streets and the fields, or from ships far at sea, and carried off to an alien world? Now I see it is true: *we are property.* The invisible ones must be watching us always. If they have need of a slave, or a subject for some hideous experiment, they come to Earth and walk among us undetected. Invisibility is the ultimate disguise. And when they find a man alone, *they take him.* A man, or a woman, or even a child—for there were the bones of several children in this awful cave as well—it makes no difference to the watching invisibles. They are hunters, and *we are their prey.*

"Something's coming," said Aleister Crowley.

There was, drawing towards us, a definite *thump . . . thump . . .* it sounded like the approach of some creature with only one leg, leaping and bounding along on its solitary limb. I did not want to see the thing's face.

The cavern we had entered was a *cul-de-sac.* The only way out was the way we had come: through the tunnel in which the approaching *thump . . . thump . . .* could be heard growing steadily nearer.

We both had our revolvers out, and trained them upon the entrance to the cavern. "The Keepers are returning to the cage," said Crowley.

I nodded, and cocked the hammer of my weapon.

Thump . . . thump . . .

The faces came.

A procession of faces approached down the corridor; disembodied faces, each one terminating in a chin and a bit of neckless throat. The faces bobbed and drifted several feet above the floor of the tunnel, and I realised that they were remnants of invisible men. Their faces were daubed with some sort of pale greenish clay, apparently for ceremonial purposes. The rest of their bodies, untouched by the clay, remained invisible in the cave light. There were six of the faces approaching, and as they entered the cavern the first of the bodiless visages turned its eyes towards me and spoke:

"You will come with us," said the face, in harsh-tongued English. *"Both of you, come. Our Lord the Dreadful Eye is curious to see you, before you are killed."*

Crowley pointed his revolver at the bodiless head. "If there's killing to be done, I could slaughter you right where you stand."

"Perhaps. But the sound would fetch others, and you would soon be surrounded by our Dreadful Lord's disciples. Obey his will instead, and perhaps he shall grant you a swift and painless death."

And all the heads, the floating faces, turned and drifted out of the cavern, clearly expecting us to follow. I gestured to Crowley. "Let's come on, then."

"What, and get killed by that Dreadful Panjandrum? Not likely!"

"Don't play an ass, man," I told him. "The invisible men already know we're here; they shan't likely let us leave. I've come all this way to save Vanessa . . . or to *avenge* her." I checked my revolver. "This Dreadful Eye's the johnny that I want. Let us meet him."

I went down the tunnel, with two of the drifting faces grinning horribly on either side of me; the shaft had widened sufficiently to permit us to walk three abreast. I heard footsteps behind me, boot nails on stone, and I knew that Crowley was bringing up the rear.

After some twenty minutes we came, quite suddenly, into an underground room of such vastness that it could have swallowed Westminster Abbey. The place was well and truly *huge.* I stood still in amazement, and Crowley muttered to himself in some ancient tongue.

The room was filled with invisible men. And invisible women, as well, although I could see no sign of Vanessa. All I saw were the faces, thousands of visible faces atop unseen bodies: grotesque, half-human faces, all bedaubed with the pale green clay that rendered visible their features. And as I entered that cavernous room, the thousands of disembodied faces slowly turned and silently regarded me. I saw a thousand sets of lips drawn back obscenely, to reveal a thousand sets of ghastly teeth, half visible, all gleaming in the light within this room.

The source of all the light, I now discovered, was an altar in the centre of the place. The altar was shaped like a hexagon, parallel to the floor of the chamber. In its centre was set a smaller hexagon, roughly three feet across, fashioned out of some black-faceted crystal. At each of the altar's six corners a bonfire was blazing.

There was naturally some quantity of smoke, ascending from the bonfires towards the ceiling of the chamber and disappearing up a shaft in the roof towards the surface of this alien world.

"We may have to escape up that chimney flue," Crowley whispered, nodding towards the shaft. "All the other passages have sentries . . ."

"*Silence!*" roared a voice. A face appeared above the altar, with two hands floating beneath it. Another invisible man; but this one was evidently in authority here: unlike the others, his hands were coated with the same sort of pale greenish clay that distinguished his face.

"*Silence!*" bellowed this creature, gesticulating with his clay-crusted hands. To the disembodied faces floating near me he spoke: "*Iklakic hnai kavnoklor. K'dee!*"

With a howling, with a screeching, with a sound like some great hooting ape tribe, they took me. I felt a dozen sets of invisible hands clutching at my arms, at my face, at my legs. A score of invisible arms passed me over the mass of jeering faces, hoisting me towards the altar. In the confusion I saw Crowley receiving similar treatment. We were brought to the edge of the altar and flung atop it like sacrificial goats.

"They certainly devote attention to their guests," Crowley muttered to me.

"*Silence!*" repeated the leader. Watching us struggle to our feet, he rasped: "*H'klau vednishc thneklac g'thnöi.*"

From somewhere outside the chamber there arose a great clankering sound, drawing gradually nearer.

Crowley heard it too. "They are bringing the prisoners," he said.

"How can you tell?" I asked him.

Beneath his beard growth, Aleister Crowley's face was suddenly pale. "Don't you recognise it, man? The sound of *chains*. I would know that sound on any planet in the galaxy; chains are chains no matter what sort of being creates them."

From a tunnel at the far end of the chamber, the prisoners came. They were naked, except for their shackles. And I saw, in an instant of horror, that the prisoners were *humans,* from Earth.

Most of the prisoners were men; several were women, and towards the end of that wretched procession was a girl who could not have been above fourteen years. They were all of them gaunt, emaciated to the point of starvation. Their hands were shackled behind each one's back, and a long chain—passed through metal collars forged round each prisoner's throat—linked them all together. The prisoners' faces were thin and very nearly fleshless, to the point of being merely living skulls. Their eyes, in their starveling sockets, seemed glazed over with dust. On each one's face was an expression of the most insurmountable despair, of fears and agonies scraped raw and forbidden to heal. When I saw their sunken faces, I suddenly knew what it meant to be damned.

"Crowley," I said. "This is monstrous."

"*Look there,*" Crowley whispered hoarsely, pointing. At the end of the prisoners' chain dangled two *empty* slave collars, awaiting new occupants.

I *knew* this parade of living skeletons; I had seen them in nightmares. They were the people I have read about who vanish from the surface of the Earth, without a trace. Was one of these prisoners Andrée, the French aëronaut, who had been plucked from the sky one brief year ago, in 1897? Neither he nor his hydrogen balloon had ever been found. How many of the men standing before me now had stood, twenty-six years ago, on the deck of the *Mary Celeste?* And how long had these others been trapped in this place?

Vanessa had told me that the Earth-born who came to her homeworld always chose to remain, willingly. She had not mentioned chains. Did Vanessa lie, then? Or had these people never been enslaved until the coming of the Dreadful Eye?

Behind this legion of walking cadavers came another chain, longer than the first. There were shackles and collars attached to it at intervals, and amongst the dungeon irons I saw movement: stains of dirt and filth clotted on bodies I could not perceive; *invisible* bodies. These prisoners were natives, then, of this alien planet.

I heard a shout. One set of shackles strained towards the altar; the face within the slave collar was invisible, but the feminine torso beneath was a definite pinkish flesh-colour. The rose-tipped hue of those trembling breasts was the product of my own tattoo needle . . .

"*Vanessa!*"

I rushed forward, but several of the invisible brutes held me back. I struggled, whilst the prisoners were led up a flight of stone steps to the top of the altar. And now no restraints could contain me. I broke free of the invisible clutches, and reached my Vanessa —chained Vanessa, limping Vanessa—at last. I took her lash-scarred body in my arms, and pressed my face to her trembling lips.

"Vanessa . . . my darling . . ."

She had barely the strength left to speak. "I knew . . . *I knew* that you would come," she whispered, and then collapsed in my embrace.

The clay mask and disembodied hands of the invisible leader came forward. "*You will let go of her, manling.*"

I confronted him. "Are you the Dreadful Eye?"

"*No; I am his High Priest. The Dreadful Eye, may he stalk in darkness forever, soon arrives.*" The clayed lips of the High Priest grimaced obscenely. "*Our Lord the Dreadful Eye approaches, to pass judgement on all who oppose his rule.*"

"Well, tell him to ruddy well get a move on," I shouted. "Let him show himself. I want to see this two-penny tyrant who hides behind his underlings and calls himself the Dreadful Eye."

"WHO CALLS?" said a whisper behind me. It spoke in the very quietest of tones, yet the voice penetrated to the darkest corners of my mind. *"MANLING FOOL, I AM HE WHOM YOU SEEK. TURN ROUND AND FACE THE DREADFUL EYE."*

The High Priest shuddered, and fell moaning to his knees, with his hands shielding his prostrated face. Before me all the thousands of invisible worshippers, the sea of masks, flung themselves face-down upon the cavern floor. Several of the shackled prisoners on the altar cried out in despair, and a few of them fainted. I felt a cold wind suddenly spring up at my back, and I knew that it came from the thing which inspired this unreasoning fear. So I turned then, and I faced the Dreadful Eye.

Hovering above the black stone in the centre of the altar, perched in midair at a point slightly higher than my head, there stood a disembodied mouth. A mouth by itself, with no neighbouring face. It was faintly transparent; I could distinguish the lips, and the teeth, and some glimmerings of tongue, yet I could also see *through them* all the chamber beyond. A ghost mouth, with no body beneath. The mouth drifted towards me, and spoke: *"WE MEET AT LAST, MANLING."*

"Well, you meet *me*, at any rate," I answered. "You still haven't shown yourself. I should never have thought, from your name, that the Dreadful Eye consisted solely of a mouth."

"I HAVE EYES," said the mouth, and as it spoke it flickered out of existence, to be replaced by a pair of smoke-coloured eyes. They turned in their sockets and regarded me for an instant: lidless, unblinking. There was, in those silent watching eyes, something genuinely *dreadful*, and unholy. Then they vanished, and were replaced by the mouth. *"I HAVE EYES, AND A MOUTH, AND MANY OTHER PARTS,"* whispered that hideous orifice. *"I SELDOM FAVOUR MY SUBJECTS WITH MORE THAN A PORTION OF MYSELF, UNLESS NECESSARY."*

Aleister Crowley stepped past me and faced the grey mouth defiantly. "What d'you want with us, Gob-Hole?" he asked, and then gestured towards the slaves. "I demand that you release these prisoners, and return us all safely to London. Hop to it, Gape-Face!"

"*FOOL!*" The floating mouth bellowed in rage. A sudden flash of violet-coloured light filled the chamber, and a roar like a thunderclap, and Crowley instantly doubled over in pain. His hands clutched at his forehead, his fingernails digging into the flesh. His eyes rolled back within their sockets until only the whites could be seen.

I drew my revolver, and fired a bullet through the centre of the Dreadful Eye's hideous mouth.

"*FOOL!*" howled the dangling grin. My bullet passed through the wraithsome grey lips, and struck an invisible man at the foot of the altar. I saw his clay mask twitch, and he yelped like a dog.

There was something very wrong here. The Dreadful Eye had struck down Crowley easily, with a blast of such force that Crowley was still moaning and writhing in agony. But with so much power available, why had not the Dreadful Eye also unleashed it towards *me?*

The invisible disciples advanced to attack me atop the stone altar. I fired a shot into the thick of them. But they were hundreds, and I had so few bullets left . . .

"*KILL HIM!*" screeched the Dreadful Eye's bodiless mouth.

The High Priest rushed towards me, his clay-daubed face and hands visible, the rest of him unseen. "Come, *you're* worth a bullet, at least!" I shouted, and fired point-blank at his gibbering face. The clay mask cracked open and shattered into fragments as the High Priest toppled backwards and died.

A mass, a wave, a torrent of disembodied faces poured up onto the altar: a hundred throats howling blood-lust all at once, and ten hundred more behind them, chanting: "*Tekeli-li! Tekeli-li!*" Invisible teeth bit flesh, and I bled. The prisoners, naked in their chains, made a creditable effort to aid me. Several of the stronger ones flung themselves between the tide of invisible creatures and myself, and this gave me three precious seconds in which to reload my revolver before, screaming in agony, the prisoners were crushed beneath the horde of invisible feet. Most of them died, I believe, very quickly.

I could not see Vanessa . . .

I fired again, aware that I was merely postponing the inevitable. I recalled Crowley's warning that I must save the last bullet for myself . . .

Aleister Crowley, just then, revived. He rose unsteadily to his feet and drew his revolver, yet he was obviously still in great pain. He fired. The invisible mob fell upon him, snatched him, and held him aloft. Crowley fired again, but his aim was off. His bullet missed the mask-faced horde entirely, and struck the black-crystal hexagon at the high altar's centre. The crystal shattered, and . . .

"NO! OH! AWAOHHH!"

The scream filled the universe. The invisible men, overrunning the altar, dropped back. The mouth, the fragmented face of the Dreadful Eye, grew suddenly huge and monstrous in the space above the altar. The terrible mouth, the ghastly eyes, and the nose appeared, running into each other like melting quicksilver, and the face was distorted in an agonised scream. I saw, for perhaps one full second, the naked face of the Dreadful Eye revealed. I shall see it, in my nightmares, forever.

The masks of the invisible men rose up from the floor of the chamber and regrouped to mount a fresh attack.

"Bloody hell!" shouted Crowley. "Look at *this,* lad! *Look at this!*"

"KILL THE REBELLIOUS ONES!" The voice of the Dreadful Eye was everywhere at once. His face—his eyes, his gaping great mouth—had vanished, and now a clutching disembodied hand floated in the space above the altar, beckoning its disciples to the attack. The fingers of the hand were twisted, gnarled, with long talonous nails. The hand, I noticed, was a *left* one, as though the Dreadful Eye might be left-handed.

And then ten or a dozen of the invisible brutes caught hold of me, seizing my arms and my legs and my throat.

I remember calling out Vanessa's name. I heard no answer.

Crowley fired his revolver again . . . not into the invisible horde, but directly into a cavity in the centre of the altar, where the black-faceted crystal had been. *"Call off your dogs,* you in there,"* Crowley shouted to something unseen, *"or the next bullet's* yours.*"

There was, for a moment, absolute silence in the chamber, and then I heard the rasping voice of the Dreadful Eye:

"RELEASE THE HUMANS, AND LEAVE US," it commanded. *"I WISH TO DEAL WITH THEM ALONE. OBEY ME."*

There was some murmuring at this, from invisible tongues, and several of the Dreadful Eye's disciples seemed unwilling to obey this new command. At length, when it became evident that the majority of the disciples would submit, the others assented as well. They let go of me and left me where I fell. The only sounds were the steady *thump-thump* of invisible feet—a procession of alien initiates departing—amid the moaning of the wounded left behind.

I found Vanessa trampled in her chains, at the edge of the altar. The visible portions of her arms and legs seemed oddly bent, at unnatural angles. I knelt, and cradled her head in my blood-spotted hands. She was sobbing. I wiped the filth from her sores, and I wished, for the thousandth of times, that I might be able to see her invisible face.

"The pain, Vanessa," I whispered. "Is it too much to bear?"

"They . . . *hurt* me." Her voice was faint, and she sounded as though she were choking on blood. "There were . . . so *many* of them, and they all . . . *ungentled* me. All the touch . . ."

I stroked her gently. "Listen carefully, Vanessa," I said. "I love you. I shall do whatever I can for you. But without medical provisions, I very much fear that there is only one way I can end your suffering." In my pocket, I closed my hand round the revolver. "Do you want the only ease that I can offer?"

"I believe that I can . . . endure a bit longer." She was shaking. "But the pain is so bright. Oh, they . . . *kavnar faughn iklakic . . .*"

Her trembling lessened; she was unconscious now. I kissed her unseen lips, and felt a chill; Vanessa's warmth was fading.

"Let her rest, for the moment," said Aleister Crowley. "I think you'd better have a look at *this.*"

I left Vanessa, reluctantly, to see what Crowley had nosed up. He was standing directly over the hole in the altar's centre, his hands gripping the butt of his revolver. Crowley kept the weapon trained steadily into the hole beneath his feet, and stood ready to fire. At *what?* He stepped back from the cavity so that I might approach it, but kept his pistol dead-aimed at his quarry within. I knelt, and peered into the hole.

The altar, evidently, was hollow, for the space within the cavity was surprisingly large. The interior was dimly lit, but peering into the hole—whilst gesturing at Crowley to get his pistol out of my face—I could perceive the dark outlines of something within.

The place was full of machines. They were packed into nearly every cubic inch of space beneath the altar stone. Machines of such strangeness and utter complexity that I could not even guess at their purpose.

There were, crammed together underneath the altar, rows and rows of very small electric lights, winking on and off amid the shadows. A queer machine clicked at intervals and hummed to itself. There was, in one corner, a large oblong plate made of glass, which emitted a peculiar phosphorescent green glow.

Something scuttled in the shadows within that hole, like a rat making its escape behind the machines. A rat, or the Dreadful Eye?

"Over *there.*" Crowley pointed. "D'you *see* it?"

He had his Vesta-matches out. With his boot heel, Crowley smashed the last fragments of crystal still clinging to the edges of the hole. The entrance to the chamber below was roughly three feet across.

"You stay here; look after Vanessa," I told Crowley. "And see if any of the other prisoners can be helped." I snatched his packet of Vestas, and before Crowley could stop me I drew my revolver and lowered myself halfway into the hexagonal cavity. I dangled for a moment at the brink of the shaft, then let go, and I dropped . . .

I must have fallen ten feet to the bottom. I landed sitting down, slightly dazed but unhurt. There was a rapid clattering sound in the darkness, and I quickly struck a match.

Something moved, and I expected it to be the Dreadful Eye.

It was a man, a stout and nervous little tremblesome mouse of a man, with eyes that seemed made out of water, and a moth-eaten grey comforter dangle-knotted round his neck. He looked exactly like a clerk in some Holborn accounting house, with the sort of a face one expects to find peering out from behind money ledgers and stacks of receipts. The only thing out of the usual about him was his right hand: it was swollen, and bound up with some torn strips of cloth, through which had seeped some quantity of blood. I struck another match. The little man saw me. He whimpered, and withdrew a bit farther into the shadows.

"Mr Dreadful J. Eye, I assume?" I asked the tremblous little man.

"Er, ah, well . . . *no,*" he stammered. "Th-that is to say, I . . . um, *yes.* But not *exactly.* Y-you see, I . . . well, *no.*" He blinked at me, and mopped his brow with his left-hand shirt-sleeve. "T-t-tell me, sir: h-have you ever been to Brighton?"

I must have goggled at him. *"What?"*

"D-did you n-n-never go to Brighton Pier as a child," began the quiversome trembling man, "to s-s-see the Punch and Judy shows? I did that once." The stammering little fellow managed a nervous smile. "And d-d-did you n-never wait until the per-per-formance was ended, when the Devil carried Punch away to Hell? D-did you never l-li-lift a c-corner of the cloth of the p-puppet stage, expecting to . . . to see another glimpse of Master Punch? I . . . I have d-done that, sir. Can you im-im-imagine how it felt for me, wh-when I was six years old, to d-di-discover that Punch and Judy and Jack Ketch the Hangman were only p-pup-puppets, made of wood, and th-that their actions were controlled b-by an unseen puppet master? Have . . . have you n-never d-done this, sir, as I did once?"

I dared not let my guard down for an instant, for fear that

this stammering little man might be the latest of the Dreadful Eye's disguises; yet the nervous fellow seemed to be wholly incapable of guile. "I think I see what you're driving at," I said. "You mean that the Dreadful Eye was just a hoax, an empty marionette . . . and now *you*, the puppet master, stand revealed."

"Good heavens, NO!" The little man began to quiver like a frightened rabbit in a cage. "You . . . you've got it back to front! D-don't you *see?* The Dreadful Eye is the puppet master, and I . . . oh, God! . . . *I am the marionette!"*

And then he suddenly collapsed, in a dead faint, face downwards, as though his strings had been cut.

This was a rum go, right enough. I found a ladder stowed between two of the strange machines; I hallooed up to Crowley, and between us we managed to fetch the little man up through the hole to the top of the Dreadful Eye's altar.

Vanessa was beginning to stir; I rushed to her side, knelt before her, and asked how she felt.

"It still . . . *bites,"* she said, trembling. "The torture-masters touched me in the darkness . . . but I *knew* you would come . . ."

I kissed my Vanessa. She was still in her chains, but now she regained sufficient strength to use her shape-changing ability slightly; just enough to briefly narrow her limbs and slip free of her chains and slave collar. I assume that the Dreadful Eye's prison warders had kept her too weakened to manage this before. "I feel . . . some more of good now," she murmured, in half-remembered English, and as my hand touched her face I could feel her invisible smile.

Three of the other enchained prisoners—two human, one outworlder—were still alive, although barely conscious. Crowley and I did what we could for them.

All the other slaves, human and alien alike, had died in their chains; I felt that their deaths should not pass unremarked. "We must give them a decent Christian burial," I said to Crowley.

"Christian? I'm a pagan myself," answered Aleister Crowley. "As for a burial: we're already at least two hundred feet underground. How much deeper would you propose that we dig?"

We cremated the dead prisoners' remains in the bonfires surmounting the altar. I said a prayer over each body as I consigned them to the flames; their souls, I hoped, might find some comfort now in Jesus. Meanwhile, Aleister Crowley offered a benediction in some ancient tongue I did not recognise, voiced to some dark elder god. And Vanessa, as soon as she had strength enough to sit upright, whispered a prayer for the dead in her own planet's language.

Then, at prayers' end: "Who's *he?*" Crowley asked, indicating the rabbity little man whom I'd found. Even in his unconscious state, the stranger was still trembling.

"Whoever he is, I've some questions for him as soon as he comes round," I said. "He seems to know some secret of the Dreadful Eye."

"He'd better know some way we can get out of here," said Crowley. "Have you forgotten the army of invisible men? They're sure to kill us, if we try to escape from this place."

Third Day

Having done all I could to lessen Vanessa's pain, I was reluctant to tarry any longer in the Dreadful Eye's altar chamber. But Vanessa was too weakened to travel just yet, as were the other three slaves whom we had rescued. There seemed, at the moment, less danger in staying here than in attempting to leave: the Dreadful Eye's disciples, ordered to stay out of this chamber, would almost certainly be waiting just a little way beyond if we endeavoured to escape.

I found that I could remain awake no longer; the best scheme, for now, would be to regain some slight strength. Crowley offered to stand watch whilst I slept. I took what ease I could, on the altar top beside Vanessa, and after a time I was prodded suddenly awake by the toe of Aleister Crowley's boot. "Aroint thyself from Morpheus, lad," he said. "Our blinky-blighter has regained consciousness."

The nervous little man whom I'd discovered was beginning

to revive. He blinked, rubbed his head, and sat up slowly. *"Oh!* Oh, dear *me!* I'm still *here!"* he stammered. "Th-th-then it *w-wa-wasn't* a n-nightmare!" He peered round, saw us watching him, and blinked again. "Who . . . who are *you?"*

"We shall introduce ourselves later," said Crowley. "Who are *you*, Blinkibus?"

"M-m-me?" The little man blinked more rapidly than ever, and peered round the room exactly as though he were a rabbit exploring its hutch. "Why, I, er . . . this isn't *England,* then?"

"Does it *look* it?" asked Aleister Crowley, stepping over a heap of extraterrestrial corpses.

"N-n-no." The nervous little man blinked again, and he plucked at his bandaged right hand. "B-but I had r-ra-rather hoped . . ." He paused, took a deep breath, and then let it all out at once: "My name is George Cyril Ampleforth, of Number Twenty-three, Cricklewood Lane, London."

"Alias the Dreadful Eye, no doubt," said Crowley. "I should never have guessed that the most bloodthirsty interplanetary fiend in the galaxy props his feet up at Number Twenty-three, Cricklewood Lane."

"Let me see him," said Vanessa, very weakly. She stood, ignoring my protests, and tottered forward. As soon as George Cyril Ampleforth caught sight of Vanessa's gaunt naked form—her visible limbs and torso, with no visible hands, feet, nor head—he turned pale and tried to hide behind Aleister Crowley.

"Oh, dear *me!"* he squeaked as Vanessa came towards him. "W-wh-what . . . whatever is *that?"*

"I am a victim of your lord, the Dreadful Eye," said Vanessa. "Stand still and let me get a look of you." She clutched the trembling Ampleforth and drew him closer to her invisible face. She appeared to be gazing directly into his eyes. She examined him at great length, and then at last she released him. "No," she said, with some trace of regret. "No, you are not the Dreadful Eye. But *his mark* is upon you."

Then she fainted again, as I held her. "She wants food and medical treatment," said Crowley. "I could do with a few drugs myself. I say, Ampleforth: is there nothing to eat in this place?"

"To *eat?*" For the first time, the little man looked almost happy; we had evidently touched upon a subject very dear to him. "Oh, *yes!* Yes indeed, and no mistakin' it! Wait right here!" Ampleforth scurried back to the ladder, and disappeared down the shaft beneath the altar. He returned a moment later bearing a wicker picnic hamper. "There's bread, and cold chicken, kidney pie, and a flask of Bovril," he told us, eager to please. "A bilberry tart, and soda-water, and some bottles of ginger-beer." He set down the hamper and started handing round its contents. "Here, tuck in, *do!* There's plenty."

"It may be *poison . . .*" I started to say, but when I saw how hungrily Crowley scoffed down a chicken wing I abandoned that notion, and reached for the dinner. Despite my own hunger, I took round some food to the three remaining slaves whom we had liberated, to see if any of them were conscious enough to take nourishment.

It appeared that two of them had died while I had slept. I tried to feed the third—a man from Earth; European by the look of him—nonetheless, and I thought I detected some glimmer of life returning to his face. Then I tucked into the food with a will. Vanessa plumped for some of the kidney pie; I shall never get used to the curious sensation of watching her eat—of seeing the food torn to shreds in midair by Vanessa's disembodied teeth within her invisible mouth, and watching the bits tumble down her half-visible throat.

Ampleforth, having somewhat recovered from his initial nervousness, kept up a constant stream of stammerings throughout our repast. I was far too hungry to engage in conversation—I had not eaten in nearly three days—but Crowley was as voluble as ever. "Come, Ampleforth," he prompted, "tell us all you know of the Dreadful Eye, and when we may expect him to return . . . and, while you're about it, explain your own *rôle* in this affair."

"Yes, please do," said Vanessa, whilst I poured her some Bovril. "I sense, Mr Ampleforth, that there is nothing of evil in you . . . yet some evil has clearly used your mind for its feeding place."

And then Ampleforth spoke. I took out the tattered remains

of my memorandum-book, and—borrowing Crowley's penknife to sharpen the last of my pencil stubs—I proceeded to set down the length and breadth of Ampleforth's revelations. With many hesitations and asides, and constant pluckings at his blood-stained and bandaged right hand, he endeavoured to render some accounting of himself. I have transcribed as much of his tale as I could, taking care to delete the frequent ejaculations of "Oh, my *goodness!*" and "Dear *me!*" that constantly peppered his recital.

What follows, then, is the tale of his ordeal.

The Ninth Part

THE NARRATIVE OF GEORGE CYRIL AMPLEFORTH

(Ampleforth's tale:)

"It began with a shop, sirs. Ampleforth's Medicines & Lozenges, I called the place; a proper croaker's chevvy. You've heard of my chemist's shop, of course? Oh. Well, never mind, sirs. The shop did little custom, and business fell off considerable.

"One day, in July of 'ninety-seven, during Her Majesty's Jubilee, a boy came into my shop. He had an earthenware jar; it could have been a hundred years old, by the look of it. The lad said he'd found the jar in a pit, near the excavations for the hydrogen balloon works, at Cricklewood Aërodrome. He'd no idea what it was, and thought as I was a chemist I might care to analyse it. I put the jar down and when I turned round again to thank the lad the little beggar had legged it. Disappeared.

"I unstoppered the jar, and poured out the contents: some sort of pale greenish powder, it was. 'Strewth, that powder had the most peculiar odour; as soon's I whiffed a smell of it I come over all queer-like. Looked it up in my big three-volume pharmaco-what-d'ye-call-'em, and couldn't find aught of greenish powders . . . except copper sulfate, and such, and this weren't in the sulfate line. So I funneled the powder back into its jar and took it home. I suppered, but I didn't eat much: I could still smell that powder, and it fair took the skin off my appetite. So for bed.

"That night, sirs, I had the most shiverous dream. I could see, with my eyes closed, a *face* peerin' at me. It had saucerish eyes, and not much of a nose; no, nor much in the way of ears, neither. Mouth like a great hairy slit, with six grins' worth of teeth. And the thing had a . . . a *hand,* ye might say, all with clawed finger-tips. The thing *beckoned* to me, grinning horrible out of its gape-agog slit-face, and it *whispered* to me, about things that I . . . well, never you mind *that* part.

"It was that powder, I tell you, as was nightmaring me. So I took the jar out behind-house and I dropped it down the convenience. Yes, the earth-closet. I went back to bed, but I still couldn't kip much.

"Next morning I opened my shop. And the first thing I saw, sirs, sitting smart as you please on my counter, was *the earthenware jar.*

"Now this was beginning to deeve me. I took the jar—I could feel the powder moving inside, soon's I touched it—and I ran over to Clutterhouse Farm, next the balloon works and the aërodrome field. I found a pit, thirty foot deep if it were an inch. Flung the jar down it, I did, and kicked a good five foot of earth over it. Then I went home. Thought of going back to my shop, but . . . well, I decided *not* to. In case the jar might be . . . well, you *see.*

"That night, as soon as ever I went to sleep, the face came back. This time it was closer, and I could see a bit more of the body all dangle-down aneath the neck. I woke up shouting and sat up with all the bedclothes tossed about. My hand touched something sitting on the nightstand, and in the dark I knew straight away what it was. I lit the gas, to turn on the lights, and on the nightstand there was . . . yes, *the earthenware jar.*

"I got dressed, and took a coach to Charing Cross with the jar in a satchel. I got off at Hungerford Bridge and walked out over the middle of the Thames, where the river twists a bit—yes, King's Reach, just past Cleopatra's Needle. I took out the earthenware jar and felt the powder moving inside it. I opened the jar and tipped it over upside down like, meaning to pour the stuff into the river current.

"Well, just then a cold wind springs up out of nowheres. The powder falls out of the jar, riverwards, but the wind blows the pale green stuff back into my face. I dropped the jar; heard it splash into the Thames, right enough, but the powder was mostly on *me.* By the time I stopped coughing and spluttering I must have swallowed about half of the powder, and inhaled the rest. Nasty stuff.

"I took the next coach destinating to Cricklewood. Halfway there—round about Bayswater—it sudden becomes very crowded in that coach. I turn towards the bloke sitting next to me, and it's *him*—the face with the eyes, and the beckoning hand—come to ride in the coach, though I doubt he'd bought a ticket. *'Hallo there, Ampleforth,'* he whispers, and I screamed. The rum thing of it was, couldn't nobody there in the coach see the ugly brute except *me,* no matter how much I shouted and pointed. The driver put me off in Maida Vale; claimed as his coach was forbidden to transport lunatics.

"I started walking home. I got as far as Kensal Green, when something tapped my shoulder. I turned to look, and . . . yes, it was the face.

" *'Let's have a chat, Ampleforth,'* says the thing, always whispering. Oh God, that voice was horrible. It sounded like chalk and fingernails riding a slate, with screeching alley cats besides.

" 'You know who *I* am,' I said to the face, as soon as I'd managed the nerve for it. 'But I don't know *you* . . . no, nor don't *want* to.'

" *'Permit me to introduce myself,'* the thing whispers. *'I am called the Dreadful Eye.'*

" 'You'll be called the Bloody Nose,' says I, 'if you don't nip it out of here, and leave honest people be.'

" *'I have need of your head, Ampleforth,'* says the whispering thing. *'Let me borrow it, pray.'*

"Then the thing just reached out, with those claw-fingered hands, and took hold of my head. I could *feel* the claws digging into me and I screamed Neddy Jingo. Then I suddenly felt myself being pulled *right out of myself,* as if something were tearing me apart. And then all sudden-like I'm *outside my own body,* looking at myself. I see my body standing empty, and the Dreadful Eye clambering into it.

"Well, then my body grins, and yells: 'Life! *Life!'* It started clattering away, acrost Kensal Rise, whooping and shouting like a proper Tom o' Bedlam.

"Now, I hadn't any legs, as my body—which I hadn't got— was wearing 'em, but I just *thought* of going after that thing in my body, and blowed if I didn't start to follow it. My body starts leaping and bounding down All Souls Avenue, screeching *'Life!,'* and I go rushing after, trying devilish hard not to lose sight of it. How I could *see*, without any sort of eyes nor head attached to me, was something I couldn't rightly explain at the time.

"The thing in my body rushes down Kensal Rise, and I follow behind, and as we come into the Donnington Road a coach drives up; a horse-car diligence. Well, the coachman sees my body coming towards him, whooping *'Life!'* at the top of its lungs, and he reins in his horses. But he's not quick enough, and my body slaps head-on into the coach . . . and at that instant, sirs, even though I'm not inside my own body, I *felt* the pain of that full-tilt collision.

"The accident, sirs, knocked the *thing* proper out of my body. Claws and all, I see it moaning on the kerbstones, in the Donnington Road. Well, I thought of as how it would be nice to get back inside my body . . . and then I *was* inside it. One of my shoulders was bleeding, where the horse-car had struck it. I ran away and left that horridous thing the Dreadful Eye lying there. I was glad to be shut of him.

"That night I slept like a top. Next morning, when I opened my chemist's shop, my shoulder still dinged me a bit, so I took off my shirt, and painted the cut with arnica. It stung, of course, but I felt the pain fading. I bandaged the cut and put my shirt on, and just then the Dreadful Eye walks right through the solid wall of my shop and squats on the counter. *'I have come for your head, Ampleforth,'* he whispers, gentle as death. *'Keep quite still, if you please.'*

" 'I'm blowed if I'll be killed by the likes of *you*,' I told him.

" *'Killed? My dear Ampleforth, I have no intention of ending your existence. I merely intend to step into your body and cast you out into the shadow realms, naked, without form or flesh to inhabit. After that, you may do as you please.'*

" 'Hardly sounds fair to *me*, then, does it? Eh?'

"The Dreadful Eye looked at me, with that horrible face. *Do you speak to me of fairness, man?'* he whispered. *'Ampleforth, I am older than Time. When the dawn-men walked the Earth and did the first evil to one another, I was there. For most of my millions of years, I have not owned a body. Sometimes—now and then, amongst the corridors of Time—I have seen mortal bodies that I coveted and I removed their human contents. Oh, they fight. Yes! Yes! They squirm, but I peel away their skins, crack their braincases open like walnuts, and I fling their naked souls whimpering into the shadows. Then I enter the brain, climb into the skin, try on the face, and I walk amid the world of living men. Each body, Ampleforth, serves my needs for a time—ten years, or twenty—before it moulders and corrupts into blackening putrescence, and I am a bodiless outcast again. Oh, Ampleforth! I have walked through seven thousand million years, and for only some few fragments of that time have I worn flesh. Is this fairness? I shall now take your body; it will last me some five or six precious years, before it crumbles into filth and I am forced to seek another form. Ampleforth, that is as close as I can ever come to fairness.'*

"Says I: 'You're the Devil.'

" 'No. The Devil is an amateur; he simply isn't in it. The Devil was an angel once and could become one again if he would only go with cap in hand and ask for his old job back. But there is nothing of angels in me, and never can be. Look at me, Ampleforth.'

"I had my eyes tight shut, but I could still see him. 'Go away!'

" *'Look at me.'*

" 'Shan't!'

"He grabbed me then, and started clawing at my forehead, trying to get in. I tried to fight him, but my hands went right through the ugly brute's jabbering face, like he weren't even solid. And then something happened.

"In the struggle, I pulled open the cut in my shoulder from the carriage accident. It started hurting again. Well, the Dreadful Eye suddenly *screamed*, and then he vanishes.

"I did some thinking on that, until I twigged what it was:

the Dreadful Eye, he can't keep hold of a body whilst it's sensationing *pain*. Living all those years without a body, he hasn't got much experience of pain; it's a thing he can't handle. It was *pain,* sirs, as made him vacate my body, when the coach struck it in the Donnington Road.

"I hoped I'd seen the end of him, but boiled if he doesn't come walking through the wall again, Tuesday next. *'No slacking, Ampleforth,'* says he. *'You've worn that body long enough; give someone worthier a chance to inhabit it.'*

" 'Here, why don't you go trouble some *other* bloke?' I asked him. 'Someone who won't mind you a-prigging of his body. This Oscar Wilde fellow, now, in the papers: I'm sure *he* ain't getting much use out of *his* body, considering where it's been lately. Go bother *him.'*

"The Dreadful Eye raised his claws. *'Alas, my grip upon this particular world is more tenuous than it might be. I cannot enter the living flesh of any Earth-born form, unless it first ingests the powder. You have taken the powder, Ampleforth. Now I shall take YOU!'*

"Those claws reached out for me again, but this time I'm ready. I slapped myself, in the face, just as hard as ever I could.

"It hurt, sure as crumpets. The Dreadful Eye jumps back, and I see I was right: he won't enter a body that's feeling *pain.* But he stays, watching me, and after a bit my face stops tingling. He slithers forward again.

"I slap myself again, and he draws back again, and waits. But we both know the same thing: I can't just keep slapping myself forever. I'm bound to stop some time, and then he's *got* me.

"I needed to keep him away whilst I figured how to get rid of him permanent-like. I took a blue-glass medicine bottle and smashed it. The Dreadful Eye saw my plan, but I was too quick for him: I grabbed a sherd of broken glass and cut the palm of my left hand. There's the scar of it there *now* . . . y'see? Just there. I was careful not to cut through any tendons, nor any particularly interesting blood-vessels. But it *hurt,* and the Dreadful Eye howled something fierce; apparently, now that he'd worn my body, he could feel any pain that hurt *me.*

"The Dreadful Eye just scarpered up and vanished, but I knew he'd be back. I put some alcohol on the cut, so it wouldn't go septic, and I tried to think on a way to be shut of him forever.

"I didn't much fancy the notion of cutting myself every couple of days for the rest of my life. I'll have you know, sirs, that I am highly allergic to pain.

"Well, for three days or so, the Dreadful Eye came dancing at the doorstep of my mind. I'd have a shave in the morning, and in the looking-glass I'd see him watching me. So I'd snick myself with the razor, and he'd screech and go away again.

"The worst part was that I got so little *sleep*. I'd lie abed nights and feel the pain in my shoulder or my hand. After a while it would stop hurting, and I'd begin to drop off to sleep, and then he'd *come:* through the wall, through the floor, trying to sneak into my head. I'd wake up, *fast,* and pinch myself. He'd leave, but after a while he'd come back.

"On the fourth day, I thought of a way I could sleep: laudanum. Tincture of opium, we call it, in the chemists' trade. I'd a good quantity of the stuff in my shop. I was dead tired from never getting a decent kip's worth of shut-eye, and I couldn't see any other way out. I'd have to hurt myself as bad as I dared, and then take a dose of laudanum so that I could sleep through the pain. My *body* would still hurt, so that the Dreadful Eye wouldn't dare get inside it, but my *mind* would be feeling no pain. It was dangerous, but I couldn't see no better course of action. I *had* to get some sleep.

"Now, no self-respecting chemist keeps batches of laudanum lying about: that won't answer. You've got to make it up fresh, y'see. I keep the opium powder in a barrel in the cellar of my shop, and the alcohol in a fireproof canister aback the stairs, to do the tincturing with. That's your laudanum, gents: powdered opium and ethyl alcohol; but in the proper proportions, mind.

"I lit a candle and went down-cellar to fetch the ingredients. And then I heard something whisper my name. I look up . . . and there, at the top of the stairs, with a grin on his face, sits the Dreadful Eye.

"*'You're for it now, Ampleforth,'* whispers the thing. *'You can't get out of here unless you get past ME.'*

"I saw him squatting in the darkness, watching me. And I said, just then, the very first thing that come into my head; a little song I'd heard once, when I was a lad:

> *'As I was walking up the stair*
> *I saw a man who wasn't there.*
> *He wasn't there again today;*
> *I wish, I WISH he'd go away!'*

"The Dreadful Eye applauded: *'Excellent verse, Ampleforth! Such a sensitive soul! Such an elegant mind! Such a pity that I am now going to tear it out of your skull, kicking and screaming, while I put your body on. Your flesh is mine, Ampleforth.'*

"And then the Dreadful Eye reached up, with one ugly-clawed hand, and *he shut the cellar door.* I heard it lock, click-shut tight. Then he reached *through* the door, like a ghost, and I heard him draw home the bolt. I was trapped.

"*'We shall sit, you and I,'* said the thing in the cellar, *'until you cannot stay awake any longer, and your body screams for sleep. When you awaken, Ampleforth, you will be a soul without a body, cast adrift in the shadow realm.'*

"*'Not if I can help it,'* I said. I was scared, and no mistake. But I meant to stand and fight against this bodiless bastard. *'You haven't podgered me yet,'* I told him. *'I could burn myself with this candle, or cut myself on a bottle. At the first whiff of pain you'll leg it out of here, and then I'll break open the cellar door and escape.'*

"*'I have waited long enough, Ampleforth,'* said the thing. Just then my candle went out . . . and I hadn't got matches. *'We are alone in the dark, Ampleforth,'* said the whispering voice. *'You are alone with the greatest and most unrelenting evil in existence. We are fighting a battle, you and I, and the prize is your life-flesh. Eventually you must sleep, and then the prize will change hands.'*

"I reached for a morphia bottle, ready to smash it and cut myself. *'Keep away,'* I said, *'or else I shall damage the goods.'*

" *'I think not, Ampleforth. We are in nearly total darkness; you cannot see to hurt yourself properly. What might begin as a finger slice could result in wholesale amputation. And this cellar is quite dirty; to cut yourself here, in this place, would be to flirt with gangrene, and a slow and agonising death. No, Ampleforth: you daren't risk that, and we both of us know it.'*

"Well, he was right on *that* score. I sat down against a barrel of quinine, and I tried to keep awake. And the thing in the dark at the top of the stairs started whispering to me, whispering the most horrible notions. I was never much a praying man, but I started praying *now,* to blot out the whisper in the darkness. Next I sung every hymn in the Bishop's. I started out with 'Old Hundred,' and went on with 'Nearer, My God, to Thee.' It helped keep me awake, y'see, and I thought the creature might fear the music of God. But he sat there, he did, and he kept on whispering those nightmare things.

"We waited, the two of us, for I don't know how many hours: I couldn't read my pocket watch in the dark. I thought of killing myself, which would leave my body too spoilt for *either* of us to use. Several times, in that cellar in the dark, I thought of slitting my throat on a piece of bottle glass. I'd come to that desperate an end.

"I felt myself drifting to sleep. I fought to stay awake, sat up, and blinked. The Dreadful Eye had been sitting at the top of the stairs. But now he was sitting two steps farther down, still watching me. I lit into the first verse of 'The Son of God Goes Off to War,' and two choruses of 'And Did Those Feet in Ancient Times,' and pinched myself to stay awake. It was getting difficult . . .

"Then I realised I'd started falling asleep again, and I slapped myself a few times to wake up. I couldn't see very much in that cellar-dark, but I could see the Dreadful Eye. He'd moved down to the middle of the stairs, and he was grinning at me . . . *waiting.*

" 'Go away, there,' I said. 'I don't mean to co-operate.'

" *'I have waited so long for a mind to inhabit,'* says he. *'I can wait, if need be, a bit longer.'*

"I felt so tired by now that I decided I *would* shut my eyes for a few seconds, only ten precious seconds, and then open 'em again; then I'd be sure to stay awake. So I tried and shut my eyes, and when I blinked 'em open again the Dreadful Eye was squatting on the bottom step, just an arm's reach away from me . . . still watching, still waiting.

" *'Prepare, Ampleforth.'* And now he'd moved again, somehow, although I hadn't seen him do it. He was squatting in the darkness right beside me. *'Prepare yourself,'* he whispered. *'Submit to body-theft!'*

"Then he reached out again and touched my forehead; his claws felt like icicles slicing into my brain. Then I felt that queer awful sensation of being torn right out of my body, and the world all twisty wrong and inside out. Then I suddenly wasn't tired anymore. I was lying on the ground beside the coal bin, and I could tell without looking at myself that I hadn't got a body anymore.

"Something was moving in the shadows near the coal bin, and I knew what it was: it was my body. There was, on its face—on *my* face—the most horrible expression; half a grin and half something I hope to never see again. The Dreadful Eye was wearing my face.

"The thing ran up the stairs in my body, and I sort of floated along right behind, bodiless. When the Dreadful Eye got to the top, he rammed his fists—*my* fists he'd stolen!—right through the cellar door, flindering the wood, and he ripped the door clear off its hinges. I'd never known my body to have such strength when *I* was wearing it.

"The next weeks, sirs, were positive agony. I'd no body now, and I discovered that I didn't want for sleep nor eating. A soul with no body wrapped round it never gets tired, nor hungry. I followed the Dreadful Eye and watched him do as he pleased with my body. I was helpless to do aught to stop him.

"He sold my chemist's shop out from under me. He kept a few bits of the chemical apparatus, and some compounds and drugs, and carted them off to my house. Sold the furniture out of my house, too, and most of my clothes. Anything he could turn a shilling on, he sold . . . and spent most of it on lab equipment. He built some sort of apparatus; I couldn't understand more than a tenth of it, but the thing was most definite electrical. Acid cells and crystals and long coils of wire stretching hither-forth. *Silver* wire, if you please; the ordinary copper sort wasn't good enough for his liking.

"My body still had to eat, so the Dreadful Eye fed it, though he cursed the time and money he spent filling its belly. The rum part was, *any* food was much the same as twelve others to the Dreadful Eye. He'd make a slap-up nosh out of treacle and eggs, and raw pork, and some burton, and a tin of jellied eel, and a bottle of vinegar to wash it down with. Either he couldn't tell the difference 'tween one sort of belly-timber and the next, or else he didn't much care. Perhaps, since eating was a new experience to the Dreadful Eye, he enjoyed experimenting with different tastes and such. I'm still minded of the time he went for six days in a row on nobbut raw fish and butter.

"He built some awful machine. It was mounted on wheels, like a caravan, and had ever so many batteries attached. There was a black canvas hood that swung over the whole of it, to hide the machine—I could figure *that* much—though what the thing-ummy contraption was *for* I just never quite twigged on.

"Sometimes, wearing my body whilst he built his machine, the Dreadful Eye would accidentally hurt the body. He'd whack my thumb with a hammer, or stub my foot, and we'd always *both* feel it. He would let out a howl, and I'd see bits of the Dreadful Eye come poking out the edges of my flesh. When I saw *that*, I'd try to crowd in, to take my own body back, and push the squatter *out*. But I couldn't do it. 'I can feel you, Ampleforth,' he'd say, and it fair drove me sick to hear his voice coming out of *my* mouth. 'I can feel you,' he said, 'and I know what you want. But you won't have it.'

"He slept when my stolen body needed rest. I tried getting back into my body when he slept, but I couldn't. There was something that felt like invisible ice, damp and cold, just underneath the skin of that body all the time.

"The Dreadful Eye finished building his machine . . . in

August, I think; I still tried to keep track of the date. I was floating, all bodiless, about six feet above him when the apparatus was finished.

"There is a hill, sirs, halfway 'tween Cricklewood and Willesden Green, where Melrose Avenue meets the turning of Walm Lane. The Dreadful Eye wheeled his barrow-gadgery thing to the top of that hill, about noon of a day, with the black canvas hood up, so no-one could see the insides.

"The Dreadful Eye stood on the hill, looking down at the people in the roads below, and the children playing street games, and a cart horse, and a vicar on the steps of St. Gabriel's Church. 'Oh, humans!' said the Dreadful Eye, wrapping his words in my stolen mouth. 'Humans! If you only knew what a tremendous gift you have: a solid body, a genuine *life* . . . and at the end of that wearied life, a peacement. I envy you this, for I am doomed to be immortal. You have what I do not, humans . . . and nearly all of you *waste* it.'

"Then he reached out a hand of my body he'd stole, and he switched on the awful machine.

"At first nothing happened. But faraway-like, I heard a rustling, of a *something* crawling towards us in the grass along the hill. It came from west, and east, and roundabout us. The *whatevers* that surrounded that hill all came closer.

"Then I saw something move in the grass. It was a rat, but with something uncommon strange about it. There was *fear* in that rat's eyes, and although it came closer I could tell by its eyes that it would rather run away. But it *came*. And then a sparrow, and two starlings, all cheep-a-cheeping with fear. And then *worms,* sirs, came out of the ground. Then flies were next: hundreds of flies, all come swarming round the black-hooded machine. And toads, and ferrets, and a badger. All the beasts and the insects. And them as had faces, all the faces wore *fear*. The Dreadful Eye stood in his boots at the top of the hill, and he laughed. 'It begins!' he shouted. 'My task here has begun!'

"His machine somehow started all this. That contraption under the hood, it was shaking and juddering, and it gave out a sound: loud and high, like a factory whistle. It summoned the beasts . . . and they came, with the fear in their eyes.

"I flung my bodiless self against the Dreadful Eye's machine and tried to shut it off . . . but I just passed *through* it, all ghostlike. I was just a sort of an undressed *mind*, with no body, y'see. Like a balloon with the skin taken off.

"Then the Dreadful Eye stopped laughing. 'The *humans!*' he shouted. 'Why don't they respond to my summoning?' He looked down the hill, towards Walm Lane. The cart horse as I've mentioned was trying to unhitch its traces, straining towards the top of the hill and the beckoning machine. But the people nearby all behaved just as normal as Tuesday. 'I did not realise,' whispered the creature wearing my body, 'that the inhabitants of Earth were so strong-willed as this.' Then he noticed the animals that were gathering round him, all tremblesome. 'The experiment,' he whispered, 'ought not to be a *total* loss.' The Dreadful Eye turned away for a bit and adjusted his machine. Then he turned round again, with that horrible gape-a-grin, and he said to the animals: *'DIE!'*

"They all *died*, sirs. Some of them, it was quick. Some others—the badger, a cat, and three dogs—took the longest to die. And all their faces, when they'd finished twitching, still showed *fear.*

" 'If you are watching, Ampleforth,' said the thing wearing my flesh, 'I congratulate your fellow humans on the strength of their soul-force. *You* succumbed to my will, but only after ingesting the necessary powder; I have not the resources just yet to mix sufficient quantities of that substance to enslave all the people of Earth. I shall have to pull up stakes here and seek some other world, some species possessing souls more ripe for harvesting, more swiftly dominated. But I shall take your body with me, never fear. I shall hunt a new species, and feast upon their souls, and grow stronger. And *then*, Ampleforth, when I have fed, I shall return here to Earth, and start again. The souls of your man-race, Ampleforth; they are *mine* now. It only remains that I claim them.'

"Then the Dreadful Eye switched off his machine and

wheeled it home. I followed him, sirs, in my bodiless fashion, determined to hit upon *some* way to stop him.

"He built another machine in the cellar of my house. This machine had a huge sort of funnel on top and ran on batteries, as we hadn't got electric wiring in that district of Cricklewood yet. He fills the funnelish part of that machine with lumps of coal; big as walnuts, they were, and switches on the apparatus. The machine begins racketing to itself, like this: *Chunka-chunka-whoops! Chunka-chunka-whoops!* And every so often it throws in a *Tiddley-pom.* After a few minutes, a little door in the machine pops open, and out comes a walnut-sized diamond on a tray.

" 'Success!' whoops the Dreadful Eye. Then he trots upstairs and tucks into a meal of fried cucumbers, apricot soup, and a frosty glass of Thatcho Hair Tonic. All the while, there's *Chunka-chunka-whoops!* going on in the cellar. An hour later, the Dreadful Eye went back downstairs, and I ghost-drifted along right behind him.

"Sirs, the funnel of that machine had been full of coal. Now it was empty, and the tray was filled with diamonds.

"Next day the Dreadful Eye went up to the City . . . and I tagged along, floating overhead. He had fifty diamonds in a black Gladstone bag; I watched him sell some to Spink's, and the rest to the sparkle-mongers in Hatton Garden. The diamonds were uncut: he claimed he'd bought them off Zimbabwe tribesmen in Oranjemund, and he gaffed so persuasive-like that the gem dealers believed him. He took their cheques and he set up a bank account. Using *my* name, if you please.

"I couldn't figure, at first, why a johnny like the Dreadful Eye needed money. But he wanted batteries and wire to build his infernal machines; he used the lolly to finance 'em.

"He sold my house and bought a smaller place in Fetter Lane. He engaged a housekeeper to come round once a week, clean the place, and cook enough food to tide him over till the week next. Her tuck was good enough; this is one of her meals as we're eating now, in the picnic hamper.

"I tried to communicate with that housekeeper something fierce. I'd been stranded outside my own body for nearly two months, without being able to speak; I was fair going barmy from the loneliness of it. I tried tapping the housekeeper's shoulder or touching her face, but I always went *through* her. Ugh!

"In his house in Fetter Lane, the Dreadful Eye kept the cellar door locked, so the housekeeper could never go nosey-parkering down there. But *I* could get in, through the wall, ghost-like. In that cellar I watched him build his most horrible machine of all.

"You've seen the magic-lantern projectors, sirs? Well, the Dreadful Eye's machine was summat like that, only larger. A giant lantern, and it cast a violet-coloured light.

"The Dreadful Eye switched it on. The beam of light from his projector went halfway across the cellar and it *stopped,* in mid-air. Well, the Dreadful Eye grinned. He took a lump of coal, and flung it straight into that glowing violet light. I saw the coal strike the edges of the light, and then it *disappeared.* Fell right out of the universe, through a violet-coloured hole.

" '*Ampleforth!*' screeched the Dreadful Eye. '*Ampleforth! I know that you are hereabouts. You fancy that by following me you can get your body back. But I am going to a place, Ampleforth, to which I think you daren't follow, and I shall go there costumed in your flesh.*

" '*Ampleforth, I am the purest and most all-encompassing force in the universe. I am Evil. I was not born on Earth, yet I feel quite at home here. It strikes me that your Earth shows the potential to become a veritable breeding-ground for Evil.*

" '*But I shall not remain here just yet. The failure of my previous machine indicates that the minds of humanity are not sufficiently ripened towards Evil . . . YET. So I propose, Ampleforth, to use Earth—and this house, in London's midst—as a base of operations. From here I shall mount expeditions to the else-worlds, and seek alien races whose minds I can shape to my purpose.*

" '*Ampleforth, the light you see before you is a gateway. I shall enter it, dressed in your body, and emerge in some far strange domain. Come with me, at your risk. Or stay here, Ampleforth, and be separated from your birth-flesh for all eternity.*'

"Well, that wasn't much of a choice. Wherever this cove

took my body, I was meaning to follow. It was *mine,* and I wanted it back.

" *'Right. I'm off, then,'* said the Dreadful Eye, and adjusted his machine. I saw my chance, and I floated all bodiless quiet into a pocket of the waistcoat he was wearing. The Dreadful Eye, he never seemed to notice; I suppose that, as I'd got no body, I didn't take up much space. Then the Dreadful Eye he ran and *jumped* into that beam of violet-coloured light."

Ampleforth broke off his narrative just then. Aleister Crowley and Vanessa and I had been listening for the better part of an hour, keeping our silence. Now, for the first time since Ampleforth had begun, one of us interrupted him:

"This beam of purple light you mentioned," said Crowley. "We made the acquaintance of it, or its twin brother, in London. I assume that, when you and the Dreadful Eye plunged into the beam of light, you emerged on *this* planet?"

"Dear me, *no!*" said Ampleforth, taking a draught of ginger-beer so as to fortify himself. "We came out in quite a different world; much more alien than *this* planet. It was the place where nightmares come from: hundreds of 'em, all different horrible sizes and shapes, all swarming and clawing all over one another, and all of them chattering and jabbering at the top of their voices all at once."

"I have visited that place," said Crowley, solemnly. "You are describing the railway buffet at Clapham Junction."

"Please don't *joke,* sir!" protested Ampleforth, and seemed to grow a bit more stammerish. "If I m-might be permitted to continue . . ."

"We popped out, as I say—the Dreadful Eye and me, his bodiless stowaway—on a planet of nightmares. The creatures living there were great nasty droolish bug-eyed brutes, with too many legs and the wrong sort of faces. There was nothing of humans in them.

" *'My talents would go wasted here,'* the Dreadful Eye remarked. Was he talking to himself, or did he know I'd stowed along? *'This world,'* he said, *'contains brutality, and death, yet I sense little potential here for genuine Evil.'* Then he turned and jumped back through the beam of violet light. We came out again in the cellar of the house in Fetter Lane.

"I suppose I should mention the dials. The Dreadful Eye's lantern projector had a row of metal dials, with little symbols written on 'em. They weren't in English . . . no, nor Latin nor Greek. What? Bless you, sirs, I can't *read* them ancient lags, but I recognise a hepsilon when I see one. The writing on those dials, sirs, was no Earth tongue.

"The Dreadful Eye took a memorandum-book and he copied down the settings of the dials and made some notes. His writing was all the same queer alphabet as the markings on the dials: all pot-hooks and hangers. I ghost-floated over his shoulder and watched him.

"Then he twisted the dials to a new setting, and the glowing beam of light flickered and changed. He jumped through it again, with me a stowaway aboard his pocket watch.

"We must have visited, like that, some seventeen or twenty worlds. One of them was so cold that we left in a hurry. Another planet had some sort of air that my body's lungs couldn't breathe, and the Dreadful Eye came back choking and coughing. Each time we returned to the house in Fetter Lane, the Dreadful Eye wrote down the setting of the dials what had brought us to that particular world.

"I was beginning to figure out the projector. Every setting of the dials set up a gateway to a different sort of planet. There were six dials, as I say, with six possible settings on each dial. But the Dreadful Eye knew what he was about. There was *one* dial as he'd never turn at all, and another one he'd only twist back and forth 'tween two particular settings. After a while I twigged that he was deliberately limiting himself to planets where my body could survive with him inside it. After all, it wouldn't do for him to jump through the gateway and come out inside the middle of a sun, or pop out in empty space without a planet handy underneath him. The Dreadful Eye had gone to a lot of trouble to steal my body, and I could tell that he meant to keep it.

"We visited, him and me, every sort of a world: frightening dark worlds, and dead worlds, and dying worlds, and worlds that had just begun to sit up and take notice. The worlds that especially interested the Dreadful Eye were the ones with life, *intelligent* life. Every time he came back to the cellar in Fetter Lane he would scribble his notes, and then he'd squat in the darkness and speak to me—for he knew, by now, that I was always nearby—and he'd tell me what he planned for the worlds he'd visited. He told me he intended to spread Evil there, amongst the creatures of those worlds, so that he could feed on their minds in some way I didn't understand, and he'd grow stronger. And, d'ye know? The planets that attracted him the most, the worlds which he thought would make the ripest breeding grounds for Evil, were almost always the planets inhabited by things that looked like *men.*

"I lost track of the exact date, but after a while—in early winter of 1897, or thenabouts—there came a day when the Dreadful Eye set his dials and jumped into the violet-coloured light and came out *here,* onto this very planet. *'This is it, at last,'* he whispered, and I tried again to grab my body back. But the Dreadful Eye was still clutching hold of it from the inside and he wouldn't let go. *'I have found it,'* said the Dreadful Eye. *'A world that has the glimmerings of evil, to be nourished and spread. Why, I can smell the utter evil of this place. I shall establish a supply depot here and begin my task.'*

"I suppose as you know what came next. He took over this planet, day by day and bit by bit. He brought his black-hooded machine here, through the violet-coloured gateway. That machine, remember, never did yet catch hold of human minds, but it worked on the natives of *here.* Gradually the Dreadful Eye took control of more and more of the people what lived on this world. There were a few rebels, I recall, who were strong-minded enough to resist him . . . but he's rounded 'em up, one by one. There's no way to defeat him.

"I was surprised, sirs, to find *humans* living on this world: men and women from Earth, who fell through holes in the universe somehow, and landed *here.* They'd got here before the Dreadful Eye showed up, and were getting on fine with the locals.

Well, the Dreadful Eye scotched *that* lot quick enough: he'd turned the natives into mind-slaves, and he had them round up all the humans just the same as they'd caught all the rebels amongst their own people. The Dreadful Eye had some of his human prisoners executed straight off, as an example. He experimented on others, and as they died he dissected their souls to find out why they resisted his power. The other humans he doomed by working 'em to death in his slave camps. Oh, he's a *born* slave master, and no mistaking it. After he's fed on the minds of the natives of *this* world, he'll be strong enough to have another go at Earth. We've got to stop him, if it costs us all our lives. But I'm hanged if I can see a way to do it."

The Tenth Part

"DEVIL TAKE THE HINDMOST"

Date unknown; in the enemy camp

"But if all of this happened more than a year ago, Ampleforth," I asked him, "when did you regain possession of your own body?"

The stammering chemist smiled, and lifted his swollen right hand. He had kept it, all this while, bound up in some strips of cloth torn from his shirtfront. "D'you see this?" he asked us proudly, as though the bloodstains were a badge of honour. "*You* shot me, sir," he said, nodding towards Aleister Crowley. "Dear me, yes! I must congratulate you on your marksmanship. That shot you fired, which shattered the lens on the Dreadful Eye's altar, also injured my hand."

"My apologies," said Crowley. "I had *meant* to shoot the Dreadful Eye."

"And so you *did*, sir. I wasn't wearing my body when the bullet struck my hand; the Dreadful Eye was still inside it. That was *his* scream you heard, sirs; I imagine that catching a packet of molten lead must have been a queer sensation to *him*. Floating up in the air as I was, I could see bits of him popping out through the skin of my body, as he tried to stay inside it. But the pain of the gunshot must have been too much for him; he gave it quits, and I watched him climb out through my skull. I jumped right back *into* my body straight away, soon as he disoccupied it, the same as I'd done in that carriage accident. You gentlemen found me a few minutes later." Ampleforth's smile widened into a positive grin, and he did a little dance of bursting glee. "You can't imagine what it's *like!*" he shouted at us. "To have gone for a year and more without a body . . . to have done without *touching* anything, without *feeling* . . . Oh! It was *agony,* man, and no mistakin' it. And then to have them all come back at once: all the feeling, and touching, and tasting, and smelling, and breathing, and sweating, and *life!*"

My primary concern at the moment was Vanessa. She had regained much of her strength, and was now attempting to walk without aid. And yet her injuries were evidently severe; I perceived that, if we were ever to escape from this place, Vanessa would have to lean against me, and totter along as best she could.

There remained the problem of the unknown prisoner, the only one of the Dreadful Eye's slaves who had survived the attack. He was naked and emaciated; his pale flesh was spotted with scars and fragments of coagulated blood, mute symbols of the agonies which he must have endured in this place. His hair, long and unwashed, showed dead white beneath its filth. He was unconscious, yet clearly alive, for his breath came in deep hawking rasps.

"I wonder who he is," I thought aloud.

"His name is Volkert. A German, I think," said Vanessa. "We met in the Dreadful Eye's inquisition room; we were brought there to be used in certain . . . *experiments.* He told me of his service as a seaman on your Earth, and of an encounter at sea with . . ."

Vanessa paused for breath, evidently in pain from her ordeal.

"Whoever he is," said Aleister Crowley, indicating Volkert, "we shall have to leave him behind."

"You can't mean that," I said.

"What else would you suggest?" Crowley asked. "There's no guarantee that we'll ever get back to Earth. We don't know the way, and I expect we'll be attacked by homicidal invisible maniacs the instant we leave this chamber. You and I have perhaps ten bullets left between us, against thousands of invisible enemies. Judging by her injuries, Vanessa will be useless in a fight, and I suspect that this quivering Ampleforth bloke is about as useful as a bicycle in a shipwreck."

"Did I hear you mention Earth?" squeaked Ampleforth,

scurrying towards us. "Dear me! We must get home to Earth immediately!"

"I quite agree," said Aleister Crowley. "What time does the next intergalactic hansom cab leave for Piccadilly?"

"Joke if you like," said Ampleforth, finishing off the cold chicken. "When you've done joking, *I* can take us back to London." He strode briskly to the centre of the altar, and pointed to the hexagonal cavity leading into darkness below. "Follow me."

Ampleforth descended, negotiating the rungs of the ladder expertly despite his injured hand. Crowley went next, gesturing for me to follow. I was reluctant to leave Vanessa unattended, but Ampleforth assured me that she was safe for the moment, and Vanessa added that if the Dreadful Eye's warriors returned she would sense their approach in advance, and give us warning. Hesitantly, then, I descended into the altar, amongst the Dreadful Eye's peculiar machines.

There was a crate near the foot of the ladder; Ampleforth rummaged about in this and unearthed a paraffin lantern, that he bade Crowley to light. Presently the lantern's glow was flickering through the chamber. "If I didn't know better," said Aleister Crowley, "I'd swear that this lantern was made on Earth."

"Very likely it was," said Ampleforth. "I bought it from a man in the Portobello Road for eight shillings. If it had been imported from Mars, he would have charged more. The Dreadful Eye took it along when he sold my house and moved to Fetter Lane."

Ampleforth led us to a device with a rotating turret, several handles, and a large black control stud. In the turret's centre was a small glass plate, in which appeared a phosphorescent image of the altar chamber that we had so recently vacated. Ampleforth gripped the handles of the machine, and—wincing slightly at the pain to his injured hand—he adjusted the controls. As he did so, the image in the glass plate *moved* before our eyes.

"A *kinetoscope,* or animatograph," said Aleister Crowley. "The new invention that projects a moving image. I recently saw its inventor, William Friese-Greene, demonstrate a similar moving-picture projector at the Alhambra Music Hall in Leicester Square."

"Nothing of the kind," I said. "I've seen something like this in the illustrated papers. The new Garratt submarine warships have a similar device; it's called a *periscope*. We can look through it and see the whole chamber above us."

"Quite right, sir." Ampleforth nodded. "A periscope. Now, watch *this.*" He twisted the handles a bit more. In the centre of the glass plate appeared a new image: the clay-stained cadaver of the Dreadful Eye's High Priest, slumped lifeless at the altar's edge. Beside him lay his shattered ceremonial mask. "Shade your eyes," Ampleforth cautioned us.

He pressed the control stud. There was a flash of violet-coloured light, and a roar; the surface of the glass plate glowed so brightly that I had to shade my eyes. When I looked back, as the strange glow receded, I saw—in the image within the glass plate—a small hill of smoking ashes, where the corpse of the High Priest had been.

"Sacred Anubis!" shouted Aleister Crowley. "That's the same machine the Dreadful Eye used on *me!* Gave me the worst headache of my life!"

"Yes," said Ampleforth. "It's a good job that the machine wasn't at full power then; it would have incinerated your head."

"I'd look a proper toff without a head," said Crowley, shuddering.

"Yes," I agreed. "But think of all the money you'd save on haircuts. Ampleforth, how long does this machine require to reach full power?"

"Each time it's used, it wants another ten minutes to recharge itself," said Ampleforth. "Use it sooner than that, and the charge is too weak to do much damage. Why d'you ask?"

"I was wondering," I said, "why the Dreadful Eye didn't blast *me* with this device, after using it so effectively on Crowley. Come, this is all very interesting, but it doesn't fetch us *home*. Which way to London, please?"

"This is the way," said Ampleforth. "I came down to get *this.*" He took a map case from a nearby cabinet and scurried back towards the ladder. We followed him up to the altar top. Ampleforth opened the map case and unrolled a hand-drawn chart from within.

"I recognise this," said Vanessa, leaning on me whilst she gathered her strength. "It is a map of my birthworld: *this* world."

"We are *here.*" Ampleforth jabbed his podgy forefinger at a dark spot near the centre of the chart. "The altar chamber is this mark just here, you see. What we want is to escape to *here.*"

He indicated, on the chart, a sharp promontory at the edge of the alien sea.

"*That,* sirs and lady," said Ampleforth, "is our jumping-off place. Our only chance of returning to Earth. The Dreadful Eye constructed one of his machines there: a projector, like the one in Fetter Lane. The machine, if I can only switch it on, will create a gateway between two worlds. We will enter the sky-hole on that promontory, and pop out the other end within the cellar of the house in Fetter Lane."

"You are *certain* of this?" Vanessa asked.

"Of course! Whenever the Dreadful Eye went back to London—such as to fetch that food we ate just now—he would switch on that projector, plunge into its beam, and pop out in Fetter Lane."

"Crowley and I came here," I remarked, "through a vortex in Hammersmith, and we emerged at two entirely separate points."

"Ah! Then *that* sky-hole must have been made by a different projector, with a variable setting of the dials. The Dreadful Eye explained it to me once, just to mock me: he keeps his projectors spaced out acrost the planet, y'see, so's their fields don't overlap and tie the universe in knots." Ampleforth tapped the chart. "No, lads, the only projector I trust sure is *this* one, on the cliffs, because its dials are locked in place for Fetter Lane."

"How far are we from that machine?" Crowley asked him.

Ampleforth consulted the map. "About three miles, I should think."

"*Three miles!*" shouted Crowley. "Great Osiris, man! Three

miles of open country to the cliffs? We'll be easy prey for the invisible men!"

"There is no other way," said Ampleforth. "But I have a plan."

"I should bally well hope so. Let's hear it."

"You must remember," said George Cyril Ampleforth, "that the Dreadful Eye has spent a year on this world, in the inhabitance of *my body.* Lately he's developed the trick of sending *pieces* of himself on missions to elsewhere, but the principal gist of him has always worn *my body.* His disciples, sir, have never seen him wearing any other form. Our only chance to escape depends on my convincing his disciples that *I am the Dreadful Eye.* We must walk straight out of here, bold as brass. And if we meet any invisible men, I shall tell 'em I'm their boss. But we mustn't show *fear,* see . . . else they'll suspect."

I said nothing; I saw little chance of such a plan succeeding, yet I could think of no other means of escape.

There remained the dilemma of the freed prisoner, Volkert. "Are there any other humans still captive on this planet?" I asked, surveying the corpses of the Earth-born men and women who had died here.

"These were the last," said Vanessa. "The Dreadful Eye dissected the rest or worked them to death. Only Volkert is left."

Crowley had used his picklocks to unfasten Volkert's shackles; now I examined the man. By every standard of cold bloodless logic, we should have to abandon him. To hamper our escape by carrying a comatose man would be next-door over from suicide.

Yet to leave him behind in this alien place would be very like murder. If our positions had been reversed, I should not want Herr Volkert to abandon *me* here . . .

"Help me build a *travois,*" I said to Aleister Crowley.

"A tra-*which?*"

"A sledge, to carry this man. We must bring him with us."

"Are you *insane?*" Crowley's eyes bugged out and he hopped up and down. "Have you gone utterly Bedlam-bonkers berserk?"

"We cannot leave Volkert behind," I said. "The disciples of the Dreadful Eye will kill him."

"Better that they devote their attentions to *him*," replied Crowley, "and give the *rest* of us time to escape. *'Devil take the hindmost'* is *my* motto. The Dreadful Eye's projector is three miles from here; we'll be lucky to get *half* that far before the invisible men catch us. Ampleforth can't fight, with that gammy hand. You and I are ready to drop, and Vanessa is lagged. She'll have to lean on one of us every step of the way."

"I won't mind *that* part," I said, and Vanessa placed my hand to her invisible face, so that I could touch her unseen smile.

"But to drag along a *dead* man!" Crowley protested. "I swear, that takes the ruddy biscuit . . ."

"He's not dead *yet,* damn you!" I said. "We can't leave him . . ."

"I agree," said Vanessa, quite feebly. "Volkert tried to protect me in the pain-rooms of the Dreadful Eye. We are honour-bound to bring him along."

"All very well, since *you* won't be the one to carry him," Crowley said, which I thought most ungallant of him. "Bloody hell: that's my one vote for sanity and common sense, and your two votes against. Ampleforth, what do *you* say?"

"Who, *m-me?*" stammered the chemist. "Why, I . . . th-that is to say, um, well . . ."

"Come, man! Do you vote we stop jawing and get out of here with all possible speed—and sucks to honour and chivalry—or do we jeopardise our own escape to drag this load of German cabbage along?"

"W-well, I think, s-since you put it so plainly . . ."

"Yes?" asked Crowley.

"Dear *me!*" stammered Ampleforth. "I v-vote, well, that is . . ."

"YES?"

"We must bring him along," decided Ampleforth.

"Good lad, Ampleforth!" I cried, and clapped him on the back. "You've made the honourable choice."

"*H-h-have* I?" Ampleforth blinked at me. "Why, so I *have!*" And he stuck out his chest a bit farther and lifted his chin.

And now to escape. By dismantling the ladder we fashioned a crutch for Vanessa. The rungs left over, strung together with the picnic cloth and the remains of my coat, were used to construct a makeshift stretcher, upon which Crowley and I placed the half-conscious Volkert. His eyes flickered open just then, and he seemed to be trying to speak. "Courage, *mein freund,*" I said to him. "We may yet all get out of this."

"Are we ready?" asked Crowley, checking his revolver.

"We appear to be," said Ampleforth. He had taken on, these past few minutes, quite an air of authority. The blink-and-tremble man of an hour ago had vanished, and he now seemed strangely confident. Perhaps he was preparing for his *rôle,* his great imper-sonation of the mighty Dreadful Eye. He would have to be a convincing actor now, for our escape to succeed. As I watched him, Ampleforth drew himself to full height and gestured with his one good hand towards the passageway nearest the altar: "Let's go."

We set off: Ampleforth first, as agreed, followed by Crowley and then myself, we two bearing Volkert between us. The poor bloke was coming round to consciousness. Vanessa—the only one among us who could infallibly sense the invisible disciples' ap-proach, should they creep up behind us—served as our rear guard, supporting herself on the crutch, and with one invisible hand grasping tight to my shoulder. She was unmistakeably in pain.

"Can you manage to walk?" I asked, and kissed her.

Vanessa stroked a bruise on my face; I felt the pleasure of her touch, oddly mingled with a twinge of pain as she fingered the bruise. "I shall *have* to manage, won't I?" she answered, returning my kiss.

Outside the altar chamber, the tunnels branched out in a maze of directions. Ampleforth selected one tunnel, with an air of great confidence. "*This* is the one we must take," he declared, setting off down the passage.

"One would almost believe," Crowley whispered to me, as

we followed Ampleforth, "that he actually knows where he's going."

"HALT!" rasped a voice, directly in front of us. *"What is your business here, manlings?"* I recognised the thick slurring tones of the invisible race. Three faces emerged from the shadows: faces floating in midair, with no visible bodies beneath them. The invisible disciples still wore their clay ceremonial masks.

It was Ampleforth's move now: I felt my mouth go dry, at the thought of my life and Vanessa's in the hands of this stammering little man. But now he was an Ampleforth transformed. He tucked his bandaged hand into his pocket and strode forward briskly, jabbing a businesslike forefinger at the clay-masked face of the nearest invisible man. *"You, there!"*

The invisible duffer hesitated. *"Me?"*

"Yes, confound you! State name and birth-shape! *At once!* And your purpose in this particular tunnel. *Now!"*

The invisible guard made a chittering sound that I took to be his name, in this alien world's peculiar tongue. Then in English he added: *"I was present at the gathering two time-bits ago and departed with the others when the Dreadful Eye so ordered. I then . . ."*

He was interrupted suddenly, as another clay-masked face pushed forward, and its owner spoke. From the sound of his voice, this sentry was shrewder and more cautious than the first. *"Who gave you the right to interrogate us, manling?"* the second guard harshed. *"Humans are the slaves here, not the pain-lords. Submit!"*

"Indeed?" asked Ampleforth. "Then perhaps, Clever Dick, you will know me by this human body which I wear."

"I do not, man-one."

"Fool! *I am your Lord, the Dreadful Eye!"*

When Ampleforth spoke, the invisible sentry dropped back. I saw his clay mask tremble, as though he were so unspeakably afraid of the Dreadful Eye that mention of *the name alone* would bring him to the borderings of fear.

"The all-dominant Eye?" The guard genuflected. *"Your pardon, Master. I did not recognise your present shape."*

We were permitted to pass. I discovered that I had been holding my breath; I released it now, then looked back. Nothing was following us . . . at least, nothing *visible*.

"A near go, that," said Crowley to Ampleforth. "I thought you said that the invisible men know what you look like."

"Not all of them," said George Cyril Ampleforth. "The Dreadful Eye's high priests and acolytes have seen my body walking about, with the Dreadful Eye inside it. *They're* the ones who would mistake me for him. That sentry wallah spoke English; he's either done spy duty on Earth, or he's spent some time interrogating human prisoners."

We proceeded in near-total darkness. The tunnel sloped gradually upwards—a sign, I hoped, that we were nearing the surface. Our only dependable source of light was Ampleforth's paraffin lantern. Crowley wore this on a cord hung round his neck, like a glowing talisman.

The man Volkert, whom we carried between us, was passing in and out of consciousness. He threw one arm up quite suddenly, striking my face, and babbled something in ominous tones that sounded like a despatch from Hell. I was suddenly grateful that I do not understand much German. But Crowley *did*, evidently, for I saw him turn pale.

"Quiet, now," Ampleforth whispered, as we reached a sharp bend in the tunnel. "We have nearly reached the surface."

"Who comes?" intoned a voice in the passage ahead of us. Farther on, I could see the mouth of the tunnel where it broke to the surface, and the alien rockscape beyond. *"Who comes?"* the voice repeated, and I looked for the tell-tale clay masks of the invisible priests. I saw none; this new crop of sentries were well and truly *invisible*. But how many *were* there? A dozen? A hundred?

Ampleforth, brave Ampleforth, strode masterfully forward. "You know who I am, I assume?" he demanded.

"We know whom you APPEAR to be," rasped an invisible voice. *"You bear the likeness of our Lord, the Dreadful Eye."*

"Then let me pass. These others with me are my prisoners."

"I think not," spoke another invisible voice. *"If you are truly*

*the all-dominant Master, and not merely a counterfeit clothed in his
flesh, it can be proven. Speak to me, Lord, in the tongue of this
realm."*

"The *t-t-tongue?*" quavered Ampleforth, instantly dropping
all guise of authority and reverting to his blinking and stammering self. "You mean the, um, the, er, the *language?*"

I knew we were done for. It was obvious that, for all the
time Ampleforth might have spent on this world in his bodiless
state, the trembling chemist had never learnt the lingo of the
invisible race. I saw the dust on the tunnel's floor shift as the
invisible sentry stepped forward, and I could envision him leering
triumphantly as he asked, in his alien tongue: *"Gnihklag tekel
m'nee?"*

"I shall answer for my Lord, the Dreadful Eye," said Vanessa.

"Let him speak for himself," said the sentry. I saw Crowley
reach towards the pocket in which he kept his revolver; I reached
for my own, trying not to drop the stretcher bearing the half-
conscious Volkert.

At that moment Volkert's eyes opened. He screamed.

Crowley dropped his end of Volkert's stretcher, and the
screaming man fell into the dust. Crowley's revolver was out, and
he fired—once, twice, three times.

"Iklac kavnoklor!" screeched an alien voice, in a tone that
clearly meant *"Sound the alarm!"* By now I had my own revolver
out, and I fired in the direction of the voice.

"Oh, dear!" wailed Ampleforth. "Oh, we're for it now. Oh,
my!"

"Stow it, you snivelling git," said Crowley. "We've shot *these*
three, but this place will be mobbed with invisible men any moment. *Run!*"

The sailor Volkert had stopped screaming, and now he was
weeping hysterically. He seemed unable to stand. "Crowley, give
me a hand with him," I said.

"Not much, thanks. He's slowed us down enough already.
Devil take the hindmost." Crowley seized Ampleforth by the arm

and ran on through the tunnel, howling: "Ampleforth! Lead the way back to Earth!"

But it was Crowley who did all the leading; poor Ampleforth was dragged along behind, whimpering: "Turn *left*. Oh, dear! Now *right*. This is so terribly confusing!"

I could *not* leave Volkert here to die, especially since he had once aided Vanessa. I looked to her now: Vanessa seemed to have gained enough strength to hobble along without my help. Ignoring my own injuries I lifted Volkert, and hauled the white-maned emaciated man onto my back. I slung him pick-a-back across my shoulders, and started after the others, stumbling over the corpse of an invisible man in my hurry. "Hi! Crowley! Ampleforth! Wait a bit for the stragglers!"

We reached the mouth of the tunnel and made for the outlands beyond. We must have made a curious *tableau,* in that alien landscape of boulders and cliffs: Crowley first, leaping over the rocks, waving his pistol and howling frenzied remarks about Earth, London, *home,* whilst dragging Ampleforth by the wrist. Ampleforth, in his turn, was stammering his endless litany of "Oh, *dear!*" and "Oh, *my!*" and "Good *heavens!*" as he scurried along, interspersed with an occasional chorus of *"Ouch!"* I came next, staggering beneath the fitfully conscious burthen of Volkert, who, to demonstrate his gratitude, was bleeding all over my shirt. Last came Vanessa, her crutch and her visible limbs and breasts hopping and limping along, connected to her half-invisible torso and head. We must have looked like a touring company of *Derby Day at Colney Hatch* or *Bedlam on Parade.*

"Stop a bit! Stop a bit!" whimpered Ampleforth. "There's a pebble in my boot. Dear me! I'd forgotten how exhausting it can be to have a body. *Stop* a moment, sir!"

"No time," puffed Crowley, dodging in and out among the boulders all the while. "Hurry *up!*"

When we had gone perhaps half a mile from the mouth of the cavern, Vanessa risked a backwards glance. "I can see them," she said. "The Dreadful Eye's initiates. They've discovered the sentries we killed, and they're coming after us."

"How many?" I asked.

"At least twenty, I think. Perhaps more."

Twenty invisible men! Too many for us to fight, and it seemed unlikely that we could outrun them. In the distance I could hear the rumbling voices:

"Tekeli-li, tekeli-li . . ."

"If we can get to the ridge," said Crowley, "we may lose them. There are so many boulders and ravines, they mayn't find us."

I had trouble moving onward: one of Volkert's arms *would* keep dangling into my face. His head, tucked round behind my neck, was bruising what remained of my shoulder. The unfortunate man had gone into a semiconscious stupor, and his mouth, hanging close beside my right ear, kept murmuring in nightmared German.

And behind us, I heard:

"Tekeli-li, tekeli-li!
Tch'kaa, t'cnela ngöi . . ."

"Wait a bit!" panted Ampleforth, whilst Crowley dragged him along.

"No *time!*" said Crowley, and hurried along all the faster.

"I'm tired, sir!" said the stammering chemist. "And I'm afrighted!"

"Then I shall inspire you," said Aleister Crowley. "I shall recite, for the benefit and immoral inspiration of us all, as we trudge along on what may prove to be our death march . . ."

"Belt up, Crowley," I said.

"Ahemph!" As I was saying: to inspire us, as we hurry along, I shall recite a poem of my own composition."

In the fast-approaching distance, I could hear quite another sort of recitation:

"Tekeli-li, teka'ngai,
Haklic, vnikhla elöi . . ."

Vanessa heard the death chant too, for she spoke up suddenly, in an obvious attempt to keep the rest of us from hearing our pursuers, and thereby inheriting Ampleforth's panic. "A capital notion," she said, as we stumbled along amidst the boulders and outcroppings. "A good poem will entertain us as we run, and keep us from giving way to despair. Come, let's hear it."

"This poem was written by myself," said Aleister Crowley as he ran, "some seven years ago, in the spring of 1891, at the tender age of sixteen. It is entitled 'A Peep Behind the Scenes.'"

And he lifted his head as he hurried along, and recited:

> *"In the hospital bed she lay,*
> *Rotting away!*
> *Cursing by night and cursing by day,*
> *Rotting away!"*

"Here, now!" I interrupted. "That's enough of *that* rot!"

"It gets better," said Crowley, and continued:

> *"The lupus is over her face and head,*
> *Filthy and foul and horrid and dread,*
> *And her shrieks they would almost wake the dead;*
> *Rotting away!"*

"It gets *riper,* you mean," I said to Crowley. "Why not give it up for a . . ."

> *"In her horrible grave she lay,*
> *Rotting away!"*

"Perhaps," I suggested, "something a bit more *cheerful* might . . ."

> *"Rotting by night, and rotting by day,*
> *Rotting away!"*

"Oh, dear," whimpered Ampleforth. "I do believe that I am going to be ill . . ."

> *"In the place of her face is a gory hole,*
> *And the worms are gnawing the tissues foul,*
> *And the Devil is gloating over her soul,*
> *Rotting away!"*

"Is there much more of this?" I pleaded.

"No," said Aleister Crowley. "It is finished. Did you like it?"

"It was quite rotten all through," I told him. "If you wrote that when you were sixteen, you must have had a deucedly interesting childhood."

"They're getting closer," said Vanessa, glancing over her shoulder again. By now the death chant of our pursuers was too loud to be ignored. "We've a head start of perhaps half a mile; I fear it won't be enough."

I did not turn round, but behind us I could hear the encroaching refrain:

> *"Tekeli-li, tekeli-li! . . ."*

"How much farther?" I asked, grimacing beneath the weight of Volkert.

"We have still about two miles to go," said Vanessa.

"Oh, *dear!*" whined Ampleforth. "We'll never make it . . ."

"Courage, my cherubs," said Aleister Crowley. "I shall recite another poem, to speed us on our flight."

"Not like that *last* poem, I should hope," I protested.

"No fear! *This* poem is far more cheerful!" Crowley answered. "It is my own composition, devised in 1890, in only the fifteenth year of my present incarnation, whilst I was convalescing in a sickbed at the public school in Tonbridge, Kent. It is entitled 'The Balloon.' "

And he recited:

> *"Floating in the summer air,*
> *What is that for men to see?*
> *Anywhere and everywhere,*
> *Now a bullet, now a tree—*
> *Till we all begin to swear:*
> *What the devil can it be?"*

"This is a *much* nicer poem, I think, than the last one," puffed Ampleforth as he scurried along. "No mouldering corpses to attend to."

"It goes on a bit," said Crowley, and continued:

> *"See its disproportioned head,*
> *Tiny trunk and limbs lopped bare.*
> *Hydrocephalus the dread*
> *With a surgeon chopping there;*
> *Chopping legs and arms all red*
> *With the sticky lumps of hair . . ."*

"Good Lord, man!" I expostulated. "Is *all* your poetry so cheerful?"

"I'll skip ahead to the climax," said Aleister Crowley:

> *"Toads are gnawing at my feet.*
> *Take them off me quick, I pray!*
> *Worms my juicy liver eat.*
> *Take the awful beasts away!*
> *Vipers make my bowels their meat.*
> *Fetch a cunning knife and slay!"*

"Have done! This is awful!" cried Vanessa as she staggered along. But Crowley was by now in a state of excitement so extreme as to appear positively sexual; scrambling over the rocks and outcroppings, he continued to howl his obscene verse in a Hell-frenzied pitch:

> *"Come, dissect me! Rip the skin!*
> *Tear the bleeding flesh apart!*

> *See ye all my hellish grin*
> *While the straining vitals smart.*
> *Never mind! Go in and win,*
> *Till you reach my gory h—OUCH!"*

"That will be *quite* enough poetry," said Ampleforth, shutting off Crowley's last syllable by the deft stratagem of an elbow jabbed into Crowley's stomach. "My goodness! They didn't write poetry like that in *my* time, young sir! Where's your Browning? Where's your Tennyson, eh?"

And behind us, the voices grew nearer:

> *"Tch'kaa, t'cnela ngöi!*
> *Tekeli-li, tekeli-li . . ."*

I discovered, at that moment, that I could no longer go on. Laying Volkert down as gently as I could, I collapsed and fell gasping for breath. Crowley hurried on without me, dragging Ampleforth behind him, but at least my Vanessa stayed by my side. Yet I noticed she was glancing behind me, at the alien horrors approaching in the distance.

> *"Tekel elöi, tekel h'nee . . ."*

We had reached the cliffs. Peering over the edge, I could make out the shore of the outworlder sea far below me. If we should fall from here, it would be a drop of more than a hundred feet to the sea and the sharp rocks below . . .

"Halfway there!" said Ampleforth, pausing. "Chins up, all! See that promontory there, in the distance?" He extended his undamaged hand along the outline of the cliffs, towards our left. "Only half again a mile from here. There's our passageway home."

> *"Tekeli-li, tekel elöi . . ."*

Vanessa stood as erect as her injuries permitted and, using her alien ability to alter her form, she shape-changed—attenuating herself to a height of some ten feet and peering out from behind the cover of a boulder. "I can see them," she reported. "I have said that there were twenty coming after us. I was wrong."

"That's a relief," I said, gasping for air.

"There are at least fifty."

"*Fifty!* Great Pan!" Aleister Crowley had turned round and come back; either out of concern for the rest of us, or because he knew he would never get back to Earth without Ampleforth's help. Crowley gazed into the distance behind us and worked the cylinder of his revolver. "How close are they, then?"

"Perhaps a mile away," said Vanessa. "They have torches and weapons. They appear to be searching for us in quite the wrong direction: if we can only keep behind these boulders, perhaps they mayn't discover us at all."

Ampleforth whimpered, and sucked his injured hand.

Crowley glared at me. "This is all *your* fault! We'd have gone a good deal farther by now if you hadn't insisted on dragging that bleeding old sailor along with us." Volkert groaned again whilst Crowley spoke. "He's dead weight for us!"

"He is *not* dead," I countered. "You heard Vanessa say he tried to protect her; now we are honour-bound to help *him.*"

At that instant Volkert suddenly convulsed, as though in the throes of some unendurable pain. His head pitched backwards, at a most disturbing angle, and his jaw dangled open. From his throat emanated a sound that I had heard once before, many years ago, on the last night of my father's life. The death rattle . . .

I groped at Volkert's wrist to find his pulse; felt it flicker, and then . . .

"Well, Crowley," I said. "Yes, we *will* leave Volkert behind. He is dead."

"Oh, dear *me!*" squealed Ampleforth. Crowley remained impassive.

"Burying Volkert would be imprudent, under the circumstances," I admitted. In the distance, the chant of the Dreadful Eye's disciples, searching for us, was still audible. "However, inasmuch as that mob of jackals *are* going off in the wrong direction, and all of us are so tired that we ought to pause for breath for a moment, perhaps in that time we might offer a brief prayer for the dead, and . . ."

"*You* pray if you like, you confounded Christian," said Aleister Crowley. "I vote we leg it full speed ahead for London."

At that moment, Volkert's corpse suddenly opened its eyes, and sat up.

"We meet again, I see," said the voice in the dead throat, while the body rose slowly and stood up on spindly legs. "Permit me, one final time, to introduce myself. *I am the Dreadful Eye.*"

Vanessa screamed. Ampleforth fainted altogether, and Crowley and I stared as the dead thing tottered towards us. "These are not the most splendid lodgings I have ever inhabited," remarked the voice of the Dreadful Eye, from within Volkert's emaciated corpse. "Your own body, Ampleforth, was much more admirably suited to my plans than this shrivelled cadaver. A pity I had to wait until Herr Volkert vacated this flesh before I could have it. Yes, I have followed your little band all this time, from the moment that *you*—your name is Crowley, I think?—shot a bullet through Ampleforth's hand. I found the pain of that unbearable, and I was forced to flee his body."

"Go back to Hell, you monster," said Vanessa. Her invisible face was unreadable, but her body's trembling showed fear beneath the anger of her voice. "Go back to whatever Hell world spawned you."

"*You speak as though I were an alien,*" said the dead thing which contained the Dreadful Eye. "*But I am a native of this world. And I am a citizen of Earth as well. Every world which is the breeding place of evil, that is MY world; my home. My unholy crusade is eternal, and my reign is forever.*"

The leaping corpse flung itself to the top of a boulder, and it suddenly shrieked through dead lips to the darkness beyond:

"*THEY ARE HERE! I HAVE FOUND THE PRISONERS!*" The hideous thing atop the boulder bounded and capered and screeched. "*KILL THEM QUICKLY! IN THE NAME OF YOUR LORD, THE DREADFUL EYE!*"

And then I saw, in the distance, half a hundred tongues of flame: the guttering torchlights of the invisible men. They had gone the wrong way in their pursuit of us before . . . but now they turned, rapidly, and advanced towards the shouts of their master.

"HURRY, MY SERVANTS!" screeched the tyrant cadaver. *"KILL THEM, BEFORE THEY ESCAPE!"*

Aleister Crowley raised his pistol and fired three shots into the shrieking dead thing on the rock. The corpse crumpled under the impact of the bullets and toppled to the edge of the cliff. But it stood again, on broomstick legs, and capered towards Vanessa, its dead hands reaching out to encircle her throat.

"You, my pretty," the dead thing crooned as it came, *"you, my slut, my dolly-poppet, my whore, shall take the longest to die. Death shall pleasure itself with your flesh."* And the corpse fingers caressed Vanessa's throat.

"You bastard!" I howled, and flung myself at the slavering corpse. At the same instant, the dead creature snatched Vanessa, flinging her down upon the cliff's edge so roughly that she dropped her crutch. I seized it and, reacting instinctively, I swung the makeshift crutch with all my possible strength. The crutch struck the gibbering corpse across its fragile windpipe with such force that I heard the bones snap, and then the head flew off its neck. The decapitated body collapsed, in a clatter of limbs, while the head rolled away amongst the rocks, until it ended face downwards.

"Thank God *that's* over," I said, holding Vanessa.

Behind us I heard, ever louder:

"Tekeli-li! Tekeli-li! . . ."

The shattered head of the corpse suddenly rolled upright, and opened its eyes. *"You cannot destroy me,"* whispered the head, with no lungs to propel its thick voice.

I screamed, and hurried forward and picked up the head. I could hardly bear to touch it: I should sooner have fondled a serpent than this jabbering thing. *"Having one's head separated from one's body can be SO inconvenient,"* crooned the face, and I shuddered at the touch of its dead lips writhing against my fingers. *"For now I can inhabit head, or body, but not both at once,"* spoke the head. *"Which to choose?"*

> *"Tekeli-li, tekeli-li!*
> *Tch'kaa, t'cnela ngöi! . . ."*

Despite my revulsion, despite the dead mouth biting at my hand, I raced to the edge of the cliff and hurled the gibbering face as far as I could out to sea. I watched it fall . . . down, down to the water, and then it struck the dark surface of the alien sea: a small white dot, bobbing there for a moment while it jabbered and crooned, and then it sank into the darkness and distance . . .

> *"Tekeli-li, tekel elöi . . ."*

"Look out behind you!" shrieked Crowley.

I turned. The headless body of Volkert, all emaciated flesh and broomstick limbs, stood up and staggered towards me. The Dreadful Eye, it seemed, had vacated his quarters in Volkert's head and changed addresses. The headless corpse, lacking eyes or a mouth, advanced slowly, feeling its way with twitching hands. "He cannot see you," said Vanessa. "So long as he remains in that headless body, the Dreadful Eye is blind."

"I CAN SEE," said a voice, as a mouth and a pair of cold eyes suddenly sprouted forth in the centre of the headless corpse's chest.

Vanessa whispered: *"No . . ."* My revolver, I knew, would be useless against this oncoming thing. I would have to fight it with my wits and my hands. I forced myself to overcome my revulsion, as I reached out to touch the decapitated horror.

"I'll help you!" shouted someone, and I saw with surprise that it was the timid chemist, George Cyril Ampleforth. He seized the writhing corpse by its legs whilst I grasped the thing's arms, and together we lifted it. "The Dreadful Eye stole my body, and did as he pleased with it," Ampleforth hissed through his teeth. "Now at last I'll get some of my own back."

The headless corpse squirmed in our grip; I think it knew what we planned. Ampleforth and I reached the edge of the cliff and flung the dead thing out into the emptiness beyond, as the mouth within the centre of its chest emitted a screech. I saw the howling cadaver dangle in the air for an instant, and then it plunged towards the dark sea below.

The corpse, when it landed, was smashed to bits on the rocks.

"Thus ends the Dreadful Eye," said Aleister Crowley.

"Not so easily," said Vanessa. *"Look!"*

Far below us I saw a severed hand, resembling some horrid white spider or crab, creeping about among the rocks. The five-fingered thing dragged itself to the foot of the cliff, and began climbing towards us.

Then I heard, from the plateau behind us, a sound like the ringing of gongs, and a chorus of *"Tekeli-li . . ."* And although I knew that I mustn't, I turned round. And looked.

"Tekel elöi, tekel h'nee . . ."

It was the march of the invisible men. The flames of their torches were less than a mile away now; I could see the flames as they approached, and I could hear the footfalls and voices of the invisible disciples, but I could not see the fiends themselves.

"This way!" shouted Ampleforth, pointing towards the darkened promontory to our left. We scrambled towards it now, the four of us, and ran.

A wind sprang up from somewhere, the first air current I had ever encountered on this stagnating world. It grew and widened to a howl, and the chant of the invisible men was swept along within its force: *"Tekeli-li! Tekeli-li! . . ."*

"Ampleforth!" I shouted into the wind as we staggered across the plateau. "Are you *certain,* man, that we've come the right way?"

"Yes, yes!" He huffapuffed his answer as he ran. "No mistaking it. The Dreadful Eye's projector . . . 'tween this world and . . . house in Fetter Lane, is at the edge . . . that cliff." His words came in fragmented gasps, but he forced himself to keep running. "Seen it dozens of . . . times, when he travelled . . . back and forth 'tween the worlds in . . . my body, and I was . . . an outside passenger. I only hope that, when we get to the machine . . ."

". . . *if* we get to it," interjected Crowley.

". . . I only hope that the projector is functioning properly, with the proper setting on the dials."

"And what happens," I asked Ampleforth, leaping over a jagged outcropping, "if it's *not?*"

"Oh! Then we are trapped here, of course, on this planet."

"What? *Forever?*"

"Goodness, no," panted Ampleforth. "Only a few minutes more, until the invisible men catch up with us. And kill us."

"Tekel h'nee, tekeli-li . . ."

I kept running.

Vanessa could barely keep up her strength, even with her crutch at the one side of her and my shoulder to lean against at her other as we ran. Whenever either of us stumbled, I felt Vanessa shudder from the pain; her injuries must be severe beyond my reckoning . . .

We reached the top of a hillock, and I risked a look back; the torchlights of the invisible legion were less than half a mile behind us now, and drawing rapidly nearer. The ringing of their gong was deafening, and their chant was incessant, a hideous blood-curdling wail:

"Tekeli-li! Tekel elöi!"

At the top of the hill was a boulder; nearly spherical, like most of its brethren stones upon this world. Had it stood in this place since the beginning of days, or had some outworlder Sisyphus abandoned it here? I rushed to the boulder and braced myself full length against it. Crowley saw what I was about and ran to help me. Vanessa, using her crutch and a stone as a lever and fulcrum against the boulder's thick base, provided the final bit of strength.

We pushed. The boulder came loose and plummeted bouncing and rolling downhill towards the oncoming invisible horde. The boulder triggered a rockslide, and the rockslide gave birth to an avalanche. The chanting stopped, turned to shouts of confusion, and the invisible army broke ranks. I saw torches and weapons fall, thrown aside in the rush to get away.

"Look at them run!" shouted Crowley. Unlike me, he could *see* the invisible mob. "Half a dozen crushed like beetles! And another ten retreating! Oh, what a rout! This is glorious!"

"They're still coming," said Vanessa darkly. "We've crushed a few, but the others are still after us."

The chanting renewed, a gradual loudening far in the dark, but its sound—and the glow of the torches—came steadily nearer:

"Tekeli-li, teck'l hnau . . ."

We kept running. We had gained, in the rockslide, some few minutes' time, and killed or injured enough of the invisible men to thin their ranks considerably. But we were still outnumbered, out-weaponed, and they were gaining on us. . . .

"There it is!" shouted Ampleforth. *"Just ahead!"*

We had reached the base of the promontory. At its edge, among the rock piles ahead of us, squatted the outlines of a peculiar machine.

"That is the projector." Ampleforth was gasping as we clambered up the slope. "I've seen the Dreadful Eye use it. And the gateway's nearby: the other end in Fetter Lane . . ."

". . . and in London, and *home!*" Aleister Crowley pulled ahead of us, and rushed to be first up the slope. Then he froze, and his voice touched the edges of fear: *"Ampleforth!"*

"Eh?"

"You said that the hole in the sky was a globe of violet-coloured light."

"A globe of light, or a hexagon, sir. I mind that once it was a dodo-cum-hedron. Yes, it's all in the . . ."

"Where *is* it? Why isn't it *here?*"

Sure enough: as we reached the promontory, there was no sign of any violet-coloured aura like the one in Walcot Square, nor resembling the fierce glow in Hammersmith.

"I can't understand it," said Ampleforth. "I was so certain . . ."

"Tch'kaa, t'cnela ngöi!
Tekeli-li . . ."

The invisible men, with their torches upraised, were something less than a quarter mile away . . .

"We will die here," said Aleister Crowley. "May the Great God Pan deliver us. We will die in this place."

The visible fragments of Vanessa began to tremble. I held her close, told her again that I loved her, and whispered to her the things that ought not to go unsaid before the coming of death. . . .

"This wasn't meant to happen!" wailed Ampleforth. Too weakened to stand, he crawled across the promontory on all fours. I saw him slip, and he sent a small shower of stones pelting over the cliff. "It wasn't meant to end like this," he whimpered. "Not without a . . . *hullo!*"

I could hear, coming towards us, the chant of the invisible men, and the ringing of gongs, *tekeli-*closer. There was a scuttling sound in the dark, a sort of slither growing nearer: the approaching many-score of invisible feet.

I heard a sound at the base of the cliffs: a sudden hooting ululation. Down below, a great flapping white shape was rising out of the alien sea, and leaping towards us across the surface of the water.

"I've *found* it! Help me! *Quickly!*" Ampleforth was flinging stones over the cliff's edge in a lunatic frenzy, but I saw that there was method to his madness. Beneath the rubble, buried underneath a rockfall at the base of the Dreadful Eye's machine, was some sort of an electrical switch. Ampleforth was attempting to uncover it.

I scrambled up the promontory after him, tugging a boulder away and rolling it down the hill towards the invisible army approaching us. "Are you certain that this thingummy will help?" I asked, unburying the switch.

"Yes! It *must!* Stand back!" Ampleforth flung his full weight against the switch and rammed it home within the flank of the machine. There was a roar like a thunderclap, a crackling of power, a hum. The invisible men ceased their chant and broke ranks again, and several of them heard the growing roar and dropped their torches . . .

"The sky!" shouted Aleister Crowley. "Oh, my God! Oh, Jesus Christ! *Look up at the sky!"*

In the grey emptiness of that alien sky came a point, a beam, a growing edge of light. It swelled and shook itself and increased, it took the form and image of a hexagon of violet-coloured glow.

The passageway between the worlds grew to three feet across, then no larger: we would have to go through it, then, one at a time. The Opening hung in the air several feet past the edge of the promontory cliffs, and slightly higher than my shoulder. If one of us were to step off the cliff's edge, he would miss the hexagon of light entirely; he would fall past its lowermost edge and plummet to an agonising death on the rocks far below. But if we were to take a running start, to run with all our strength and speed, and *fling* ourselves beyond the edge of the cliffs, there was a chance that sheer momentum would carry us out to the waiting hexagon of light. . . .

"Can't you move that gateway any closer to us?" I asked Ampleforth. "And make it larger, while you're about it?"

The chemist shook his head. "P'raps the Dreadful Eye knew how, but all I know of his machines is what I l-l-learnt from w-watching *him.* But that v-vortex will take us back to London . . . p-p-provided, of c-course, that the set-setting of the dials has not been changed."

"And if it *has,* man? If it *has?"*

"Th-then we'll come out in someplace elsewhere altogether . . . p'raps in some other universe," said Ampleforth.

The chant of the invisibles—no longer in the distance—resumed and was now too loud to be ignored. I kissed Vanessa and looked towards the waiting violet light. "In view of the risk for whoever enters that thing," I suggested, "perhaps I ought to go first."

"No, *I* shall," said Aleister Crowley.

"Are you certain?" I asked him. "If you run and your leap doesn't carry you far enough, you'll miss the gateway, and fall . . ." I looked down towards the rocks and the sea, and the jabbering flapping white shape-thing that waited below, hooting up at us.

"Beyond that violet light," said Aleister Crowley, "are London hansoms, and buildings, and Whitechapel doxies, and a plate of bangers and mash cooking up on the gas-ring. Can't you smell it? Oh, *London!* I've got to go *home.*"

He shook my hand, solemnly, and kissed Vanessa. *"Konx Om Pax,"* Crowley murmured. And then he turned from us and bolted suddenly up the promontory's slope. He reached the edge of the cliff, and flung himself upwards and over the brink. I saw his face for just a fraction of an instant, and then Crowley's body —all flapping coat and kicking limbs—struck very nearly the centre of the violet-coloured glow. I thought I heard the brief beginning of a scream . . .

And then he *vanished.*

"Your go is next, sir," Ampleforth told me. "You, and the lady."

"Yes, of course. Vanessa next." I kissed her, and told her what I felt must be done. The chanting had now reached the promontory's edge: *"Tekeli-li! . . ."* In another few minutes the invisible men would be upon us. I could *smell* the greasy smoke of their torches.

Vanessa was too weak to make the jump unaided. I knew this, and so I stood at the edge of the cliff. She walked a little way down the slope, towards the oncoming horde, and then she turned and ran very suddenly towards me. At the very last moment, as she came to the edge of the cliff, I caught Vanessa in my arms and *flung* her towards the hexagon of light. I saw her half-visible form shape-change in midair, outstretch to touch the waiting purple light, and then . . .

. . . she vanished.

"Now *you,*" said Ampleforth. *"Hurry up!"*

The chanting was *very* close. Devil take the hindmost.

"You won't be able to jump far enough, Ampleforth, by the look of your legs," I told him. *"You* go first, and I'll give you a leg up, just as I did Vanessa. You can't jump . . ."

"Stuff and candlesticks!" Ampleforth protested. "I'll show *you* who can jump!" He took a sudden running leap, and threw himself off the edge of the cliff. I was sure he wouldn't make it, and he very nearly didn't. But at the last possible instant Ampleforth's body struck the very edge of the sky-hole passageway, and I saw him pass through . . . and he vanished.

And then the invisible men were upon me.

Something struck me in the face and knocked me down. I pulled out my revolver and pumped my last remaining bullets into the squirming mass of invisible faces and limbs that clutched at me. I struggled free, and tore my shirt nearly off in my fight to escape. Then I flung my now-useless revolver at the alien horde and heard it strike unseen flesh. And then I turned and ran up the promontory towards the edge of the cliffs and the sea.

"I'm coming, Vanessa!"

I reached the edge of the cliff, and kicked up and aloft. I jumped, head downwards, and I could see—far below me, at the bottom of the cliff—a tribe of leaping and flapping white shapes hooting, jabbering at me amid the rocks and the alien sea.

I won't make it, I thought. *I didn't jump far enough. I remember that corpse on the beach, that was drained of its blood.* All this nightmare-parade of my thoughts came in a single flashing moment, and then I struck something hard and cold and dead. It was the passageway between the worlds. I had reached it, and now it engulfed me, and then the darkness arrived . . .

The Eleventh Part

What Happened in the Cellar

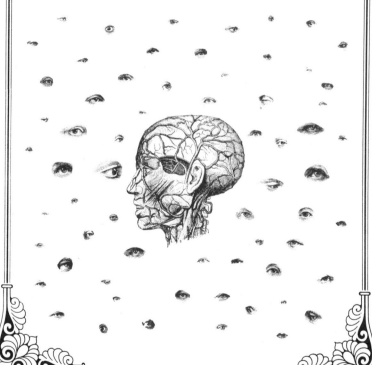

The screaming came.

In the hole between the worlds there is no sensation of any sort excepting *pain*. I hurtled through the void and felt my mind sliced and flensed into a thousand splinterings of howl. I screamed, with no mouth, with no face, with no physical body; soul-naked, huddled and whimpering in the place outside existence.

Something appeared; I found myself landing face-down, in an oblong patch of dusty earth. Something moved suddenly in the darkness and gripped me: a hand, clutching hold upon the tatters of my sleeve.

It was Aleister Crowley.

"Get up, man!" he shouted. "Mount the battlements! We're not out of this yet, by a long chalk."

With an effort, I stood. Vanessa was there, taking hold of me, kissing me, breathing life and warmth into my numbed body. Ampleforth, scuttling about in the shadows like some crazed blackbeetle, relighted his paraffin lantern. I was blinded for a moment by the sudden rush of light, and then I saw where we were.

The four of us stood in what looked like a perfectly ordinary English cellar. No, not *entirely* ordinary: in the corner squatted a peculiar machine, identical to the one on the alien cliffs. It was one of the Dreadful Eye's interdimensional projectors.

In the centre of the room, near the ceiling, floated a hexagon of violet-coloured light. I could see images suspended within it:

the cliffs and boulders of the alien rockscape, that we had so recently fled. And I could see, as well, the projector that remained there on the cliffs, keeping open the dimensional gateway.

Coming towards us—that is, the images grew larger within the floating purple light—I saw the torches of the invisible men. And I could hear voices chanting, growing louder as they approached:

"Tekeli-li, tekeli-li! . . ."

"Here they come," whispered Ampleforth. The stammering little chemist seemed calmer now, more resolute, as he awaited his death.

The glowing hexagon flickered, and then a flaming torch burst through the vortex and into the cellar. I felt the heat of the flame as it passed me. A stone, flung by some invisible hand, hurtled through the hexagon of light, and whizzed past my face.

"They'll be coming through the portal *themselves* next," said Crowley, stamping out the torch. "It's a good job that portal's so narrow; they'll have to come through it one at a . . ."

"You will die!" screeched a voice. I saw the dust on the floor billow up as an invisible *something* plunged through the vortex and bounded into the room. *"Manling fools, you will all . . ."*

Crowley fired his revolver, then let the weapon fall from his hand. "My last bullet, confound them."

Something landed heavily on my chest, and I felt the cold breath of some invisible horror trying to bite at my face, with a terrible chittering sound. Crowley grabbed the alien thing, and together we pinioned it and wrestled it back towards the glowing vortex. The damned thing screeched and gibbered and clawed at my shoulders and chest as we flung it *back* through the hole in midair, to the alien world!

"Look at 'em go!" Crowley whooped, gazing at the scene within the vortex. "The one we threw back landed on three others; knocked one jackanapes right off the cliff. The rest of that lot are pulling back."

"Tekeli-li, teka'ngai . . ."

"Only a temporary respite," said Vanessa. "We must destroy the hole between the worlds."

I ran to the projector in the corner. On its flank were six gleaming metal dials, with strange symbols etched into their surfaces. They were markings of no Earth-born alphabet. "Will *this* machine be any help?" I asked.

Ampleforth scurried over, and looked. "No; this projector's not even switched on, sir. It's t' *other* one what's causing our trouble . . . the machine on the cliffs."

"They're coming back!" Vanessa shouted.

"Tekel h'nee, tekeli-li . . ."

There was a tool chest in the cellar, beside the projector; had the Dreadful Eye himself placed it there? Now Ampleforth opened the tool chest, and produced a hammer and a screw-wrench. "It's the *dials,*" he announced. "That projector on the cliffs has its dials set for this here cellar on Earth. We've got to switch off that machine, or change the settin' of its dials."

"Which means," whimpered Aleister Crowley, "that one of us will have to *go back* . . ."

". . . or else the Dreadful Eye returns to Earth," said Ampleforth. Then he pushed past me suddenly, and ran towards the hexagon of light.

"Ampleforth!" shouted Crowley.

The chemist, wielding the hammer in his one useful hand, and the screw-wrench gripped fast in his jaws, suddenly *jumped,* and struck the glowing violet-coloured hole.

"Ampleforth, you ass!" Crowley bellowed. "Come *back!*"

Ampleforth fell, and landed in a heap on the cliffs of that alien world. We could see him, imperfectly distinct, through the aura of the gateway hexagon. We saw him stagger towards the projector on the edge of the cliff, and then he attacked it with the hammer.

"Mr Ampleforth!" shouted Vanessa. "Look *behind* you!"

Did Ampleforth hear her? It is difficult to say. I saw him turn, saw him confront the invisible men at the head of the cliff. By the number of their torches, there must have been at least a hundred of the brutes approaching Ampleforth. And then they attacked. A hundred voices howled at him, a hundred invisible mouths whispered his name, and a hundred sets of alien hands reached out, clutching at him, pulling him down from the Dreadful Eye's machine. Ampleforth, swinging his arms in great wild patterns, sent the hammer crashing down upon the howling invisible men.

Beside me, I heard Crowley whisper: "He's done for, poor devil."

Ampleforth doomed? I saw him, for one bare and final instant—coatless, his high stiff collar broken and torn, as he battled a swath through the horde of his enemies. I saw him climb to the top of the dimensional projector, as it perched at the edge of that outworlder cliff. "You've lost!" he bellowed at the oncoming mob. "The Dreadful Eye is unbodied! England is saved! Earth is free, and no mistakin' it!" I saw him stand, surrounded by torches, with the blood streaming down from his forehead. And I saw him then—this trembling little man, this stammering clerk of an Ampleforth—transformed in that last battle's moment into Ampleforth the brave, Ampleforth the magnificent. He swung his hammer at the Dreadful Eye's machine. I heard the sound of fragile mechanisms breaking.

Through the violet-coloured hole between the worlds, we saw the projector on the cliffs explode. The hideous apparatus shuddered and bellowed like some sort of wounded beast, and a thick stream of sparks erupted from the gaping wound in its metallic flesh.

And then, with a gathering roar, the edge of the alien cliff broke apart beneath the weight of so many invisible men. The damaged projector toppled over and fell towards the waiting grey sea far below. And the very last that human eyes ever saw of

George Cyril Ampleforth, he was plummeting—brave to the last —down that long awful drop to the alien sea.

If he screamed at the end, or cried out, I did not hear it.

The glowing hexagon of light within the cellar had begun to fade; now it suddenly *winked out,* and was gone. There was a sound like the popping of some colossal cork, and an inrush of air, as the passageway between the worlds ceased to exist.

The projector in the cellar, behind us, had stood silent all this time. Now Aleister Crowley strode towards it, and his fingers touched its row of silver dials. "It's the most incredible device that man has ever witnessed," he breathed. "A thousand—no, *forty* thousand different worlds to explore, and all at the touch of one's fingertips. Forty thousand worlds to witness, to explore, perhaps to rule." Crowley's eyes widened as he fondled the dials. "I *must* learn how to master this machine."

"I have seen that expression on another face," said Vanessa, "and I know what it means." She drew Crowley's arm from the projector as she faced him. "Would you really master this machine? Or will the machine master *you?*"

Crowley started to speak; I stepped between him and Vanessa. "We still don't know where we *are,*" I pointed out. "This *looks* to be a normal cellar in England—those are almost certainly English rat holes in the corner there—but just the same, hadn't we better have a look upstairs?"

"*You* go, then." Crowley glanced at the place in midair where the dimensional gateway had been, and nervously licked his lips. "I shall stay here, and . . . *dismantle* . . . this machine."

There was a hungering look in his eyes, as he faced the machine. "No, *I'll* attend to the projector," I told Crowley. "You must look to Vanessa; she is injured. Get her upstairs; look for some blankets, and food." I kissed Vanessa; the touch of her body against me felt most pleasant, but her flesh seemed distressingly cold.

I found an axe, with which I might smash the projector. I watched Crowley climb the cellar stairs, with my half-visible Vanessa leaning on his arm. Crowley unlatched the heavy wooden cellar door. "Leave the lantern there, so I can get some light," I called after him. Crowley nodded, and set down the paraffin lamp at the head of the stairs. Then he and Vanessa walked out, leaving the cellar door open.

The cellar was darker than I had realised. I went upstairs to fetch the paraffin lamp, intending to lower its wick and thus brighten the flame. I reached the top of the stairs and had only just picked up the lantern, when the cellar door suddenly swung shut, and latched, *all by itself.*

I saw the surface of the wooden door shimmer and ripple; two of the knots in the wood now grew larger, and turned into *eyes*. A thin wooden crack below them split and widened and turned into a mouth. *"We meet again,"* whispered the door, as its face looked at me. *"Had you forgotten, woman-birthed manling, that all things which are dead lie within my domain? That includes wooden doors."* And the Dreadful Eye laughed.

"But we threw you off the cliff!" I protested. "I saw . . ."

"You threw a corpse which I briefly inhabited. When you plunged through the gateway from that else-world to here, I came with you."

I pounded on the door, shouting as loudly as I could: "CROWLEY! GET VANESSA *AWAY*, MAN! HE'S HERE IN . . ."

"They cannot hear you, manling. No sound penetrates that which I inhabit, unless otherwise is my pleasure. And now, Earthone, our moment arrives."

" *'Our* moment'?" I asked.

"Yours and mine together," whispered the face within the door. *"My eternal unholy campaign must continue; thus again I have need of a body. YOURS. I shall take it, and you will become one minor fragment of my vast unending plan, one crucial thread in Evil's tapestry."*

"I decline the honour," I said to the wooden face. "My body is mine, and this world is my people's; nothing here is yours. Leave this planet, and take care not to slam the door on your way out. After you have left Earth I shall count the silverware."

As I spoke I seized the handle of the door; it would not turn. Somehow the wooden door-frame had *grown*, changing and reshaping itself to embrace the door, jamming the latch bolt. I would have to break down the door to escape. As I thought of this, the eyes within the door suddenly closed their wooden eyelids, the mouth tightened, and the grinning face vanished. *"I am here,"* said a voice at my feet.

I looked down . . . and shouted. On top of my left foot was a *face.* It had rooted itself within the leather surface of my boot top, and it regarded me grinningly. *"Curious habit of you Earthers, to encase your feet in the skins of dead beasts,"* rasped the face made of leather. Then the face disappeared from my boot top and instantly reappeared within the wooden surface of the cellar stair beside my feet. *"Down we go, then,"* laughed the stair-face, and the wooden step crumbled to sawdust.

I made a grab for the bannister; too late, for the cellar stairs *dissolved* underneath me, one step at a time. I fell, headlong, shouting thump-a-bumping down the flight of cellar stairs, to land in a heap on the earth floor below. My left leg, caught beneath me at an unnatural angle, felt as though it were on fire; I tried to stand, and could not. My leg was broken.

"The time has come to seize my property," whispered a voice beneath the stairs. I looked, and saw the Dreadful Eye's hideous face watching me. It had taken up residence in a grout of rotting fungus, at the base of the wall. *"So much death here,"* rasped the lichenous face. *"So much carpentered wood, and tanned leather, and butchered meat, and other dead pleasantries which I can inhabit. But, man-one, I have need of your body."*

"Well, you've foxed yourself," I said, gritting my teeth; the pain in my leg was intense. "Ampleforth discovered that you couldn't occupy a living body that was suffering *pain,"* I informed the Dreadful Eye. "Thanks to that cropper down the stairs, you've just broken my leg, and it hurts like Billy-O. So my body is closed for repairs. Trot along, then; get out."

"I have learnt," rasped the terrible thing, *"ways of possessing a physical form, and of evicting its rightful inhabitant, that I did not know when last I wore Ampleforth's flesh. Manling-mind, prepare for disembodiment."* The dark face approached me.

"Keep *away!"* I shouted.

"*So much death,*" whispered the face beneath the stairs, creeping towards me in a moss-trickled slime. "*You humans surround yourselves with dead things. You dwell in houses built from murdered trees. You wrap your feet in slaughtered leather. And you cover your nakedness, manling, with threads of once-living tissue: dead cotton, shorn wool, shredded flax . . .*"

The face vanished. And then instantly I felt a tightness at my chest, a tugging, as *the fabric of my shirt* suddenly rippled and *came alive,* and a hideous cloth *face* thrust its button eyes close to my head. I felt the twisting lapels of the white shirt-thing's grinning linen mouth press two tattered cloth lips against my ear, whilst the flapping shirttail of a tongue touched my face in a linenous whisper:

"*Your shirt, manling! The finest linen I have ever been pleased to inhabit!*"

I screamed, and tore the living shirt off my back. I saw the twisting fabric writhe and flicker and dance, its wrinkled face whispering promised obscenities. Then the eyes of the shirt became buttons again, and it fell . . . a heap of empty cloth.

"*And now I am HERE!*" rasped the voice, near my legs. I felt a fluttering in my trousers, and then . . . *oh, God!* The very fabric of my trousers tore and reshaped itself, pulled free of my body, and then the trousers danced a hornpipe round the cellar, whooping with glee. I saw something form in the cloth, and I beheld the grinning face of what had once been the seat of my trousers.

"*Do not be so surprised!*" mocked the hideous trousers as they capered about in the dark. "*After all, you are not the first man to have unknown dangers lurking in his trousers!*"

"Is it your intention," I asked, trying to shut out the terrible pain in my leg, "to invade all my clothes, and strip me naked?"

"*Unnecessary,*" said the trouserous thing. "*It is your body—living flesh, sustained existence—that my hungering craves.*" The face disappeared from the animated trousers, and instantly reappeared —first here, now there, next elsewhere—manifesting its eyes and slit-mouth in every piece of wood, paper, cloth, leather, dry rot, decayed fungus, or other dead tissue everywhere within the cellar, flitting from one to another so rapidly that I seemed surrounded by ten thousand whispering faces of the grinning Dreadful Eye. *"One living body is more useful to me,"* said the thing, *"than all the dead sawdust and sausages of your planet. I shall inhabit you, man-flesh. I shall reside in any limb or bone or portion of your form, and by gradual expansion claim the whole."*

"How can you take my living body," I asked, hoping to find some weapon in the knowledge, "if you inhabit only the dead?"

"A man though living is partly a corpse," the jabbering thing said harshly. *"There is within yourself a large cavity filled with dead tissue: butchered chicken, murdered potatoes, trembling wheat stalks decapitated and ground into bread, slaughtered beans, deceased tea. All once alive. Shall I inhabit them?"*

"NO!" I protested. But the face vanished, and instantly I was stricken with excruciating pain, as I felt some alien presence writhe and stir *within my own stomach.*

"So much death," said the voice—*inside* me now, underlining my screams. *"All the dead vegetation and animal flesh which you have thrust into that hole in your face congeals and forms a mass within your gullet, and I am within. Gradually, as your digestive process runs its course, shreds and fragments of the murdered luncheon within you will be absorbed by your organs and limbs. Think of it, human! Slaughtered breakfast and unliving dinner are added to the stockpile of living tissues which comprise a living man! And I, the Lord of Death, will remain undissolved in the process. I will spread my domain into every cell and pore and living molecule of your body. I have won!"*

I was too weakened to scream any longer, yet the pain grew more intense. My bladder mutinied, and I experienced the most terrible urge to be sick, to retch up this hideous writhing mass which infested my stomach, but I could not. It had taken on a life of its own, and it chose to remain within me.

"And there are other portions of a man that lie within him dead, besides his meals," whispered the alien voice in my body. *"So many million microscopic cells comprise a man . . . but every day that you live, some few thousands of those microscopic portions of you*

die. Life is merely a gradual death. Very well: I shall claim the dead cells and martyred oddments of your body NOW."

And then came a pain so all-consuming and vast that I coveted death. The gradual encroachment from within came spreading through me, taking over my body one cell at a time . . . rapidly, rapidly.

"I evict thee, Earth-one," whispered the alien Other within. *"I disembody your soul. I shall deny you access to your limbs, crowd you out of your torso, and eventually confine you within one solitary corner of your brain, whilst all your body is claimed by a new occupant. Soon, manling, soon your trembling soul will huddle for refuge within one last remaining brain cell. I shall find it, and engulf it, and then . . ."*

The pain in my body was lessening now and gave way to a gathering coldness. I had thoughts of Vanessa . . .

"I am here," said a voice just beyond my right arm. In the dark of the cellar, I looked . . . and then screamed.

The palm of my right hand was *sprouting a face.* The cold eyes winked maliciously at me beneath my fingers. As I watched, the palm slit open and formed a mouth of grinning teeth. Then a thickening nose—squat, triangular, flattened—took shape in the flesh of my hand, midpoint between the thumb and fingertips. And the fingers danced and beckoned obscenely.

"Did you know, mortal one," rasped the face which had once been my hand, *"that the human form's outermost layer of skin is primarily DEAD? So, then: I, Lord of Death, claim the unliving parts of your flesh."*

"Get *out* of me!" I shouted, thrusting my right hand away from myself. Now the hand was becoming a misshapen *head,* and the wrist was becoming a throat. The arm below . . .

I saw the axe where I had left it, on the cellar floor. Finding myself forced to become left-handed by my right hand's mutiny, I seized the axe with my left hand, and for one mad instant I considered *hacking off* my right arm, where the fiend had taken root in my flesh. *"You are not rid of me so easily,"* said the mouth at the end of my wrist. And then—God help me—I saw the eyes and the nose and the mouth of my Dreadful Enemy move *down* my hand, past the wrist, along the length of my arm, towards my face. I was dimly aware of my right hand returning to normal, as the face inhabiting my flesh crept shoulderwards, rippling along within my flesh. I watched as the alien face climbed the bend of my shoulder, crept its way up my neck, until—just when I thought that the scuttling face would interlock with my own—it abruptly circled round behind my ear, and passed from sight.

"*I am here,*" the thing whispered behind me. I felt a stirring in my scalp, and I reached up to touch the spot. Then I screamed, as I felt my fingers touch a pair of bulging eyes and a mouth and a gibbering tongue that had suddenly formed *on the back of my head.*

"*We are twins, you and I,*" spoke the mouth in the back of my head; I felt its lips move beneath my fingers. "*Such companions we make, human one,*" said the jabbering face. "*Come! Let us walk among men, you and I, on one stalk of a neck, and see what sensations we arouse. With eyes on front and back of our partnership head, no-one will know if we are coming or going . . .*"

"Get *out* of me, damn you!" I shouted. There was a stirring in my scalp again; I touched the spot, and was relieved to find that the Dreadful Eye's face had gone. But then where . . .

Something laughed.

"*I am here,*" said a voice just in front of where I sat, quite near the floor. Having lost my shirt and the greater portion of my trousers in this struggle, I was aware of the cold. "*I am here,*" came the whisperer in shadows, and as it spoke I felt something stir and come to life against my thighs. I looked down, at the most intimate part of any gentleman's anatomy, and sprouting from that region I beheld . . . the grinning head of the Dreadful Eye.

"*Did you think that you might never find me HERE?*" laughed the bodiless head, taken root in my manhood. "*Did I not say I might inhabit any LIMB, any ORGAN of your body?*" Its laugh punctuated my shouts as I tried to stand up. But my shattered left leg only buckled beneath me, and I fell and landed sprawling on my back.

"*Do not be so surprised to find me HERE,*" said the gibbering thing, dancing upright erect on its hair-covered stalk. Its mouth grew larger, whilst its cold eyes regarded me. *"For THIS is the only part of a man that has a mind of its own; it moves by itself, obeys no will but its own. Is there evil in humanity? Then that evil begins HERE,"* mocked the grinning face between my thighs. *"For here is where the seeds of all mankind's evils originate."*

"Get out! You are lying! *GET OUT OF ME!"* I shouted, gripping the axe, and raising it with both hands. I saw no other way now to separate myself from this beckoning horror, except by carving it out of my flesh. I must, I *shall* destroy this evil thing . . .

Through my pain, I heard the laugh of the intruder. *"Yes! Let me hear you cry out, manling!"* said the gleeful evil one. *"Let me hear your song of anguish, your sonata of pain! Let me hear! I'M ALL EARS!"*

And then suddenly, horribly, the entire surface of my flesh at once erupted in a vast display of *ears*. Pointed ears, twisted ears, sprouting up from every square inch of my arms and chest and face. A thousand organs of the Dreadful Eye.

"Or perhaps you would prefer," came the deafening whisper— so loud, because I heard it with so many ears, *"perhaps you would prefer to be all-seeing? Behold!"*

The ears opened, and turned into *eyes*. A thousand eyes, infesting every portion of my flesh. And I could *see* with all of them, in ten thousand directions at once. This was madness.

"Would you scream, manling? Very well. I provide the equipment. Begin!"

The eyes of my flesh swiftly widened and grew; splitting open, they formed into *mouths*. I tried to speak, and as I did so my flesh burst open in the parting of a thousand sets of lips, the darting of a thousand wagging tongues against their palates. I saw the mouths opening in my hands, my arms, my chest. And with a thousand tongues of agony, I screamed.

And then I discovered something.

My shattered left leg, alone, had not yet been transformed. My entire body was covered with mouths . . . *except for that leg.* The Dreadful Eye had said he could tolerate *pain* now, yet apparently he could not withstand it completely. Why else, with all my body to invade, would he avoid that bleeding limb?

"I think I know a way to fight you . . . *now,*" I said, with a thousand-tongued voice. The remains of my trousers were nearby; I fished out my pocket-knife and opened its blade. "Have *this,*" I said, and slashed a mouth that grew on my left arm. The mouth whimpered, and fled along my arm towards another mouth; melting *into* it, as two beads of quicksilver turn into one. Then I slashed *that* mouth—trying not to cut too deeply—and again the mouth scurried away along my flesh and joined another pair of lips, near my shoulder. Then *that* mouth became an eye, and stared at me; I tried to gouge it out with the blade, and it trembled and fled.

I was bleeding from the many tiny cuts, as I progressed. It was terrible work, but I saw no other escape. There was blood trickling into my eyes as my knife tried to corner a runaway mouth that dodged and twisted about across my forehead. I caught it, and hunted another. The galloping eyes and scurrying mouths had begun a migration *away* from my extremities, and *towards* the centre of my back, between the shoulder-blades: the only part of my body that I could not reach with my hands.

Ampleforth's paraffin lantern lay where I had dropped it in my plunge from the stairs. Having fallen on its side, the lantern had nearly gone out; now I raised it, and the cellar filled with light. "Get *out* of me," I told the Dreadful Eye. "This body's mine by right of birth. GET OUT!"

"*No, manling!*" said the enemy's voice; I felt a mouth flutter and speak, where the thing's face burst forth in the small of my back. "*I have tasted life . . . do you expect me to relinquish it NOW?*"

"I shall shatter this lamp," I said, "and let the flaming paraffin pour down my back, unless you depart. The flames may kill me; they will certainly cripple me. I would rather be free and a cripple than a whole man enslaved. Get out of me."

I lifted the lantern, ready to carry out my threat.

The enemy howled. I felt a *convulsion* in my body, a sudden vomiting of the flesh. I saw a *thing,* in the shadows of the cellar, hastily tear away from my chest with a terrible snicking sound, and then the Dreadful Eye was *there,* in the cellar before me. It had too many limbs, and its face was a hideous caricature of my own.

"*I MUST have life!*" said the gibbering mouth. Something flickered in the shadows nearby, and a large brown rat scuttled out of the darkness. It saw me and began to turn away. And then the rat beheld the Dreadful Eye, and it *squealed.* I have never seen any animal so *terrified* as that quivering rat.

"*I must have LIFE!*" howled the alien thing. And then the Dreadful Eye suddenly *took* the squealing rat and seemed to turn the creature's body inside out as I watched. I saw the Dreadful Eye *enter* the rat's trembling body and then vanish within. Now before me stood only the rat, but in the rat was the mind of an Other . . .

I reached forward and snatched at the rat. It scurried into the shadows, but I caught it by the tail and held the squirming rodent high aloft in my left hand. With my right hand, and the corresponding leg, I dragged myself along the cellar floor.

The Dreadful Eye's interdimensional projector was waiting. I switched it on, as I'd watched Ampleforth switch on the twin of this machine, on the alien cliffs. There was a crackling sound, a rising wind, as the air in the cellar began to be sucked into a pinhole of light that now formed, midpoint between the cellar floor and the rafters.

The rat squealed, its struggles growing more furious as the violet-coloured orifice of light began to widen. I waited until the hole between *here* and the else-lands grew to six inches across.

"*Now!*" I shouted, and thrust the squealing rat into the void. I felt *cold* touch my fingers as my left hand entered the Opening; I pulled away, and with my right hand I switched off the machine.

The glowing orifice winked shut, and the wind fell to silence. My left hand, I noticed, was bleeding. I must have been touching the interdimensional hole when it closed in upon itself . . . for the tips of my thumb and forefinger had been neatly *sheared off.*

But the Dreadful Eye was gone.

I had won.

A dozen rats came out of their holes, and watched me with bright-button eyes, sniffing whisker-twitching noses. "To think that a *rat,*" I said, half aloud, "was sacrificed, in order to destroy the Dreadful Eye. A rat saved mankind!"

I crawled back to the staircase. Several stairs which the Dreadful Eye had inhabited now lay crumbled into sawdust, but the rest of their stair-brethren remained. With my one useful hand, and the bannister, I pulled myself upwards one stair at a time. Gritting my teeth in the pain. I ascended. The wooden door-frame that had altered its shape when the Dreadful Eye inhabited it was now an honest respectable door-frame again. I pushed the door open and went through.

I appeared to be inside a perfectly ordinary house. "Vanessa? Crowley?" I called. No reply. Balancing myself on my right leg, with my hands against the nearest wall, I propelled myself by hops and draggings through the rooms, leaving traces of blood as I progressed.

I came to some sort of a vestibule, and the door beyond was open. I went through, in my limp-crippled state.

There was no sign of Crowley. But my Vanessa was there, on a couch, evidently asleep. The visible portions of her gaunt but still beautiful form swelled and breathed in the rhythms of slumber, and I touched my hand—the right one; it was cleaner—to Vanessa's invisible face. Her features were composed, her half-visible eyelids were shut. She was sleeping, and I have never seen her more beautiful.

The curtain behind her was drawn. I opened it, quietly, and found a window. Outside was a crossroads, and a sign read FET-TER LANE. I could hear the morning hoofbeats of the horses, the rattling trams, and the rustling coughs of the pigeons. I could smell the thousand strange and familiar scents of smoke, and fish, and horse sweat, and the factory odours, and cheese, mixed all together. In the distance, hard by to the east, the bells of St. Andrew's were striking the quarter hour, and I heard the bells of all the City joining in. I saw *London*. And I have never, in all of my life, seen her more beautiful.

A door opened, and I turned as best I could on one good leg. In came Aleister Crowley. He was still as filthy and ragged as when last I had seen him, but his arms were laden with blankets, and bandages, and medicine-bottles, and a flask of what looked to be sherry, and tins and parcels of *food.* He saw me, in my blood-stained nakedness, and Crowley smiled.

"All dressed up for a jaunt through the park, are you?" he said. I heard his deep familiar laugh. Then he saw my fractured leg, with dried blood and damp earth caked about it, and he frowned. "Hulloa, what's *this?* It appears that you've cut yourself shaving."

Vanessa stirred and awoke, and the first thing she spoke was my name. I could no longer stand; I lowered myself to the couch, and I held her. We kissed, unabashed by Crowley's presence, and I felt a trickled warmth against Vanessa's face, beside my own—a teardrop, from her alien eye. I touched my tongue to the dampness: Vanessa's tears tasted faintly of nectar; quite unlike the salt tears of humanity. I held her closer, and more than a few tears were exchanged between us, as we whispered our love. "Do as you please, then," snorted Crowley. "Since *I* seem to be the only one around here sane enough to want breakfast, I shall go ahead without you!" He tore into a packet of muffins, and reached for the marmalade pot. The last I saw of Crowley for a while, he had gone off in search of a spoon.

There would be time, I decided, for marmalade later. I had my Vanessa, my London, my life. I was in a strange house, and my injuries wanted attention—as did Vanessa's, and Crowley's—but this could all be faced later. Now, in joy and relief to have come to the end of our journey, Vanessa and I showed each other the extent of our love.

"See me," she said, trembling . . . not with fear, but with anticipation. *"Feel me,"* she whispered.

"Touch me," I answered. And at last, in the embrace of sweet London, my Vanessa and I had arrived, well and truly and finally . . . *home.*

VANESSA'S
DELIVERANCE

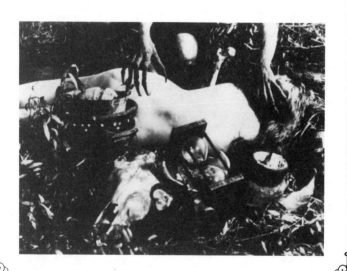

Afterwards

When one has fought one's greatest battle, and emerged victorious, there is little to do afterwards except to sweep up the corpses.

As neither Vanessa nor myself is suited for travel, owing to our injuries, it fell to Aleister Crowley to locate the nearest shop with a hire-telephone and to ring up my sister Sarah. She arrived within the hour, in a hansom cab laden with enough medical supplies to outfit the next dozen Afghan campaigns.

"Trust *you* to find a planet filthier than London to visit," she said, kissing me. "I told Henry you'd gone to America; he sends his regards, but expresses surprise that you haven't been murdered by howling bloodthirsty savages."

"I apologise for disappointing him," I said.

My leg, it develops, *is* broken: fractured some three inches above the ankle. Sarah splinted me expertly and then, determining that no other of my injuries were as urgent as Vanessa's, devoted her attentions to my alien beloved. I was left propped up on a Chesterfield sofa with a stack of yellowed newspapers, donated by my sister.

It appears that Earth has kept itself busy in my absence. I left this planet on the evening of 27 December, 1898 . . . and today, it seems, is the twelfth of January, 1899! Already the new year portends to be a fertile one.

In France, there are increasing cries for a new trial for Captain Dreyfus. Only a few days ago, the scientists Pierre and Marie Curie announced the discovery of a new substance: *radium,* which possesses wondrous properties. The frozen-faced murderer, Vacher, sentenced to death by the French magistrates for his crimes, held his tryst with *Madame Guillotine* on New Year's Eve. In Rome, they have unearthed the ancient remains of Romulus, founder of that city. In Germany, the health of Emperor Wilhelm is worsening.

In San Francisco, a woman named Cordelia Botkin has been sent to prison for flavouring chocolates with arsenic. Colonel Theodore Roosevelt, flushed with his recent military victory in Cuba, has been sworn in as Governor of New York. The United States Congress are debating the terms of their peace treaty with the Cubans.

And what of England? I find, to my delight, that during my interplanetary jaunt there has been in my homeland no upheaval more tempestuous than an election dispute in Aylesbury and the news that the East London Gas Company is raising its rates. How reassuring it is to know that—whatever battles rage elsewhere for domination of the galaxy—England stands as she stood, now and eternally.

Sarah is at this moment ministering to Vanessa. My sister has shut herself up with her patient in what must have been Ampleforth's bedroom, employed when the Dreadful Eye's purloined body required sleep. A less peculiar haven would be welcomed, yet the severity of Vanessa's injuries has prompted Sarah to insist she not be moved. As Sarah sends out no word of my beloved Vanessa's condition, I have spent the interim sleeping, obtaining some semblance of a bath, and revising this journal in my memorandum-book.

The adventures of the fortnight past have been so hectic that I have *not* been able to set most of them down on paper whilst they occurred. I had managed to sketch some brief notes while listening to Ampleforth's tale . . . but nothing at all was written, of course, while we were fleeing for our lives across the outworlder cliffs. I have therefore begun to set forth the narrative *now*, and I hope to proceed without interrup

"Excuse me."

Aleister Crowley entered, in a new suit of clothes. "Greetings, old warlock," I said as he came in. "Park your astral self in yonder chair, and give me the news."

Crowley sat down, all a-jangle with amulets. "I have just come," he reported, "from a meeting of the Hermetic Order of the Golden Dawn."

"What, in Hammersmith?" I asked.

"Er . . . well, *no*. There are some . . . *unpleasant* memories attached to our Blythe Road meeting-place of late. We have some smaller quarters, in New Queen Street. It appears, my dear needle-monger, that you have displeased the sacred elders of the Order."

"How so?"

"They hold you personally responsible for the animated corpse that walked into their meeting December last, disturbed the brethren, and then proceeded to drop dead all over again."

"Indeed?" I asked. "I was given to understand that the Golden Dawn *encouraged* supernatural occurrences."

"That is only correct," said Crowley, "when we *ourselves* are in control of the occult phenomena. To encounter supernatural forces that are more powerful than ourselves presents implications too painful to contemplate. MacGregor Mathers dumped the aforementioned cadaver in a dustbin, and Arthur Machen slipped a fiver to some business associates of mine who practise the fine art of disposing of corpses that have outstayed their welcome. The Golden Dawn has passed a resolution to the effect that your visit to our sacred Order—as well as the affair of the masquerading corpse—never occurred; in fact, that no meeting at all took place that night."

"What rot!" I protested. "I assume that Sir William Crookes, being a scientist, opposed the others in their desire to cut and shape the fabric of reality to suit their fashionable distaste for the facts."

"Not a bit of it," said Crowley. "Sir William sponsored the resolution. Seconded by Willie Yeats, who asked all present to agree that he was absent from the meeting that never occurred, as he desired to claim he was in Dublin that night. I have laboured long and hard to become an initiate of the Golden Dawn, to be privy to its secrets, and to find myself the intimate acquaintance of its influential members, yet now those members threaten me with expulsion from the Order unless I accede to their resolution. So: it seems that our recent trip to the invisible dimension, and the battle for our lives within the Dreadful Eye's domain, never happened at all."

"*You* disbelieve that, surely," I said.

"My beliefs," replied Aleister Crowley, closing one eye, "are both peculiar and unique. I profess steadfast and unwavering faith in whatever set of creeds are most convenient at the moment. I have been keeping a diary, sir, begun November last, wherein I set down the accounts of my intercourses with Magick. Now I find it inconvenient to admit that what happened has truly occurred. *Selah!* I unhappen it, and fill my diary with a fortnight's worth of fictitious days and counterfeit events, rather than pen an account of what *really* took place. If, at some future time, it should fall to my profit to unleash the truth, I shall then of course courageously reveal it."

"It is gratifying," I said, "to meet a person like yourself who has such well-defined principles. Your scruples, sir, are as steady as pudding. What becomes of your promise to chit me three hundred guineas, as payment for performing Vanessa's full-body tattoo?"

"Three hundred guineas?" cried Aleister Crowley, using his legs to levitate to a standing position, whilst his feet projected his physical self in the direction of the door. "You have evidently mistaken me, sir, for my identical *Doppelgänger,* a handsome but penniless poltergeist notorious for his generosity with my bank account. Since the supernatural occurrences which brought you and me together never transpired after all, it stands to reason, sir, that I have never met you."

"Very well," I said. "In that case, it has been a most pleasurable experience for me to never meet you, and I look forward to never meeting you again sometime. We must make a regular habit of it: let us devote one night a week to not meeting each other."

If Crowley heard this, he made no indication. He turned

and left, and at the time that I write this I do not know if I shall ever see him again.

13th January, 1899

This morning the pain in my leg was much worse. Sarah still tends Vanessa's injuries, but an hour ago she was kind enough to encase my fractured limb in a cast of court-plaster. I have asked her to let me see Vanessa, but Sarah refuses:

"She is very ill, I fear. I cannot bring Vanessa to you."

"Then I shall go to *her*," I said, endeavouring to stand.

"No. Your leg . . ."

"Bother my leg!" I stood up, balancing upon my right foot whilst looking for something to use as a crutch. "I mean to see her, Sarah. Give me a help with this gammy leg, then; if you refuse, I shall hop all the way to Vanessa."

And so, leaning on Sarah's arm, I was taken to the door of the room in which Vanessa lay. Sarah paused before opening the door.

"I believe you should know," she whispered, "that Vanessa is delirious. She mayn't recognise you."

"She will know me," I answered.

"I have done what I could," Sarah went on. "Vanessa seems to have internal injuries, but as her organs are alien I can only begin to guess . . ."

I kissed my sister on the forehead. "You are more adept, I am sure, than any twelve hackabones surgeons in Harley Street."

I pushed open the door, and went into the room, supporting myself against the nearer wall.

The curtains were drawn, and the room was in darkness. I found some matches in the bracket, lit the gas, but kept the lights very dim.

I saw a bed, and felt my way to the counterpane, ignoring the agonied throbs of my splinted limb as I knelt beside the bed.

I could see my Vanessa in darkness. The portions of her body where my tattoo needles had worked were there before me, visible. As for the rest: a silent indentation in the bedclothes, that swelled and decreased with the slow rhythm of Vanessa's breathing, showed me where her unseen face must be. I bent towards it.

"Vanessa . . ." I whispered.

Did she hear me? There was silence at first . . . and then a gentle murmuring: I saw the quilt stir as it brushed Vanessa's chin, and her breath trembled the cloth. "I am here, my darling," I said to Vanessa.

"Gnerdi klun faughnar," she whispered. *"Gnerdi hoth, chela vnakli d'vril . . ."*

The words of her alien tongue. I watched, helplessly, as my nightmared Vanessa spoke . . . to me? to herself? to some horror that whispered and stalked through her shadow-dark mind? Vanessa's words loudened, and I saw her body grow tense in her delirium's writhings. Then she suddenly sat upright in the bed; I saw the visible portions of Vanessa change shape and distend, twisting into some alien form which I could not clearly perceive in the half-light. But I heard Vanessa scream:

"Ngai! No! No! You cannot touch me now! I am become a she-human! Listen: do you hear? I speak their tongue! I have escaped you!"

I could not see her face, nor any portion of Vanessa's head. But I saw, on the far wall, the shadow that was cast by her body as she rose before the gas-light. And there was a moment when . . .

How did it happen? Does the combustion of coal-gas give off not only heat and light, but some other form of energy as well? Some ray within a portion of the ultra-violet spectrum not generally seen by human eyes? I do not know. But for a moment, in that flickering gaslight, I beheld *the shadow of a head,* and—in silhouetted profile—the outline of Vanessa's invisible face.

I cannot forget that face. It was elongated into something which had no right to be human. It was a face born in nightmares, and suckled in madness . . .

And then the shadow passed, and I saw again the naked shoulders, with no visible head.

Sarah entered and sat beside me. She took Vanessa's arm and felt for the pulse. It appeared, from Sarah's huntings, that the blood pulse in Vanessa's alien form was best detected in the underside of the *elbow,* not the wrist.

"She is fevered," said Sarah. "A pulse this fast would kill a human; I expect it's not normal for *her* sort, either."

I said nothing. I was thinking of what had happened in the cellar: of my battle with the whispering face beneath the stairs.

I have fought the most hideous thing which any man has ever faced. It *invaded my body,* corrupted the flesh, and tasted the edge of my soul. I am frightened, for I am certain that the Dreadful Eye *will* return. He still craves the death of Vanessa . . . and so long as she lives here, Earth remains a hostage planet.

I do not want to face the Dreadful Eye again. A portion of me wants to hide, just as Aleister Crowley has done, until the horror treads past. But I have promised Vanessa that I shall help her slay the Dreadful Eye. In God's name, what have I brought myself into?

Vanessa stirred again in her delirium. Her form became more human, then less so. Shifting, changing . . .

"I very much fear," said my sister, "that Vanessa will die."

All the words: the incisioning scalpel. The thought of Vanessa's oncoming death gives me pain, for I love this strange female. But at the same time I suddenly feel an intruding sense of *relief.* Yes. *If Vanessa dies, she will escape the Dreadful Eye. If she dies, then Earth may yet be saved; the Dreadful Eye will have one less reason to return here. Yes, of course . . .*

Vanessa moaned again, in her alien tongue. I found that my hands were moving—I had not consciously guided them—towards Vanessa's unseen face. My fingers crept across the coverlet, and touched the bolster underneath her head.

Oh, die, Vanessa, die, and we both will be free. You will be released from your pain, and I will be freed from my promise to destroy the Dreadful Eye. I am more frightened of his face than of any dweller out of nightmares. But die, Vanessa, and Earth will be saved. Die, and I can go back to my safe little shopkeeper's life among dust-covered shelves. Die, and I can abandon my promise to you. For I cannot bring myself to break that promise while you are alive. Confound it! I love you, Vanessa . . .

"What in heaven's name are you *doing?*" said a voice.

Sarah was gripping my arm, and I saw that I had caught hold of one of the pillows, and had raised it towards Vanessa's face. "One would almost believe that you wanted to smother her," said my sister.

Can an alien die? Is it murder to deny Earth's air to else-born lungs?

I dropped the pillow, felt it land on my fractured ankle. Just a pennyweight of feathers, but its impact as it struck my injured leg was a hundredweight agony.

I love Vanessa. I love the Vanessa whom I fancied once existed: the invisible shape-changer who could wear a hundred forms, a thousand faces. With so many different shapes from which to choose, Vanessa could become *any* woman, wearing every sort of face. *That* woman, who could be transformed by her will and my needle to any colour and shape we two fancied . . . *that* woman is she whom I loved. This trembling thing in the bedclothes, this alien invalid understudying the *rôle* of a corpse: she arouses in me an overwhelming sensation of *pity*. I love her, yes, but my instincts are no longer those of passion. My impulse is to put her out of her agony.

. . . for her own easement? For the sake of the Earth? Or merely to protect my own cowardly self from the returning Dreadful Eye?

I wish to heaven that Vanessa were conscious enough to convey her own thoughts in this matter. She is clearly in pain; does she think to endure it, or does she hunger for death?

I love her. I must kill her.

16th January, 1899

Vanessa's pain ripens and grows. I watch her, as she lies in shadows moaning, her body changing and reshaping with each spasm of her mind. I am sitting, just now, less than three feet from her bed, writing these words by the light of a paraffin lamp. Vanessa screams but does not awaken; I am powerless to aid her.

I have had time, these last days, to bring up to date my written account of what has passed. I look back at what I wrote of Vanessa three days ago—*"I must kill her"*—and I am ashamed. I love this woman; I want her to *live*. Whatever momentary madness compelled me to feel otherwise is past, and it *must* not return.

I am still too frightened to confront the Dreadful Eye.

My leg grows stronger, but remains too weak to bear me. Sarah has brought me some of her husband's clothes; I have slit one trouser leg to accommodate my plaster cast. My sister has also brought me crutches, as well as some food, and I now can hobble tolerably well. I take my exercise exploring the rooms of this house in Fetter Lane.

In a cupboard I have discovered a sack stuffed with banknotes: nearly two thousand quid. The Dreadful Eye's wealth, presumably; hoarded while he occupied Ampleforth's body.

I confiscate this rhino with a will. Now, as soon as Vanessa is well enough to be moved, we can *get out of this house,* she and I, and live elsewhere.

17th January, 1899

This morning a woman arrived on the doorstep. She was startled to see me, and asked for "Mr Ampleforth, the master." Apparently she was engaged as housekeeper by the Dreadful Eye during his Ampleforth disguise. I introduced myself as Mr Ampleforth's brother from Orpington and dismissed the woman with a gift of thirty pounds: a higher wage than most servants receive in six months' time.

The housekeeper's arrival had delayed me from looking in on Vanessa. I crutched my way into her room and called out: "Vanessa?"

She did not answer. The visible portions of Vanessa had turned paler somehow, but I could still see her, a movement in the shadow . . . was she trembling? No; the gaslight had flickered. Vanessa lay still.

On crutches, I knelt towards the bed, and felt about with one hand, seeking Vanessa's invisible face. And I prayed she was warm, while my fingers touched . . .

Ice-flesh.

Vanessa is dead.

Three hours later

Sarah has arrived. I still have difficulty believing what has passed.

Vanessa's corpse grows less visible each moment. Sarah is with my sweet alien now, while I write this. The regions of Vanessa's flesh which I once tattooed have all turned paler, as the pigment dissipates.

I do not know what shall be done with Vanessa's else-world remains. She deserves a decent Christian burial . . . a *burial,* at least, with the hope that whatever alien god received her prayers will now accept her soul. A closed coffin, for obvious reasons, and a churchyard interment. Vanessa wanted to live as a woman of Earth . . . now, at least, she will be buried as one.

She was born on a far-distant world. If her flesh is buried *here,* will her soul ever find its way home across the stars?

And the Dreadful Eye has won. I cannot hope to stop his interstellar conquests, but I pray that he will wage his battles *elsewhere.* Earth has dictators enough of the home-grown sort; we have no need to import them.

Sarah is calling me. I must see what she wants.

I shall finish this later.

Seven o'clock, Tuesday evening

It is torture, and it started with a kiss. In the past quarter hour I have endured the most painful bitter intimacy of my God-abandoned life. I write down what has occurred . . . but I wish I could tear the agony out of my mind and pin it squirming to this page.

When Sarah called, I crutch-hobbled my way to the bedroom. Sarah was there, and . . . Vanessa, *alive!* She seemed very weak, but sat propped up in the pillows, and was asking for me.

I dropped my crutches, and—ignoring the pain in my agonied leg—I knelt by the bed, all my weight on my uninjured limb. I held Vanessa, and we kissed.

Her lips were colder than I had hoped.

"It seems," said my Sarah, "that Vanessa's race could teach our human species a thing worth the knowing. They've a trick rather like the hibernation some Earth creatures undergo, to slow their metabolism, and reduce their body heat. But I never guessed . . . well, a drop in temperature of nearly forty-five degrees . . ."

"My people call it the frost-sleep . . ." said Vanessa. Her voice was still weak. "A bodily function used at very last resort, to permit the physical portions to heal . . ."

To *heal?* Then Vanessa would *live!* I held her again. "Is there anything you require?" I asked of her. "Food, perhaps, or . . ."

"A piece of beef-meat, uncooked, would go well, please," she said, and Sarah went pattering to fetch it. "But what I desire most urgently," said my alien lover, now that we were alone, "is certain knowledge: have we escaped the Dreadful Eye?"

"He is gone," I replied. *Gone for NOW,* was my unspoken thought.

"Gone? *Where?*" Vanessa asked.

"He followed us back to London," I told her. "He attacked, and took possession of my . . . hmmm, that part is best kept unrevealed."

"Where is he *now,* please?" persisted Vanessa.

I kissed her forehead; the flesh was still cool, and held a taste I had never detected before. "The Dreadful Eye is well and truly *gone,*" I told Vanessa. "He needed a body to inhabit, so he took possession of a rat. I switched on the Dreadful Eye's projector, and when the dimensional gateway appeared I threw him back . . ."

"*Then he still rapes my homeworld!*" howled Vanessa, struggling to rise. "You sent him back there, *and my people are still unfree!*" She sat upright now, her breasts and half-visible shoulders heaving as she rasped and hawked for air. "*I must go back, and . . .*"

"*No!*" I said, standing up so suddenly that I forgot my injured leg, and nearly fell again. I had forgotten what Ampleforth had said: that the Dreadful Eye's projector in the cellar had its dials set for Vanessa's homeworld! Now I envisioned Vanessa renewing her battle with the Dreadful Eye, and myself honourbound to go with her. For *I* had flung the Dreadful Eye back through the portal, to Vanessa's world . . .

"No, Vanessa." I spoke, having no idea what to say next. "It is not what you think."

"Please explain."

"That is to say . . . I *did* put the Dreadful Eye into the dimensional portal." I could hear my own voice, feel it form in my mouth, but my mind did not seem to be governing it. The lie created itself. "I sent him through to . . . an altogether *different* planet. Not yours."

"The dials of the machine," Vanessa answered, "were set for my birthworld."

"I changed the setting of the dials," said the lie that wore my voice. "The interdimensional gateway from Earth to your planet shifted to some *other* world; I do not know where. I caught a glimpse . . . I believe the place is uninhabited . . ."

"*Thank the destinies,*" breathed Vanessa, and her body relaxed against the coverlet. "Then my people are free at last," she said.

"Yes," I lied.

"And the Dreadful Eye is gone forever," she said.

"Yes," I lied.

Vanessa touched me, her unseen fingers tracing the forms and ridges of my face. "I love you," she whispered.

"And you arouse in me, strange Vanessa," I answered, "a greater love than I have ever felt for any other woman."

It was the truth.

We drew closer. My hands, my sweat-and-England face, sought Vanessa's shadowed countenance, and we joined. At the parting of our kiss, Vanessa shape-changed one of her arms to twice its customary length, and grasped Sarah's medical bag. She brought this bedwards, and extracted a small phial of salve. "Will this adhere to my skin?"

"I suppose it might," I answered.

"Then please apply it," breathed Vanessa, "to the remnants of my body which your needle never touched. I want you to *see* me . . ."

I followed her bidding. Vanessa lay quietly, her chest rising and falling in rhythms of breath. The invisible lids of her eyes were apparently closed.

I opened the salve pot and touched my fingertips to the substance within: the soft cream, lightly flesh-coloured, with its sweet peculiar odour, felt warm against my hand.

I touched Vanessa's invisible face with my salve-moistened fingers, stroked the cream against the high ridge of her cheekbone. A smudge of the salve adhered to her unseen skin, transforming it into suddenly visibled flesh.

I kept working. Vanessa's alien form had often altered its shape in the past, refashioning itself to suit my wish and Vanessa's will. But now Vanessa's flesh was no more pliable than any Earth-born woman's. Did she hold herself rigid, to make a better canvas for my art?

I enfleshed her with both of my hands, rubbing the salve into the soft concentric curves of Vanessa's ears, and working it as firmly as I dared into her nostrils. Vanessa showed no discomfort. I flesh-painted her chin and the arch of her throat.

Vanessa's forehead, now emerging visible, proved to be high and prominent; I had expected no less, to house the wisdom of two worlds. As gently as possible, I stroked more salve into the hollows of her eye sockets. Yes, her eyelids *were* closed; whilst I coloured them, I could see the flesh ripple as her eyes moved beneath the brief surface.

Her mouth was next. Vanessa's lips were gently closed. I

kissed them again, and then applied the warm salve. Next I fleshened her temples and shoulders.

Done. And now there couched before me, eyes closed, the new face of Vanessa.

I have read that our universe is infinite. I am perfectly willing to assume that our ant-hill humanity is merely one of many thousands of sentient races, strewn among some million habitable worlds, interspersed between many billions of suns, amidst the countless and innumerable galaxies. I am prepared to accept this as fact. But I *know,* and I always *shall* know, that in all the endless universe beyond—in all the mere infinity of space and time—there is no beauty to compare with the image of Vanessa's bright face.

Vanessa opened her eyes very slightly; the eyelids were visible, coated with salve, but I could not see the eyes contained within. The empty sockets regarded me. "Did you know," said Vanessa very softly, "that, whenever any of my people die, in death we revert to the shape we possessed at our birth?"

The flesh of her torso, where I had long ago tattooed it, now grew pale, milky, clouded like barley-glass, and I perceived that she was scarcely breathing.

"*Vanessa . . .*"

"There is darkness," she answered. "All is shadow and dim. But oh, my darling Earth-born! If my love for you were the sun, you would be blinded by the light . . ."

Her body, the else-woman flesh, dimmed and faded. Vanessa's portions which I had once injected with visible pigments were turning *invisible* again. Some chemical process within her was breaking down and diluting the pigments, absorbing them into alien transparence once more. Her woman-formed flesh, as it vanished, began to shape-change into some else-thing.

"*Vanessa! . . .*"

I probed the air to find some portion of her invisible self, touched her flesh, and felt . . . a *winterness.* Her skin had been cold once before, during Vanessa's grim frost-sleep. *This* was colder, more intolerably wintered. As I watched, water droplets condensed, ice particles formed against her crystalline flesh, revealing the barest outlines of a frost-covered shape that was rapidly losing all semblance of humanlike form.

Vanessa was . . . Vanessa *is* . . . and most decidedly this time . . . at the end of her pain.

My beloved is dead.

The Last Part

THE THING IN THE EARTHENWARE JAR

1.37 a.m., Wednesday
18th January, 1899

It is dark while I write this. I can still see Vanessa . . . that is, I see her *face,* the death-mask moulded in salve with my fingertips. The mask of Vanessa floats, silent and still, a few inches above the indentation of the pillow. Her head, between pillow and mask, is invisible . . . and her body lies unseen as well.

My last hope is that Vanessa's final moments were pleasured by the lie that I told her. If she *believed* that the Dreadful Eye has been destroyed, that her people are free and the battle is won, then my falsehood eased her death.

And the lie I told at sweet Vanessa's death now extricates me from my promise to her. The Dreadful Eye's conquest resumes, but I have ferreted my way to the sidelines. *My* battle is done.

I should be pleased, and yet I am disgusted with myself.

20th January, 1899

Sarah and I have made arrangements for Vanessa's burial. We have dressed her—or rather, *Sarah* clothed Vanessa's invisible flesh, whilst I fumbled at lacings and button-hooks. Vanessa's burial clothes were purchased by Sarah with a portion of the bank-notes that I found. Now my alien Vanessa is garbed in the disguise that would have given her the most pleasure to wear: the costume of a fashionable young lady of London.

The coffin will be tightly sealed, but—should some inquisitive gravedigger broach it—Vanessa's black gloves and burial veil should keep her invisibility secret.

Sarah's husband Henry has been helpful after all. He knows some fellow at his club, who knows some Whitehall minister, who is an intimate friend of a boon companion of a casual acquaintance to the Archbishop of Canterbury. Favours were asked, debts recalled, and the *denouement* is that my Vanessa will be buried as swiftly as possible, in Nunhead Cemetery near Peckham Rye. A small headstone will be her grave marker. Certain minor details, such as the filing of a death certificate, will be dealt with in a highly original manner.

My injured leg will require another several weeks to fully heal. I am a leaping-jack at best, until that time.

But, crippled or whole, I owe Vanessa a debt. If the Dreadful Eye comes back to Earth, if he who has slain my strange female returns, I shall destroy him, or die in the reckoning. I owe Vanessa this.

If I can kill the final Enemy, then two planets—my own and Vanessa's—are saved. And if the Dreadful Eye kills *me,* then at least I will rejoin my Vanessa in death.

21st January, 1899

I have just come from her burial.

This has been the most painful of days in my life. Sarah and Henry arrived in the morning, with a livery hearse. Henry still does not know, will never know *who* is in the coffin, nor the circumstances of her origin and death. Sarah has told him that the occupant was a lady of my intimate acquaintance. No more will be revealed.

Because of my injured leg, Sarah and Henry suggested that I remain in the hearse whilst the rest of our funeral party went on to the grave site. I ignored their protests, and crutched and hirpled my way to the burial. I watched as the sexton's spade bit into the earth, and the coffin was lowered.

Forgive me, Vanessa, for wishing your death. And forgive all my lies. I wish that everything I told you had been true. But the one vast bright undying truth is this: I love you, strange Vanessa.

The interment was completed, and we slowly returned to the hearse. "Lean on me, if you like, old fellow," said Henry, offering me his nearer arm. He is not a bad sort, after all.

On the ride back from Nunhead Cemetery, I sat in the rear of the livery hearse, with my injured leg propped up along the seat, my sister and her husband in front of me. Our talk carried little of moment until the hearse reached Holborn Viaduct, when Henry suddenly asked me: "Why didn't your gentleman friend join us at the gravesite?"

Thinking of Crowley's betrayal, I said: "I have no friends. Except yourself, sir, and my sister."

"But I distinctly saw him," said Henry. "A man in an Inverness cape. He came up to the gate of the churchyard, but would not go in. He watched us bury your lady-love."

So it *was* Crowley, then, I am sure . . . for that is just his sort of fancy. His confounded pagan worship prevents him from setting foot in honest Christian graveyards.

And now it is ended. Yesterday I rung up estate agents in the hope of obtaining lodgings elsewhere, for this house in Fetter Lane is *evil*. Let the damned place be shuttered and boarded, and on some reckoning night—when my ankle has healed, and when the neighbouring houses have been afforded all possible protection—then I shall return in the dark with a paraffin lamp and some rags. Then this hideous house—and the squatting machine in its cellar—will be swallowed in flames.

22nd January, 1899

I am writing this by the early-morning light of a streetlamp, underneath a stone arch in St. Bride Street, hard by Fetter Lane. Tonight a nightmare arrived on my doorstep.

An hour ago I was asleep, in the Fetter Lane house. It was my habit to sleep upon the downstairs Chesterfield couch, with my splinted limb propped up. I could not bring myself to sleep in the bed in which Vanessa had died. In my sleep, I encountered a dream.

In my dream I awoke and discovered my leg was now perfectly healed. Such dream-cures are common; amputees, for example, often find themselves whole in their dream-forms. In my dream I stood up, crossed the room, and gazed out of the window, into Fetter Lane. Across the way, beyond the Holborn Circus streetlamps, I beheld the figure of a man. He was waiting in the shadows, and I knew—the way we know things in a dream—that he was watching *this house.* Through all the layerings of dream he was so indistinct and distant that I could not see his face, but I saw that he was wearing an Inverness cape.

For a long moment's waiting we watched, without moving: I observed the dream-man, and he stood pondering the house in which I slept. Then he alighted from the kerb and slowly walked across the cobbled Fetter Lane, towards the house.

He walked like a beetle, some scuttling thing which crept out from the dark underside of nightmares. He hobbled and lurched, in a drunkard's approach, and came forward in diagonal meanders.

As he came closer, I still could not see his face. The mantle of his Inverness was thrown across his features. Shadow-masked, he drew nearer. Then I *knew,* with dream-certainty, that this stranger was watching *my* window; looking *through* it, seeing *me.*

I have never, in any previous dream, felt a sensation of *temperature.* Yet now in this dream I experienced a growing wave of *cold* that gnawed at the remainder of my soul.

Now the dream-stranger stood, directly outside the dream-window of that dream-imagined house. My dreaming self gazed out at him, and he in turn was looking straight at me.

In my dream then I reached towards the mantle of his cape, to excavate the face within. But my dream-hand was stopped by the window glass between us.

Then the figure in the Inverness cape reached up, undid its cloak, and thus revealed to me its face.

At that instant I awakened, screaming.

I awoke on the couch, and my leg was still splinted, with my crutches near to hand. So it *had* been a dream, then. Yes. And now I stood up, on one leg and both crutches, and—realising that there was no-one at the window after all—I turned round to reassure myself, and looked.

A face was peering through the glass.

The eyes regarded me for an instant, and then the figure turned and melted into the night. But I had seen, and recognised, the face.

It was the dead engine-driver, who mocked me in Hammersmith. It was his *corpse,* at least; another mind now occupied his skull.

The Dreadful Eye has returned.

I left the house at all speed, cursing my crippled leg for slowing me up. I took only the clothes I now wear, and the banknotes I found, and the journal in which I now write this.

The hour is wanting ten minutes of dawn; come the sunrise, I shall find other lodgings. *I shall not return to that house.*

10th February, 1899

Nearly three weeks have passed, and the Eye has not found me. Where is he? What does he want?

I have obtained lodgings in the Belgravia district: at Eccleston Square, behind Victoria Station. I have sent word to Sarah, telling where she might find me.

My leg is healing admirably well; Sarah has removed my splintings, but I still have much court-plaster and bandage-wrapping with which to contend. Three-fourths of me is human; my left leg resembles a mummy in the British Museum.

No-one knows me here, and that is how I prefer it. The neighbours are quiet enough, but the lodger upstairs keeps three dogs whose demands to go out are both frequent and boisterous, keeping me awake at inconvenient times.

I have given two hundred pounds to my sister and her husband for their trouble with Vanessa and myself. The remainder of the bank-notes I acquired will sustain me for the present. I now spend nearly every moment awaiting the inevitable visit of my Enemy.

How did the Dreadful Eye return to Earth? And *how* did he regain possession of the engine-driver's corpse?

Sarah tells me that the plaster cast may soon come off my leg. I await such a time. Confound this itching!

18th February

Still no sign of the Enemy. I am getting about more of late, most frequently by cabs, for my leg is still brickled. I recall that George Bernard Shaw, when I met him, was likewise crutched and bandaged in the identical limb as myself. Perhaps that accounts for his pepper-box temperament.

I saw Aleister Crowley yester-evening. I was cabbing it down Regent Street, and—passing St. James's Hall, where a performance by Moore & Burgess's Blackface Minstrels was about to commence—I chanced to see Crowley in the ticketers' queue, a slender youth of twentyish beside him. I bade the cabman drive closer, while I rolled up the isinglass window shade and, leaning out Crowleywards, said: "I should like to have a word in your ear."

The self-appointed wizard Aleister Crowley took one look at me and fled towards Piccadilly, howling: *"I have never seen you before in my life!"*

"These rum 'uns comes out early-like, as the weather gets warmer," observed my cabdriver.

So I am alone, then. Vanessa is dead, and all the rest who shared in my adventure prefer to claim it never happened. Sarah and Henry remain on the sidelines of this battle; when the blood harvest begins, I pray it will spare those good people.

6th March

What in God's name is the matter with those *dogs?*

10th March

I have taken the cast off my leg, with the aid of a blunted razor. So I am a two-legged man again; *that* much freedom I have. I still limp, and have obtained a Malacca walking-stick to hasten my progress.

I was right, I think, to remove the plastering myself, without prevailing on Sarah's help. I do not want her to visit me here, in Eccleston Square. For I cannot be certain of it, and yet—I am increasingly convinced—there is something *very* wrong with this house.

11th March

Confound those dogs! Their howls are maddening. . . .

12th March

Ugh! Rats in the walls! Yes, and crawling across the wainscoting. Great fat hairy ones; I've killed two with my Malacca stick, and sent the others sclattering. I don't wonder that the dogs upstairs have been howling again.

I *shall* change lodgings at once. Today is Sunday; tomorrow I'm off for the estate agents. I don't much fancy this.

13th March

If there is a God, then I pray to Him: let this be madness. Let Reality melt, and make all that surrounds me be dream-things. I cannot bear what has occurred.

I awakened this morning, some time before dawn, with the sensation that *something* was watching me. The paraffin lamp on the bedstand was out; I poked about for a match to relight it, when a voice quite suddenly whispered:

"Permit me."

The lamp lit; I did not see how. I turned down the wick to increase the dim glow, and I beheld my visitor.

It was a man made of sawdust and orange rinds and sausage casings and rot. All the dead things conspired to create him. In the lamplight, I could not perceive his face. But I knew who it was.

"You have come, then," I said.

"Evidently."

It was futile, I knew, to attack him. And useless to run. "How did you get back to this world from the invisible place?" I asked my unholy visitor.

"I never left. I have remained here on Earth."

"Rubbish, sir. You inhabited the body of a rat—a very excellent costume; it suits you most admirably—and then I pitched you through the Opening between the worlds."

"You pitched a rat, perhaps," said the dead thing. *"But there is more than one rat in the cellars of London."*

Now I remembered: the rat in the Fetter Lane house had wriggled free of my grasp, and scrabbled into the shadows. I had snatched it again, flung it into the dimensional void . . . but now it seems that, in the rat-infested darkness, I had caught *the wrong one.*

The stench of my visitor was nearly unbearable. *"Enough of rats,"* said the collection of dead bits before me. As it spoke, different fragments of itself began to seethe within its surface. *"I have come here on business."*

"Whose business?"

"My own. I made an error on that last world, the alien one, by

endeavouring to possess the minds of all its inhabitants at once. The process dissipated me, as I was spread amongst too many different victims."

"When one applies for the office of galactic overlord," I remarked, "one must expect risks to go with the job."

"Just the case. I am beginning again now, on Earth, and with a different strategy. I now propose to steal the mind of just one man, and to infuse it with all my grim knowledge and thoughts. This man —a marionette, manipulated by myself—will commit the acts of evil which I require to sustain me."

"I thought you tried that once before," I said, "with Ampleforth."

"No. That was eviction; this will be abduction. With Ampleforth I stole the body and inhabited the brain, but I evicted the mind and the soul. This will be different: the man remains within his skull, imprisoned in the flesh, whilst I control his limbs and faculties and speech."

"You might at least take the body of a dead man, then. That engine-driver . . ."

"Corpses nourish me but little. Even Ampleforth's body had begun to putrefy while I was in it, for his life-force had gone elsewhere. I require a living body, with a living mind and soul to sustain it, and to absorb the body's pain. I cannot endure pain; Ampleforth discovered that. Pain drove me out of his flesh. Ah, but NOW—as landlord of a living human brain, with its rightful owner my unwilling lodger within—I can control the brain's neural pathways, just as a stationmaster guides the railway switches. I shall connect myself to all the pleasure centres and motor neurons of the brain, and leave attached to their original owner all the sensory ganglia which transmit sensations of PAIN. Then I shall savour all the ecstasies of flesh, whilst evading the agonies."

Hoping to dissuade my visitor, I said: "Surely no human mind could sustain you forever."

"These are details," answered the visitor. *"The mind which I inhabit will last for a few years; perhaps twenty, or fifty. After that? There are minds here in plentiness. I feed on souls, and I have hungered so long. Your planet's citizens offer me a banquet of minds, a*

harvest of intellects on which I may feed—one by one; a procession of souls. I can dwell amid Earth-minds for centuries."

I knew, from terrible experience, that I had absolutely no way to stop this unliving thing. "And whose mind," I asked, "have you selected for the honour of containing you?"

"Human-born, have you not already guessed?" The sawdust man reached out towards me. I saw the dead fingers lengthen and attenuate; they writhed about like tentacles quite near my eyes. Death's fingertips, they lengthened to enfold me. *"I offer you a partnership,"* whispered the deathness.

"I decline."

"You have no choice."

"Why *me*, of all possible people?"

"Because I have already tasted your thoughts. I have gnawed at the crusts of your soul, and I hunger to consume the parts remaining. And besides, you and I, we have something in common."

"Pray, what?"

"The she-one."

"Vanessa?"

"Aye. Vanessa."

"We have nothing in common where she is concerned," I said to the listening dead thing. "I *loved* Vanessa. I love her now, even in death. You hated her, sir. You abducted her, tortured her, and killed her."

"Do you think," my dead visitor whispered, in a voice so very quiet as to barely touch the threshold of my hearing, *"do you think that, because I am alien, that all within me is alien as well?"*

"Explain yourself."

"Have you not learnt the reason why I sent my invisible minions to London, to find your Vanessa? Have you never discovered why I brought her back to the alien world, and bade my torture-masters perform their specialities upon her? Did you never suspect why I witnessed their unholy rites, whilst they tortured Vanessa? Pain—my own pain—is intolerable to me, but the pain of another feeds my ravenous great hunger. I tasted Vanessa's sweet agonies. I savoured the roots of her glittering fear. The sensations of shame and humiliation which her captive mind emitted were like sweetmeats to me; I de-

voured them. And I was present at the moment of her death—you did not see me, but yet I attended—and I assure you, human one, that the instant of Vanessa's bright agonied death was an orgasm, sir, for myself."

Now I felt a new revulsion for this hideous thing, surpassing all my previous emotion. "What did Vanessa ever do," I demanded to know, "that it pleasured you to end her existence? Why did you hate her?"

"*You have misunderstood me,*" said the dead one in the darkness. "*Do you think that I tortured Vanessa, stripped naked her soul, fed myself on her pain, and consummated her death for such an insignificant motive as HATE?*"

"Then why did . . ."

"*For the greatest of all possible reasons,*" said the beckoning horror. "*I loved her.*"

14th March

Will those dogs never stop?

The rats have come back now. I have killed several. The others watch me, regarding in silence.

The rats are continuing their work. I can see them, as I write this. A constant eddy of rodents scuttles in and out of the room— through the walls, through the windows and grate. The rats come, and each one bears in its quivering jaws something *dead:* a bit of maggoted meat, a mouldered carrot, decaying fungus, some cloth. Each carrion fragment is added to the mound in front of me, and each rat hurries away again to find another remnant of deathness. The mound of dead things grows larger every moment, as each further bit is deposited. Already the heap begins to assume a most ominous shape.

The rats and I are not alone. A thousand faces regard me. The faces have sprouted from every dead surface, each once-living part of the room. Anything fabricated from *wood,* or from *leather,* or *cloth*—everything has a face, and it watches me. Even the flame of the gaslight has taken the form of two eyes and a flickering mouth, for the coal-gas itself is the fossil remains of plant life and primordial beasts who died long before the Jurassic. The paraffin lamp, too, sprouts an animated flame; I quickly shut it off, but it returned of itself.

The faces whisper to me. Sometimes, amongst them, I can make out the features of persons once known to me: my mother, my father, my brother James who died in infancy. There is one large and gibbering head just above the chimney-piece; its face resembles Ampleforth's. New faces arrive, and I look amid the gathering horde for one particular countenance, but I cannot find her. A thousand faces, yet never among them Vanessa's.

One mercy remains to me, at least. The clothes that I wear remain inanimate. This memorandum-book, constructed of paper and pasteboard, pulped from once-living trees, shows no sign of conspiring against me. The ink in my pen—coloured vegetable matter—is dead as well, but does not yet writhe within my grasp.

I am hungry. An hour ago I went to the larder and began to eat. A potato in my hands suddenly opened its eyes, and some bread and cheese came alive in my mouth. I spat them out, flung the foodstuffs away. I watched my breakfast crawl across the room, adding itself to the gathering mound on the carpet.

My hunger grows steadily worse. Meat and vegetables croon to me from the larder. I must not submit . . .

The mound of dead things still grows. Somewhere, buried within it, is the vacated form which the Dreadful Eye wore. After speaking to me of Vanessa, he *left,* and the collection of sawdust and rot which had carried him here scattered lifeless on the hearth. Now the rats are adding to it.

There! I have just now killed another rat, with a brick. Its brothers add its crushed remains to the thickening mound while I watch.

A procession of ants has arrived, each one bearing a crumb. These are added to the pile.

I wonder why the dogs have stopped howling?

All the faces babble madness. A few, here and there, utter fragments of coherence in the all-surrounding croon. Why do they keep me here?

The mass of dead things in front of me moves now. It rises and stirs, and fills all one end of the room. It presses itself against the faces which sprout from the walls, and as I watch all the faces descend from the walls in some fashion, attaching themselves to the mound. Now the thousands of eyes turn towards me, the mouths begin to speak.

"Are you ready?" says the Dreadful Eye, in a voice with a thousand dead tongues.

"You might at least let me finish *writing* this," I answered, scrawling down those very words as I speak them. "I had hoped, since you left, that you mightn't return."

"I had an errand, necessary to perform before I might take over your body."

"You had no difficulty before, in Fetter Lane," I said. "You nearly took over my body *then,* in the cellar."

"Yes, and would have pushed out your mind. But this time I mean to retain it. I control what is dead, but to suppress your living mind I need assistance from elsewhere. I took the liberty, therefore, of having a prescription filled."

Just then there was a knock at the door. *"Answer that,"* said my dead visitor.

I must see who—or what—has arrived. Perhaps I may be able to resume this narrative later. The rapping at the door is most insistent.

TO WHOEVER FINDS THIS

If I can trust my pocket watch, I have some twenty minutes left. Perhaps that is just enough time to set down what has occurred.

In my dark flat in Eccleston Square, I had opened the door just in time to glimpse a small figure—it looked rather like a young boy—running off down the stairs. "I say, *wait!*" I tried to run after him, but the wooden door of a sudden changed its shape, sprouting arms which twisted round me. I struggled, but was pulled bodily back into the room.

The doormat was cocoanut-matting, I think. It had been

made of *something* formerly alive, at any rate. Now it humped itself up, like a stickled hedgehog, and walked on its corners right into the room, whilst the door closed itself. A packet, done up in brown paper, and presumably left by the boy—if it *had* been a boy—was astride the animated doormat.

"Open it," said my visitor, the Dreadful Eye.

I tore away the brown paper, and took out its contents.

The packet contained a small earthenware jar. On its surface was pasted a label: TO BE TAKEN INTERNALLY. The jar, when I opened it, held a quantity of pale green powder.

"This is the stuff you gave Ampleforth," I remarked.

"Not the same, but very like," said all the faces of the Dreadful Eye. *"You will be so kind as to swallow it."*

"And then . . . ?"

"On a man of your size it requires, I should think, about an hour to take effect. You will lose all control of your body, yet remain conscious. Your flesh will submit to my needs, and permit me to enter. Thereafter, I control your body's movements, and I sense its stimulations. You will be blind, deaf, and mute, shuttered up within the attic of your mind and receiving no sensory stimuli—except when your body feels PAIN."

"I should go mad within a fortnight."

"There are those, I believe, who would say you have touched madness already. Enough talk: consume the powder."

"And if I refuse . . . ?"

Instantly, a hundred dead parts of the room sprouted limbs. Fingers, hands, arms grew out of every place made of wood, cloth, or leather. My cotton and celluloid collar grew tight across my throat, and my trousers stirred threateningly. The leather belt encircling my waist began to mutiny against me.

"You can be forced to obey me," came the harsh reply.

"How? By violence? If you hurt me, you render my body unsuitable for a new tenant."

"I can render you unconscious," said the thing, *"and while you remain in that state the ants will feed you. There is a good ounce of powder in that jar . . . but one grain at a time, a thin trickle of*

ants conveying the powder past your lips and then into your throat
. . . it can be done. I may wish the rats to assist them."

I shuddered. "You've won, then."

"Of course."

There was still one brief hope, if I only had *time.* "Do I
swallow this stuff?" I asked. "Or inhale it?"

"Just as you wish," said the mound of dead faces. *"The powder may even be injected, if a hypodermic syringe is available and
such are your tastes. Or swallow it, and I'll permit you a tumblerful of
water afterwards, to wash it down."*

"Very well."

Still *one* possible hope . . .

I tasted the powder. It was bitter, and I felt my gorge rise.
All the dead faces watched as I managed to swallow the stuff.

A coat-stand walked into the room on its wood-spindled
legs. Clenched in its upper row of hooks, it held a glass of water,
presumably obtained in the kitchen. "Cheers," I said, taking the
glass, and I tossed down the draught.

I was aware of a peculiar buzzing in my skull . . .

"And now we are twins of the mind," said my peculiar visitor.
*"I have a toehold on your brain already and cannot be dislodged. Not
even I myself can now sever the link. Do you wish one last morsel of
freedom? I permit it. Until the powder takes effect, you may do as you
will. Run away if you like; when the powder takes hold of your mind,
I shall be there, alongside you. Within you."*

"Suppose, before the hour is up, I try to fox you?" I asked.
"I might, for instance, try to kill myself . . ."

*"I think not. Ampleforth might have committed suicide, but
your mind is more tenacious than his. One of the reasons why I have
chosen you."*

The buzzing, in the back of my skull, had grown louder. As
there seemed nothing to stop me, I turned and fled. The door
opened by itself, and I ran from the flat, my injured left leg rioting
with pain. Somewhere hard by Victoria Station I summoned a
cabman. I have managed to jot down these last few pages in his
carriage, as I rushed towards my destination.

And now I am *here,* within the house in Fetter Lane. The

windows were boarded up, as I had left them. I broke in and went down to the cellar.

I found the Dreadful Eye's machine. It was encrusted with cobwebs, but appeared otherwise as I'd left it. By following its cables, I have located the projector's power source: an electrical generator, concealed behind a false wall of plaster and lath. I have shattered a hole in the wall, so that I may get at the generator.

There are a pair of insulated gloves in Ampleforth's tool chest, and some wire. I know little of electrics, but now speed is more essential than skill.

I have severed the cable between the interdimensional projector and its generator, and then *mended* the cable—spliced it as if it were rope—with some lengths of the wire. I have switched on the projector. The humming started almost immediately, and soon a sphere of violet-coloured light began to form.

Darling Vanessa, I lied to you before, when I said I had changed the setting of the dials upon this hideous machine. Now I entruth that dark lie: I have torn off the cobwebs, and now I *have* altered the settings of the dials. The gateway between dimensions that once linked this cellar to the cliffs of your world, dear Vanessa, now leads to some other world, *elsewhere.* A province unknown.

The wires with which I spliced the electrical cable are too weak, apparently, to maintain such a strong surge of current for very long. I have read of electrical explosions. Give me only a few minutes *more,* and then it will not matter if this whole damned house explodes. I have faith in the Metropolitan Fire Brigade of London.

And there *will* be a fire. I have sprinkled the workings of the Dreadful Eye's throbbing projector with the contents of Ampleforth's paraffin lamp. The flame, when it arrives, will be industrious.

I shall place this memorandum-book inside the metal tool chest, and pray that it survives the coming blaze.

The buzzing at the back of my skull has grown louder, and now it sounds like the beating of wings . . .

Five minutes left, at best. Perhaps less.

Just as I failed to save Vanessa, there seems to be no way to save myself. The Dreadful Eye has chosen me as the next receptacle for his evil. But perhaps I can save *Earth* from his unholy campaign.

The sphere of violet-coloured light still hovers, waiting. I can see another shape begin to appear within the thing: it is a hexagon, I think. I plan to wait until the last possible instant before the Dreadful Eye clambers into my mind and takes control of my body. In that last instant of humanity remaining to me I mean to take a running start towards the glowing gateway beyond the machine and fling myself into its interdimensional void. The Dreadful Eye, perforce, will be hurtled through *with* me. Wherever we emerge—in empty space, or on some barren planetoid—*there* the Dreadful Eye must achieve his domain. Not on Earth. Nor on Vanessa's homeworld. I have lost my strange beloved, but now I complete my last promise to her: now, Vanessa, I *have* freed your people. . . .

Perhaps, by some tenuous chance, I will defeat the Dreadful Eye. If I do, and if I can find my way back to this dimension, I shall somehow return to Earth and set down the account of my fate in this journal.

If this page is the last one I write, then I have lost. Eventually the Dreadful Eye will find his way back through all the universe's corridors of worlds, and revisit the Earth. It may take weeks, or centuries: infinity is not so vast as my enemy is. If my own body fails him, he will occupy another. *But he WILL return to Earth, and plague humanity anew.*

He may arrive disguised as anyone, concealed in any human form. He will grasp whatever mind and soul may suit his purpose. You who find this, take warning: he may walk beside you at any moment, wearing your neighbour's face. Tomorrow he may enter *you.*

Now the beating of wings has grown louder, and beneath its under-edges I can hear . . . yes, it starts: the whispering voice at the base of my skull.

I am no longer alone in this cellar.
EYE CAN SEE ALL THE